PRAISE FOR *KINGS OF BROKEN THINGS*

"Set during the Red Summer, *Kings of Broken Things* perfectly encapsulates both the frailty and darkness of the volatile period that saw the end of World War I, the shift from an agrarian to industrial society, heartland baseball, and the brutal lynching of Will Brown that led to the Omaha Race Riot. Powerful and resonant, this book's relevance, in the context of today's concerns, cannot be overstated."

—Julie Iromuanya, author of *Mr. and Mrs. Doctor*

"A beautifully written novel about an ugly, tumultuous time in history, *Kings of Broken Things* is an exciting, gritty portrait of a corrupt American city on the edge of self-destruction. It's a novel that simmers, like Doctorow's *Ragtime*, leaning forward always toward its powerful final chapters. Whether writing about violins or baseball or bordellos, Wheeler demonstrates a dazzling talent for bringing history alive, offering breathtaking insights into the hearts and minds of these immigrants and outsiders."

—Timothy Schaffert, author of *The Swan Gondola*

"The rhythms of baseball run through the prose of *Kings of Broken Things*, as the game becomes a gateway into the stories we tell ourselves about America. This is a book that questions those stories and gives itself over to the conflict at the core of them, all told in sentences that skip along like a perfectly struck ground ball."

—Matthew Salesses, author of *The Hundred-Year Flood*

"In this beautifully written debut novel, Ted Wheeler takes us back to a crossroads in American history, a time full of the innocence of our childhood when the joys of simple pleasures were beginning to be tainted by the growing awareness of a darkness at the core of the American Dream. Set in Omaha, the contradictions at the heart of those living in the heartland are tested by the foreboding shadows of racism and hatred that finally explode into a lynching of a black man in downtown while white crowds look on. How could the good people of Nebraska have committed and tolerated such a brutal act? Wheeler's novel explores the world that created this terrible moment, and the aftermath that continues to punish a city known for having rigid discrimination and oppression to this day. Indeed, this is a novel for our time as we collectively face an uncertain future and ask ourselves how the daily shootings and injustices can be stopped. Wheeler possesses a powerful voice that reminds us that wrong doesn't become merely historical; it lives forever, no matter how hard we try to erase the memory. Readers will learn from reading this novel, experience empathy, and perhaps read the daily news with greater compassion. I recommend this novel be read and reread."

—Jonis Agee, author of *The Bones of Paradise*

"In this marvelous debut novel, Theodore Wheeler's clean and unsentimental prose takes us into the rough streets of Omaha's River Ward at the end of the First World War. Wheeler skillfully wields historical facts and imagination to give life to immigrants and the sons of immigrants as they are swept up in American ways—from baseball and election politics to the tragic lynching of a black man named Will Brown. This is a book whose characters and scenes will stay with you long after you've turned the last page."

—Mary Helen Stefaniak, author of *The Cailiffs of Baghdad, Georgia*

THEODORE WHEELER

KINGS OF BROKEN THINGS

A NOVEL

Little
a

Text copyright © 2017 by Theodore Wheeler
All rights reserved.

Published by Little A, New York

www.apub.com

Amazon, the Amazon logo, and Little A are trademarks of Amazon.com, Inc., or its affiliates.

ISBN-13: 9781503941472 (hardcover)
ISBN-10: 1503941477 (hardcover)
ISBN-13: 9781503941465 (paperback)
ISBN-10: 1503941469 (paperback)

Cover design by Faceout Studio

Cover illustrated by Christina Chung

Printed in the United States of America

First edition

KINGS
OF BROKEN
THINGS

Prologue

To the boys who lived on Clandish Street, those who were too young to fight in the war on either side, the world was smaller than the newspapers suggested. Maybe they'd heard the names of generals like Foch or Hindenburg or Pershing, but these names had no bearing on their lives. They worried about the names of ballplayers and boxers instead. These were boys whose only shoes were baseball spikes. Who carried a mitt everywhere, just in case. Who stole packs of Sweet Caporal cigarettes to acquire the Ty Cobb card inside, then smoked the cigarettes too, because why not? Life was simple for them, for a while. Pleasant noises came from the homes on their block. A hausfrau singing in Plattdeutsch loud enough to hear from the walkway, the woman proud of how she slipped through her aspirated syllables and spit her *t*'s. Sweethearts, arm in arm, struggled to find privacy as clans of siblings escaped their houses before the sun set. Dogs let their tongues wag in the heat, bellies bulging in the dirt, full of table scraps, chicken guts, and pork rib bones.

People watched each other from porches after dinner, their attention caught in particular that summer by a girl with a space around her on the walkway because nobody wanted to come close. *Oh? Didn't you hear?* The girl slender and dignified. She clutched her man's elbow. *That's Doreen, yeah? No, that's Carla. No, that's Evelyn. No. That's that girl Agnes.*

She was a pretty girl, with blond hair and an erect way in her back, prettier than most. This girl walking down the street, her man's arm around her waist. *Don't you see her? She was raped last week.*

It was remarkable to the boys to see a woman who'd had it done to her like that. A girl shuffling along with her wrists bruised purplish, her skin thin at the bruises, like a rotten tomato under the plant where the good tomatoes grew. A girl who wore elegant dresses. Who put curls in her long, fair hair.

Everybody had a theory about how these things happened, especially later, when the mob caught one, a black man who did bad things to a girl. They would wonder about it in Omaha for years after the fact. What went through his mind? What was he thinking when the cops handed him over? This one they caught, this Will Brown. They'd wonder if his ears worked, if he was able to hear what that mob promised to do to him. They'd never know. No more than fifty people had even heard of him the day he was arrested, but the day after, Will Brown's name was on the lips of every person in Omaha, after what that girl said he did to her.

The boys who grew up on Clandish would think an awful lot about the folks who were around those years, the war years, the Red Summer that came after the war. This was the neighborhood they'd claimed, and it would go up in flames. They would be the ones to set it on fire.

THE OPEN CITY
Spring 1917

Consider Karel Miihlstein. In 1917 he was eleven years old, new to Omaha, fresh off the boat when he met the boys in the school yard. He was from Salzburg, he said, but had come from Galizien, over there, where the Eastern Front of the war was being fought. His father repaired musical instruments; his mother had been a famous actress and singer, out in the far reaches of the empire his family fled from. But his mother was dead by then—she'd died back there—and maybe this was why his family had to run from Europe in such a hurry like they did. And, of course, there was the war.

Karel was an interesting kid. He had talents. His English came off as well as his German. He could run. He was bigger than most boys his age and knew a little violin when pressed to play. But these were inessential skills. That spring Karel got to know the boys on Clandish, so he learned how important it was here to be good at baseball.

Once the weather turned warm, the boys divvied into teams. They were the oldest in their school, eleven, twelve, thirteen—at the end of boyhood.

Karel wasn't the last one picked that year, even though he didn't have a clue how to play. There were two others who were known to be horrible at baseball, for reasons that couldn't be helped—one whose rickety legs were being straightened by iron braces and another whose hair was kept shorn to eradicate the bugs that plagued him. So Karel grinned when the captains from one team grabbed his arm and pulled him to their side before it came down to the final pick. Alfred Braun and Jimmy Mac, boys from his class, were the two who picked him. It wasn't until then that they asked if he even played.

"I never held a baseball before," Karel admitted.

"You kidding?"

"Can you throw?"

It was no use lying. Once they fetched a ball and Karel sort of flipped it sidearm to Alfred, sort of rolled the ball in the school yard gravel, they saw all they needed to see.

Jimmy Mac slapped his hands to his face. "Oh, Jesus. Why did you send us this one?"

Karel didn't know what to do. He pulled his arms into himself, felt his shoulders shrink as panic crept over him.

"Hold on now," Alfred said. "That's bad, but you're not the worst I seen. Not for a first throw. We're just going to have to fix you, yeah."

"Sure. Don't worry." Jimmy Mac dropped his hands to his side and smiled. "We won't let you down."

Workup was played in the school yard that first week of spring. A real game wouldn't form until the next week, when the captains could be sure where each belonged on the diamond. For the initial days a boy took his shot at every position in turn. They rutted out base paths with the end of a bat, folded felt jackets into squares for first, second, third. Home plate was a cap. The school owned a bat—a stubby red thing with a hook screwed into the handle so it could be hung from a coatrack. The boys could borrow the bat whenever they wanted, so long as they put it back where it belonged. A couple of boys had ball gloves but most didn't. A boy should get used to cradling a ground ball soft with his hands or to knocking it down with his chest, or if he was chicken, to turning and giving chase as the ball rolled by. A glove wasn't all that important, not how the boys saw it. The hands were important.

Karel stood back to watch near the schoolhouse. A redbrick building with a bell that was surrounded on all sides by flat ground. From what his father had told him to expect, the school on Clandish was what Karel supposed all the Middle West should look like: a large building with a Stars and Stripes snapping from the top of a flagpole, straight rows of desks and inkwells visible through the ground-floor windows.

The sun was warm on Karel's skin those afternoons, when kids shed their jackets as soon as they stormed out over the threshold of the schoolhouse door. Still, Karel would have been warmer if he'd moved like the other boys, chasing the ball, swinging lumber off shoulders, over heads, lining up to cover the school yard flats and urging each other to hustle in high-pitched barks. Karel followed their moves. Boys crouched half to the ground, hands on knees, socks pulled high. One threw the ball and another caught. Karel didn't like the idea of playing a position so close to the action. The catcher in particular risked his teeth, squatting where the bat was swung. Out in the field would be better, Karel figured, where he could stretch his legs, hunt the ball, and be expected to catch it only on occasion, but he was afraid to voice his assumptions, to stake claim to a job he might fail at.

The two who'd picked him were skilled ballplayers. Karel tracked their movements. Jimmy Mac was redheaded and skinny, with long arms to pluck the ball from the air. He ran, reckless and daring, squared liners up to his face to see the ball coming, the protecting mitt just in front of his nose. He did better in the outfield. Alfred was shorter, dark and compact, and was more comfortable patrolling the infield, where it was a credit to be close to the ground.

After a while these two pulled Karel from the schoolhouse wall to teach him how to field. "Bend your knees," they told him. "Reach for the ground. Pick grass if it helps." They bossed him around until he could drop into a fielder's stance on his own and bounce from his hips, where his muscle was, and not look like an idiot doing it. Then they rolled a ball to Karel and made him bat it back with his hands. Harder each time. The three of them in a triangle, in defensive stance, slapping the ball back and forth.

After a while the boys said that was enough. It was getting dark.

Karel thanked Alfred and Jimmy Mac for showing him how to play. They said not to worry. They hadn't really taught him anything yet. And it was true. Karel would learn much more about baseball—he'd be the best of them by the time he was finished.

"You live with Missus Maria, yeah?" Alfred asked.

"Sure he does," Jimmy said. "I seen him before. You got all sisters, don't you?"

"Yeah."

"That's fine. They're pretty."

Karel didn't like to talk about his sisters. The elder pair teased him a lot and were too old to care about anyway. But Karel's other sister, Anna, was only a year older than him. He protected her.

"Don't you think they're pretty? Your sisters?" Alfred sucked on the pit of a cherry. He kept fruit in his pockets, stolen from the market, like lots of kids did.

If Karel was going to make friends with any of the boys, he could do worse than Alfred Braun and Jimmy McHenry. Sure, Jimmy was measly faced, Irish, and Karel had been warned against trusting the Irish. Then there was Alfred, who had wide hips and a big rump that ballooned his trousers in back. He never wore a belt, because he didn't need one. Alfred didn't have baby fat on his cheeks either, a strange thing for a stout boy, like all his mass should erode to his feet. "You're turning conical is all," Jimmy sometimes teased, cinching his own narrow shoulders to mimic Alfred's form. "A walking, talking dunce cap. That's what you are."

Neither Jimmy nor Alfred came from model families. This made Karel feel better about the boys. Like he was one of them.

They had questions for Karel now that he was on their team. What work his father did and why his sister Anna was pulled from school.

How Karel lived in New York City for a year after he came over, saw the Statue of Liberty, and went to the Polo Grounds once, but only because he and his father took the wrong Ninth Avenue El transfer and ended up in Harlem by mistake, and not necessarily to see Christy Mathewson and the Giants play. Even though he didn't know who the ace hurler Christy Mathewson was, the boys respected Karel once he told how he'd escaped from the war in Europe. He and his father and his sisters had run halfway across the continent to board an American ocean liner in Bremerhaven. There was fighting where he lived before that.

"Is that why you haven't got a mom?" Jimmy asked. "Did she die in the war?"

"Yeah," Karel admitted. "She was killed."

He felt himself toughen, saying that, staring past those boys into the street. He hadn't been able to say it before. It was his mother who Karel took after. She'd had a round face and big cheeks and strong shoulders, like Karel did. He didn't really remember her—his sisters told him these things. That's how he knew anything, secondhand. He had to accept what his sisters said—how his mother was beautiful, and cruel sometimes if she felt like it, and how she was killed, in Austria-Hungary, in northernmost Galizien among the Carpathian Mountains, by Tsarist Russian soldiers? by a Serb assassin? by a stray bullet? Karel knew nothing about that. His sisters wouldn't tell. He didn't want to know how it happened anyway, not as a boy. She was his mother. She'd smiled at him, tucked him into bed, then lifted him from his blankets in the morning and fed him sugary bits torn from a marzipan pastry. He remembered that, didn't he? That was all he had of her.

The other boys looked at Karel different once they knew how he'd ended up in Omaha.

Consider that two years had passed since Karel and his family fled Central Europe. Tsar Nicholas sent Cossacks to fight in the Carpathians, and that was bad news. That was why Karel and his family had to run. Cossacks had it out for Jews, and Herr Miihlstein had lost enough of

9

his small family already during the early days of the war. The remaining Miihlsteins were lucky to get out so easy and still have enough money to find a place in New York for a while. Then a job at the Musik Verein in Omaha came open when the man who'd held it died of consumption. Miihlstein took the job, dragged his children across a continent for a second time, and rented the attic where the deceased had formerly lived. Things would be easier this way, since that was where all the deceased's work was left, what was Miihlstein's work now. And, needless to say, Frau Eigler was looking to fill the room.

Karel and his family were a bit different than the rest of the boys and their families.

Consider that there were five Miihlsteins altogether. Karel, Anna, the two older sisters, who were off six days a week cleaning streetcars in an immense underground garage, and their father. Herr Miihlstein was a lanky man with short arms and a thin mustache that was often stained by his lunch. Karel didn't look like his father. He had darker hair and skin, and was broad in the shoulders. His feet were so big he could hardly keep shoes that fit. Sometimes he wore his father's, which fit just as well, at least when Karel was eleven and hadn't yet outgrown them.

Miihlstein worked nearly all day and night in the attic of the Eigler house. He hummed along as he measured string or reinforced the neck of the viola he was charged with reviving. He squeezed the wood to put it under stress, to find the reason it didn't sing right, then rolled a red felt carpet over the worktable and pulled all the tools from his kit to examine them, to make sure each was still fit. Little cans of lacquer and thinner pressed on the felt. Tools pulled from nooks and leather slots. Waffled metal files, awls and emery cloth, spools of catgut, spare pegs, clamps, chisels, a skinny metal hammer. Wood shavings popped from the block plane as Miihlstein revealed new fingerboard then sanded it round. Notches were filed and awled for strings, the fingerboard painted an ebullient, endless black. Miihlstein's wire glasses rode down his nose on a bead of sweat. He bit his upper lip, sucked the prickles of his mustache into his mouth to concentrate. He engaged a single instrument a whole week or more to repair it, like this viola, stretching and tuning and playing, humming along as he plucked and bowed, until: "Perfection!"

The whole rigmarole bored Karel. He hated to be stuck in the attic dormer. There were two beds, a rocking chair, a sofa draped in yellow chintz. He and Anna devised docile and melancholy games to occupy themselves before supper, imaginings that often involved the war. Karel's favorite was to play army surgeon with Anna's rag doll. She allowed this. There was great commotion in Karel's mind as the doll was rushed from an open battlefield—a circular woven rug strewn with sock garter barbwire and newspapers crumpled into craters—to the great bed where the girls slept. Under the bed the real fun began, their legs stuck out opposite ends. Because she was sickly herself, Anna had a nicely dark mind for details. She described a simple shrapnel wound in an arm. But then! Then the ambulance was hit by mortar fire and overturned on the road, the poor souls inside tossed on top of each other. Broken bones now, fractures, splinters of glass and head wounds. "The driver died at once," Anna hushed. "A tragedy, for he was greatly loved by his wife, as all in his village knew."

Once Anna completed her treasury, Karel took over. The poor soul was in real trouble. Only one thing could save him. An amputation. Karel pinned the rag doll to the floorboards and revealed the yellowed cloth skin. He sawed with the edge of his index finger and tucked, as if Anna wouldn't notice, the doll's arm into its dress. The dress was back in place, the sleeve folded up. At first the poor soul was saved, lifted from the operating theater and slid under the blankets atop the bed. "You're in luck," Anna said to the poor soul. "Nothing but raspberry torte for a year." Then things took a turn for the worse. The poor soul couldn't be saved after all. They enclosed the corpse in a white paperboard box—the rag doll corpse-like already, as they saw it—and took the box out back of the Eigler house to bury it in the garden.

Karel worried his new friends from school would find out how he played with Anna. It was shameful, of course. A boy shouldn't enjoy carrying on like that with a doll, not a boy who was nearly twelve. He resolved to end his childishness. Soon, anyway.

Maybe Karel was too old to play such girlish games—but it was how he and Anna spent time together. By age eleven Karel was aware of how Anna was different than other kids. How she didn't mature the way she should, because she was stuck at home with her illness, at Herr Miihlstein's insistence. So she remained the same age, played the same games over and over, obsessed over the same old gossip, the same books of Viennese poems. Anna liked playing with Karel, with her dolls, and that was fine with him. Karel loved his sister—all three of his sisters really, but Anna the most—and he didn't know how else to spend time with her.

Anna always wore a white straw hat when outside. It was dented, the brim slightly twisted, but she kept it clean and a purple ribbon was attached and neatly tied. She believed the hat made her beautiful. She was right. She wore a matching lavender overcoat, and the way she smiled, black hair swept around her face, her overbite and pointy nose and dark eyes, how she sat in the grass to weave wildflower stems together for the dead—the boys on Clandish would never forget her. The times they caught a glimpse of Anna on a chair by the doorway as they walked by the Eigler house, Anna sitting in the front window, Anna planting flowers by the lattice skirt under the front porch. She spent most of her time doing craftwork up in the attic dormer where the Miihlsteins lived, so it was rare for a boy to even catch a glimpse of her, a boy stopped on the walkway to stare up into a window of that grand Victorian house where Frau Eigler took in roomers during the late years of her life.

After the box was buried, a prayer sung, Anna and Karel retrieved the doll from the damp spring soil. Anna didn't have so many dolls, even rag dolls, to leave them interred. "He's alive!" the two of them chanted, pulling the rag doll from its now-muddy box. "He's alive! The boy's alive!"

Maria Eigler must have seen the two of them burrow in her daffodils. "Stop it!" she snapped, surprising them as she rushed out the back door. "You shouldn't do that. The woman across the alley lost two babies these years. Both of them she buried in little white boxes, yeah."

Maria hushed at them, a hissing, cutting kind of inflection old women perfected, those years especially, the war years. Each reproach made Karel feel miserable and small. He covered himself with his arms. Anna was shrinking too. She clutched the doll to her chest.

"Leave her alone," Karel shouted. "Can't you see she's crying?"

He popped off his knees to shield Anna, rallied up his fists, trembling. It was instinct to dig his heels in once he saw his sister frightened. She was as delicate as a doll, her skin porcelain white, her hair limp in pigtails. When she pulled off her glasses to dry the lenses, sores bloomed on the bridge of her nose.

"What's wrong, Karel?" Maria released her skirts and patted the wrinkles she'd made in clutching. "I don't know why you act this way."

"We didn't do anything!"

Anna stood and secured the hooks of her glasses behind her ears. "Stop that," she said to Karel. "You know Frau Eigler doesn't mean it."

Karel was ashamed already and couldn't take Anna scolding him. Once he dropped his fists, Maria swooped in to hug the both of them. He let her.

He wouldn't have liked to admit this, but Karel felt better squeezed to Frau Eigler's soft hips, her body padded by layers of skirts and underskirts, her own well-buttered girth below that. Her body bounced into his as she walked them to the back door. He felt lighter being jostled.

Maria sat them at the table inside and apologized. "It isn't your fault," she said. "I was being a ninny. I hadn't thought of your mother when I yelled at you."

Karel hadn't thought of his mother either, playing the burying game. Maria always wanted to talk about his mother. That made it hard to be in the house too. He could take her doting on him, calling him downstairs to taste her stews or Danish pastries—which was fine, better than fine—or how she sent him on errands to the market for quince or meat, or to a chemist for alum powder. Karel just couldn't stand it when Maria brought up his mother.

If he was better at baseball, Karel realized, he could leave the house whenever he wanted. If he was an important player on a team, if the other boys saw him as rough and strong and one whose body could defeat other bodies, then Karel could go anywhere he wanted. He wished he knew everything there was to know about baseball. Rainbow throws and hard slides and how to hit too, to hit bombs. He'd know more and play better than all the other boys, he decided. They hadn't even trusted him with a bat yet, but he'd learn how to swing one. Then he'd have a place to be.

Maria told Karel and Anna they couldn't chant about baby boys coming alive if they wanted to dig in the yard. "We won't," Anna promised.

"Yeah, Frau Eigler. We won't dig in your garden again."

She laughed at Karel. "Good. What a domesticated boy."

Karel stayed late in the school yard those days. He watched boys play ball. Learned the language. Stinger and blooper and daisy cutter. What was meant when one boy urged another to toss the onion or crack the willow.

Older boys hung around the ballfield to check on a little brother or pick up a cohort. The kind who hung around the outdoor market all day, who wore drab clothes like most working class, but wore them stylishly, with derby hats set back on their heads to let loose a flourish of bangs. Karel had seen enough bad things to avoid boys like these, those who fidgeted on their bench all day in class, if they were in class, who couldn't wait to sneak away downtown. A boy named Ignatz was the toughest of this type at Karel's school. An alleged Serb, Ignatz was tall and snub-nosed and still attended the lower school even though he was fourteen. Unlike the others, Ignatz didn't run in a group. He was a crew unto himself. He was terrifying.

Ignatz came over to the ballfield and knocked the cap off Alfred Braun's head one of those days. "Hey, Freddie," he said. "Your dad's bothering folks at my dad's warehouse again. He's got no business there. Everyone's tired of him."

Alfred snatched his cap from the ground, then smiled, broad and impish. The ballplayers rushed in to see what would happen to Alfred. Karel stayed to the back. Ignatz looked like he'd toss Alfred over the fence. He was angry and mean, his cheeks swollen. He was too ugly to be anything other than tough. That puggish face, the nose smashed up into two fleshy holes.

"Tell him to stay out of the warehouses," Ignatz said. "They don't need any organizers down there."

Karel hid at a corner of the schoolhouse until Ignatz left. A thicket of junipers grew in a way that created a tunnel where branches shied the bricks, where the airy dust off the bark coated his teeth. Mostly it was girls in the hollow. Karel was used to girls. Each cordoned a space where she could set up house, a sitting room, a kitchen, an opening between limbs an anteroom, then tended a stove or shook out sheets or put a baby down or swept dirt with a juniper branch.

"Is that you in there?" Jimmy Mac pushed through the stingers to see inside the hollow. "You're on our team," he said. "You don't got to play with girls."

Karel returned to the light, facedown as he crouched out. Evergreen needles had worked over the side of his shoes, into his pockets and his hair. He shook his head to dislodge them.

"Come on." Alfred tossed a ball to himself. "You got work to do."

They went back to the drills from before. In triangle, rolling the ball to each other, training their hands to anticipate bounces, how the ball played on gravel, on grass, on rubbed-smooth slabs of rock-hard dirt. "Step back," Alfred ordered. All three did. "Again," he said after the ball looped a few more turns. With every step back Karel had to slap the ball harder, until he picked the ball up and slammed it on the surface to bounce it over. "Good," Jimmy said. "You're getting the hang of it." Each time a new hop played on Karel, his hands learned what to do. He felt his chest fill and warm. The boys backed ten, fifteen, twenty feet away, until Karel could rear back and glide grounders in return. He caught barehanded and threw before his palm felt the sting. He felt surer in his body. His arm found a slot he could throw from and strike where he aimed without aiming. Alfred and Jimmy tossed just as hard to Karel. He liked that. They didn't ease up on him. He bounced on his hamstrings in the stance. Got used to the short hop so the ball came to the meat of his hands instead of his wrists. He was getting better and better until the ball turned a rock and came up on him, right to his lips, and got him.

His mouth watered. He breathed in without letting out. Went to his knees to feel what happened. Heard the others gasp, heard them running to see if he was going to bawl about it. But the shock wasn't so bad. His lip swelled but there wasn't blood. Karel felt splinters in his mouth, a front tooth chipped. The surface changed as he ran his tongue over his teeth.

"Took a bad hop on you, yeah?" one of the others asked. "Sure it did."

Karel rubbed the chip with a finger. The rough edges of it, a wedge of tooth gone. He searched the inside of his mouth with his tongue for broken pieces. Grit over his other teeth now, at the back of his throat.

"I need a glove," he said.

Alfred disagreed. "A glove can't help if you don't know how to use it."

16

Of course, it was easier for those boys to say so. Both of them had gloves of their own.

"Where you going to get it anyway?" Jimmy asked. "Will your dad buy one?"

"No," Karel said. "I can't ask him for something like that."

Alfred came up with a plan the next week. If Karel wouldn't ask Herr Miihlstein to buy him a mitt, then Alfred would get one from his own father. Emil Braun talked more baseball than anyone and had connections on the Southside team. "Come with me," Alfred said. "My pop will know what to do."

The Brauns lived in a gray, rotted tenement building near the rail yards, a German cluster on a hill south of Clandish, closer to Poppleton and Fourteenth, where freight rails cut through and sidings bunched out in clovers, and the rumpled brown bluffs of Iowa were visible over the trees, the steel girders and granite blocks of the UP railroad bridge where it spanned the river. They dodged the soapy drips of linen that hung heavy on lines attached to the eaves of splintery lean-tos. Younger kids turned gymnastics on a wagon in the alleyway, near a rut of muddy water, shirts falling over their faces as they walked on their hands or sprung over the side of the wagon. They danced in spasms when Karel looked at them, to impress him in some way, the logic of a show-off five-year-old.

Alfred's father opened the door when he heard them in the hallway.

"What are you doing here? I'm busy today."

Alfred ignored his father. He ushered Jimmy and Karel into the room past Braun. The man wore only trousers and suspenders, with one foot bare and the other in a red sock. A few scraps of clothing were scattered here and there that Alfred rifled through. There were no books, no newspapers. No window, no air stream. Bedsprings sang through the wall from next door. It was a rotten place. Karel felt lucky to have a whole attic loft for his family, up top where a window caught the breeze. Six people here crammed in a room a sixth the size of Maria Eigler's attic.

"Where is it?" Alfred asked. "Just saw it this morning."

"Where's what?"

"The mitt. The ball glove."

To stay out of the way, Jimmy and Karel sat on the bed. On the far side of the mattress lay some saltines and the greasy end of a summer sausage. A carving knife was on a table nearby, next to a canister of snuff.

Braun took Alfred under an arm and swayed to the corner. "Don't you see I'm busy?"

"No. With what?" There was moaning from next door. Braun pounded on the wall and told them to shut up, but it made no difference.

"It's Karel," Alfred explained. "He wants to play ball but doesn't know a thing about it."

"What do you mean? That boy?"

Alfred wrenched his arm free to dig under the bed. "Don't you got a glove for him?"

Braun smoothed the skin of his forehead as he stared at Karel. He was a short man with narrow shoulders and a gelatinous middle, and was bald on top. He took two steps across the room to lift Karel's wrists and feel for muscle.

"Okay, okay," Braun said gaily, mocking like he was impressed by Karel, or possibly was actually impressed. "Let me think a minute. This isn't the first boy I ever seen in this condition. It isn't always fatal."

The bedposts squelched against the floor from Alfred scuttling underneath. "Here's mine," he said. "Ain't we got another?"

Braun didn't answer. He reached across for a saltine to crunch while he deliberated.

"Stop digging, Alfred. Come with me. This will be better luck. There's someone the boy must meet. If he wants to be a ballplayer, then he'll do this. Trust me."

Karel looked to Jimmy, but Jimmy didn't have an answer either.

Emil Braun was a curious man. The way he squawked instead of speaking, some in German intonation, some Midwestern.

Meeting Braun changed something in Karel, freed him, but he wasn't sure why. He knew his own father wouldn't approve of him being here. Herr Miihlstein wasn't a wealthy man, but he had a reserve about him, his mechanical good manners, the dignity to which he clung. The whole family had squeezed into four seats on the train passage to Omaha rather than splitting up and risk getting stuck next to some scoundrel. Miihlstein refused to allow a baggageman to check his tools either. He held the black leather valise on his lap the whole trip, over two days, until every con man in the compartment suspected he carried something of greater value than he actually did.

Karel didn't care for manners. He liked Emil Braun, even though the man was strange. Maybe because of this. When Braun stood to grab a shirt and ratty overcoat off the back of a chair, Karel stood too.

He followed as Braun navigated odd-angled tenement rows then rushed across Clandish into downtown. Braun moved with busy purpose, even though he didn't have a job like most fathers. He didn't even associate with musicians, like Karel's father, but held several posts for which he was remunerated in different ways. Deacon of their tenement; attendant for the streetcar workers' union; secretary of a political group that met in the basement room of a tavern, SOSA, the South Omaha Social Anarchists. Braun was not hired muscle, as he claimed to Karel that day. But he could talk—he never stopped talking—and there were opportunities for men like him, even if most folks down on the River Ward didn't consider what he did to be legitimate work.

It was meteorological phenomena Braun talked as he led the boys north. "It's the big guns in France that make the wind gust so much this spring," he claimed, circling his arms in the damp air. "Mortars make the wind strong. It's changed weather across the globe. More the cannons fire, more the wind blows. It's proven. The generals will ruin everything."

When they crossed Cuming Street, it was clear where Braun was taking them. This was the big thing that spring, heading up to the Northside. Boys on Clandish dared each other to sneak through this black neighborhood, all the way to Lake Street, to prove they weren't chicken. They called it No Man's Land, where black folks lived. There weren't big houses up there, not where they went, but shacks and four-family homes set back from the road at odd intervals. Some had glass windows, some didn't. Some were sided by tar paper or cedar shakes. Men walked out shirtless. They crouched and squinted at the white kids rushing down the block.

Braun dragged the three boys to a shack set back in the weeds of an otherwise empty lot. The door pitched open halfway when he knocked, its latch broken. A smell of rendering pork leached out. Jimmy Mac whispered that they should get out of there, but Karel didn't move. None of the boys moved. They huddled behind Braun, peeked around as a woman with a red kerchief over her mouth came to the door and asked who it was.

"It's Emil. Tell Josh."

They went inside when beckoned. A man sat on the floor in the room that wasn't the kitchen, a shoeshine kit open in front of him as he wiped grime from his brushes with a rag. He was skinny and missing teeth. The bony points of his shoulders tented the wool shirt he wore; his long arms snaked around the room when he reached for something to pull from his kit. He didn't have legs, Karel saw. Both pant legs were pinned up to stumps.

"This is Josh," Braun said. "He was once the finest ballplayer any-one knew in North *or* South Omaha." The boys clustered by the door now that Braun moved inside. "Tell them," Braun said. "They don't believe me."

The man, Josh, laughed to himself, then snapped a rag at the boys. "Don't listen to Emil. He's a bullshitter. A certified bullshitter."

Braun crouched to joke with the man. They shook hands so Braun could pass along some coins in charity to Josh, just Josh, who once ruled the Whites-versus-Negroes series they played in Rourke Park on the Fourth of July, a cripple now who used to sweet-talk a screwball and blister Braun's thumbs when they both still played. Josh was a big deal here in his neighborhood. Everyone on the Northside came to talk to and honor Josh with their respects; to hear how things used to be and argue if they were better off ten, fifteen years ago, than they were now; to learn how Josh gripped a baseball to throw a two-seam sinker or a forkball or his famous screwball. He'd show any boy the grip if the boy said he dreamed of being a great pitcher, though few had hands large enough to palm the ball the way Josh could. Emil Braun came up here to pay his respects too, to talk to a man he considered a friend, even though Braun didn't exactly belong up here on the Northside.

"I was a Southsider," Braun told the boys, "a second bagger. You believe that? I was good."

"No, he was not," the man laughed. "He was not good."

"Eh," Braun said. "Easy for you to say."

Karel tried to listen, but he couldn't follow. Instead he crept near a doorway to look in on the woman. She mixed sand-like spices in a bowl, aromatic and strong, spices that burned his nose, which was maybe why the woman wore the kerchief over her mouth. Karel didn't want to think what might be under the kerchief. A meat cleaver stuck from a wooden block within her reach, blood-heavy around the blade. "What are you doing to the meat?" Karel asked. She didn't answer.

Braun pulled Karel back. "This one never played baseball. He's fresh off the boat."

"Is that right?"

"Yeah. Tell him something, Josh. I brought him to meet you. He should meet the best."

Karel didn't know what to say as Braun nudged him close to Josh. He'd never seen a black person up close and wasn't so sure he wanted to, there in the dark of the shack. The smell of shoe polish, the rendering from the stove room. Karel leaned in. He felt he couldn't help leaning, the others heavy behind him. Josh stared back, his eyes brown and orange.

"You were a ballplayer?"

"Hurler, kid. I was the hurler."

Josh pulled a baseball from his leather kit, one of a few there, and tossed it in the air to distract himself, higher each time, until it skimmed the ceiling.

Karel glanced to where the man's legs were missing and wondered how that happened. Was it an accident during a game, like Karel's chipped tooth? But much, much worse? Was he sucked into some slaughterhouse apparatus? Did he fall from a boxcar? The ends of his pants were damp where the stumps were, spotted with blood and yellow.

"Yes, kid. I was the best there was."

Josh's hands clawed over the baseball's skin. He roughed up the thread. The ball spun and spun, stopping only when he changed grips. Two fingers uncoiled to fork over the red seams, then together in salute along one. His thumb dealt back and forth to spin the bottom. His palm over the whole ball. Massive hands with pink insides and nails where they weren't blacked with Shinola. "You want to be a ballplayer?" he asked. "Maybe a hurler like I was."

"Yeah."

"Take this." Josh arched the ball across the room, soft, so Karel, sucking his lips to protect his mouth, could trap it against his belly. "You want to be a ballplayer, carry a ball with you. Toss it. Get a feel. Squeeze the thing if you want to. Just know about it."

Karel took the baseball with both hands to glance it over. The cover browned, a fingerprint here and there in polish. The seams were rough and scuffed his thumb. This was his ball. He'd carry it in his back pocket like Josh told him to.

Braun put his hand on Karel's shoulder then crouched down to look at the ball. "You want to know about Josh? Should I tell you? Do you want to know where his legs went?"

"Shit," Josh objected. "Don't start in, Emil. This has got nothing to do with that. I'm trying to help this boy, like you asked me to."

"Josh enlisted. He volunteered! Was a buffalo soldier. You know what that means, boys? He left his legs on San Juan Hill, that's what. Gave both legs for Cuba's freedom. A fine thing to do, yeah? I won't quibble with a man who gives up the prime of his own life for others to be free. But what did he get out of the deal? Where did he end up?"

"Don't insult me. Don't come here and bring up bad things."

"I'm not! My friend. It isn't your fault. It's Teddy Roosevelt's fault. A sick game aristocrats play, one designed to destroy good men like you. Woodrow Wilson does it too, now that he's been reelected. He's found a new war. Every ruler craves war to destroy the lives of common men."

"Don't put me down. Not in front of your boys. Why'd you bring them anyway?"

"I'm not! You don't understand."

"Go on, boys. Get on out of here so I can talk to Emil. Okay? Go on."

Braun put an arm across the doorway. "You boys know I love him, yeah? You can see?"

"Go on," Josh repeated. He slid around on his backside to wave Braun away. "This is my house."

Braun stayed to plead his case as Karel and the boys rushed to the main avenue, where a streetcar line ran. The rails and electric wires led the safest route to downtown.

23

The boys hurried, but not as fast as they might have the days before this one. If someone stopped them, asked what they were doing up here where they didn't belong, they had an answer. They'd been with a friend, Josh Whatshisname, the greatest Negro ballplayer there ever was. Karel had a baseball to prove it. Josh's thumbprint right there on the cowhide.

Once they reached Clandish, Karel slipped off to Maria Eigler's for supper. He wasn't the only one. All along Clandish front doors opened and slammed, folks headed in for the evening, home from work, home from school, just home, no explanation needed. Smoke curled from chimneys. Light leached from windows to color walkways gold. Even though the sun was nearly set and the wet wind blew hard from Europe, Karel wasn't cold. The excitement of having friends kept him warm. These weren't the musicians his father knew, they weren't his sisters. They were boys. Troublemakers. At supper he wouldn't tell what he'd been up to all day. That he'd been to the Northside wasn't something his family needed to know, or that he'd been inside a tenement, or where he got this baseball from. He wouldn't have to tell these things to stop his sisters from teasing him. They'd see on his face that he'd been running with the boys.

He was capable of trouble too.

He wasn't far from home when the bully spotted him.

"Hey! You're friends with the Braun kid, yeah?"

It was Ignatz, from the school yard. He rose from the stoop of a house and hopped down to the walkway. Karel barely went up to his chest.

"You shouldn't be friends with a Braun. They're bad people," Ignatz said. "Freddie's not so bad, but the others are rotten. You meet the father?"

"He's nice," Karel said.

"You're new here, I know that. You don't know nothing."

Karel reached to where the baseball was. He could feel it in his back pocket even without touching, but his hands moved in a nervous twitch to double-check, which was a stupid thing to do. Ignatz would want to see what Karel was hiding.

"See that house two down? That's mine." Karel looked to Ignatz's house, how it sunk into a depression where the alley ran, small and wood sided and cream colored, split into apartments with doors on either side of the porch. It had none of the elegance of Maria Eigler's house. "I'm not trying to make you mad, but tell your sisters. Yeah? The older ones. Shit, the little one too. I won't hurt her. If they want some company, some late night, that's where I live. You tell them that I said they're invited."

Ignatz put a hand on Karel's chest.

"If they knock on the window, I'll let them in. All three at once if they want."

Karel pushed Ignatz. Punched his hands as hard as he could to knock down the bully. But Ignatz didn't move. Strong and fat, Ignatz absorbed the blow. Only his clothes were dented.

"What's wrong with you? Don't do that."

Karel pushed again, this time knocking Ignatz off his stride. Karel pulled his arm back like he was going to swing, but Ignatz was quicker. Karel went down in the mud.

Ignatz came at him, so Karel kicked. He felt the ball in his pocket, on his back hip. He bicycled his legs to keep Ignatz away. He wouldn't give up the baseball.

Ignatz grabbed one of Karel's shoes to stop the kicking. The shoe popped off in his hand. "Okay," he laughed. Grabbed for the other shoe, took that one too. "Listen," he said. Ignatz tied the shoelaces together, yanked them tight, swung them around, and tossed them in a whimsical, jerking arc so they snagged over the electrical wire that hung above the street.

"Steer clear of the Brauns. That's all I'm saying."

25

Karel slipped into the alley after Ignatz got him, near Maria's daffodils. The soil felt damp through his socks as he huddled along the garden. His clothes were dirty.

Maria was in the back window, where the kitchen was. Light shone out from the glass onto the lawn. Supper was almost ready. She twisted and reached, bent and stirred. Whenever she lifted the lid off a pot the glass steamed and changed the light. After a while Maria disappeared. They were eating. Karel still watched the window, saw nothing but the back wall. He'd have to go in before long and say what happened. His father, his three clucking sisters, they'd all understand how he was pushed down and slugged in the gut. How an older boy took his shoes and tossed them over a wire. His sisters would coo over him when they heard. They didn't expect him to defend himself. His father would congratulate him for coming through the ordeal without a shiner. Maria, he knew, would pour a tall glass of milk and serve cake for dessert. He'd rather be whipped for losing his shoes—that was the truth.

Consider Jake Strauss. Things were pretty good for Jake in 1917, the year he turned twenty. Where he came from wasn't such a great place, up north along the Missouri River, in Jackson County. He'd had a lot of trouble there. Something with a guy Jake had roughed up—a guy his age who'd spread malicious rumors about how Jake's mother caught the crab louse from a Chinese rail worker—and the people in town didn't appreciate how Jake took revenge by smacking that boy twice with a pick handle. (Once for his mother, once for his baby sister—both of whom died a few years before, up there in Jackson County.) Jake's father was a German pastor, which only made the situation worse, so Jake ran off in the middle of the night before that other boy tried to rebalance the scales by inflicting fresh calamity on the Strauss family. Jake grabbed twenty dollars from the drawer in the kitchen, saddled his horse, and rode to Omaha. That's when his luck changed.

He tied his horse to a drainpipe in an alleyway on the northern outskirts of downtown Omaha and took the twenty dollars to a saloon called Mecklenburg's, where he joined the food line then stuffed his mouth with angry bites of rye bread and fatty meat at the bar. Everything in Mecklenburg's tempted him. Kippered herring, sardines, onions, radishes, pumpernickel, smoked Schwarzwälder ham. He gorged because nobody stopped him. He ate seconds and thirds. Had beer after beer and let the foam dry on his lips, then arched back tall on his stool when he was done to watch others hustle for food. He liked it here on the River Ward, on Clandish, everything so German and open to those who'd ask for it, which was different from where he came from, a small town where they shut up anyone whose voice even hinted at the Germanic. Jake should have looked for work or a room, but beer made him feel better. It was good beer. Cold and uncomplicated. He set his hands on his stomach to feel his guts swell with suds.

Later on he found himself standing in a row of tents along the muddy banks of the Missouri, a dozen or less of the tents pitched from the southern tip of the pig iron mills under the Douglas Street Bridge to the northern edge of the warehouses. Some kid from the saloon brought him there and told him he'd have a good time.

As Jake stumbled along, he felt a bawdy heat radiate from the flats, from open fires and juiced-up men, from rosy-cheeked women who circulated the crowd, from kids with trays tethered over their shoulders who sold tobacco and a drink they called mulberry wine. Heat from his own body too, jacked up on booze and the desire to live like a young man wanted to live, without consequences. From the mud itself. From the burning solder soot that pumped from mill chimneys and rose above the industrial dusk of the valley. The odor was overwhelming. Jake didn't understand how a river so big, that moved so fast, could smell so bad. He smoked to mask the stench, but the cheap tobacco sold here only made things worse. Jake had to laugh at it all. Even after all the beers, he was a little embarrassed at how drunks dipped forward on shaky legs and relieved themselves where they stood. Or how others slopped happily to a tent flap and peeked in at a naked woman. If a man liked what he saw, he entered. The spectacle got Jake going, desire at war with shame. The rude caterwauling inside the tents. Pinned to the front were hand-painted flyers advertising some exotic fantasy—Mother Russia, Queen of Siam, Country Schoolteacher, the Nun—but inside the women more or less looked the same. This wasn't a high-class joint with women of alien color or a traveling lady like Calamity Jane. This was rutting. These women were desperate.

"Here we go." The boy who'd brought Jake pushed to an open tent. "She's just your speed—the Old Gray Mare!"

Inside was a woman, as promised, curled to the back of her cot, the arcs of her body hidden among puffs of yellowed linens. Jake smelled her body before he saw her. The saline tang of sweat and semen was thick.

"She'll check you," the woman said. She flapped an arm to a child at the dark end of the stall. Jake hadn't noticed the girl, maybe six or seven years old, in a shabby orange dress, her face smeared with mud. A washbasin and some balled soap were on a nightstand.

"Open your trousers," the woman ordered. The girl approached. "She twists your thing in case there's the drip. She washes everybody. That's the rule."

Jake wouldn't move. The girl made a grab for his belt, but he swatted her away. Her face lit red as she stared up to him. "I got to."

"Go," he whispered. "Leave me alone."

It wasn't long before the woman leaned over to see what was keeping him. Her jaw square, her nose broad and flattened.

"Set down, Minnie," she said. The girl took her spot next to the nightstand. A sneer mirrored in both their faces. "Come on. You don't got to wash either. Just hurry."

Jake wouldn't move. He didn't understand what was wrong with this woman, with all these people down here on the flats. He felt like a boy, stubborn, inexperienced, because that's exactly what he was—a country boy, he realized.

"Why's a little girl here?" he asked.

"You're with the Episcopals?"

"No. I need a place to sleep. I want the girl to leave."

"You can't flop here."

"I got to sit down."

"Somebody'd grab her if I set her out there alone. She's only safe if she's with me."

The woman patted the cot, but Jake didn't move. Something came over him. The grease and vinegar of the saloon food, the pilsener, the woman's sour smell, and the girl.

"You'll get us in trouble. If the mack comes by . . ." The woman looked at the girl.

She pulled the straps off her shoulders until they hung over her belly. The chemise she wore spread and collapsed to bare her chest and ribs, the skin ruddy and scratched, specked with insect bites. Jake tried to look away from the woman, but he didn't want to see the girl either. He didn't know where to look—the woman's gnawed-at flesh, her opening legs, or the girl hunching into herself.

The woman followed his eyes. "Set next to me. Minnie ain't for sale."

"If I give you extra? Can she wait outside?"

"You paid, bunny. You can have me a little while before you leave, or you can just leave. The girl stays here either way."

"I didn't pay."

"You down here, aren't you?"

"What do you mean?"

"Are you stupid? They took it!"

It wasn't until he was out from under the bridge that Jake admitted his money was stolen, that the boy from the saloon had robbed him while pushing him around the flats. Jake slid to a stoop to catch his breath then laid there. He was too trusting. Too stupid. Why had he run off from home in the first place? He took that twenty dollars, most of his father's savings, and he'd lost it. He couldn't ever go back.

A smoky voice came from inside. "Can't sleep on the stoop. It's fifty cents for a bed inside." Jake peered into the shadow of the doorway. It was a flophouse. A sign said this.

"Fifty cents," the voice repeated.

Jake saw the glint off a knife in the shadow.

So how was he lucky? Penniless in a new city. No relations. No connections. No job.

He was lucky because he met Tom Dennison the next day. Folks on the street told him where to find the Old Man, what they called Tom Dennison. They told him the Old Man would help.

Tom Dennison ran things in Omaha those years. For three decades he had a hand in picking who'd be on the winning ticket each election and was on the board of the gas, electric, and water companies. He owned the police force more or less, everyone knew that.

There was a guard outside the door on the street, outside the tobacco shop where Tom Dennison kept an office those years, where a dark staircase led up to the second floor. The guard was roughly the same height as Jake but thicker through the legs and chest. "You need some help, pal?" the guard asked. "You need to see Mr. Dennison?"

Jake didn't move. The guard was Chip Lee. Jake recognized him right away. Chip had been a big deal when Jake was a kid. A prizefighter. All the boys pantomimed his style, the square stance Chip used in his prime, before he was KO'd in three consecutive bouts. There were scars along his jaw, Jake saw, and cloudy discolorations below the lobes of his ears. Chip patted the pockets of Jake's suit and felt along the belt line, then showed Jake up the staircase and stood behind him in the doorway.

The upstairs office occupied the entire second floor. File cabinets stacked everywhere like card catalogs in a library. Autographed photos of movie stars on the walls. Charlie Chaplin and Buster Keaton, Lillian Gish. Ballplayers like Ty Cobb, Grover Cleveland Alexander, Three Finger Mordecai Brown. Pictures of racehorses draped in red roses. Nearly a dozen men lingered under the photos, hands in their pockets. The lights were dim except for one bulb that beamed down over a small pine desk, a desk positioned so close to the entrance that there was just enough space for Jake to slip inside before he was stopped. The lightbulb hung down in his eyes, forcing him to stoop to the desk and squint to see the woman there, her orange hair wispy and pale in the light. At the far end was a larger desk, behind that a rollaway safe. A window let in a wash of sunlight and backlit a man working at the desk. Tom Dennison.

The woman on the platform tapped her nails on her desk until Jake stopped staring around her. Her face was an unearthly white under the bulb. "What do you need?" she asked.

"To talk with Tom Dennison. That's what they told me."

The woman pulled out a black ledger and flipped to a tabbed section to consult its pages. The writing was small and packed tightly, but Jake saw some of what it read, references to the Brandeis department store and the Omaha Electric Light and Power Company, to the Paxton and Fontenelle hotels, to grocery stores, steelworks, lumber and coal companies, trucking firms.

"Tell me where you come from," the woman said. "You're a farmer, right?" Her hair was short and curly, held aloft by some chemical element. "There's something we have going. You'll like it." The woman flipped through the ledger again, scratched something down on a page, then stepped around her desk. "Take this to the Flatiron, and they'll have something for you."

She handed Jake a slip of paper and said he could go. But Tom Dennison waved Jake over first. "Jim Dahlman sent you, is that right? He bailed you out?"

"No, sir. Folks on the street said to come."

"You're not a drunk? Is that what you're saying?"

"No, sir. I want to work."

Jake stood there while Dennison inspected him. Jake was tall, pads of muscles strained against his clothes. He looked over his shoulder to where Dennison's bodyguard waited.

"Is that Chip Lee watching the door?" Jake asked. He lowered his voice so only those around the desk could hear. "We all wanted to punch like him back where I come from."

"That so?"

32

"We followed him in the papers." Jake hunkered down to protect his midsection, he put up fists and bobbed on the balls of his feet. It was Chip's old stance, solid and square. Jake felt his face turn red, seeing Tom smile.

"Chip was pretty good in his day. He was famous up around your parts?"

"Yeah. He was."

"Where was that? Where you're from?" Jake didn't want to say, but he let on, slipped the words *Jackson County* out the side of his mouth. "Sure. I know the place," Dennison said. "I lived near there, in St. John's, when I was a boy. With the Catholics there."

"Yeah? Is that a fact?"

"It is."

Jake had Tom Dennison's interest. This is why Jake was lucky.

"Did you get in a little trouble up there?" Dennison asked.

"I did. I hurt a boy in a fight."

"Well, that's fine. That doesn't mean a damn thing to me. Why would I care if you clipped some guy? So long as the guy deserved it."

Jake found the back of the Flatiron that afternoon, the long rounded butt end where the service entry was with its iron doors painted green. Trash cans lined the wall, empty produce crates, stacked milk bottles. A hotel occupied most of the building. This was on St. Mary's Avenue, where downtown edged against the ethnic neighborhoods. Folks wandered here, passed through from north to south, or back the other way, the block specked with filling stations, printing shops, bail bondsmen. The hotel itself was newly made of tan brick and glazed terra-cotta limestone. The restaurant on its ground floor was elegant and smelled like buttered bread rolls and onion soup through the window. Jake didn't understand why he was sent here, but the man at the service door was ready for him. "You're Strauss," the man said. "I'm the foreman."

Inside, the foreman pointed to spigots dripping with water and four large washtubs near the basement office. He tossed a hunk of soap to Jake and said to wash up. Jake hadn't washed since he left home and didn't realize how filthy he was until grime streamed off him and settled in the bottom of the washtub. His skin burned raw when he finished, from pumice in the soap. "You ready now?" the foreman asked. He was middle-aged, short and muscular, clean shaven. A certain kind of purpose buoyed his accent. "This is hard work," he said, "but you get clothes, three squares a day. If you can dig and push a wheelbarrow, you can handle it."

"We're digging?"

"Of course we're digging. Making tunnels. It don't matter where we're making tunnels to, so never mind that. Do what I tell you—that's your job."

Speed was the first order of business in the tunnels, the foreman made this clear. Wood frames were put up every few yards to prevent cave-ins. Bare wires hung from timber to light the work. The corridor was just wide enough for two men to sneak by. There was hardly room to stand. Once Jake entered the tunnels, that day and the ones that followed, lucky Jake, he'd spend the whole shift stooped over.

There were other men Jake was introduced to, the rest of his crew. Reinhold Bock dug out the edge of the corridor with a pick or shovel or hatchet, whatever it took to expand the path. His was the dirtiest job but also the most important. The others depended on his progress to keep busy. "You won't see him much," the foreman said. Reinhold burrowed deep into a space only big enough for his body and his tools. Dirt flew out over his dangling legs. The next two cleared away what was picked off by Reinhold, shoveling debris into wheelbarrows, and this was where Jake came in. His job was to make sure the work kept moving. He filled in when necessary, lugged dirt and rock out the tunnel, erected frames to keep the corridor from collapsing, steadied beams with his shoulders while others clamped and hammered them into place. Jake mostly shuttled back and forth along the corridor. What the others removed, he piled outside the office. So much debris by the end of the day that they could hardly pass when it was time to clean at the washtubs. It was cramped down there anyway. Besides the foreman's framed office there were tools lying around and washtubs stacked up and street clothes waiting on hooks, their clothes and the clothes of the dozen or more men working in other corridors. There was a telephone on the wall. Jake didn't understand how it worked, but by the next morning the basement would be as clean as ever. Trucks had to back up to the service door overnight to remove the debris. "They load out and dump somewhere," Reinhold said. "A farm. Or in the river."

The shifts were ten hours long, six days a week. It was hard, but Jake liked the work, or at least the idea that he had work. He was lucky to get this job but wouldn't have minded being in the open air. The weather outside was nice those days. It was spring. Sunny, clear, getting warm. He saw so little sun. Mostly he was bent over a wheelbarrow to go back and forth underground. A job that was easy enough to master so long as he didn't get lost. The tunnels spindled off in an impossible web, so Jake followed the track he wore into the loose tunnel bottom, tried to line up the raised patterns left where chunks of the iron wheel broke off. He played games like this to do something besides just pushing loads.

Digging a tunnel under the city wasn't all that strange, he learned. Tunnels spidered all over: from the bargain basement of the Brandeis department store to banks across the street, from office building to office building. Jake worried the paths might cross and they'd bust into a neighboring tunnel, a legit one, and get caught at whatever they were doing. Reinhold said not to worry. "This isn't my first job. You dig for a while, turn where they tell you. Before long you pop up in some basement. It's a hotel. An office that belongs to the boss. Who cares?" Reinhold wore a soft cloth cap to cover his baldness. Its ragged brim edged over his eyes. "I wasn't the one who told you. But Mr. Dennison's got tunnels all over town where he holds things. Here and other places. He just don't want folks to know. It's his prerogative, yeah. He's the boss."

Jake imagined that maybe Reinhold was the architect of all these tunnels. That he alone knew where to burrow and what the point of it all was.

Charlie Pfister and Joe Meinhof were the middlemen in the operation. Half-brothers, they argued throughout the day, over the work, over what tools belonged to whom, over anything. Meinhof had a neat fop of hair he kept parted and oiled, with the sides of his head shaved, a style Jake hadn't seen before. His face was pinched with nervousness. It made Meinhof conspicuous, his eyebrows arching wrinkles into his forehead, a dimple in his chin. Charlie was more at ease. He had a thick mustache and a way of angling his ear when he couldn't hear what was said.

At the end of the day their crew and the others packed outside the foreman's office in the hotel basement to disrobe and scrub off their daily grime, bent double still, this time in a washtub. The foreman set out sponges and paper-wrapped bars of hotel soap, then collected the work clothes in a wicker hamper for the laundry. All the while, Charlie and Joe Meinhof bragged about what went down in social clubs nearby, near fanatical now that the shift was over and they could celebrate. "There's girls, Jake." "And beer!" "You have to come." Once outside the steel door, Meinhof reached up and put his arm around Jake to pull him down Clandish.

Jake ate at Mecklenburg's with the other men nearly every night once he was drawing a wage. "I was here before," he told them, hunched over the bar. "Got tricked out of my last dollar."

Which was true. This was the same place from his first night.

Things had worked out well enough for Jake, but thinking of how he lost the family money made his stomach shrink, and he didn't want to feel that way.

✳

The first time Jake saw the Eigler house he worried he had the wrong address. The homes at this far end of Clandish were too nice, the avenue too residential. The street was paved and washed. Houses were made of brick and stucco and occupied by only one family. The foreman wrote this address on a scrap of paper and sent Jake here. Maria Eigler, the landlady, led him upstairs. His room was on the second floor overlooking Clandish, and was oversized, with an armoire. He didn't have to share with anyone. The only other tenants were a family who lived in the dormer, the Miihlsteins. All but the boy had glasses with mangled steel frames. The girls wore their hair long over the padded shoulders of their dresses. Silke, seventeen, was vibrant and kept her back straight and blushed dolorously when Jake looked at her. Theresa, fifteen, her hair combed off her forehead, was more outgoing. She laughed a lot, a silly kerfuffle that was contagious.

The Miihlstein boy was square and unexceptional among his sisters, Jake thought. Karel walked around shoeless when Jake moved in—strangely, since they weren't that poor. Jake didn't worry. From what Maria said, their mother had apparently died on the boat to America. Karel was allowed to be a little strange then, even though Jake wasn't sure this story was true. There were rumors about every foreigner that could either be believed or not.

Some evenings Jake skipped Mecklenburg's and ate supper at the Eigler house. Maria's dining room was full of wonders. Wainscoting went around the walls to keep the plaster from denting; bookshelves stuck out to catch the feet of Jake's chair; the hard-used furniture; a lamp in the corner; charms and oddities she collected; a darkening portrait of her late husband, August Eigler, a railroad man in the railroad's first days here. Jake thought there was something generous and noble in the way Maria and the Miihlstein kids gabbered to each other and passed food around a crowded table. The dining room warm with steam. Silke and Theresa across from him giggling. Karel squeaking his chair, spilling milk, telling of stray cats he knew. When supper ended,

Maria spread a stack of newspapers over the table. She cross-referenced with an atlas to see where positions on the Western Front had switched. Karel asked Silke to point on the map where they'd lived in Galizien, but the girls were weird about it. Each of them selected different spots on the map, within Austria-Hungary and beyond, where each was born, and disputed which village in Galizien they'd lived the last few years. It was confusing. The boy demanded to know where Maria was born too—the custom for those who were countrymen, as all but Jake were Austrian. Maria and the Miihlsteins were of opposite ends of the empire, but all had been to Vienna. Maria urged the Miihlsteins to tell stories about Viennese *plätze* and the aroma of real coffee as it could only be savored in Wien, and told how she was homesick, Maria interrupting the kids along the way until she realized how much things had changed in a relatively short amount of time, from when she was born and then left, until the others did the same. Anna, the frail one, changed the subject. "Where are you from, Jake?"

"My town isn't on this map," he said, then he pointed out the north-facing bay window. They were perplexed by what they saw. An overgrown cottonwood, an outhouse that had been converted into a toolshed, a tiny bungalow squeezed in along the alley. "That way, six hours upriver by horse," he explained. "It's called Jackson County."

Jake pointed to Danzig on the map when he finished joking, because he knew Jackson County wasn't what Anna meant when she asked him where he was from. "My dad is from around here," Jake explained. "South a ways from Danzig, in Kreis Schwetz." The kids were pleased at what Jake showed them. Silke explained. "We've never lived with a Prussian before," she told him.

"You still haven't," Jake insisted. "I've never been to Prussia. I was born in Nebraska."

"It's the same thing," Karel said, but Theresa cut him off.

"Don't argue. If he says he isn't from there, who are you to disagree? He isn't."

Maria mounted a stool in the parlor to watch families promenade home from social clubs. An alcohol lamp hissed beside her as she puffed smoke from a hand-rolled cigarette out the window and gossiped about neighbors. Who worked what job, who the odd ones were, whose faults were well known, which boys were troublemakers. There was something of an old farm woman in Maria that Jake observed. How her hair was pulled tight in a bun and had paled more orange than gray with age, but was thinning, her forehead elongating, her features moving closer to center. It was a sort of skepticism that affected itself in Maria, a weariness in her face.

She rolled cigarettes to keep her hands busy. Tins of them were all over the house. Jake liked the way sweet Virginia tobacco smelled when she scooped it up with papers, the wood and cherry of it, the robust spirits of dried leaves before they burned.

"Where's your dad?" Jake asked the kids.

"Upstairs," Silke said, folding the newspaper to put it away.

Herr Miihlstein must have thought he was alone, bent over his table to perform some delicate task in only his undershirt and shorts. With a small brush he blacked the neck of a violin, pausing every few strokes to sharpen the bristles between his lips. Jake should have left the man alone, but he was fascinated by the attic. Beside Miihlstein's tools and worktable there were projects of all kinds scattered about. Plaster models. Tangles of copper wire bent and joined to look like flowers. Papier-mâché dolls hung on string from the ceiling. Sheets of corkboard had been installed on the walls of the dormer where they lived, where crosshatched prints from the ladies' section of the paper were pinned, popular songs and cartoons. Bits of English primers too.

It was Anna, Miihlstein's third daughter, who dipped into these arts to decorate the scrupulous attic. She was too sick to go to school. This is what she did instead.

Jake leaned further up the stairs and caused a riser to squeak. Miihlstein noticed him then. "Come and see," Miihlstein said, smiling as he set down his work. He waved Jake to a sofa. On the table a portable burner was heating a teakettle.

"It's hot," Miihlstein said.

Jake regretted coming up. It was warm outside. Spring came too late, then burned off too soon, and it was near sweltering in the dormer. He'd wanted to invite the father out to the porch to enjoy the evening and a beer, but now was stuck as Miihlstein poured tea from the kettle.

Miihlstein was peculiarly formal about serving, his elbows held high, still in his underclothes. "There's no cream," he apologized, pouring his own tea. He reclined then, crossed one leg over the other, and nodded to drink. His glasses kept fogging over. Jake was embarrassed for the man, but he took the tea and sat back to watch it steam. His hands were sore from pushing the wheelbarrow. He had to palm the dainty cup from the bottom.

When Jake asked Miihlstein if he liked it here in Omaha, Miihlstein said it was suitable. Although it troubled him that he couldn't find an opera house. "There isn't an opera house," Jake explained. "Just small theaters. The big ones you see downtown, those are movie palaces."

"No? When I agreed to come, they told me there was an opera house."

"There used to be something, a prairie one, but it burned up. They rebuilt it," Jake said with some hope, "but now they're going to tear that down too because it's old-fashioned. I'm sure that's what they were talking about, whoever told you that."

Miihlstein asked if Jake was from Omaha. Jake said where he was from. "But still Nebraska, yeah?" Miihlstein asked. "That's close to here?"

"A day away, depending."

A drunk feeling covered Jake's mind, so he set his cup back on the table.

"Is that brandy in the tea?" he asked.

"Wine."

Both of them laughed.

"I don't know you," Jake said.

"No. We aren't acquainted."

"I don't even know your given name, Herr Miihlstein. Yeah? Where are your trousers? I'd like to know."

"It's hot. I can't take the tea otherways."

Miihlstein glanced away, apparently more annoyed than embarrassed. Jake waited for him to say something more about it, but he didn't, just bounced his foot. His legs furred over with hair.

"Where exactly are you from?" Jake asked. "I heard it different ways from your kids just now. Vienna? Lviv? Warsaw?"

"We're getting serious now," Miihlstein laughed.

He coached his kids to be coy like this too, Jake realized, as a way to protect themselves.

"We were in New York," Miihlstein said. "Before that, Europe."

"Yeah? Was your wife with you then?"

"She wasn't in New York. Is that it you're asking? She died before."

Jake said he was sorry to hear that. He asked if the kids got into trouble much, not having their mother around. Something Jake knew about, of course, his own mother having died when he was a boy. Lucky Jake.

Miihlstein sat back and looked to the rafters. "Ah. It's complicated. There are many ways to think about the feelings on the children's mother. There's what science has to say. What Freud said of mothers. Jung and the collective memory. Symphonies in the key of D minor."

"It isn't everything," Jake interrupted. "Not having a mother."

Jake and Miihlstein sat back to watch each other. It was only when Jake lifted his teacup from the table to drink that he remembered Miihlstein was in shorts and undershirt, and how this made his glasses and mustache look funny.

"Tell me about your mother," Miihlstein said.

Jake took his time to remember her. "She pushed me off her lap to fluff her skirts when it was hot. There was a hook-shaped scar on her knee. She'd cut it on a broken soap dish. She wrote all the time. In diaries, journals, on whatever was handy. Her hair turned blond in the summer. I was there when she died. A little older than Karel, but not by much. I don't know what else to tell. Twelve years isn't very long to have your mother."

It surprised Jake to say all that. He hadn't said more than fifty words on the subject since she'd died, and he hadn't mentioned her at all after he pummeled that boy who defamed her.

"Can I trust you?" Miihlstein asked.

"What do you mean?"

"Are you a liar? Is that the right word I'm saying? You're a liar?"

"I'm not."

Miihlstein frowned. He uncrossed his legs and leaned forward. "Would you keep track of my boy?"

"Karel? How do you mean?"

"Keep him out of trouble. Do you understand? There's these lousy boys he runs with from his school. Your mother died. So you understand."

"You can trust me," Jake said. He knew he was making a mistake. "I'll take care of Karel."

"Good." Miihlstein refilled their cups. He sat back to sip, recrossed his legs. "I feel better. You are a good person, Jakob. A decent one, is that right? This is something, I feel, people must say to you often. Yeah?"

Karel's shoes were still up the wire. He could see them from the dormer window. "Let Maria buy you new ones," Anna pleaded with him. But Karel didn't want new shoes, he wanted his current ones to not be hanging above the street. His sisters teased him for being a stubborn brat, but he'd have rather walked barefoot than have an old woman bail him out of trouble. "There's nothing spoiled about bare feet," he said. Maria agreed. If Karel wanted to ruin his feet, that was up to him.

His feet suffered from his preference. The soles cut by rocks and broken glass. The skin blistered, black and dry, the nails of his big toes gone ingrown. On the porch in the evening, his feet looked even worse than Jake's.

Karel spent a lot of time with that big farm kid in the weeks after he moved in, watching him stretch out to erase the crick in his back. Young, tall, and daring, an athlete with light hair and strong jaw. Maybe Jake Strauss wasn't the quickest wit, but he wasn't pretentious either. Jake talked American. Karel wanted to sound like him and watched his every move. How Jake unwrapped his swollen feet and dipped them in the steaming water of a zinc tub. How he swirled his toes to dissolve Epsom salts. "You too." He pointed to Karel. "Those Tarzan feet need some work." Maria dragged out a chair so Karel could partake. Both boys with pants rolled to the knee, Jake's socks draped over the handrail to freshen. It stung as the potion seeped in Karel's sores and cuts, but he wouldn't complain, because Jake didn't.

Jake was enormous. He worked some secret job. Had money in his pocket and stayed out late sometimes to meet women, surely to meet women. When he asked why Karel didn't wear shoes, Anna burst out with the truth. Some bully stole them off Karel's feet and tossed them over the wire. Jake stood in the zinc tub to inspect the hanging shoes as they turned with the breeze. "Those yours?" Karel wouldn't say. "Why didn't you say something?" Jake asked, stepping out from the water. "Jesus! To just go barefoot when it's easy enough to snag them."

He went to the house next door, where a painter lived, and asked after a stepladder and a pole. Barefoot himself, a wooden pole in one hand and a beer in the other, Jake fished the shoes off the wire as traffic swerved around him. He returned the ladder and pole, tossed the shoes up to the porch, and sat back with his feet in the tub next to Karel's.

"Not too much worse for wear," Anna said after an inspection.

Jake laughed and gulped the rest of his beer. "I wish that bully was here now," he said. "We'd show him something."

"He doesn't live around here," Karel lied. He felt his face burn, could feel himself becoming as small and as young as he really was. "He won't come back."

"Better think again," Jake warned. "You're going to see him. It's going to happen. Don't think it won't." Karel couldn't look at Jake. "What are you going to do when you see him? That's what you have to ask. Prepare. Plan it out, yeah. Stand up for yourself."

Karel took his feet out of the Epsom water. "Do you want more?" he asked, pointing to Jake's empty glass.

Karel hid in the back of the cellar for a while, getting the beer, beyond where potatoes and beetroots banked against a wall, beyond a twisted mass of flower stems hung upside down, where the booze was stored. Maria had socked in a lot of booze. She bought half the store from Hiller's Groceries at a close-out sale because the state prohibition was coming. Maria had kept tabs on the liquor market like a ticker-tape reader on Wall Street tracked the price of wheat or steel. She picked up a case of Lewis Hunter Rye for $9.75, one of Cedar Brook Bourbon for $10.50. She'd packed in a lot of beer too, with Karel's help loading down the steps, into a compartment near the coal chute, the ceiling low. He felt safe, alone under the floorboards. The tip of his nose damp with the raw air. Cool and damp. Buried like a cagey old mole. The longer he waited in the cellar, the more he could see in the dark. He found framed pictures and held them to what slivers of light there were. Painted portraits, an old one of two girls clutching small white dogs to their laps. Dozens of crates stacked in the back holding who knows what. The wood of the crates like raw clay, brown and sagging. When he lifted one it fell apart in his hands and crashed to the floor. Karel waited a moment, crouched and still, his hands in filth. Surely Maria would have heard. She'd come for him, wondering what took so long. Nobody clambered the stairs. Nobody called through the floor. Karel smelled the must of what fell out. Union Army uniforms, blue flannel and wool, two or three once-intricate medals that disassembled to components when he touched them. A saber guard and scabbard, the blade missing. Maria's husband had been in the war. These were his things.

Under the uniforms and scabbard Karel found an instrument case. Inside was a violin and bow. There were no strings, the fingerboard was loose. If Karel squeezed its body the violin would crumble. Maria never mentioned a violin. Maybe she'd forgotten about it. Maybe the violin was her husband's, that August Eigler, dead long before Karel was born.

Inside the case he found a dagger with a wooden handle. He put the dagger aside, pressed the crate together as best he could, and packed the army clothes inside, shoved the crate back where he found it, then examined the dagger. The blade was tarnished and dull, glazed by black gum here and there. The handle was loose but it held together. The dagger would stab.

Karel wrapped the blade in a handkerchief and secured it in his belt line.

He washed at the kitchen sink upstairs. "Did you find what you were looking for?" Maria asked. She was making lemonade in a glass pitcher. "I don't mind if you have a look around. There's lots of treasures there."

Jake was ready for the beer. A plate of anchovies and crackers was on his lap.

Karel wouldn't tell what he saw in the coal cellar, certainly not the dagger. It was a nice thing to sit and breathe and drink from a glass in quiet. He let the lemonade pucker his face.

"This will be a fine summer," Jake said. He drank the top off his beer, held out a swaying finger to touch the breeze. "Don't you believe me? I'm a farmer. The good weather is coming. Sunshine, I expect. And we have plenty of booze stored in."

It was liberating to sit on the stoop early in the evening in those middle-spring hours when it was warm enough for Karel to roll up his shirtsleeves, like Jake told him to, and let the air hit his skin. This was the main promise of spring. There would be more of these to come. Barefoot (by choice) and comfortable, reclined in a sturdy chair. No mosquitoes yet, no bearing-down evening swelter. There were twin cherry trees in Maria's yard, in full bloom at that moment. One's limbs curved over the crest of the other's crown, where evening light dipped over the ridge of the house to illuminate its stark white petals. The whole world was green in those hours, breezy and clear.

"I shouldn't like to sit so much," Jake said. "That's not the way it's done where I come from. You're supposed to keep busy. Dawn till dusk and all that, yeah."

"This isn't a farm," Maria pointed out.

"You're right. I should be lighthearted."

Karel would remember what Jake was like those first months he came to Omaha. He was alive. He was free and strong. Karel wanted more than anything to know what it felt like to be Jake Strauss on those spring evenings as they watched the gloaming peter out over Clandish. To sweep blond hair behind his ears and flex muscles with every move. To gulp beer and mug witty about its quality. To have people dote on you. To be comfortable in this. There was no need to sneak off those nights.

Jimmy Mac had news. He'd heard from his brothers about an Irish girl a few blocks over who, for a penny, let a boy see but not touch the orange hair that grew among the freckles of her pubis. "You won't believe it," Jimmy said. "No joke. A real burning bush!"

All the boys had heard about this girl. She lived south of the train stations in a mansion cut six ways into apartments and had set up shop under the porch. Stairs zigzagged up both sides to reach the second and third floors of the house. Where the porch wrapped around, there was a loose confederacy of belongings. Washtubs, fishing poles, two chairs with the seats missing, a doctor's cabinet fished out of hospital rubbish, a pile of old coats where calico kittens made a nest. Boys in bunches of fives or sixes made their way to the under-the-house girl once word spread. On the day Karel and his friends went, a few others were sneaking out around the porch.

"She's working," one of them said, "but better hurry. She might get shut down soon."

Karel followed where the boys pointed. On the porch near the kittens was an old woman. "That's her grandma," one of them said. The woman was dark and ancient, Russian looking, so maybe not the girl's relation. She moved only slightly in her chair, like the breeze rocked her, and stared out at nothing, dead except for her eyes.

"Does she tell?"

"Not yet."

"Maybe she's dumb and can't, old as she is."

"Maybe. Maybe she doesn't care."

"I think she's dead," Alfred said.

The boys gazed with audacity for a moment, thinking what a story it would be if they found a dead grandma. She didn't flinch, some vulgar boys all but daring her to, until she leaned back to clack her chair into the siding of the house.

"Jesus," Karel shouted, standing firm with the dagger inside his belt. "She's a witch!"

The other boys left laughing. Karel felt fine with the way he handled himself. Omaha wasn't such a big place, the River Ward surely wasn't. He knew they'd remember he was the one who called the old woman a witch then snuck under a porch to gander up her granddaughter's dress. He was no sissy. Whatever he had to prove to the others he was proving.

The air was damp under there. Some bricks were strewn about to gather moss where the girl waited. She was older, maybe fourteen or so. She sat on a stool, as silent as her grandma, except the girl smoked a cigarette. Bars of light stroked in the smoke where it came through the lattice. The girl didn't say a word when the boys advanced. Alfred held out a penny and she took it. "Two more," she said. "Price has gone up." He handed over what she asked for. Then she lifted her dress and they saw the orange between her thighs. They dropped to their knees. The puff of orange, the fold of skin like she'd been sliced there. How bizarre an invention was this girl. Jimmy Mac moved close, reached a hand out to touch there, but she snapped closed.

The boys stayed a moment longer, snickering. Jimmy apologized and asked if she'd lift her dress again. She wouldn't, not for less than a nickel each now. They still gaped at her, at her lap, knowing what it looked like under her clothes.

※

The boys wandered the Ward the rest of the afternoon, to an alleyway junk shop in the market to look at greasy postcards and tattered ball gloves and brass bedposts and odd parts from dilapidated machines and houses. The guy who ran the shop cleaned out the rooms of the dead if no family or church did it first. In a glass case near the cash drawer, he had a collection of medals from the Civil War. These weren't for sale, but he showed them off to the boys, crosses and stars of brass and gold. "Looky here," the man said. "A Confederate." And it was, tarnished and tattered, the bluish ribbon torn. Karel thought to show the man the one in his belt—a Union officer's dagger—but he worried the man would take it for his collection. They left, went up Pacific to the railroad tracks and over into the tenements, standing tall as they wandered. Karel could die happy, seeing what he'd seen, the burning bush. He walked without aim. Whatever good there was in the city would come to him.

By the courthouse, around the block from the YMCA and the night school, Jimmy Mac went to stare up at the busts and engravings carved on the facade of the library. Sophocles. Goethe. Shakespeare. Curly haired, wigged, chinless men sometimes. Sometimes fiery eyed and crazed. They were poets or something. The boys guessed what those masks meant, death masks, the shadow of the library stretching over the street by then. City and county offices had let out, and lots of people were around to crank over car engines or hop a streetcar. The boys floated in the mass as they stared up at the masks on the library. Schiller, Wordsworth, Homer.

Staring up like that, they were the first to see. An airplane flew over, a hundred feet in the air, no more. White canvas wings and wire struts, its blurring, roaring propeller. The boys shouted "Look!" and all the grown-ups froze to do so. A biplane. Karel saw its machine gun. He saw the pilot's leather head and goggles, the rest of the man enwombed in the plane's fluttering thorax. The pilot did a turn over the courthouse and returned flying upside down. He rolled the biplane twice again until it was headed north and then was gone. Like that. They heard the propeller racket slip across the Ward then waited in silence in case the plane circled back.

Folks spoke quietly at first. "I suppose it's gone." "Maybe." Some waited, but the spell broke once they looked down from the sky. Karel and his friends were the last to give up waiting. They waited near the street to get out of the walkway and watched the clouds for another miracle. They moved to the library side to look north, but the biplane didn't return.

The boys moved on too, down the sidewalk to Eighteenth Street toward home. They permitted themselves to talk about it. To say, finally, "Boy. Did you see that? What a day!"

"Think he's one of ours?" Karel asked.

"Yeah. Sure he is. Fort Omaha is up that way. There's a field there."

"Oh." Karel had never seen a plane up close and rolling. He didn't think of it as an enemy plane, as an asset of the Triple Entente against the Central Powers, even though they were adversaries by definition, Karel being an Austrian on his papers.

The boys weren't paying attention. Just walking. They didn't see Ignatz running at them. "Did you see?" Ignatz shouted, his shoes slapping the pavement.

"The flyer's gone," Karel said.

"You saw?"

"Yeah."

"It just went by," Alfred said. "You missed it."

Ignatz looked like he almost didn't believe. He paced to the end of the block and back, staring at the sky the whole time. He didn't watch where he went. He didn't need to. The clerks and stenos parted out of his way. An angry, puffing bull.

"There was a real flyer," Karel said. "Leather cap and all."

"No shit," Ignatz said. He straightened to catch his breath.

The boys waited to see if they'd get it bad or if they'd be let off. Karel hoped Ignatz would leave them alone. Jake had told him to stand up for himself when he saw the bully, but Karel didn't want to fight. He hoped there would be words, that they could forget what happened before and be nothing to each other from now on. But it didn't work that way. A bully needed no reason.

Ignatz shoved Alfred into the bricks of a building. He grabbed Alfred's collar and was going to slug him. Ignatz felt slighted and was going to take it out on someone. Alfred was going to get it, with nowhere to run. No clerk or steno was going to stop boys from being boys. If Ignatz slapped Alfred around, that was fine to a grown-up.

It wasn't fine to Karel. He couldn't stand to see his friend punched, to stand by and wait to see if he'd get punched too. Karel wanted to do something to stop the bully, and he had the dagger.

He pulled the dagger from his belt and posed the tapered end at Ignatz. "Leave Alfred alone," he shouted. "He didn't do nothing."

"What's wrong with you?" Ignatz said. He released Alfred to grab for the dagger, but he couldn't get it. "What is that?" he asked. "You take it from the junk shop?"

"It's an officer's blade. It will do you good enough."

Ignatz was too quick, too much older and bigger. The dagger only bought Karel a few seconds before Ignatz slapped it from his hands. The blade rattled to the pavement between their feet. Ignatz grabbed Karel then heaved him off the walkway and pinned him against the bricks.

Karel kicked at Ignatz's stomach, slapped at his ears as much as he could with his arms held. It didn't make a difference. Karel looked into Ignatz's face, the meat of his lips as they smiled wet with the juices that ran out. The grip tight under his arms. Karel hurt everywhere. Felt the grasp closing and winced to blackness. This was it. His turn.

Karel was on the ground as he opened his eyes to light, crumpled on his knees, liquid streaming from his mouth as he gasped. Jake was there, a few others, in clean white clothes. They had Ignatz cornered, took the lids off trash cans and banged them together. They shouted and mocked punches so Ignatz had to cover himself. There were about a dozen men around. Working men, playful and mean. They had a boy who thought he was something tough and they had to prove he wasn't.

Ignatz's shoes were shucked off—Jake's idea—and the men took turns throwing them at the roof of a building. Ignatz chased after but couldn't outrace the men, the group of them, and had to watch again as his shoes spun up three stories and came tumbling back.

Karel wasn't exactly sure what was going on. A couple of them helped him up, one who introduced himself as Charlie. Karel said nothing. He watched as Jake chased Ignatz down the street, kicking at the bully's socked feet until Jake let him go.

"What sort of plan was this?" Jake asked Karel. "Let him pin you to the wall? Get strangled?"

"I got a couple shots in," Karel said.

"Yeah. You got a shiner too. Bet you didn't know that, huh?"

Karel felt a knot swell under his eye where Jake poked. The men said that was okay. Ignatz was bigger. What did Karel expect?

"Come on. You boys fought. You come along."

The men pushed to make room at Mecklenburg's bar, pulling the boys along with them. Alfred and Jimmy had been in a saloon before, but this was a first for Karel. The men lifted under the boys' arms, dropped them on stools, then laughed along as Joe Meinhof argued with the bartenders. "What do you mean, how old are they? What's that matter?"

The saloon wouldn't serve kids, not with the statewide prohibition of all alcohol sales.

"Near beer?" the men objected, once the bartender suggested it. "What's that?"

"This one's got a shiner," Jake shouted, bucking his arm around Karel, "and you don't think that deserves a real beer?"

"What rot! You want these boys to eat some near-meat and near-bread too? How about some near-air to breathe, dummy? How'd that suit you?"

Mugs were presented to the boys and they were urged to drink. Joe Meinhof apologized for not being able to get them the real thing. "You get in a real fight, might as well get some real beer for your trouble."

Near beer was horrible, bitter and effervescent. "You don't have to drink it," Jake said, but Karel did anyway. So did Alfred and Jimmy Mac. How couldn't they? A group of real men were toasting them. The boys clanked mugs together and swigged as they looked up at the rowdies cheering on. They met all the men. Jake Strauss, Karel's savior, blond and grinning. Joe Meinhof, who crouched when he spoke to the boys so they saw his half-crazed eyes. Charlie Pfister, who was an old man to them, with his big mustache turning gray. There were others too. Ingo and Heinz and Konrad. Dairymen. They smelled like sour milk and sweat, and brought plates of roasted meat to the bar for the boys to feast from. These were superb men. They gloried in life. They yelled, doltish and unabashed, and called each other names. They wrestled to prove their points. They cussed in German and English and Bohemian, worldly men that they were. Karel cursed them in Yiddish and earned a slap on the back for his talent. They were gods.

Karel watched Jake, Joe, and Charlie most of all. He knew they were up to something secret. They dressed like dairymen but didn't smell like sour milk. When they'd left work, it was the Flatiron they came from, a luxury hotel nowhere near a creamery. It was a mystery.

Somehow it was brought up that the boys had seen the Irish girl's burning bush that afternoon. Their stools were spun so they faced the men. "A girl your age, with that?!" "She's got to be older. She is? I knew it." "Is she still there, you think? Tell me how to find her." The boys couldn't stop laughing, seeing the men worked up. It was a big joke. "Fuck off," Alfred said. His voice hadn't dropped, so his cursing was hilarious. *"Verpisst euch!"*

Joe Meinhof set the dagger on the bar in front of Karel. "This yours?" The men took turns jabbing the blade in the air like they skewered a Rebel, or a Yankee, or whichever. "Looks like it's hardly holding together," Joe said. They'd all seen Karel drop it. Karel took care to not pierce himself as he took the dagger back and slid it into his belt.

He slid off his stool to find Jake, who leaned into a table off in a corner with some women. When Karel came over Jake waved them off, women with grand curly hair and cherry lipstick, who glared at Karel as Jake slipped away. Jake led to the sill of the window and motioned to sit. They watched outside as workers rushed home or to another place. There were more than just swillers on Clandish. There were families, a mother dragging her brats to the stairs of a *Verein*, where it was good to bring kids along, for there was dancing and food and refined attitude in *Vereine* if you were a member. Karel tried listening to what the mother told her kids as she brushed them along. He couldn't hear. The barroom was so loud that only a streetcar could dint the noise inside Mecklenburg's.

Karel noticed how Jake watched the mother get her children inside the club, he too trying to hear. They looked to each other, embarrassed. Karel waited for Jake to say something, to make a joke. Jake licked his lips to think.

When he did speak, Jake explained how, if he stayed late enough, a man met women in saloons. This was not the advice Karel expected after they'd watched that mother rush by with her kids. "I blush when women touch me." Jake pulled Karel close to confide. "The type you find here falls in love instantly when you blush, so long as you're good looking. It's easy. You don't have to say a thing about love. You hardly have to talk at all."

If Jake let it play out, he told, soon enough he'd be up in an empty room to screw on the floor. Sometimes the women he went with were professionals. Sometimes they weren't. He didn't always know the difference. "They want money, I pay. Why would I care? It's perfection. Absolute perfection."

Jake admitted that he didn't know why he told these things to Karel, but he went on for a long time, said he never licked snatch when the woman asked him to. It was too tart, he explained, like these were fine things for a boy to know.

Karel had to interrupt. He wanted to talk about the fight with Ignatz.

"What if you weren't there today? What do you think would of happened?"

"Who cares?" Jake said. "I was there. This happened."

"Yeah. But what if you weren't?"

"Coincidence rules all, *Schatzi*. Don't let it bother you when good things happen. Or bad things, yeah. It's just things."

Jake was drunk. His cheeks hot, eyes deep and wet. Karel felt a little strange himself, though he'd only had near beer. Maybe it wasn't near beer.

Things had gotten out of hand at the bar. Jimmy Mac danced with a woman named Carla, much taller than Jimmy, with bright-red hair curled loosely atop her head. Jimmy had red hair too, but his mother kept his cut short. He was scrawny, like all Irish Karel knew. Skinny legs and arms that were eaten up by hunger, kind of hunched over, if tall, from being bowed double at Catholic mass all the time. Carla looked like a giant over Jimmy. There was no crick in her back. Her chest stuck right out. She wore a yellow dress that filled over itself in layers, a long seashell necklace that slapped Jimmy in the face as they clopped back and forth in front of the bar. Jimmy didn't seem to notice the shells smacking him. He beamed from ear to ear.

Karel had another glass, Jake next to him, clapping his hands with a dozen others as Jimmy and Carla danced. Karel would have clapped, but he held his glass with both hands near his mouth. He felt like he and his friends were men. If only the bartender would allow them beer beer. If only he felt a real drunk instead of this jolly strangeness. Manhood wasn't so far off. He would be twelve before long and things would change for him. He knew this. His changing was a fact, something he felt in the air.

It wasn't long, standing around with his glass, before his father was at the bar to retrieve him. Someone must have seen Karel sitting in the window and sent word up to the Eigler house that the young Miihlstein boy had been roped into some gallivanting spree at a beer saloon. Herr Miihlstein was calm as he grabbed Karel. He merely said it was time to go. Yet as he was so quiet in his manner, it caused a disruption among the people standing by, those who wouldn't have noticed if he'd screamed. Herr Miihlstein in his boxy European hat and black suit, his delicate wire-framed glasses—the folks in Mecklenburg's noticed that. The clapping stopped.

Jake apologized to Herr Miihlstein for not asking permission before bringing Karel down this way. Miihlstein said it wasn't necessary to apologize. "I'm taking care of him," Jake insisted. "There are no worries here."

"What about his bruised eye?" Miihlstein asked. "Who gave him that?"

"Well . . ." Jake laughed. "Would you believe a mouse socked him with a brick?"

As they left the festive end of Clandish, Karel tried to explain about near beer.

"You shouldn't see things like that," Miihlstein objected. "You don't belong there. It's nighttime. Time to be home."

Karel saw after his father said it. The sky was black. It was late.

Consider Evie Chambers.

The trick for a woman like Evie was how to pass time without getting in trouble. She had a dozen ways to kill an afternoon. She listened to records in the morning. Tipped some wine after lunch while she bathed and perfumed to ready herself. Most of all she worked on her clothes. Her mother had taught her how. Evie believed sewing was such a low thing then—she was right about that—but in time she learned there were lower occupations. Now even something simple like a slip gave her the chance to complicate its design, to make it intricate, perhaps needlessly so. She was glad her mother showed her how to do these things. Life would have been so boring if it wasn't for designing her own clothes, for her records, and the long walks she took in the mornings when she could get out. The thing with the man was something else.

Consider that Evie was nice looking and fair skinned, that her hair coiled languidly on its own without having to be relaxed. She had thin lips and small teeth, and smiled nice, and moved graceful, like her hips had knowledge in their curves and dimples. They did. Her mother was never pretty, or at least her mother hadn't been pretty for long, Evie didn't imagine. Evie was more like her father. Her father had run off too. She remembered these things as she sewed. How she'd told her mother, leaving, that sewing was the only thing Evie got from her. "That's all that's worth taking," she'd said. Running off wasn't enough for people like Evie, when she was sixteen years old and wanted to dance in the majestic halls of a grand city. Chicago, New York, Paris, Zagreb, Timbuktu. The precise geography of her ambition was cloudy. What Evie knew was that she wanted to wear the most elegant costumes and carry herself with perfect sangfroid—to meet men who were loose with money, so she could get some money for herself. Evie was twenty-six in the spring of 1917. She missed her mother like she never thought possible before those days. Because her mother couldn't hide what she was, couldn't escape, not like how Evie and her father did. They were the guilty ones, Evie and her father, with delicate features and soft voice and light skin. Evie's mother couldn't hide, couldn't pass, not like Evie could. Which is why Evie liked living on Capitol Avenue in Omaha, a block that was equal parts elegance and squalor, one where people let irregularities slide. There were places like Capitol Avenue in Topeka, where Evie came from, but too many people knew her in Topeka. Even if life in Omaha wasn't so great, she was judged here more by what she did than what she was. In a way, at least. What she looked like, not who she looked like. What she was, not who she came from. Even though this was the truth of the matter as she knew it, Evie couldn't speak this plainness of her desire to her mother. Not when she was growing up and not ever. It had been nearly ten years since they'd spoken. Evie was fairly certain she'd never speak to her mother again.

If Evie had too much wine, she put the tools away to keep from mangling the fabric or slicing open her arms. Those big shears. The razor blade, the sharps. If she was at the table thinking about her mother, then it was time to stopper the wine. Then she bathed, she perfumed. All the things required of a kept girl waiting for her man.

Ugo Daniel would come around seven in the evening. He put money down to keep the rooms. He had a key. Evie kept an eye on the street so his arrival never surprised her. She was ready to greet him, to have a drink poured, a record spinning, a party started and waiting for him. Ugo, always fashionably late. He bought her things—silk stockings, a powder puff, a rabbit fur coat, nothing actually too expensive. She didn't complain about the shabby presents because he was an easy one to handle. Nervous, glancing, spastic in his way, but too self-involved to give her trouble. He spent more time in front of her mirrors than she did. Dressing and re-dressing, preening himself. He claimed people were after him—he had to look good. If he didn't bring along dinner, they ordered in from a restaurant down the street (chop suey was her favorite) and then ate at her table. Evie made a habit of finishing only half of what he got her, no matter the portion. When she ate around a man, she had half. It was a rule.

They ate at the same table where Evie sewed during the day, an oak slab gouged and slashed from use. Ugo never asked about the abused table, nor the bolts of fabric she kept, nor the wire dummy in the corner she used to shape her dresses. Maybe he thought these were merely things all women had. Ugo wasn't so smart. Evie may not have known what he did during the day—whether he had a family on the side in addition to his kept woman—but she knew he'd inherited his money. He'd escaped Europe on a friend's yacht with the family fortune in the early days of the war. A story he told all the time.

After dinner and wine and coffee and wine, they'd go to bed. There was some theater involved then. A feather boa could be ruined between her legs if he bought her one. That happened more than once. Evie knew she looked good. She had energy, a wonderfully pale complexion, a great supple essing of neck, shoulders, and breasts. She knew how to make herself look like she was in love. Evie felt like a movie star doing things with the boa, more like a Talmadge sister than one of Marnie Chambers' brats of Topeka, Kansas. She looked like Natalie Talmadge. That's what she told people to shape how they saw her.

Ugo wasn't the first of her men, he was just the latest. She knew enough by now. He wasn't so bad. Wouldn't beat her. Never threatened to kill her. Wasn't so large. The routine didn't hurt; it was just routine. That's what he laid down for. The worst part was that people asked about Ugo if they had an idea who he was. Was he dangerous? Did he hit her? Some people got aroused hearing such things. Evie took a little extra on the side from some gamblers who asked questions like these and more. Ugo didn't know about that. Evie wouldn't tell him. He gave her some too, of course. She spent it all, every dime. It was too much money for something as simple as being an old man's girl, and the only thing that made what she was doing right was to make the money disappear. She wasn't so naïve anymore to not think what the money meant, or who it was coming from, those gamblers.

That year a swindler they called the Cypriot was the main obsession on the River Ward, on Evie's street too, even more than the battles in Europe. That's what people talked about. The Cypriot was a numbers guy from Chicago, some said, a policy man looking to wheedle in on established terrain. There were stories about his being a ladies' man, a brute. This excited a lot of the girls Evie knew. Some of them said he was a rogue Ottoman assassin trained in Constantinople. That he was a secret agent here to meet other secret agents. Or to knock off a dancer at Chez Paree. It made no sense. One day the Cypriot was a celebrity criminal from the East Coast. The next, girls insisted he was involved with Gavrilo Princip and the Black Hand, that he'd had a role in planning the murder of Archduke Franz Ferdinand and Duchess Sophie, and he was on the run from Sarajevo. Everyone agreed the Cypriot was an important man. He had money, he dressed exquisitely, he kept a girl somewhere in Omaha, in the brownstones north of downtown. The whole bit.

It wasn't Evie's job to worry about Ugo. But she did. Folks said they'd kill that fink Cypriot if they found him. There was a bounty at stake. These were maniacal people who said these things. If they thought Ugo was valuable, or dangerous, they'd do bad things to him. Evie knew Ugo wasn't the Cypriot, if there was such a thing. Ugo wasn't a threat to anyone. He was a silly man.

Still, she worried. He might go missing if someone got the wrong idea. Some days she watched out the window and imagined he wouldn't come back. She wondered, would it be up to her to go looking for him?

She didn't really know what Ugo did when he wasn't in her rooms. She just knew he was prissy and self-conniving and tended to think of himself as a rougher man than he was. He liked to come at her from behind, her lying flat, he pushing her face into the pillows until down seeped into her mouth. She felt small when he did it like that. His body compacting hers. At least she didn't have to look in his eyes when he did it that way. He'd sleep soon enough, curled into himself. He preferred that Evie sleep naked. But once he was asleep, she rose in the dark to find her pajamas folded on the dresser, or she'd be cold.

He didn't touch her when she was sleeping. With some of the others she'd had to stay awake all night and not disturb the covers, so nothing happened she wasn't ready for.

In the morning she helped Ugo dress if he let her. He mostly liked to do it himself, especially the final stages of his costume, the collar, the jacket with the pink silk lining, an ivory comb he scratched through his beard. He flattened his brow with a tip of his pinky finger, flashed eyes at her in the mirror, a threatening motion, maybe not. He straightened his eyelashes, blinking rapidly along an extent of pointer finger. Evie along, ready with his coat.

He placed her in the window when he left. He liked to stop and look back and have her stare down, half-undressed, like she craved him. He liked to have people on the street see that.

Then she could close the shades and forget. It was a long night's work. Not the easiest way to get by, but she didn't know of any easy way. This beat dancing for dimes in some crummy hall to a two-bit band bored by its own miserable sound. At least Evie had her cutting table to go back to. Her own two hands warmed the slab when she spread fabric over and marked chalk where chalk should be marked.

Some of those days Evie dreamed about what it would be like to own a garment shop, to make a living selling clothes to other women and not be beholden to wicked men to get by. In some ways her mother, a seamstress from Topeka, had lived this life already. Her mother doing business out of that shabby front room, inching along on the pennies and nickels she earned by darning socks and patching trousers. Evie wondered, if she tried to break out on her own, could she do any better than her mother had done? These were the kinds of unanswerable questions she considered when alone at the sewing table with only her wine and her tools and the memory of her mother.

One evening Maria pointed out a girl to Jake. Tall, slender, with a small, well-shaped face. Her name was Doreen, and she'd have looked dignified, except she was unwell. Her hair thin, her face discolored by clouds of yellow and green. Jake couldn't take his eyes off her. He tracked the red of her dress as foot traffic washed around her on Clandish. The dress was old-fashioned and out of season, too heavy for the weather. She was bundled up, and everyone knew why.

She clutched a man's elbow to inch along the walkway. "That's her betrothed." Maria's breath came over the sill, sweet with tobacco. "What a shame. The wedding's been put off. That's what they always do when the scandal's in the papers."

She and another girl had been raped that month. Black men were the ones who did it.

Jake had never seen anything like the Fourth of July in 1917. There wasn't anything like this before, as a matter of fact, celebrating Independence Day while fighting a world war. Flags flew over all Omaha, the reds, whites, and blues of the US, France, and Britain. Every neighborhood helped move the celebration along. Even if there was disagreement, if President Wilson should have got them roped into the European war or not, the River Ward wasn't going to miss out on a party like this. The tunnelers got the day off, despite it being a Wednesday, and they were in Mecklenburg's early that morning to drop dimes on the bar and bicker before heading to the parade, where spectators packed both sides of Farnam on the sidewalks and lawns that fronted the courthouse and city hall. The parade was to honor the military. This went without saying. Every civic event was obsessed with patriotism that summer. They called this one the Kick the Kaiser Parade.

When the tunnelers got to the parade, Red Cross nurses in white-winged hats marched along the streetcar tracks. Contingents from army and navy brass bands followed, then a handful of blimp pilots from the academy at Fort Omaha. Bunting draped from the windows of city hall. Flags flew from atop the *Bee* newspaper and Omaha National Bank buildings. Businessmen held pickets painted with slogans against the Kaiser, making fun of his wooden arm, warning that America was coming. Novelty Old Glories were sold, noisemakers and popguns too, paper hats, fireworks and hot dogs, lemonade. The pavement was littered with debris, the walkways packed with people caught up in a fanfare. Merchants in fruit-sticky aprons, office girls in blue dresses, primped schoolkids and frazzled teachers, Civil War veterans with bronze service tokens pinned to their lapels. There were drums and bugles, full brass sections. A group of frumpy girl stenographers near Jake sang the national anthem, impromptu, a cappella, in an ecstatic patriotic joy.

Word started going around that morning about the rowdy celebrations that took place in Europe overnight, how a million Parisians cheered as doughboys marched the Champs-Élysées. All those Frenchies were elated about reinforcements coming over on boats. In Omaha, a place those boys came from, the reality of what America was in for on the Western Front was starting to hit home. Conscription had begun. Over two million young Americans would be selected for service. Meanwhile people read aloud from front-page digests and marveled at the calamities that would soon involve their sons and neighbors. Long-range German railway guns shelled London in June, with mortars blasting sixty miles distant; meanwhile the English tunneled under enemy lines at the Messines Ridge in Ypres and killed thousands of Germans when they detonated six hundred tons of explosives in the mines. The war had already been going on for three years and nobody knew when the fighting would stop. The only certainty was that Americans would soon number in the dead.

Jake hadn't wanted to go this far uptown, he'd wanted to see a big wrestling match that sounded more entertaining. No-neck Marin Plestina from South Omaha was going to face the handsomely coifed Henry Ordeman of Minneapolis in an auditorium that wasn't all that far away from where the annual Interrace Game was to be played between Northside and Southside baseball squads. Jake was outvoted by his friends, though, because there was no price for admission to the parade (the wrestling and baseball were two dollars each) and the tunnelers wanted to save money for drinks later on. Jake had spent most of his time in clubs and saloons after what happened with Karel, feeling he should avoid the Miihlsteins until any hard feelings blew over. Even though Karel explained it was just near beer he drank in Mecklenburg's, and Jake confirmed this, Herr Miihlstein kept the boy under lock and key for the rest of the summer. Jake felt bad about that. It didn't occur to him until later that Mecklenburg's operated illegally during the state prohibition. "What if there was a raid?" Herr Miihlstein had asked. "How would you feel if the boy had been arrested?" Jake shouldn't have promised to look out for Karel. That's where he went wrong.

There was food at the parade, near the courthouse steps, so Jake ate. He bought a grilled hotdog and a Nehi cola, then a scoop of pistachio ice cream and some roasted nuts. No matter how he passed the afternoon he'd go to the Potsdamer later, a dancing club. Jake couldn't lose. He wore a gray cap, wool trousers, a whitish shirt. He was excited to be up where the important buildings were. The six-story clock tower of the post office, banks with marble festoons, municipal shrines where politicians did business. Just the year before, President Wilson gave a campaign speech on this spot. Jake stood where the grandstand had been.

He looked to the parade, to the crowd. He smoked to pass the time. That's when he spotted the girl, the one who was raped in Riverview Park. That Doreen. She was only twenty yards away, steadying herself against a light pole. She wore the same red dress, torn and dirty now, not so red. Her hair was thin, unpinned and breezy about her face.

Street kids surrounded her. You couldn't stop and talk to a kid like that or else a bunch would move in. That was how the girl screwed up. Now she was in trouble. Maybe she asked what occasion it was or if they'd buy her a lemonade from one of the vendors. Then the street kids noticed her. They pulled at the loose seams of her dress. Called her a tidbit, a chippy. Asked who she worked for, or if she was looking for a mack.

Jake shouldn't have been bothered—she wasn't his sister, she hadn't been his fiancée—but he wanted the kids to leave her alone. She screamed, but it only egged them on.

"We should do something," Jake said to his friends, the other tunnelers. "We could drive them off if we tried."

"Cut it out," Charlie barked back. "It's not our business."

Jake turned red. "We can take them. If we have to fight, I know we'll win."

"Think a second," Meinhof said. "Remember where we're at, Herr Jakob. It would be Huns attacking the boys. They'd have us hanging from a tree before you know what."

The girl shucked off into the crowd anyway and the gang left her alone. They were just picking on her, reminding everyone of her misery. Street kids were the least of her problems.

It was a relief to see dancers take the stage at the Potsdamer, once Jake and the tunnelers arrived at the club. They spoke their mother tongue here. Smelled and tasted and handled their own food, at the pinnacle of culture as they knew it. A sensational concurrence of music and communion. There was five-cent beer, and the price of admission included a glass of Rhine wine, or something like it. Even though Nebraska was officially a dry state now, little had changed on the River Ward. City authorities made no effort to enforce the law. Many saloons stayed open and, at least in Omaha, the prohibition flopped. Barkeepers kept the beer flowing, moving quickly so the taps rarely closed. A glass was filled with frothing amber then replaced by another before much could spill. Patrons moved at a corresponding pace, they had to, trading dimes for beers in a single motion, their combined mass a cloud of felt hats and rosy faces. The pitch smell of the mills lingered in and out of clothes and skin. Oompahs pealed joyously, openly, by a brass band that throbbed the crowd with dance music until the well-greased hustled to an opening and circled recklessly with their fellows. On stage the girls were lithe and graceful with long kicking limbs, except for one who had short, strong legs, the most athletic, who leapt with rousing quickness. The routine was disorganized, but Jake liked it. The girls were pretty. The skimpy outfits they wore looked like tiger pelts. Furry ears rounded out of their hair. It was nice to watch a band play, to lean into a balcony rail and enjoy music, to watch a twirling baton spin between the drummer's carousel fingers, and smile as the stick, snatched midair, made the bass drum boom.

More friends showed up. They all got drunk and took up the news that was parsed near constantly in places where they could speak freely—politics, war, the Cypriot.

Joe Meinhof was already exasperated. "I knew this would happen. It's no coincidence this all started once the Cypriot showed up. And a bunch of *Schwarzers* moving in to take jobs. What's happening to those girls. It's the Cypriot! I know it."

Jake focused below, where the crowd was busy. Young men looking to get sauced mobbed the kegs of beer and pushed each other around, the same brand of street kids who harassed the girl at the parade. They were out of place, with their tilted hats and clipped English, and that they didn't dance. They didn't even sway or tap their feet. They weren't German.

Meinhof went on, his back to the room. "It wasn't like this before. Blackies with their paws on a woman. It's chaos they want. That's why they're here."

Joe Meinhof was the kind of guy who had a dozen theories for any debate, who existed beyond logic. His face had a nervous quality because of the wrinkles in his forehead, that odd fop of hair on his head. He was a small, bewildered person.

Charlie, Meinhof's half-brother, didn't buy these kinds of conspiracies. "Don't make yourself crazy," he said, moving closer until both brothers leaned on the railing. "What a stupid thing to say. How does having women raped help anybody?"

"Okay." Meinhof smiled, an amused lilt to his voice. "Not all blacks are rotten. There's some bad eggs. I don't like to have to repeat this. But the rapes. Those poor girls. That's the kind of thing that's going to happen more and more until a blackie's held to task."

Jake wished they'd shut up. He hated talking politics, and how angry some of them got, himself included to be honest, thinking about a girl being taken advantage of by a black man. He'd think about Charlie's question for a long time after, following the logic that it could somehow help those in power to have a girl raped.

Jake was tired of his friends. How their faces drooped longer and their lips wavered open to preach some injustice or another until the debate spiraled to the irrelevant. Jake didn't want to hear what his friends said. They were just as hateful as anybody. That didn't make things better. Jake stepped outside to have a smoke. Once he breathed different air, he decided to head home.

It was late evening. The sun labored to set in the July lethargy, stopped at its vanishing point to smolder, its light turned red in wisps of smoke. Hundreds of folks congregated on Clandish. They packed walkways to light off ladyfingers and roman candles. It was too hot to sit inside, a southern wind gusting furnace air and silt. Jake wandered the boulevard. He watched families outside their homes and smiled at those he knew, friends of Maria. Almost all houses on Clandish were wood framed. Newer, smaller homes crouched in under the eaves of big ones like Maria's two-and-a-half-story Victorian down the block, so narrow that alleys between houses became shallow ditches and truncated backyards overflowed with native trees—ancient black walnut, bur oak, and cottonwood. Fragrance seeped from these trees now like it did at no other time of year. Jake caught his breath in the familiar bouquet of a mature tree's leaves. He picked the aroma out from urban odors and remembered what it was like to stroll in the forests and orchards at home, the walkway dimpled with the remains of cherries.

Jake loved the trees back on the homestead in Jackson County. He'd felt safe in them. Lindens, ash, hickory, plum, and one plane tree he could make out from half a mile away, tall and white and ancient. Its ashy limbs glowed incandescent in morning and evening light, somehow brighter when everything around was darker. Holy in the way it shined in the gloaming of a summer evening, and that it lived at a parsonage. The tree looked like it had a halo, like it was God himself.

Jake imagined what Maria and the Miihlstein kids had devised to savor the evening that Fourth of July. He was miserable, ambling alone in Omaha. What he saw on Clandish reminded him of the way folks back home used to talk outside church on Sundays when the weather was nice. He remembered how they sang hymns inside the sanctuary. Afterwards there would be a picnic under the trees of the parsonage, or they would go to a neighbor's house to eat in the shade of a vine-heavy pergola. Every Sunday was a holiday. They sang out in church because there wouldn't have been music if they didn't. There were so few of them it didn't matter who had a nice voice or who had trouble staying on key. There was no one else, nowhere outside of them, the body they made together back home in Jackson County.

The noise stopped him in his tracks. It didn't register what was happening. Some arguing a few blocks back on Clandish. Shouting between young men then a pistol shot. Jake heard. He headed back to see. Back into the people who ran up the long hill of Clandish. Women in summer dresses, hats flying off their heads. Men sprinting away. "A kid started trouble," one of the fleeing said to another. "Some paddy cop tried to nab him." A woman knocked into them. "It's the Cypriot!" she shouted, arms crossed over her breast. "It's him!"

Something whizzed by Jake's head into a storefront. The muscles in his neck and under his arms gripped into him at a shattering that grew louder, faster, as the storefront window cleaved from its frame, its fantastic dissolution against the pavement. Jake tucked his chin to his chest to shrink his face into the mass of his torso. He turned to look, and the window was gone. A man rushed inside, to the hardware store, then tossed out hoes, shovels, an ax, to who'd take one. He slapped a pick handle into Jake's hand and shouted, "Tear them up!" He meant the cops, who were running by with batons. Jake turned the pick in his hands to examine the grains and cracks of its wood handle. The memory of how to swing was locked in his arms—like when he'd whipped that boy back home. He let the pick fall to the ground. He didn't want to use it. He'd stay out of trouble.

They ran with weapons and tools, the folks on Clandish Street, ready to find the Cypriot and take him apart after that woman shouted the name. But the man was hard to find. There were so many rumors about what the Cypriot looked like. How could anyone recognize him? In the meantime guys grabbed merchandise from knocked-in storefronts. Drunks broke things because they could. Most men on the Ward had been drinking since morning to celebrate the holiday, and now they had this to celebrate. Something free for the taking. Street kids made a terrible racket when the cops tried to carry them off, but more boys pushed through all the time. The cops couldn't keep up. Even little kids leaned out windows to fire roman candles and taunt a cop. Flares and shining orange sparks rained down. The whole thing that much better with a rocket's red glare. Who could disagree? Most of the boys on Clandish were involved in some way. Shouting out windows and stealing candy and catching hell from a man who knew their parents and ducking around the sidewalks, trying to keep from getting slugged. A melee like this was somewhat common, every couple summers when the heat got to people. A melee was a great thing in the way a street kid saw the world: all the yelling and violence. The desecration of buildings that appeared indestructible. What did it matter to break a window? What did it matter to take a knife and gash the wood of a door? The world, this city, it all seemed permanent. Nothing, the boys believed, would ever change Omaha. They wanted to leave a mark, even if that mark was vandalism. The boys felt it was a fundamental right to slur cops. They were entitled to toss a brick down the street without concern for where it landed. Most of the men on Clandish felt the same way. Why should a boy have felt any different?

As Jake snuck through the melee, a woman ran up the back of his legs. She screamed, "My boy! Where's my boy!" She found *her boy* cracking a man with a baseball bat. Jake rubbed the tendons behind his knees as the woman ran off. He was still unscathed by that point. Many weren't so lucky. A guy collapsed by the door of the Potsdamer, laughing to himself. His mustache thick with blood that dripped on his shirt and vest. His nose struck flat against his face. "Good shot, Paddy," he laughed. *"Sehr gut, sehr gut."* "You okay, buddy?" Jake asked, leaning in as blood erupted from the guy's nose, spraying him with red. The guy laughed louder, even as he choked and sputtered. And Jake wiping blood from his lips, spitting, disgusted. It was impossible to just wipe the blood away.

Some still were drinking inside at the Potsdamer, but the show was over. Performers waited at the door to see if kids would come back through to cause trouble. It was strange to see them from the street. Burlesque next to bassoonist, lithe vocalist hugging the arm of stout gymnast.

Jake's friends were on the balcony. Meinhof, Reinhold, Charlie, a few others from the tunnels. "Are you still here?" Charlie asked, swaying, a glass of green wine in each hand. Charlie rubbed the splatters on Jake's shirt, somewhat amused when his fingers came back sticky with blood.

They moved to the bathroom to watch from a window.

Rumors of a bounty on the Cypriot's head went around. Tom Dennison was the one offering. In his drunk, Meinhof bragged that he was going to spot the Cypriot and run down to beat the tar from his bones, then carry him up to Dennison for the money. Jake pretended to ignore Meinhof, but he didn't back away either. He scanned the faces below and dreamed of the reward. He knew only that the Cypriot had a beard and was foreign—from Cyprus, whatever that meant—and that there was some deformity in the shape of his eyes. A lot of men on the street looked a little like that. How was Jake supposed to pick?

It was close to midnight before the melee petered out and Jake could tread over the debris to get home. Broken glass, trampled hats, splintered wood, casings of rockets and firecrackers, shotgun shells. Most people on the street now had been caught in the fighting and finally had a chance to walk home, shirttail untucked, hat in hand. Jake saw fireworks burst not so far away. Big shows were starting in Field Club and on the Gold Coast, in the moneyed wards. Jake saw the explosions, distant above rooftops like flowers, but was too far away to hear them go off.

On his street, things were changed. The lunchroom Charlie ate at on Sundays, a chair stuck through its door where the glass used to be. The shop where Jake bought chocolates, looted of its confections. Bakeries and canned goods stores, their shelves emptied and toppled. The sign for Mecklenburg's Saloon swung by a single chain above the sidewalk, but at least its windows were intact. A line of bouncers stood guard outside with maplewood paddles.

It was like Jake had never been on Clandish before, the neighborhood misshaped like it was. He noticed flagpoles atop the *Vereine*. None of them flew flags during the war, so he hadn't noticed the poles. He'd never seen the trees that grew behind Mecklenburg's, or that they were sycamores. Clandish felt small. He heard bands play exuberant foreign anthems in Little Sicily. He saw fireworks explode in jubilee uptown, in a different place altogether.

There was music when Jake got to the Flatiron near 4 a.m. He was in early for work. A band inched through a final set of slow and melancholy improvisation in the basement club. The cornet on a hazy, unending solo, the drummer patting a snare half-asleep because his hands couldn't stop moving, a punctuating tweet from a clarinet now and then. Jake wanted to get through the service entry fast and start digging, he came early because he couldn't sleep, but two teenagers leaned near the door, a boy and a girl.

He sometimes saw kids like these jiggle the handle of the locked club door in the afternoon, or stumble up the steps broke in the morning. The Flatiron was irresistible to thrill-seeking children. Not the kind of person who lived and grew up on Clandish, but rich kids who'd developed a taste for what they called jungle music, who snuck around more or less constantly to find a way in where they weren't wanted.

The boy at the service door pulled a flask from his jacket and handed it to the girl. She was smart looking. A girl nearly of age, in rings, pins, and furs, a dress cut so a man's gaze drew to the sateen that clung to her taut virgin bump. This girl shouldn't have been on the Ward, a girl from a nice family who had a lot to lose. Jake got aroused at the sight of a rich girl. But that guy was with her too. There was always a guy. This one older, a college boy in a bow-tie costume, white gloves and patent leather shoes. It ruined the fantasy to see the kind of guy a girl like that hung on. Cocky ones with new speedsters and roadsters of bright yellow and red. Warren or Scotty or Tim racing off in ivory suits and skimmer hats to a surfside jazz club hidden in a clump of cottonwoods along the river, an all-night juke joint where they could find illicit goods like fried catfish and cold beer. Boys who bought gifts for their girls with money made clerking part-time at Daddy's office. And the girls. Prim and pretty with powdered faces, lips rubbed red with jelly bean guts. Lillian, Maud, Bernadette, Carol. Girls who kept Mother's flask of brandy in a fluff of goldenrod dress, who caused a scandal when they came home hammered and crashed into the maid's room by mistake.

The dandy sneered at Jake as he tipped his flask. He said something under his breath about the way foreigners dressed. Jake hadn't changed his clothes. He'd forgot about the blood that speckled his shirt. The dandy muttered to the girl again. He whispered "Hun" so Jake could hear.

Jake wanted to say something in return. With a heavy accent. Like a Katzenjammer Kid comic strip. *Vot's der bich idea?* he'd say. *Chust vait! Efery dog vill got his day!* But he stayed silent. They would have laughed at him if he talked that way. He intimidated boys like the dandy, he didn't need to say anything. He muscled his shoulders back, his chest out, and the boy and girl looked at their feet then cleared the doorway. They swigged from the flask, walked away. Jake went to work. He'd forget them once he was in the tunnel, scraping out the end of the apse.

※

He was alone with the sound of his shovel cutting dirt. The clink of
metal chucking rock. The flame sizzle of a lantern with condensation
on its wick. There was constant vibration from above, something nearly
silent, an inner-earth rumble he didn't notice if others were there. He
liked to inhabit this noise when he was alone, to estimate how many
thousand vibrations from around the city merged to make one growl.
He'd worked a couple hours. The others would be there before long,
hungover but ready to go. He tried to get as much done as he could first.
Fixed a rhythm with the pick, sliced its blade into deposits of clay. Took
his shirt off when he got going. Leveraged rocks loose with an iron rod
and relied on the work to calm his mind. The cadence of digging, the
feel of metal and wood tools—they reminded him of home. He'd be
farming now if he hadn't run off, so it was a comfort to imagine pilot-
ing a mule plow and turning over furrows, the sun not yet full over the
horizon. Jake missed his animals, his trees. He pictured rolling green
hills, his stomach muscles tight, and a horse at full gallop climbing the
angles of a pasture. There was the mound of sod where the old dugout
had been. The corn up past his knee now that it was July. He recalled
picking beetle bugs off potato leaves to drop in the kerosene can and
fishing milkweed out of the soil with the tip of a spade. He just about
felt light strike his skin at sunrise, a warm embrace around his shoulders
and neck. Nothing could make him forget his connection to the land,
the farm and his family, the woods and streams he played in as a boy.
He'd have given anything to keep the kind of peace he experienced in
the woods as a child, his mother near him, before he lost her. He'd felt
extraordinarily alive. Connected to the world as he knew it then. That
peace was lost to him now. How he'd planted a line of bur oak along
the road one summer. Grew them from acorns. How there was rhubarb
and artichoke in the forest. Wild strawberries. He owned these things.
They owned him too. The bur oak, the rhubarb, the woods, the hills.
They all laid claim on Jake.

He almost felt like he was back there, the sun on his neck, when he heard a noise behind him in the tunnel.

A man was groping along the wall in the dim glow of the lanterns. Jake heard feet shuffle over the rocky floor, something dropped to a plank, and pebbles scattered. He tipped the beam of his lantern, angling its housing with the spade he held to see a stranger turn into the apse. "Nobody's supposed to be down here," Jake said. His voice was quiet and shaky, he was embarrassed that he'd been caught dreaming. He let the lantern swing from its hook. The flame flickered as a man came into the light, a man who leaned close and squinted to see who was there.

"If that is true," the man replied, "then why are you here?"

Jake held the spade crossed over his chest, showed it to the man to answer. The man's eyes changed shapes as he tried to see, half-blind without his glasses.

It came together in a flash. That this was the Cypriot. He'd hid in the tunnels, a bounty on his head. It didn't occur to Jake that he might be wrong. This was the Cypriot.

The man was in bad shape, his fine costume torn and muddy from scrabbling in the tunnels. Bruises marred his jaw, only partly hidden by his beard. He wasn't as big as the rumors said he was. His body was soft and round. He looked prissy, the way he lowered gingerly to his knees to feel along the tunnel floor.

Jake saw the glint of a lens further down, but he didn't move to pick up the glasses. He backed into the apse and gripped tighter the spade in his hands. His breath stuck in his throat. He wanted to leave but would have to cross the Cypriot to reach the open end of the tunnel.

"They were crazed up there," the man said, back on his haunches. There was liquor on his breath. "Is it all finished? The fighting?" He looked for his glasses again, edged the wrong way, closer to Jake and the tools. "Is there a way out of here?" he asked.

"I don't think so," Jake said. "These tunnels aren't open."

"I slipped down a window. A stroke of luck, getting away. At least till I got lost."

The man scrabbled on his hands and knees to search for his glasses. He skimmed over the handles of shovels, picks, axes, each one strapped tight in a bundle.

Jake wrung his palms over the shovel he held. He wouldn't cross the man. "Why were they after you? Did you do something to start all that?"

The man bent forward to grope the wood handles. He loosened the strap.

Jake wanted out of there. His legs weak. A streetcar rumbling above them, its vibrations coming, making the lights flicker. The man lunged as Jake blinked with the lights, and Jake was hit, struck across his forearm. His air escaped. The man swung again, but too high. The handle he swung scraped the tunnel ceiling and stuck a second, so Jake pushed the man back.

It felt like Jake's arm was broken. But he wasn't blind in agony. He felt the pain-thrill rise in his heart. When the man came back he dodged the slashing handle. He drove into the man again with his spade and this time shoved him over the bundle of tools.

The Cypriot opened his mouth to speak but Jake swung and connected on the ribs. An echoless thump forced air out. He got the man good.

Nine more times Jake did this. Spade levered across his hip. He felt ribs disconnect from meat. The Cypriot grasping a tool handle between strikes. Then the Cypriot, the Cypriot's grasping hand, released without grabbing.

Jake thought he'd killed the man. He'd felt the body give even on the first blow. But he touched the man's throat and felt blood pump. He turned the body over. The eyes gazed out with animal fright, like the body would rise up and run down the tunnel. The body didn't move. The eyes followed Jake as he dropped to his elbows.

77

"He's dead," Jake said to no one. He watched the body rise and flounder. There was gurgling from the mouth. The head tried to rise but then sunk. Jake saw his own bloody hands. He cupped dirt from the apse and rubbed until there was mud.

The others arrived. They turned pale when they saw the man on his stomach. His mouth bubbled blood. Jake sitting there with the spade over his knees.

"There was an accident," he said.

They didn't accuse Jake of anything. They carried the body to the foreman's office, where a telephone hung on the wall. Tom Dennison would need to know.

A BRAND FROM THE BURNING
BURNING
Winter 1918

Karel was sore the morning after his father found him at Mecklenburg's. Sore from his fight with Ignatz, in his face and ribs, and in other ways. His head hurt. His stomach was upset. Silke and Theresa explained it to him. Karel smiled, a sick smirk he felt twist on his face. "I'm not joking," Silke said. "You were drunk."

"It was only near beer," Karel said. "Don't be a fool."

Karel hoped his father would forget the whole thing as soon as the shiner went away, but it didn't work like that. The bruise faded in a week; Karel was locked in the attic all summer. None of the boys from school would see him for months as he worked with Miihlstein in the attic, handed over tools when asked for them, learned how to apply lacquer and screw-down clamps without crushing the often flimsy wood. Karel didn't really enjoy the work, but it was something to do. Otherwise, he would have gone half-crazed cooped up like that. Even Miihlstein himself, the old hermit, got out more than Karel did. On weekends Miihlstein met some Paris bohemians to play for tips outside Continental restaurants. Miihlstein on a hurdy-gurdy of the Hungarian style he'd picked up in Galizien, cranking out a buzzing noise for the Frenchies to paint a melody on. He gave Karel a chance to come along if the boy learned to play. He even offered to make a new hurdy-gurdy from a violin that would be Karel's own. Karel didn't go for that.

On days he was lucky, Maria sent Karel to the coal cellar to unearth some old dress or a sachet of papers, a bottle of sherry she'd deprived herself of on an unfortunate, moralistic whim. Karel didn't care what he was supposed to retrieve. If it meant rooting in antiquities, that was good enough. He could fill a whole day down where it was cooler. He'd tried to help Anna with her crafts the first few weeks, but the way she worked frustrated him, how she scribbled with a nub of pencil or bent strands of wire this way then that. "What's that you're making?" Karel had bugged her. Anna turned her back to ignore him, and eventually her scribbles took shape. An octopus drawn in the overlaps of the repeating loops of her cursive *a*. A hare kinked out of wire. When Anna finished, she turned to show Karel. Almost always it was a discernible something, and looked first-rate, he had to admit, most of the time. Karel wasn't artistic at all, even when he worked a project through in his mind first and tried his hardest—like when he bungled the repairs Miihlstein was making on an instrument. Karel limited himself to handing over tools instead. Any idiot, once he learned its name, could select the right gauge awl for the man requesting it.

When school began in the fall, Karel finally escaped the attic. He worried that the other boys might have forgot about him, but he shouldn't have. Alfred Braun and Jimmy Mac were dying to hear what happened to Karel that night they took initiation in Mecklenburg's.

"Jesus Christ!" Alfred said. "You get locked up or something?"

"Missus Maria told us you got in big trouble about what happened down there, yeah."

Explanations were tendered once the boys had a chance, after school the first day of fifth grade. How Jimmy Mac's mother was magically ignorant of what happened. Jimmy stank like beer when he came home late, red-faced and aquiver from dancing with a painted woman. But his mother said nothing. She let him go off to bed and even sleep in late the next morning. If his father had been around—if Mr. McHenry wasn't out even later himself—then Jimmy might have earned some blows. As it was, he was left to wonder why he got away with carrying on in sin. Jimmy contemplated this mystery a full month before he carried his troubles to a kneeler one Sunday. Looking up at the Savior on a crucifix, Jimmy realized that the Lord saw all and remembered all. He promised to never do something like that again—not till he was older.

As for Alfred, there was no doubt Emil Braun would hear about his youngest boy being in a beer saloon. He did. But Braun didn't punish Alfred, didn't lock him up, didn't leave him to come to terms with a mass of guilt on his own—the penance his friends faced. No. If Alfred found himself at a bar, then Braun figured the boy was old enough to see certain other things too. Thereafter he took Alfred to the Jobbers Canyon labor market twice a week to show what it really meant to be a workingman. That which wasn't revelry. To face down a hiring manager, to make yourself appear useful, or else.

Once school started, Karel and Jimmy Mac came along to the warehouses too, early mornings before the tardy bell rang. There were fields of warehouses that backed to the river, block after block, their brick walls stenciled with the names of owners. Wholesalers and creameries were housed here, hoarders, manufacturers, middle men. "Butter, tools, furniture, grain, meat, nails," Braun shouted. "Anything that can be shipped and purchased elsewhere, you'll find it here." Rubber tires flew from window to window across an alley, four stories up. The pavement was laced with spur rails, from one loading dock to another, but the real action took place in the alleyways. That's what Braun showed the boys—outside a warehouse on 6½ Street, where jobbers felt out soft spots along the hiring line. Many jobbers were German, or Germanic at least. Karel could tell from the tones of voices, the varieties of cadence, the burly shapes of bodies. Once Braun and the boys fell in with these men, it was impossible to escape their halting mass. Interlocked at the elbows and hips, all crushing forward, acting on a rumor of who was hiring that morning and for what. At a certain time a green slat door rolled open and a manager emerged, buttressed on each arm by a thug.

Karel climbed a drainpipe to see. The manager was short and fat and wore a coat that went to his feet. He held a clipboard, to which was fastened the list of jobs. He looked between list and crowd. Those nearby stood taller when the manager's gaze moved over, chests puffing, backs lengthening. He spoke English first. Shouted the rules of how this company did business: what they paid, what work was to be done, what kind of worker was wanted, whether lunch was served. When he finished, the manager repeated the instructions in German, then Italian, then Lithuanian. His hired muscle joked the whole time, aping the instructions in Irish accents for a group of micks near the dock. Some workers were picked right away. Regulars with the company who climbed the concrete ledge of the loading dock, slipped past the muscle, and pooled together inside the building. They smoked cigarettes and waited for the other elect. All of them dressed in white denim overalls and hats with black bills, a few women with hair pinned under their caps.

Alfred pointed out that Ignatz was one of these regulars now. He'd graduated in. His mother and father—it was incredible to Karel to think about that ogre having parents who could boss him around, bullies even bigger than Ignatz—made him stand to be judged in the jobber market after he'd come home without his shoes that time the tunnelers took revenge on him. His parents weren't as forgiving as Herr Miihlstein. Ignatz's hair was short and greased to one side of his head. He looked better that way. His body had changed too. He was solid, in the face and the way his shoulders and neck were one bulging quantity now. His work had taken him over, Braun explained. "The boy is his job." Ignatz didn't care about dominating the block like he had before. He was plugged in, picked out right away and given a deal he found acceptable. Young, healthy, uninjured. What did he have to care about? They gave him money.

Dozens of jobbers pled with the manager, those who didn't get work. "My son's sick," one shouted over and over. Another confessed that his wife would leave him if he came home empty-handed again.

Desperate for a position, these men said nasty things to each other. "Out of the way, cripple. You're not wanted here." Spitting the words. "Move on!" They shoved in front of each other, elbowed stomachs and pinched sides to make a rival look hunchbacked or crazy.

Once the spots were filled, the manager promised to call the cops if the leftovers didn't move on. The doors slammed shut.

"You think you're men, yeah?" Braun asked the boys. "This is *men*."

All autumn and winter Karel followed Emil Braun around the River Ward. To meetings at a Southside saloon that flew the black flag of anarchy, where both the bar and the cellar below were filled with stockyard workers and smelled like the manure on their boots. To a church luncheon in Florence, where Braun lectured on white slavery—a topic he knew about, since his niece was kidnapped some years before, when she was fourteen, and later found in a brothel in Salinas, California. If the infield was dry and the north gale let up a few hours, Braun took the boys to the ballfield at Rourke Park to toss a ball around. Karel was still a little clumsy in his game, but he'd hit a growth spurt and was now the biggest among the boys his age. Three inches taller, a good deal stouter in his shoulders and legs. He felt less like a neat little boy. Less precious. He felt tough and ugly. His hair cut short, slobbily, by Alfred, so his ears stuck off his head. He learned to throw from one of those ears like an infielder, as Braun had when he was a second baseman for the Southsiders. There was simplicity on the diamond when Braun and the three boys staked out the four points to whip a ball around the horn. Crisp baseball was the only thing that could awe Braun into silence. Then he let the boys chatter. *Put some mustard on it! Out of the dirt! No rainbows! Let me hear ya! Keep up the pace!* The faster they moved the warmer they got. The warmer they got, the less dumb they felt playing baseball in December.

Karel took to the game that winter, in the cold. He found a mitt in the junk store and Maria bought it for a Christmas gift. Old and greasy, perfect, an undersized infielder's glove like what Braun had. Each night Karel groomed his mitt. He oiled and cared for the leather, flossed grime out its seams with his father's tools. Karel toiled over his glove at the worktable, touching elbows with his father on the red felt, tonguing the chip in his front tooth, the war wound from his first days playing. Over and over he popped his fist into the leather to understand where the ball would stick. Miihlstein hated that and asked if Karel absolutely had to make that sound. "Sure I do. That's how I know it's perfect. Don't you like that sound? Don't it sound perfect?"

Anna tried to talk Karel into sticking around afternoons, but it was no use. He'd never do crafts in the attic if he could run around a ballfield instead. He'd never fiddle with instruments like their father did. She must have seen that Karel was an animal of a different breed.

But maybe he couldn't see Anna clearly those days either. How she hadn't grown over the summer and autumn and was shorter than he was now. How she hadn't changed at all since they'd left Europe. Sickly and small, her face framed by dark hair where her nose, eyes, and chin came jutting out. She wore the same few dresses for years, like a doll. Even more peculiar was that she didn't have her hair cut anymore. She didn't need to. Over the course of February everything appeared normal. Then it hit him. How Anna didn't come downstairs to eat all week. How the skin was mucus yellow under her eyes. How she woke in the middle of the night coughing. How her pleading stopped. No more *Come home*, no more *I miss you*, because Karel didn't have time to waste now that he was free.

On one of the warmer days in March, Karel persuaded Anna to accompany him on the streetcar to Rourke Park. He had a surprise for her. Anna wrapped her wrists and neck in rags and kerchiefs. She wore double socks and topped it off with her favorite lavender overcoat, cinched tight around her narrow waist, like it might blizzard. Karel laughed as she bundled. He was going to show her. The local ball club was having a tryout, and the boys were going to watch.

Every year on the Fourth of July, he explained, a team of whites from the Southside played a team of Northside blacks in Rourke Park, with its big green grandstands and outfield fences and perfect lines of turf and chalk. Come summer, even the dirt would be immaculate. This was the highlight of the year for most warehouse workers, for stockyard and slaughterhouse veterans, almost every postman. Anybody who held steady in an integrated profession lived and died with the Interrace Game. The teams traveled some in the summer months, a weekend exhibition here or there, but Independence Day was the pinnacle of glory on their schedule.

Emil Braun was at the tryout, on the field side of the fence. He waddled out to pester the players who knew him, to remind them that he was one of the founding members of the Omaha Baseball Club. The ballplayers teased about how, once he quit playing, a mudder like Braun went from short-but-quick to short-and-fat all at once. Braun took the ribbing. He didn't mind so much, and it was true—he was stubby legged in his brown pants and suspenders, his flop of hair trailing off the wrong way. As long as he could pester, they could tease. It was an even trade.

With some doing he talked the ballplayers into letting Alfred, Jimmy, and Karel shag balls during batting practice. They rushed the field beaming when he told them, seeing why Braun had hinted that they should bring along their mitts. Karel was going to show off for Anna. She'd see what he was up to all the time after school, why he didn't come back to her and the attic.

Out in the field Karel sprinted and jumped and snapped the ball from the ether with his leather. He made sense out there. Grown men in wool getups shouted out his talent as he ran down a fly and launched the ball back to the dirt. It was fun. Even the first time he caught a screaming liner, when the ball stung his palm so much—using an infielder's glove where it wasn't suited—that he threw the glove down and hopped with his hands between his thighs to make the pain go away. Even in his short pants and the flapping sleeves of a white flannel, he belonged out there. Anna might not understand the rules, but she should understand her brother. She'd see him the way the boys on Clandish saw him. The way he outran his awkward friends. The way his hair shimmered in the breeze, the way his shoulders widened as he caught his breath, or standing back in the grass, legs apart, knees bent, his eyes unblinking toward the backstop waiting for the smack and zip of a batted ball, until one came to him, like it wanted to be caught in his webbing, like it needed to be. And he was still new to the game, which made everything more exciting. If he kept improving, who knew where baseball could take him.

Some players took a liking to Karel. The Sutez brothers, George and Bill, who were captains of the team. They played pepper with him, as a goof, smacking a ball around at close range to see who had quick hands—something Karel had trained at with his friends. He could keep up with the men, and they liked him more once they saw how soft his hands were. Bill Sutez was handsome and well built. He had all his teeth and they were straight, not a minor accomplishment for a guy who liked to brawl like Bill did—although his ears were stretched back more horizontal than what looked normal and were cauliflowered, so not all was right. During batting practice Bill lounged in the dirt near the on-deck circle and dared hitters to foul one off his chin, laughing louder each time a ball missed him. George Sutez was the older brother, the catcher. He perked his lips when in concentration, showing off his front teeth like he was simple. The guys called him Ducky because of the way he waddled behind the plate, more comfortable in a crouch than standing upright.

Karel held his own during pepper. He couldn't help laughing at what anyone said to him afterwards, he was so happy, with Anna watching up behind the chicken wire in the grandstand. He couldn't contain himself on the ride home, bouncing from bench to bench on the street-car. Anna kept telling him to sit down and be quiet. She was ashamed at how he acted, her cheeks red, how she couldn't look any of the other passengers in the eye. Karel knew something was wrong.

She confined herself to the sofa the whole week after. Sulking, Karel thought. Jealous of what he could do. He bugged Anna to go outside. To meet some girls, nice ones she would get along with, not like some of the mad Irish lasses he tangled with at school. She didn't feel up to it, she claimed. She was too tired. She had her own plans. Karel believed otherwise, that the idea of enjoying herself was frightening. She'd blossom too if she was free like Karel. The more her arts filled up the attic, he noticed, the sicker she became. Her work evolved into stranger and stranger forms. More abstract, more sinister.

Karel would have to come up with something that would save her.

A fter he beat the tar out of the Cypriot, Jake asked for an election job and Tom Dennison gave him one. Everybody on Clandish heard about this. A story too good to not repeat. How Jake got in good with the Old Man by taking out the Cypriot, and how Jake owed everything he could give to Dennison from then on. Not only had Jake been shuffled around the police and any charges they might bring, he'd been promoted. With Tom Dennison to thank.

So Jake and his crew worked franticly through winter. They did spoils. They played tricks on reformers and the reformers' friends. They made speeches and shouted down speechmakers who were against them. It was an election year, 1918. They canvassed every day. Billy Nesselhous (number two in the organization) was their professor. Machine lieutenants ran from job to job, man to man, house to house. They pranked stodgy old men in uptown mansions who opposed the machine ticket. They slurred anyone who disagreed with them. Made false reports and bribed officials. Occupied street corners. Flaunted unrefinement. Jabbered a pitch in the muck of the river flats to convince the drunk and desperate that any new politics would be bad news for dirty habits everywhere. There were plenty of old tricks, like expanding voter rolls with the names of the dead in the Mormon cemetery. They devised their own too, like uprooting the Liberty Gardens of ladies' club presidents. If Jane Addams or Fighting Bob La Follette came to town, or if the archbishop of the Roman Catholics wanted to obstruct, every lieutenant would be there to jeer when the machine needed him to.

The election men Jake worked with made the most of their nastiness. That was part of the job—making sure people out in the suburbs were afraid to mess with a machine man from the city. Foreigners made boundaries obvious; members of a ladies' club would avoid the River Ward if they thought it was full of the Hun. Who cared if society ladies hated them? It didn't matter. On the Ward, where things did in fact matter, there was some stature in being one of Tom Dennison's men. Foremen let them alone in Jobbers Canyon. They had friends on the police force. Joe Potash, the detective in charge of organizing raids on saloons and brothels, was a Dennison man through and through. Same with Harry Buford, who drove Dennison's car as part of his police duties, not to mention the police chief himself, Gentleman Jack Pszanowski. Election workers did what they wanted on the Ward. Cops winked complicit no matter what. It was an astonishing identity for a young man to take on, especially if he was the wrong kind of person. Ingo Kleinhardt, as a case, had a dark complexion and divots around his eyes. A long scar veined his jaw, something he got during a disagreement with a tenement deacon. Ingo was in disagreement a lot, with people he shouldn't have been. He had four young kids but didn't mind getting hurt so long as he got to hurt the other guy too. Ingo was never going to be what anyone considered the cream of the cream in decent society, but men like him were the bread and butter of a political organization. Hard-drinking, chain-smoking, whore-mongering men who'd landed where they belonged.

There were a dozen of them in their election crew. Dennison gave the job to Jake and let him bring his friends along. Joe Meinhof took to the work right away, but Reinhold begged out after a week, preferring life as a tunneler. Charlie turned Jake down flat. He enlisted in the army because he was tired of being called both a slacker and a Hun. He didn't want to listen to it anymore and would be on a battlefield in Flanders by the spring of 1918. Others were happy to join up with the machine. Konrad, Paul, Rudi, and Albert left their jobs as dairymen. From the warehouses came Ingo and Heinz. It didn't take long for a daylighter in Jobbers Canyon to figure his fortunes would be brighter working nights for Tom Dennison than pleading with a hiring manager each morning. If you worked hard for Tom, he'd at least be loyal. That was a hell of a lot more than any other job promised.

Jake didn't even try to argue with the logic. Those days the machine was perfect.

He sifted in waves of daylighters late that February. It was a cool morning. Men scattered along Tenth Street in a broken single file toward the mills. Jake took aim on them, set his shoulders wide so they couldn't slip by. These were repairmen for the Union Pacific. The world's largest welding yard was close by. Its workers wore patched overalls, denim jackets, floppy felt hats made heavy by oil and soot. They stared at Jake through tired eyes, annoyed because he strode headlong against their current, a footstool in his arms. He liked facing workers alone. There was a thrill in their menacing looks when they turned to see why Jake, square jawed and blond, had made himself vulnerable.

"Have you given any thought," he shouted, "to what will happen to your jobs if the ticket of Edward Parsons Smith takes the ballot this year?"

He wore new trousers, a starchy shirt, black suspenders clamped to his belt line. His hair was trimmed neat up the side of his head. Madge Holloran, Tom Dennison's secretary, took him to the Brandeis department store the morning he started. He got a whole wardrobe. Madge paid cash. Navy and gray wool suits, matching vests and shoes, a pocket watch, a half-dozen shirts with underclothes. He was given brass money clips for his new reserves of cash. One for his own stash and another for what belonged to the machine.

Some jobbers stopped on the walkway to inspect the gold chain that hung from his vest. The jobbers were jug-eared. Their skin burned red from arc flashes and showers of sparks. Some chewed bread crusts.

"You got the chance to improve your life," Jake told them. "The fine luck of choosing between two slates of very different men. If you want blue laws down here, vote for the other guy. If you want a closed-up town, vote for Ed Smith. It won't make anything better. It won't stop crime, no matter what any brass band reformer says."

Stumping like this was dangerous. The war was on. Every day more boys returned from overseas crippled or limbless, or with some twitching neurosis caused by mustard gas and shell shock. To mount a stool on a street corner for any purpose other than proclaiming America's greatness was risky. That was why men stopped to watch. They looked at him with half grins and raised eyebrows, waiting to see if a fight broke out. If there was no fighting the men spoke up with complaints. A few of them pulled on Jake's sleeve. "Is there a party? With girls?" "Don't you have any whiskey?" "How about silver dollars?"

Evie Chambers was at the back of the crowd that morning. Jake spotted her, her body an apparition among the shoulders of jobbers. He lost his words when he saw her. The brown curls and sloping neck, the way her eyes flashed desperation.

"Give us something!" the jobbers shouted, angry at being ignored. "Can't you get me a better job?" "Yeah! How's about yours? You're not doing it!"

Jake didn't hear the men laughing. He stared at Evie. A black cap secured by pins was nearly swallowed in the mass of her hair as she pushed through the crowd. "Don't you know what you did?" she asked. "I know it was you. You're the one."

This is how Jake met Evie. She thumped his chest with her fists until he stumbled off the footstool to an uproar of cruel jobber laughter.

"You're the one who took him," she said. "You owe me something for that."

Jake tried to lay hands on her shoulders but she slapped him away. "I don't know what you're talking about," he said.

"Yes, you do. There was a bounty. That's why you did it."

Jobbers shoved him against her. "Go on, honey. Take what's yours! Beat it out of him!"

"You have the wrong guy," Jake insisted. The way she looked at him was pitiful. Her lips pale with sorrow, two flat curls of hair not quite covering her ears.

"I should say it's you. You're the one who did it. Everyone knows that."

Another girl came rushing down the sidewalk.

"Evie! They're putting you out! All your stuff and everything! I knew they'd do it the moment you left."

He followed them north of Dodge Street, the confrontation conveniently displaced. He couldn't stop watching the girl. Her name was Evie. That was what the other one called her. Jake repeated it under his breath to remember.

She argued with a man at the top of a stoop, slapped a clutch of papers out of his hands. As the man bent to pick them up, Evie chased after two brawny black men with a dresser hefted between their arms. She told them to put it back. The two acted like she wasn't there, careful not to touch her, to not look in her eyes.

Jake recognized the street they were on. This was where he arrived on the Ward, where he'd tied his horse up and let it get stolen. These townhomes were his first glimpse of Omaha. Almost nice ones, jigsawed together from curb to curb, brownstones too close to industry and the pig iron cauldrons of mills, the constant rolling of steel and tails of factory smoke. The windows here framed with lace valance or blocked out with velvet. The doors with stained-glass panels and heavy brass knobs. A sleek Packard Twin was along the curbstone, all shine and varnish. More than a dozen people stopped here now to see a woman put out. Street kids, businessmen in derby hats. Mostly it was women who pulled housecoats over their shoulders as they stood in the street, who bit their lips, or clutched hands to their necks. One wrung her fingers in the folds of a silk kimono. A few of the crass couldn't wait to inch over and examine what the evictors brought out. To finger a stole or lift a hairbrush studded with rhinestones to her thick-powdered face.

The two evictors wore overalls, shirtsleeves rolled up. They looked like twins, balding on top, with hair so short it revealed their greasy scalps. The rent collector was a beanpole. After Evie yelled at him, he backed away and left the work to the others. One emerged from the door with a tuft of gauzy material hugged against his chest. The second followed with a leather footstool. Evie grabbed the fabric and rushed up the stairs to toss it in her rooms. There was no way she could match their pace. Her belongings cluttered on the sidewalk. Furniture and clothes, a Victrola cabinet with a stack of records, a crate of wine bottles, a lounger of threadbare green upholstery, a pillow to match. The evictors carried a vanity, bottles clinking inside. A short cabinet meant to rest on a dresser that only went to the evictors' knees when they set it down. Evie rushed behind in a panic, rambling to herself. She checked to make sure none of the bottles had broken, lifting a decanter into the light to examine its rosy liquid. It was a useless thing to do. A second later she chased a boy making off with her rabbit fur coat. Once she had it back, she slipped her arms inside and wore it over the pea coat. Nobody else could grab it. But girls walked off with skirts. Kids took her records. There was talk of renting a truck to load the furniture, and a merchant who'd give them a fair price. All her things would be gone before long. She'd end up on the street, like the girl at the parade the summer before.

Jake approached the rent collector and asked why Evie was being put out.

"Her man got himself killed," he said. "She's got no one to pay her rent. That's how it goes. Don't give me shit about it. There's nothing I can do. She stayed on a lot longer than she should of." Indignation squeezed his elongated features, the thin mustache under his nose. "I hate it when they yell at me. There's nothing wrong with putting a girl out. She won't be on the street for long, a pretty one like her. Don't feel sorry for her. She's got it good."

Jake asked if there was anything he could do.

"You mean for *her*? I wouldn't do that if I were you. Don't get involved." The man shook his head. "All these buildings are owned by madams."

"Brothels?"

"Mostly." The man glanced to his paperwork. "Not all of them. I run this building, and there's no whores who live here. Not the way you mean it."

Evie splayed on the steps, an arm over her face, the rabbit fur coat bloomed out to reveal her legs. The evictors wouldn't step over her. They looked to the rent collector and shrugged.

One of them bent to pick her up after the rent collector said to, but when his hand touched her elbow Evie scrambled to the sidewalk. "Don't let her inside," the rent collector shouted. The evictors stonewalled her when she ran back with an armful of garments. Gowns fell to the steps as she plowed into them, then fell to her knees. She didn't cry, though. She fixed eyes on those who stood by to watch her struggle, the ones who walked away with her things. Ruby sequins littered the pavement. Black downy feathers and torn fabric.

"Listen," Jake said. "What's it cost for her rooms?"

"Sorry," the rent collector laughed. "I can't rent to you."

"I want her to stay. How much for two months?"

The man turned. His features narrowed, the mustache trembling.

"Hundred ten," he said. "That's in cash, per month. On the spot. Take it or leave it."

Jake didn't flinch.

"I'll get you money for the rooms. But something fair. The room isn't worth that much."

The rent collector turned and walked to the steps. He snatched a dress from Evie and tossed it on the pile at the curb.

"You can trust me," Jake said, trailing. "I work for Tom Dennison. How's that for credit? I work with him directly. I swear it."

The rent collector stared Jake in the eye. "I don't believe you. Anyone can say that."

"It's true."

"What's Tom Dennison need with you? Don't waste my time, or I'll tell someone about your lying. Then you'll be in real trouble."

The rent collector turned to pull another gown from Evie's grasp. He tugged at the material, stretched it until Evie let go and thumped down hard against the steps. She stared at Jake as she had before. She expected him to do something.

Jake had to help her. He took the rent collector by the collar and dragged him down the steps. He slammed the man against the wall, once, to stop his floundering, and then again, because he could. "Don't have to do me any favors. I work for Tom. Call me on that."

The evictors were stunned. Jake slammed their boss into the wall again.

"Put her things back," he told them. He took the papers from the rent collector, folded them carefully, tucked them into his jacket. "You'll get a fair rent. Just let the girl alone."

He returned the first chance he had, two days later. He carried a brown paper package on his arm and wore the best of his new suits, a blue handkerchief in the breast pocket. The suit fit snug around his legs, shoulders, and arms.

She opened the door before he even knocked, clutched a robe as she pulled him inside. The furnishings were familiar. The portrait of the sickly girl, the shabby lounging chairs he'd seen cluttered on the sidewalk. There was a pile of clothing in the corner, a brass bed and legless vanity in the other room. Her belongings were thrown around like this was a hotel room. Evie kneeled at the dressing glass, where her combs and cosmetics were, and anointed herself with some alcohol-rich mixture. She was calmer, her body softer, the curls in her hair relaxed and dry. She wore a pink kimono. With perfume bottles unstoppered the rooms smelled like lavender and sweet wine. Jake waited in the entry, the package held to his gut. Evie glanced to him in the mirror as she smoothed a red element on her lips.

"What were you up to today?" she asked. He said he'd worked. "Don't you want to tell me? I'd like to know what you're up to, but you don't have to say."

Jake looked around. He was under a spell, his flesh alive at the idea of being here. He'd been with plenty of women in Omaha, too many really, but never one who was so girlish and sensual. He could smell her perfumes, her velvet furniture. Neither kitchen nor bedroom was closed off. There were openings where doors had once hung, hinges still screwed to the frame, the main room divided by a canvas screen draped with her clothes. Jake set his package on the radiator then entered the kitchen. He poked at a bread crust to find its underside moldy. Greasy sandwich wrappers were on the counter, fruit peels in the sink, wine bottles along the baseboard. The milk box in the door was empty.

He leaned out the doorway. "Don't you eat?"

"Why not? When there's good food, I eat it."

Past-due bills from a laundry service scattered the counter, weeks-old grocery receipts.

"Why don't we get some food?"

"No money for food," she said.

"I can pay, yeah? We'll go anywhere you want."

Evie stood on her toes to kiss him. She moved dreamy and graceful, brushing things as she slipped behind the screen to change. He felt the mark her lipstick left on his cheek.

"Anyway. I don't go out. I take deliveries." Her pink kimono floated up to land near him. She smiled from around the screen. "They treat me poorly out there. You saw that."

She emerged in a sundress that drifted over her body, advanced on the balls of her feet, all limbs and round angles. Swinging arms, dress straps off her bare shoulders, toes curling into rug fiber. She hummed a tune as she moved clutter from one spot to another. Plucked garments from the floor and laid them on a chair back. Swept newspapers off a great oak table that took up much of the room. Dozens of suede shoes were sown around, her rabbit fur coat hung over a wire dummy near a rack of feather-garnished hats that would have been scandalous in Jake's hometown. The rooms were cool and drafty, but Evie didn't seem to notice in her sundress.

Jake's collar had doubled over itself at the back of his neck, so she reached to fix it, ran her fingers between the layers of fabric, around his neck, to his chest, until it laid right, then patted the breast of his jacket and pushed back on his shoulders to erase a crick in his posture.

"Don't slouch, honey. You got nothing to be ashamed of."

Blood throbbed in Jake's ears. He felt himself blush, seeing how her top three buttons were undone, and how light from the window shined on her sternum. She breathed. She smiled at him. Her lips pinched when she smiled. It suited her. Hers was a melancholy beauty. The way her eyebrows arched, how curls framed her cheeks, one catching at the corner of her mouth.

"Don't stand there," she said. "Aren't you here to give me something?"

Jake nodded.

"Well, where is it, you brute? Where's my present?"

He stumbled back to snatch the package from the radiator then pulled her to the Victrola cabinet. "I bought these," he said. "Boys ran off with yours."

"That's what happens when they toss you out. Haven't you been to an eviction before?"

Jake hadn't but didn't say so. He tore the paper to reveal an Enrico Caruso record. The clerk at the Brandeis department store had explained that anyone with a phonograph had to own a Caruso. There was a Rachmaninoff. Another with oldies by Paul Dresser and Harry Von Tilzer. All were suggestions from the clerk. Jake didn't want Evie to think he was simple. There were compilations of Tin Pan Alley hits, Scott Joplin's "Maple Leaf Rag."

Evie held out the Joplin to see its sleeve before she placed it on the player and lifted the needle from its cork spool. "This one I had." She turned the side crank to wind the spring motor. Once the deck was spinning, she put her cheek against Jake's chest so he could put his arms around her. He moved to open space—the music playing, the chiming rises and descents of hothouse piano, the hectic jittering—so they could dance. Her body close to his as he smelled the top of her head. The oil of her hair.

She restarted the Joplin when it finished then led him to a chair, climbed over his hips. "This is awful nice," she said. She moved fast.

Once Evie kissed him, he thought too much about what was happening. Would she like what he did? Would he lose it quick? Would she want to see him again after? He didn't know what to do with a woman like Evie. It was different with her. The girls he was used to tended to lie there and let him finish at his own great speed. But Evie paced their bodies. Kissed his ears, rubbed the back of his neck where muscle knotted, squeezed his legs with her legs, moved his hands to her thighs and her goose bumps. Some part of her always in motion touching him. Jake needed to forget himself. God, he was sober. Why hadn't he stopped for a drink on the way? Her dress flowed up with his fingertips, it was amazing. She undid his belt but he blocked her hands from doing more. She unbuttoned his shirt, slowly, until he couldn't wait any longer and shucked it over his head. He grabbed around her waist. Kissed her elbow. Jake liked this girl. He'd helped her out because he liked her, not to earn favors. Now this. He wanted to be inside her, further than anyone ever had before. He wanted to win, to see how rough she'd let him be. She reached between his legs but he blocked her. She laughed finally, and kept at him, because this was funny, wasn't it. He chuckled. He didn't understand what he was doing. He wanted to bust out. Nearly exploding in his shorts. But still he stymied her. Fought her hands, wouldn't let her take his penis out. Their hips knocked, their hands and legs and mouths worked desperate. She breathed and deepened and rubbed on his leg. Mounted over him on the chair. Between her thighs, her swollen, her wet, on his knee. Kissing. Her back arched, unarched. Her breath came out of her.

They sat locked in position. Evie's skin was dark in the dressing glass. She held him, her face hidden in the crook of his neck. She didn't move but to breathe.

Jake didn't know what to say. It was embarrassing how he hadn't done it to her. All of this went too easy for a girl he actually liked. He'd never tried it sober before, still hadn't. Never in the daylight.

He'd be good for her next time. He'd show what he could do.

"I got to go to work," he said.

She straightened and smiled, her cheeks flushed. "You'll come back and see me?"

He went to a grocer right away. "I want the whole works. Your best fruit. Vegetables. Green beans, spinach, pickled beets, strawberries when you get them. Canned meats, bread, milk." Jake leaned into the counter over the grocer's wife as she jotted down his request. He had to make things up to Evie. It was that simple. He pulled the neat fold of machine cash from his pocket and slid it from hand to hand. Nobody would care, he told himself. Nobody would notice if he diverted a little cash to Evie. Jake didn't have enough of his own money to do something like this. It was only by sneaking from the clip of cash that Tom Dennison had given him that he could afford to pay for Evie's room and now some groceries too. He wanted to be a big shot. Jake couldn't help himself. He smelled Evie's perfume on his face, was still half-hard and aching.

"I want the best you have for as long as I can have it," he said, then slapped two tens on the counter and wrote Evie's address in black wax on a paper sack. "Send it here. Say JS sent it."

Consider Tom Dennison: most people couldn't tell a thing was wrong in 1918, but things weren't going so well for him. It was an election year. The coalition Tom put together had been in charge over twenty years by then. He ran everything in town. The board of commissioners, the utilities board, the police force. He had the mayor on his side, of course. To a guy on the street the Dennison machine looked rock solid. But Tom would have known the inside workings of everything and how fragile his organization actually was. It all depended on the vote. Any single election year could topple what he'd built. He wouldn't have been able to rest, thinking about that.

To top it off, the opposition paper was making him out to be a crook again. They did it to annoy him. Tom had never stolen anything a guy wasn't willing to give of his own free will, through carelessness or greed. Tom was a gambler. This was the profession he claimed—not *boss*, as the opposition paper called him, not *crook* or *embezzler* or *racketeer* or anything else. Being a gambler was an honorable thing, as far as Tom knew. A gambler didn't steal. He won.

This time he'd done nothing. A traveler's wife had some jewelry stolen from their room. The hotel manager said to go and ask Tom if he knew who took it. Tom could have left them in the wind. He didn't know who took the jewelry, a diamond necklace and ring, not offhand. But Tom was a decent man. He found out. Some grifter came through on his way to Kansas City and somehow talked the woman out of her possessions. These things happened. How this woman ended up alone in a hotel room with a man she just met, that was her business. Tom didn't care. He tracked the thief down to KC and made sure the woman's things were expressed back with apologies. Nothing was lost in the deal by anyone. Everyone was happy, save the grifter. But then the *World-Herald* had to run a note on it, a paragraph or so, with a quote from the woman. She blabbed Tom's name. It wouldn't have been a big deal at all if it wasn't for the name Dennison being mentioned next to the name Pendergast. If Tom was connected to Pendergast, who was known for running a crooked machine down in KC, then a bunch of people in Omaha were connected to Pendergast too. The inference wouldn't sit well. Tom knew how important it was to run things clean. It wasn't enough to just do right.

That was why he was going to Frank's house for lunch. To square things with the benefactors. Frank spoke for the benefactors. He was important. He paid for things. So there would have to be an explanation for the article. Tom and Frank alone. A sit-down in the wallpapered front room of Frank's house, some ham sandwiches and beer. Tom wouldn't even take the beer. He didn't bother with spirits. That was the truth. People might not believe it, but that's how it was. Tom asked for a glass of milk, and the maid went to get it.

"I hope it isn't your stomach," Frank said. He laughed and Tom laughed too. "A grown man drinking milk."

Frank was tall, good looking, his dark hair combed back, charming in his way. Rich, connected, unperverted. He came from a good family and married into a better one. Tom considered him a man. That was important. Frank was somebody Tom could talk to. He was younger than Tom—Tom turned fifty-nine that October—but that was okay, most people were younger than him those days. They'd figure things out, and then Tom could tell the boys what to do. They'd keep things up and running in this town just as long as they could.

Tom felt fine during lunch. The ham was all right. Ribbons of fat gelled cold through the meat, there was Dijon mustard and paper-thin slices of onion. Frank wasn't even mad about the thing in the newspaper. "I want to talk about the vote," he said. There was a city election in three months—it had been twenty years since the slate Tom backed lost an election. "Oh. Nothing to worry about there," Tom said, naming off what good news there was to tell. The sound health of candidates on their ticket. The stifling of scandal. How they even got the Germans on Clandish over to their side this last year, because Wilson promised to keep the country out of the war and it got him elected. Sure, Wilson backtracked on that, but Tom didn't think most voters would hold a grudge.

"You got it under control is what you're saying." Frank sat back and dabbed his mouth with a napkin. He'd put too much mustard on his sandwich and the overspill kept him occupied.

Tom didn't say much—he rarely did—but the thought of the vote wore him out. He had a bad feeling this time. Leaning back into the fine sofa, full from the milk and ham, he murmured something about this maybe being the last time he ran an election, and how it bothered him that the odds might go against them.

"What do you mean by that?" Frank leaned in to stir his coffee. His mouth turned down, his face still and smooth as ivory. "We're going to lose? That's what you mean?"

"No," Tom said. "I don't mean that. It's just a feeling. Something strange."

"Jeez. Is that what you actually think? What are we paying you for?" Frank stood to look out the curtains. "Think you can still handle the job?" he asked. "Think you're up for another election? Think it's time to quit? Let somebody else take a hand at the trigger?"

"Sure," Tom said. "Sure, I'm fine."

Tom told Harry to drive the Olds 45 up north of the city. He wanted to see some countryside. His doctor said he needed rest, that he should avoid the office for a while, get as much fresh air as he could. It was what doctors always said: fresh air, clean water. Tom was inclined to believe them, he just didn't know how to implement such advice. He could head home early, surprise Ada. He could skip out to his kennel. There were some new fox terrier pups, he could see how their training was going. Or the stables. Tom owned the fastest palomino pony in the world.

Tom didn't do any of these things. He had Harry drive in the country. A long drive would give him time to come around to what Frank had said.

He didn't feel at all well. Headaches, heartburn, he couldn't breathe sometimes. That's why he had milk at lunch. Why he chewed mint leaves in the car.

Tom let the Olds do its work. A car was splendid magic. Man's greatest invention, this Olds 45. There was dark-green paint encased in wax, prime oak in varnish for the wheel spokes and dash, chrome mirrors and light cans that shined brighter than anything. Its tires roared some incantation when they hit gravel. Tom loved that car. He could take in the view, hills of grass, streams and ponds, a deer buck confounded at the Olds's cantankerous passing by. Tom was tired of going station to station. Breakfast table to office, office to Frank's house, back to office, to lunch, to office, to home, to supper table. He spent a lot of time in that Olds too, from point to point, but at least the scenery changed. He leaned back where the vinyl roof curved down, where nobody saw him hiding. Tom had a good life, but he couldn't take seeing the same old mugs at the office all the time, not for the whole day, not anymore. He needed something else.

It was no small matter that Harry told good stories at the wheel. In addition to being Tom's driver, Harry Buford was a cop, so he kept a treasury of dirty jokes. Jokes about priests and nuns. About schoolteachers and students. The confessions of deranged citizens. Funny stuff, and most of it true, if you believed what anyone told a cop or what cops told each other. In the car Tom could laugh as much as he wanted. He wasn't giving anything away if it was just him and Harry. So they drove. He spent too much time in the office, cooped up in a dark room. It bugged Tom that he didn't know how it would all end. Would he sit in his office and wait for a stroke to take him? To wipe out that great analyzing mind of his? Would the end come in the backseat of his car, the car gliding along? Would Harry even notice if the big one took Tom away? Would Harry just keep on driving? Maybe Tom was already dead. Maybe it didn't matter if they won the vote next time or not.

He should be so lucky.

Tom spotted Jake Strauss when they were back downtown. He had Harry roll the Olds up behind and lowered the window. "You got a minute?" he asked.

A Thompson submachine gun lay on the back bench next to Tom, half-hidden under a plaid blanket with a pistol clip jutting from its housing. The kid didn't see the gun until he was settled. He nearly jumped out of his skin when he did see it—a gun like that, what doughboys used to mow down German shock troops in the trenches of Flanders. Tom reclined behind the black canvas roof and drummed the stock of his gun. He never rode without it. The blanket that covered the gun draped over his legs in such a way that he had a clear path to the trigger.

Those days they took more and more of these trips around the city. Tom saw how Jake was comfortable in the dark-green touring car, the two of them in the back, even though he'd never been in a luxury car before. "I rode on a flatbed truck," the kid admitted, "but that was back home." In Omaha, in the first months of 1918, the kid shared the backseat of a smooth-running Olds with Tom Dennison. How exhilarating it must have been for him.

Tom had picked the kid out. Some of the older guys didn't like it, but Tom didn't care what they thought. Maybe he saw something they didn't. Some potential. Some dumb ambition. Some glint of himself as a young man. Tom didn't have a son. Everyone knew this. Two boys had been conceived a long time ago. One was miscarried. The other died as an infant.

This wasn't about that. The kid impressed Tom, that was all. Jake was good. He believed in the method Tom taught. Was eager to learn. Was strong and confident in his faith. He spread the gospel. Violence didn't freeze him. Sure, the kid didn't say much about himself or why he'd come to Omaha in the first place, but Tom admired that too. Why should a man uncloud his past? All the kid talked about was the weather up where he came from, the crops they grew, how his father ran a little church business out of the farmhouse. It was a bland life out there on a farm, and a guy like him wanted adventure. But then, why didn't Jake find a recruiting station and enlist? All the adventure anyone could ask for was free for the taking in France just then. The American Expeditionary Forces would have been happy to have him. But Jake wasn't like that. He hated guns. He told Tom once that he'd bought a revolver—in case it was needed, you never knew—but he didn't like holding a gun. Didn't like the smell of guns. He hid the revolver under his mattress and hadn't fired the thing once, hadn't even let it see the light of day. How do you figure a guy like that? Timid a lot of the time. But he did bad things to people. The foreigner in the tunnels, that Cypriot. Jake would beat a man near to death—it was in his eyes—but only in the right situation. Whatever that meant to him. Then ask him to flash a pistol to set some crooks straight, he'd shake his head. "I'd rather not," he'd say. "Get Meinhof to do it."

This bothered Billy. Billy Nesselhous was Tom's right-hand man, so Billy did some checking on Jake. Some things about the kid's mother turned up, quite a lot about his father, who got into trouble when he was young. There was an incident with a pick handle where Jake came from, how he struck down some boy and hurt him bad. This didn't bother Tom the least bit. Tom did things like that himself as a young man, back when he was a rambler, in Leadville, Colorado, in Salt Lake City, in Montana boomtowns that came and went before they even made it to a map. If you won, people were going to resent you. That's how it went.

Billy even had the kid followed. Weekly reports were compiled from the start. It was suspicious to Billy the way Jake came in after he took out the Cypriot and asked for a job connected to the vote, like the kid had ambitions contrary to Tom's. So they heard about Jake Strauss walking Clandish Street and Jobbers Canyon. They heard about him skirting the slag fields by the iron mills. He handed out cards for jobbers to bring to the polling room so nobody forgot the names of the candidates. "Tell them Cowboy Jim sent you," he'd say, just like he was supposed to. "Say Tom Dennison wants you to work. The foreman will know what to do." The kid jabbered until his voice gave out, spouting off about what Mayor Dahlman meant to the River Ward. He staked out saloons, hospitals, barbershops, bakeries. He talked to anyone who was good-natured or stupid enough to listen to an election man. This was all on the up-and-up. So Tom arranged some bigger game to see how the kid would handle it. A grocery truck was to be lost in the tenements. The kid was instructed to point the truck onto a dirt path where nobody from a main street could see. He rode the runners to toss off sacks of flour and rice, kegs of lard, tins of canola oil. War rations ate through most of the food poor folks had access to, so Tom commandeered a fruit truck to mete out apples and tomatoes, then watched a ways back as Jake carried off the plan. Kids swarmed out from every cranny as soon as the truck splashed into the muddy yard, tipped off by curiosity, boredom, hunger. They shimmied out on the bare limbs of trees to see in the back of the truck.

These jobs were like feeding the masses, but it was no miracle. The arrangement went off smooth because Tom had an edge over the underlying interests. The fruit company happened to be the same that was awarded a contract to supply the city fire company with produce. They were willing to lose a little if it meant business ran as usual. Once the truck was empty, Jake told its driver to cross into Iowa and report a highway robbery to the sheriff of a small county, one disinterested in big-city politics. An insurance company would share the loss if the produce was reported stolen. If the insurance man complained, Tom reminded him of what he too owed. The whole operation ran smooth. The kid played his part to a T. Even Billy had to admit that.

The Olds drove up north to where the roads were a mix of crushed red brick and mud. They saw mangled bodies here. This was what Tom wanted to show Jake. People struggled with legs bent the wrong way. Sleeves hung empty below a stump. Pant legs dangled or were pinned. Kids in barren yards watched the Olds swerve chuckholes. They twisted their feet in tufts of calf-high grass. Some had hands tucked into sleeves of greasy leather, facing the one who wagged a broomstick over his shoulder at the end of the block. Women dunked laundry in washtubs under the eaves of single-story shacks. There was the husk of a burned-out house, a stripped-down Model A sunk in mud to its fenders. A steam engine puffed behind the buildings, dredging sewer sludge north to a canal that went to the Missouri. Old and not-so-old men loafed outside a yellow building. None of them spoke when they saw the car. They stared silent as it moved along.

When Harry went to turn around, a man crossed in front of the Olds. He was middle-aged and bent toward the road as he stumbled. A rheumatic. Tom leaned forward to see what the holdup was. And he saw this man, fingers bent broken, unable to close, limbs joined at odd angles. No part of his body could flex straight. Scars covered his face.

Men twisted in chairs along the storefronts, the hard labor of their lives fixed to their bodies. Tom explained how thousands of them were coming north to fill stockyard positions as locals enlisted in the war. These neighborhoods were overflowing. Every morning, trucks owned by stockyards rumbled in to trade night for day workers, then returned in the evening to reverse the exchange. Most of them were scabs. It was better than sharecropping. Even if they might end up with a broken leg splinted by a nearly straight elm branch. Or lying on the planks of a walkway with nowhere to go. Or missing chunks of their ears from the cutting apparatus. Or knocked stupid by a stampeding bull, jabbering and drooling, face swarmed with flies.

Tom asked Jake if he'd ever seen a black person before coming to Omaha. He hadn't. Stories about the blackies of North Omaha were common where he came from, he said. So-and-so's cousin got raped because she lived alone in an apartment. A guy's sweetheart groped by blacks because she wanted to sit in an air-conditioned theater to watch a movie. But no. There weren't people of color there. No Greeks or Turks or Italians either. He'd heard of buffalo soldiers camped at Fort Robinson and Negro sodbusters—Moses Speece and his brothers near Broken Bow—but he'd never seen a black person before coming to Omaha.

Tom had come from the same area as Jake—one county over, in fact—and he knew how it was up there in the northeast part of the state.

The car was stopped, so Tom decided to call a boy to him. The boy was on the corner with two girls who must have been his sisters. Hair stuck out from their heads like it was pulled that way. Tom asked about the boy's family when he was close enough to hear, how many kids there were. Was the boy born in Omaha? Did the boy's folks plan to stay? He asked, "Do you know who I am?" The boy shook his head. Tom smoothed his thumb along the stock of his machine gun. "You don't recognize me?" The boy turned his bare feet in the road, looked to his sisters, his skin ashy from the dust. "I'm Tom. Tom Dennison. You think you can remember that?"

"Yessir. You Tom Dennison."

"Good." Tom slid a roll of cash from his pocket. He counted out thirty dollars with his gun hand and handed the money to the boy. The boy's jaw nearly dropped to the road. Tom told Harry to drive on.

"You understand why we do these things, don't you, Jake? If that boy sticks around, or even if he don't, as long as he survives to be a man, he'll never forget me. He'll tell his kids and grandkids about the time this fellow named Tom Dennison made him rich a few days. If they've never heard of Tom Dennison, then he'll tell all about my generosity. That's why we do these things. So that boy remembers."

There was a banquet that night at a warehouse cleaned out for the purpose. Mayor Dahlman would be there. Frank would be there. The city commissioners. Billy set it all up. A regular thing in an election year. There would be a big spread. Rotisserie chicken and roast duck with apricot jam, mashed potatoes still steaming they were so hot, canned carrots and peas and tomatoes, white bread with butter and orange marmalade. There would be wine and rye whiskey and a keg of Storz Triumph that had been held over for the occasion.

Tom didn't feel well, but these kinds of things were necessary from time to time. He'd rather be at home with his feet up by the fire, his daughter Frances beside him, Ada bringing broth. The doctor said Tom should have shook off what was bothering him by now. It had been months. Still some illness dragged on him, a little bit more each week. Walking pneumonia, the doctor guessed. Tom's breathing was bad. Ada said he'd had an apoplexy. "Wouldn't that explain it all," he mocked her. "My brain broke." He felt bad about his repartee later, but setting his wife straight was a necessary thing. Ada couldn't keep going on about it like that, not with an election to win, not with Frank and the benefactors showing doubt. Tom had his hands full enough without worrying about water filling his lungs or his wife thinking he'd had a stroke.

Billy Nesselhous stopped by Tom's house before the banquet to talk things over. Billy was the only one Tom was honest with about being sick. They'd known each other a long time. Billy had been a rangy street kid himself once but was short and fat now, almost all his hair gone, his nose swelled up like a red balloon. Tom figured he had no room to judge. He probably looked worse. Two old gamblers. Partners of the famed, now-defunct Budweiser Saloon. It was Billy who helped Tom set up his first policy wheel and gambling room when he came to Omaha. Billy was from here and knew the lay of the land, and they had mutual friends in Denver. That was enough in those days.

Tom was in the kitchen when Billy arrived. He'd changed into his tuxedo and was having broth to warm up. Ada offered Billy some, but he'd had whiskey on the ride over and the broth wouldn't mix well.

Billy wanted to compare notes on the election to make sure he was up to speed. It was his feeling that they'd pull it out again, easy, and he tried to convince Tom to share his optimism. Cowboy Jim Dahlman, their incumbent mayor, took first in the open primary a couple months before, which had surprised Tom. Maybe it surprised nobody else, but that didn't matter. Primaries were bullshit. Particularly when nobody was eliminated. Billy was persistent, though. He said Tom read too much into the threat of reform. Tom got to feeling down and unnerved himself, and maybe even Frank, talking about losing. "You spooked yourself." Billy fiddled with the silverware. He didn't like having to be the wise one. "You feel bad, that's it. What was it the doc said? Wandering pneumonia?"

"Walking."

"Sure. That's it. But you got to keep your chin up. Tonight especially. We don't win without these men. Keep the money flowing. That will make you feel better. If we take this election, you'll be tip-top in no time."

Maybe Billy was right. Tom felt bad, and that was what made him think they'd lose. That was all. He'd feel better when they won. Winning always did that. If they held on through the municipal vote two months down the road, he'd collect from who owed him. It would be summer. He'd head out with Ada to San Diego like she wanted. If they took the municipal, he'd feel fine.

"I think you're onto something," he told Billy. "I feel better already."

"Sure you do. You just need some cheering up. That's what I'm here for."

They went through it again and Tom did feel better. The fear of losing had dragged him down, that was all. He never could stand somebody getting the better of him.

Maybe it seems peculiar that Evie and Jake fell in love so quickly. But it was a common occurrence at the time. People fell in love over the course of an afternoon, in a moment out on the walkway if it was a nice day, and were married by the nearest justice of the peace if it felt right. It happened that way for most people on Clandish. If two people loved each other, they loved each other. Why shouldn't they be together?

They weren't married, so maybe it wasn't love, but Evie got Jake to herself evenings in her rooms, and she made the most of what time they had together. She was content to cloister away with him, to listen to Irving Berlin and eat soft green apples, to read aloud from the clothbound Ovid he bought, one that reminded him of the library his father kept back home, he said. She cooked in sloppy, eclectic styles. Sautéed catfish with onions and peas. Hot potato salad. Buttered noodles, vegetable chop suey with wild artichokes. He ate quickly then finished what morsels Evie ignored on her plate, the half she left untouched. Jake was such a country boy. He sometimes drank a whole quart of buttermilk with dinner. He came to her pretty much every night as winter turned to spring, his arms full of presents he'd bought for her—more records, new bottles of roseate perfumes. It was nice to have him up in her place. The gamblers Evie worked for had let her keep the room, even after Ugo vanished, and said they'd get back to her when they needed something. Whatever you want, she'd said. She didn't want to lose the room, even if that meant she owed the gamblers. Of course, she didn't tell Jake about the deal she'd made. He had his secrets, Evie figured, his little sneaking from his boss, and she had hers.

She and Jake told stories from when they were kids. Games they'd played; people they recalled randomly, for often tawdry reasons. That made them merry. They talked about what they read in the *Metamorphoses* and listened to hot jazz on the phonograph. She said dopey things to him, like "Don't fall in love with me," and, "If you were smart, you wouldn't be here," and he acted like she was teasing. She prepared baths. Mineral-rich, nourishing baths she concocted with great care. He stopped by to warm and wash, to lay in the water with his woman.

Usually there was an errand Jake's boss required that would take him away. But some nights, like this one, Jake was free. By the time he made it through the door she was up on her tiptoes to kiss him and remove his jacket and toss it over the wire dummy. When she veered to the bathroom he followed, his eyes on the short gauzy skirt she wore, the green and white stockings. He said it was amusing how she made her own clothes. The mere idea of Evie set to a chore, her face busy in concentration, her idle hands made tense and precise. His amusement bothered Evie when she remembered all the garments she lost during the eviction. Clothes she'd made herself, gone because Jake didn't speak up sooner. But how could he have known all that?

Evie held out awhile after the first time, when she'd rubbed off on his leg because he wouldn't go inside her. His discretion threw her off. It was strange compared to how things usually happened on her block. The next time, when he tried to move his hand more liberally up her thigh, she twisted away. She kissed him these early days, let him do with his hands everywhere but between her legs. Evie didn't understand where this fresh modesty came from. New barriers were erected. Ones she'd never had before. Chastity had never been her thing, not even as a girl. Now she'd gone virgin somehow. This wasn't something Evie understood, but she was game if Jake was. When she resisted, it was his turn to say dopey things. "I was wrong about you. You're a nice girl, aren't you? Stuck in the wrong part of town." What was she supposed to say to that? Nobody had ever talked so dirty to her. "Whatever you want," she said, then slapped his hands away. This made him even hotter. She could feel the way he boiled. His face red. His blushing.

Above her, bathtub bottles lined the window, varicolored salts and powders inside the clear glass of apothecary jars. Evie mixed potions in the water then turned to undress Jake. She was pleased undoing his buttons, in whisking away his pants before they pooled on the damp tile. She led him to water and held his hand until he was submerged. She undressed herself then, sat on the stool to cleave the stockings from her legs. She turned away to pull the blouse over her head, crossed her breasts with an arm, and stepped into the water to nestle between his legs. The water was scalding, but Evie didn't care. She liked it best when the water burnt. Their bodies turned red where they were wet. She rolled over after a while to kiss him, to let his hand skate along her jaw to her shoulders, down her back to the rise of hips, back and forth, until she finally let him inside. She gasped when he slipped the threshold at last, because a man always liked the sound of air escaping her lips at the moment he pushed inside.

There was conflict in the way they made love. Like neither of them had ever done this before. Jake never came, for one thing. They did it long, hard, slow, fast, in various modulations and strengths. They tried different things. Sometimes the water went tepid, but they didn't care, moving slow, barely going, because the discipline this took made his eyes roll back in his head. Still he didn't come. It wasn't bad that he didn't. It was just peculiar to leave off unfinished. His member red and raw, still apt, if agitated, vibrating.

Evie didn't mind what she looked like below, even if her parts were as much of a mess as they felt. She'd earned that.

She posed naked in the parlor mirror to put her hair up, arms and elbows raised as she wrangled wet curls. There were shadows in the hollows of her armpits where soft hair grew. She turned her hips from side to side to examine her body—the neat puff of hair on her pubis, the way her nipples pointed cockeyed as she swayed. Jake came up from behind, fully dressed, to put his hands over her breasts.

"The nipple on that one always was wrong," she said, her mouth turned.

"This guy?" he asked, squeezing the left one.

"No. The other."

He turned her around to have a look, but she walked away before he could see the defect. She put on her robe and sat by the window to cool off. The night was going fast.

"You think I'm a fool, don't you?"

"Of course," he laughed. "They're tits, yeah? They're good."

Evie played like she was angry. She wouldn't talk. She looked out the window at some man rushing up the avenue. The street was always busy after suppertime. A perfectly legitimate man, normally good for something, would have a few drinks at dinner, and that indiscretion, before long, would lead up the steps to a madam's parlor. The guy would be lost to a wicked imagination the rest of the night. It was no secret how that happened.

The way things went between a girl and guy was a funny thing to Evie all of sudden—secure in her rooms with Jake—but she didn't let on her good humor. For Evie, playing sad was part of the game.

To raise her spirits, Jake told a joke about a pastor's wife who ate only lamb meat. "Don't you get it? Lamb meat!" A grin broke through. She let him hug her from behind, his arms over her shoulders to reach inside the fold of her kimono. She wasn't really mad at him.

Evie turned her face up to his. "Are you okay? You're all red. You're sweating."

Jake's cheeks were red. His neck and chest too, something more than blushing. His hair hadn't dried after the bath because he sweat.

"You made me this way." He laughed in a dull sort of way.

"Shouldn't you go? If you're coming down with something?"

Jake looked ill—and he must have felt miserable from the way he tried to keep her from examining him—but he acted like his condition was a joke. He wanted to stay, he said. Workers in the machine didn't get many nights off during an election. If he spent this one sick in bed, he'd never get it back.

"But maybe you're right," he said. "I'll get some wine. We've got to keep up our strength."

In the kitchen, after he put the corkscrew to a bottle, Jake rifled in paper sacks on the floor that were half-filled with tins of canned meat. There was deviled ham, beef au jus. What remained of the food he sent over.

"What's the big idea? Don't you like canned meat?"

"I'm sure it's fine," Evie said. "But I don't eat the stuff. I'm a vegetarian."

This seemed to strike Jake dumb as he stood there with the wine. How many wisecracks about eating meat were spinning gleefully in his brain? He didn't let slip even the first of them. The corner of his mouth turned up as he drank. "I didn't know you had principles."

In fact, Evie hadn't eaten meat in years. She'd been to a lecture once that extolled the virtues of purity and temperance, back when she was new in town and worked nights in dance halls. Prudish old women in heavy wool skirts and plain white blouses lectured on various topics to young women who lived on the River Ward and gave out free dough-nuts and coffee to those who would spend a morning seated quietly on a bench and be berated in good faith. Why vegetarianism should stick in Evie's mind and not a bit of the rest about chastity and restraint was a funny thing to her. Evie thought she was being cute, refusing to consume meat in a city known best for stockyards and slaughterhouses, and the habit stuck because she felt better only eating fruits and vegetables. She was a little insulted that night with Jake, that he hadn't yet noticed this about her, even though they'd been seeing each other for months. Evie never served meat, and only rarely fish, when they ate in her rooms. Young men had always been and would always be self-involved, she figured. It shouldn't surprise her if Jake couldn't see past the end of his nose.

They sat up and had wine by the window. After a while a pair of bottles sat empty on the floor next to them. Jake looked worse. His stomach made curious, loud noises. He refused a soporific when she offered one, even when she insisted. "Don't worry about me," he said. "I've got a good heart. It will take more than a fever to slow me down." He wanted to stay next to her. It was something Evie couldn't argue against, the street busier than before. Stray men reeled drunk along the curbstone, either leaving a palace or looking for one that would take them in. Girls worked the walkway now that it was getting late. Cheap girls. Desperate biddies, or older ones too staggered by Chinese opium to keep a room in a respectable joint. A man might have too much shame to snatch a girl off the street early on, but that changed after midnight if he was too broke or too drunk to take his satisfaction indoors. If he was looking after midnight, a man took what he could get, in an alley, in the back of a car. Jake and Evie watched these characters couple off. It was fascinating how a cake eater talked to a girl, both discreet and pantomime, and how she drew him in. It was better than any melodrama the theaters put on.

Evie explained how false the whole performance was, but that it could be pleasant sometimes. "If he's genteel" was how she put it. "Like you." She'd worked in dime-a-dance halls when she came to Omaha, even though it turned out she wasn't much of a dancer. She met a lot of weird men that way, a few nice ones. Jake looked uneasy when she talked like that but didn't make her stop. It was true, anyway, that there was something charming about Jake, even if it wasn't gentility. How he stared off blankly, mislaid in the world; how he grimaced in silence when at a loss for words, his mind grinding; how his hair flopped over his forehead, how a cowlick spiked up in back, Jake unaware until his woman was there to tamp it down; how he wore mud grained in the creases of his palms; how he dressed, not quite sloppy, but with mere deference to neatness. It usually wasn't this easy with a man, but Evie liked taking care of Jake.

His feet were on the windowsill, Evie under a blanket next to him in the wide seat of the high-backed chair. Outside, a white woman walked arm in arm with a black man. An umbrella dipped intermittently over their faces, but you couldn't mistake them. The two were married, Evie explained. "Not legally. They just live like they are." This neighborhood was integrated, which was something that drew Evie here even though it made her worry sometimes that she might be labeled as high yellow by the black folks here. If black folks didn't see her as white, that would change how everyone else saw her too. She worried constantly that somebody might call her out for pretending to be something she wasn't—but, really, what was the difference? Either way she was a kept woman living in a notorious part of town. To what lower station could they consign her? Even when a person did inspect Evie closely, if they seemed to gaze into her on the street—making her wonder if something was wrong with her fingernails, the palms of her hands, the shape of her ears or teeth, which was why she never ate in a restaurant, on the off chance that an inquisitor might trap her at a table—even then the person doing the inspecting always mistook her for an Italian, Albanian, or Gypsy, assuming they saw anything at all to question.

It was distressing to see a couple like the one out for a walk in the misting rain, the avenue disrupted because of them, and the peculiar intimacy of two people sharing an umbrella. Evie watched, drawn to this affection between different tribes, as if there was a halo of light around them. The couple budged down the walkway, not looking up at any of the windows to see who saw them.

For a long time after they passed, Jake watched the walkway where the couple had been. Evie stared into his reddened face, his wine-purpled lips, his blank eyes. What was he thinking? He said he felt the cold from the window in his feet. She curled around his middle and asked again if he'd lie down. He shook his head in a perturbed way.

"Do you know," he said, "when I first saw you, I thought you looked familiar? You weren't, though, yeah. I didn't know you. I hadn't ever known anyone like you. What are you, Evie? What makes you so new?"

She didn't want to hear him talk like that and spoke over him to get him to shut up. She told how her mother was a seamstress and that she didn't really know her father. After four children the man ran off to Nevada to find gold and silver and never returned. Evie had some schooling where she came from in Topeka, but only enough to meet a few boys, and she regretted she hadn't had more. It was her brother who supported the family when she was young.

"He wasn't any good." Evie opened another bottle of wine and turned the radiator full open. A rusty, damp smell filled the room as the heat banged on. "Ben found work when he was sober. He was a house painter, which isn't bad money, you know, provided you'll work when the boss says to." Ben died when Evie was little. He fell asleep on some railroad tracks one night, drunk, and was run over by a train. That was the end of him. Evie shrugged as she told about his dying, as if nothing could have stopped it from happening. "His body was sliced into segments. They had some trouble burying him like that because Mama bought a coffin with a glass front on it. When the pallbearers moved the coffin, the different parts of him slid around inside his suit. It was pitiful. Poor, dumb, Ben. His corpse wanted to roll up in a ball."

The undertaker couldn't talk Evie's mother out of buying that nice coffin. Ben was the only fool in the cemetery for their part of town with a glass-front coffin. Nobody understood why a seamstress with three kids left to care for wanted to be uppity about the one who died.

Evie didn't shed a tear as she told the story. She wasn't emotional at all. To say one's history in a clear and even voice made it almost whimsical. She was born in Kansas. Her father ran off. Her brother was dissected by the iron wheels of a train. He was drunk. He was stupid. What else? In the end, another possibility didn't matter. There was what happened. That was all.

Her mother was put to taking care of the remainders alone. Evie helped out some with the sewing. She learned to cut cloth precisely and stitch with a treadle machine. She went to school when her help wasn't required. As the youngest she got more schooling than her siblings. The high school was integrated there in Topeka; it always had been. That was where she met boys, and not just those from her neighborhood. Rich and poor weren't so segregated then either. Evie met lots of boys she wouldn't have otherwise.

"That's all they wrote for me," she tried to explain. "You know how it is. A girl is either nice or not nice. That determines everything. A nice girl sits in the parlor with a boy who visits. A not-nice girl is snuck out the back door. We didn't have a parlor in our house. We had sewing tables and wire mannequins. We had customers. Our parlor wasn't a frivolous place. You couldn't even pretend it was. Not that I ever dreamt of bringing boys there to see my mother."

It was near morning by the time they went to stand. Half-asleep in the chair, awake only by the sheer will of talk. Jake couldn't get up when he went to. He staggered and fell back. She had to help him make it to bed.

Nobody would ever figure out how the Spanish flu began, or why the virus transformed the way it did, but they knew that recruits at Fort

Riley, Kansas, were the first to come down sick. When Fort Riley dough-boys were shipped abroad, they took the bug with them. A plague like this never would have spread around the globe if it wasn't for the war. Americans brought it on transport ships, in their uniforms and sputum, and gave all of Europe the bug. From there to Australia, Egypt, Turkey, Siam, Russia. Nobody then knew much about what would become Spanish influenza. In the next two years over fifty million people would die of this flu that didn't act like the flu. The young became deathly ill, while the old and frail were spared. It would take down hale men and vibrant women in their prime in a matter of days. They'd all know somebody who would have it happen like that. Starting Monday morning normal and cool, by Wednesday the same person would be burning out through their skin in an infirmary, quarantined by public order. By Friday there'd be a funeral. Not that you'd risk going. Nobody would understand how that happened. Streetcar drivers and nurses would wear white surgical masks to protect themselves from the vibrions. It would be a plague covering the earth—something biblical—and at the same time the whole world was at war.

The way Jake moved in and out of tenements, he was bound to catch something. That March, he did. It was up to Evie to care for him. She fed him broth and brandy, left the radiator open to keep the room hot, hoping to melt out his bile. She stripped him naked because he sweat so much then covered him in blankets when he complained of the cold. He ranted and raved. Didn't know what was going on, gripped in fever and fatigue, still half-drunk. She was half-drunk too and couldn't figure out what to do. Should she send for help? Should she call the gamblers and ask them? His condition changed so fast she didn't know what to say. Jake had a hacking cough and spit up blood. Then all of a sudden his skin turned blue—dark blue, like he'd been dipped in ink. She had no idea what to do about that. She didn't know what sickness turned a man blue, as if suffocating, except he wasn't. Jake looked like he was from another planet with his blond hair and blue complexion.

Despite all outward appearances, maybe he wasn't breathing. She worried he might die. But then his skin turned back to normal. Not normal exactly. He was a feverish red, but at least he wasn't blue! Who would believe that?

The spot of blood on his pillowcase was what caused Evie to seek help the next day. The blood came from his ear. Evie corralled a boy on the street and sent him to fetch Maria Eigler.

Maria thought she was up in a palace at first, being in the district. She asked who the madam of the house was. "These are my rooms," Evie said. "It isn't like you think. Me and Jake. We're friends."

Maria knew what it said about a woman who had rooms furnished like this down on the lower River Ward. "I don't care who you are," she said. "I'm here for Jake. That's that."

She carried a basket with raw eggs inside. She cracked them into a glass Evie fetched and made Jake down the yolks and whites. She fed him pieces of raw onion and strung a bag of camphor around his neck. He calmed down then. He slept.

It must have occurred to Evie that she could leave. Maria would take over—a car could be arranged to take Jake to a hospital. Evie didn't have to suffer his illness. Yet she felt something change inside. She wanted to stay. She had to. Jake needed her.

"I'll take care of him," Evie announced. Maria hesitated, thinking it over before she went. She left behind the eggs. "He must drink one every hour. Keep up his strength."

Word reached Tom Dennison that Jake was sick up in a girl's room. Dennison came personally in the evening to see for himself. He brought a bottle of Irish whiskey and a physician and peeked in the bedroom to have a look. The bottle was inside the sleeve of his overcoat, his massive hands palmed around the base, as the doctor listened to Jake's chest with a stethoscope.

Evie hovered in the kitchen doorway to hear what Tom Dennison would say. He didn't say anything. He waited for the doctor's verdict then tossed the bottle to the bed, where it submerged in the blankets. Dennison was only there a moment, to see Jake for himself, to hear the doctor say Jake was going to be fine. "It's only the flu," the doctor said—a comment that became rare the next couple years. He left a roll of surgical gauze at the bedside for when the bleeding came back, along with a case of capsulated powders. Something to bring down the fever and a purgative.

Dennison stopped on his way out. He took off his hat. "Some of the boys didn't believe Jake was really sick. They said he faked so he could stay with his girl instead of working." Dennison looked Evie up and down. "You're the girl?"

Evie nodded. She'd met Billy Nesselhous before but never Tom Dennison.

He left without saying another word.

In moments of lucidity Jake acted ashamed about being laid up. He begged Evie to not look at him. She shut the curtains and dampened the lamp until it was too dark to see much except the warmth of the sunset around the windows. Jake was embarrassed, but he needed her. When his fever grew worse, as it did in cycles, or when his throat tore raw from hacking, it did him good to see her rushing to douse a handkerchief in camphor. He drifted in and out during the worst of it. Each time he woke up the first thing he'd see was Evie in the corner. She made sure of this.

He went into panics about footsteps from the hallway, the sounds of neighbors coming and going. In his fever people paced around him. He pleaded with her to keep his persecutors out. She had no idea what he meant. He talked about the crab louse, about pick handles and tools ripping at his body, about a child buried alive. He ranted in German half the time. She'd never heard his whispering, guttural, sometimes plaintive German voice. He relived arguments with his brother, with his father, with folks she'd never heard of. He apologized profusely, guilt ridden in two languages. "I'm sorry. I'm sorry. We buried her."

Tom Dennison's doctor stopped by four times daily, although he never did much besides operate a thermometer as far as Evie was concerned. Some friends visited the third day, Joe and Ingo, but they didn't stray in from the hallway. Jake was sleeping anyway. Evie let them see him laid up a moment then whisked them down the stairs.

It produced such amazement to see him knocked down. She couldn't help but flit around in helpful ways, a stern, wary smile on her face. She promised to stay until he was better. "So you won't have to worry where I am," she said. He'd have worried what she was up to if she left. He had no concept of time and place and couldn't figure why Evie was with him and not somebody else. "Why me?" he pestered her, and not Joe or Ingo or Ennis the Irishman, whoever they were.

There were times she thought he was a goner. She'd stay with him until he was better, and in this way he'd have to get better.

The fever lasted four days. She was an impassioned nurse. Held cool rags to his forehead. Covered and re-covered his kicking limbs in afghans. Changed his sheets if the chamber pot spilled. Kissed him incessantly. She didn't care if she caught whatever it was he had; how extraordinary that was. She rubbed his body with alcohol. She soothed him. She promised he wouldn't die. She pressed her head into the pillow beside him and kept it there a long time. Somehow Maria Eigler tracked down a crate of oranges—which was a miracle, given the war rations—and Jake had to drink the juice even though it burned his throat. It was a simple matter of whether or not Evie could keep up his strength. She made him take turnip broth and a beaten raw egg every hour. She didn't let him forget for one second he was being taken care of and was going to be fine.

And then, suddenly, he was.

Evie sat crooked on the edge of the mattress, propped up by an arm. Jake woke and saw her.

"Does your face hurt much?" she asked.

"Don't touch it," he said, shying away, his cheeks still swollen and inflamed.

"Would it bother you if I opened the window? The weather turned nice." The sun shone through in a brilliant rectangular mass. The spring air was warm and lively, an alluvial bouquet blown in from the country. Once a window was open, Evie realized the room had filled with the base odor of turnips and vomit, one that strengthened as it thinned, the memory of it, because she hadn't noticed before.

"Do you think you could eat something? I'll get whatever you want, some mashed potatoes or meat."

"I'm hungry."

"I bet you'd eat anything so long as it isn't turnips and orange juice."

"Some chipped beef sounds good," he said, "if you have it."

Sure, there were tins of meat. She went to the kitchen then came back with chipped beef over toast. Evie chatted the whole time he ate. She was taken by the feeling that Jake wouldn't have survived without her. She saw him warm inside too, his health returning. Every note of music was profound to him. Every bit of food was gravy. Most of all he loved on Evie, and she soaked it up. She'd stayed with him. She'd made sure he saw the other side of his sickness. She could have dumped him off in an infirmary or sent him home with Maria. But she hadn't. She stuck by him even when it meant she might be infected. She'd surprised him with the way she acted. It made him bashful. He hadn't expected her to be like that—she hadn't either.

She told him how Maria stopped in with eggs then a crate of oranges. How his skin turned alien blue for three hours in the beginning. How a doctor came four times a day to listen to his insides. How even Tom Dennison made sure he was okay and brought whiskey as a gift.

"How did everyone find out? Were you going around telling people I was sick?"

"No," she said. "The River Ward knows these kinds of things. You have no secrets."

C onsider Anna Miihlstein.

She never wanted to come to Omaha in the first place. Living in the Bowery wasn't the greatest either, when they first arrived in America, not with the Second Avenue Elevated running right by their window and the screams from down the hall in the middle of the night, but at least she'd heard of New York City. The truth was that Anna missed being a Salzburger. Forget Omaha, forget the Bowery, forget Galizien. Anna's desire went way back. Maybe they'd been poor in Salzburg, and they had been, six of them then trying to get by on what meager work Herr could find those days. Their mother had alienated everyone—Frau Albina Tropsch was blackballed in Salzburg because of her outbursts— but the city was nice. What Anna remembered. What Silke and Theresa had told her about. Promenading riverside along the Salzach on cobble-stoned roads. Rolling around in the hills. Swells of music from the Mozarteum conservatory. *Apfelstrudel* and white sausages. Anna didn't remember so well. She was only four when they left for Galizien. But she remembered the feeling distinctly. Sitting along the river in the summertime, the grass tall and clustered with clumps of satisfied folks. Women in hats and dresses. Girls who worried the hems of their dresses so the fabric didn't stain trouncing through the grass. This was living well. Being healthy and free and fruitful. The Miihlsteins had left all that behind. And now Anna wasn't so sure a reality still existed to match the feeling she had, not anymore. The way things were talked about, the way the dailies presented the news from Europe. Franz Josef had died. The empire would fall. This was a very sad thing to Anna. As if there could be no more white sausages and green wine and apple strudel with vanilla sauce, never again, not in Austria. There would be no more wearing white dresses and sunbathing by the Salzach.

She'd never return to Salzburg, of course. Regardless she held on to this feeling about the way things ought to be.

Maybe because of this Anna went to considerable lengths to care for her white straw hat, what Frau Eigler called Anna's Sunday hat. It was the only one the girl owned, after all, and she was conscientious about keeping it clean and preserving the integrity of the brim and band, or else it would sit crooked on her head and all would be lost. Anna was sure. Otherwise, if she didn't keep busy, Anna worried about her family: if Karel was getting in trouble at the school he attended, if Herr was doing enough business to make the move to Omaha a success, if Silke would find someone to appreciate her despite her shyness, if Theresa hadn't made a mistake quitting school to take a job with the streetcar company. Anna, stuck in the attic, worried about many things. So she allowed herself some vanity when it came to that hat. How she washed the straw every other week in the kitchen sink. Carefully untied and removed that purple silk ribbon before sinking it in warm water, and formed deftly the straw weave, dabbed with a delicate washcloth Maria allowed her to use, careful to not dent the crown or let it sag out of shape while wet. Sometimes she had to reshape the brim with the steam from a teakettle. That was a difficult task to manage. If a girl wasn't careful she could make things much worse, trying that. But Anna was very careful. Even if it required great diligence for an entire morning. She'd wash and shape and set it out to dry. She'd replace the purple ribbon.

Anna daydreamed about other hats she'd someday own. If she had some money, if she didn't rely on Herr for everything, then Anna could afford all sorts of hats. Gigantic ones with wide brims washed out in clouds of virgin white tulle. Silk turbans from the Orient topped with peacock feathers. Dapper canvas safari hats. When she was older, she'd have a job in an office, her own desk with locking drawers, a brass nameplate affixed to a wedge of stained pinewood. She'd seen such desks in New York when she followed Herr around as he looked for work. Those women behind the desks—somehow it was almost always women Herr begged a job from, in the offices he solicited, women who turned him down flat. "I'm sorry. I can't help you," they'd say. Anna beside her father, holding his hand, listening and staring at the nameplate on the desk. Did these women polish their brass every day? They must have.

This was before Anna was really sick. It wasn't until a doctor in the Bowery insisted that Anna stay in bed for an entire month that her illness took over. A month in bed, no sun, no air. Only water and Cream of Wheat. Who wouldn't feel like dying was preferable? Herr believed what any quack told him those days and then refused to listen to any doctor thereafter, since the advice of counterfeit physicians only made things worse. Foremost among Herr's ideas was to relocate to the hinterlands. Get some fresh air, get some sunshine. Herr was told about a job in Nebraska, and that Nebraska was in the hinterlands. Herr thought he was onto something. He didn't know that factories and steel mills existed in Omaha too. Or the three biggest employers here were a lead mill, a soldering plant, and, of course, the stockyards. So much for fresh air.

Herr locked Anna up even more in Omaha. He was probably a little embarrassed about how things were turning out for her. She'd never been sick in Salzburg, after all. A healthy child, engaging and boisterous, sunbathing along the river, frolicking in the Alpine hills. Now this.

Frau Eigler had her own remedies for what mystery plagued Anna, most of which involved eating large amounts of food. All sorts of meats and broths that would fortify a person. Fresh fruit wasn't so easy to come by those days but was served when possible, in thin slices with granulated sugar. This seemed to work, except that Anna's body couldn't hold greasy food or pulpy fruit. She was prone to nausea if she overate, and to diarrhea generally. Not to be discouraged, Frau Eigler had Anna drink dandelion tea, then choke down as many spoonfuls of pureed oat straw as she could stand. After Anna refused to submit to these cures, powders made from watermelon and cucumber seeds followed, mixed with warm milk.

"I'll give this one week," Anna finally said. She was tired of having to submit to every possible tonic dreamed up by those who lived in the Eigler house. "If it doesn't work after a week, you leave me alone."

"Sure thing," Maria promised. "Just try this one and see. It'll work."

"What is it?"

"Just milk, *Mädel*. Milk and some powders. You can't taste the powders. Not much."

"That's what you always say."

"This time it's true. Believe me."

"Then you'll leave me alone? No more sneaking potions into my food?"

"This will work. Then that's that."

Of course the new concoction did nothing, the cucumber seeds and milk.

Anna wasn't sure what she was sick with. It wasn't polio. She could walk. It wasn't cholera or flux, although there was the diarrhea to consider. Her bones hurt. She was knock-kneed, that was all. She was frail. There was no need to make a whole study of it. Her nose was thin and a little crooked—should they alert the Imperial Academy of Sciences about that too?

Anna wanted to be left alone. She was tired of being the subject of amateur experiments. Tired of everyone watching her and asking how she was. She was fine. That's right. Perfectly fine. So long as she spent the whole day indoors, up in an attic dedicated to her own disquiets, her crafts, her worrying about what Karel might be up to, her reading. Anna knew something bad was going to happen. She thought it would happen to Karel, but she wasn't always sure about that. Maybe it just involved him. Which meant maybe it was something bad that was going to happen to her. She didn't want anything bad to happen to her little brother, who wasn't so little anymore. She worried about him. This was the only way they communicated.

Karel was always trying to save her when he was around. It was annoying. She didn't need saving, not by him. He had these ideas about what Anna needed. These schemes of his. *Hiking!* There's a whole park out by the river, three miles wide. Didn't Anna know that? *Calisthenics!* She'd be amazed at what good some jumping jacks and knee bends could do for her temperament. *Posture!* Karel sneaking up behind her, crossing his arms around her chest and lifting so her back popped and her blood could flow freely to exorcise her bad humors. Anna screamed when he did that one. Why couldn't he warn her first before grabbing her and making her body crack?

That summer after Karel was found boozing in Mecklenburg's Saloon was stifling for Anna too. Not that Anna was complaining about seeing more of her brother. But the way he talked to her, his insistence that she cheer up. He was becoming such a boss.

"What are you doing there?" he'd ask her, up in the attic. She wanted to tell him not to bother her, that he should be quiet. But she wouldn't risk a demand like that. Karel was sensitive. He wouldn't talk to her the rest of the summer if she said something like that.

Anna said, "Just watch." There on the sofa in the attic. A sketching pad on her lap, some charcoal in her hand. Most of the time she just let her hand go as it wanted to go. Made one mark, then another. Curled out shapes with the curves from the first letter of her name. Drawing the shape of an *a* was fun. Before long, small shapes turned into bigger ones. She'd been drawing leaves on a tree, she realized, an aspen tree. She stroked two parallel lines in the middle of the mess. "There it is," she said.

"Why didn't you just start with the trunk?"

"It wasn't there yet."

"What does that mean?"

Anna hated having to explain things to Karel. His turning more and more red, until he grabbed the pad and charcoal to show her how to do it. He drew a straight trunk first, thick, with roots flaring where the ground must be. A decent enough start. That was how most people thought of a tree. Then branches, a bit too angular, funnel-like, a metallic kind of shape, Anna saw that right away. "Oh, hell." Karel stopped drawing. He realized then. It looked bad.

Karel didn't bother drawing the leaves. He scowled at Anna like it was her fault he'd drawn a strange, dead tree. "I'm sorry," Anna said. Then, "Give me that, you klutz." She tore the page out from the pad and put it on the table. Over those weeks a new pile grew there, separate from the neater stacks of Anna's crafts. This one of objects Karel had botched.

Once summer was over, Karel didn't stay around the attic much. He was free again, off with his friends. If his being in the attic didn't cheer up Anna then being gone might do the trick. Karel was such a boy about things. He couldn't understand.

More and more he was out with that Emil Braun character. With Alfred Braun and Jimmy McHenry. Anna hadn't met these people, but she heard about them from Maria. Maria knew about everyone and everything on Clandish. That was how it seemed from the kitchen. How Karel was getting good at baseball. Baseball wasn't played in the winter, not properly, but that didn't stop him. He got better and better. He'd stay out until after dark. He'd miss dinner. Then, once spring broke, he took her down to that game. The tryout. That was all it was, some grown men playing with each other. Anna had only ever seen boys play baseball—out in the streets of New York, with broomsticks and a pink rubber ball—and hadn't thought that grown men would play the game too. Men who took things serious. Who glared and spit and kicked at the grass with cleated shoes. Who only cracked a smile when one of them did something wrong or was hurt. Anna didn't understand why her brother wanted to spend all his time with these men. These were the kind of men Herr taught them to avoid.

Karel was making a mistake—that's what Anna thought, sitting there in the stands at Rourke Park. He hadn't thought things through.

Anna was going to tell Karel that he shouldn't be out with rabble like these. He should stay home to make something of himself, learn to play the violin properly so he could find mannerly employment later on. He was so good at reading and languages. English in particular came easy to him, while Anna struggled to speak anything but Deutsch. Karel was wasting his time playing baseball. Anna was going to tell him, but then she saw how he moved on a ballfield. How he covered space. Graceful in the way he drifted over grass, feet barely touching ground, his spine lengthening with each stride. He stood easy and told jokes. He belonged. That was why Anna had trouble talking to him on the streetcar ride back to Clandish, and the weeks later, when he kept at her to get out more, to make friends with some girls who went to his school. She couldn't talk to Karel anymore, not like she used to. He kept at her, told her she should be more like the girls from school, girls who sounded horrible, crass, dirty, whose fathers worked in mechanic shops.

"I'm sick," she'd say. "Did you forget that, Karel? I'm not at all well."

It was reasonable to most people on Clandish that Anna might be bitter, even at her age. The situation wasn't fair. Karel was her little brother, and before long he'd tower over her. He was strong and his body electric. He jumped down the six steps of Maria's front porch when he left for school and didn't even quiver. He landed, stiff then lithe, like a gymnast, wished her *auf Wiedersehen* then dashed down the avenue. Nobody could say that was fair. Older sister Anna slinking to the attic, legs shaking, remembering the sound of Karel's feet hitting the pavement after leaping from the porch. Her legs would snap if she tried something like that. Poor girl.

She barely made a sound upstairs. Hung her straw hat on the balustrade. Curled under a quilt. Lay there a while on the sofa. Listened to Herr working away. He wouldn't bother her. Not right away. Herr's hands were busy restringing a cello whose tuning pegs kept unwinding. He didn't offer much company to his youngest daughter, even if they were in the attic together most of the day. Between the string section of the Musik Verein and the horde of amateur fiddlers lurking in immigrant Omaha, he was kept busy year round. If only he charged what his services were worth and worked at a quick pace, Herr could have made quite a chunk of profit. If he made more money he wouldn't have to work as hard. Anna understood how these things went.

After a while Herr took a break. He started his tea and perched on the edge of the sofa while he waited for the kettle to whistle. "What's wrong, Mädel Anna? Can't you tell me?" Anna hidden, the pattern of the quilt illuminated green and gold from the lamplight on the other side. "Will you sit up? Won't you read awhile?" Herr shifting his weight and stretching his arms around the lump on the sofa. Anna the lump. "Don't go away from me, *Mädchen*. I won't lose you. I won't let you get away."

Anna couldn't help it. She sat up and let the quilt fall and leaned into him. A silly man. He was small, like Anna. He didn't eat much. She felt his ribs rise and fall through his shirt.

"I'll read a bit," she told him. "Now leave me alone."

Anna began to miss certain crafts she'd done the spring before. Some favorites that Karel had stuck in the coal cellar. A pony she'd bent out of scrap wire, a little carved elephant with an Oriental-looking gem drawn on its forehead, a yarn June bug. She wanted to have these special ones in the attic, the best of the best, so she slipped through the kitchen and down the steps into the dark. There was a lightbulb, but, when she pulled the string, the weak filament did little good. Lit the landing, bled but little into the deeper shadows. Anna sat on the bottom step to let her eyes tune to the dark. After a moment she could see why Karel liked it down here. Nobody came looking for you. Nobody was looking at you. They all must have thought Anna needed their company, that she couldn't stand to be alone and waited all day for her siblings to return—and she did, the unfortunate part about it. The house was always occupied. Maria around in the parlor, the kitchen, the front rooms. Herr all day in the attic. Even Jake Strauss coming home late in the morning, bursting into the bathroom to wash at the sink, even if Anna was in the bathtub or using the toilet. Anna liked Jake. She did. But he had a habit of embarrassing her.

Down by the banks of beetroots and mass of dried flower stems it was different. Maria was too old to use the wobbly cellar stairs anymore. And nobody else cared to come down. The cellar was full of what most folks would consider junk. The junk represented new worlds to Anna. Not only did she find stacks of her own work but other treasures too. Ancient ones, which were the best kind. She poked around. Looked in crates without digging deep. She was curious what Karel had been up to down here and mined for evidence. Paths had been cleared through the junk, so she could wander from wall to wall. The dirt floor turned over fresh where a crate had been dragged across the room. Crates stacked four high in their new spots, as high as they'd go before tumbling. There was scrap metal in the back, the frame of an old bicycle. There were some paintings, some plaster busts of Viennese composers—Schubert, Haydn, Beethoven, Mozart, of course—small busts about the size of an infant's head. Even Anna's crafts had been sorted into stacks. Her drawings. Her clay. All the wire work hung from a floor joist with tacks, so they swayed a little as she approached, vaguely alive and menacing. Anna was moved, seeing this. Her eyes wet. Nobody was watching as she let a tear brim and fall. Karel was always trying to fix things for her, wasn't he? He hadn't thrown her works away, like she'd feared, but preserved them in this secret place they shared. At least Karel did right down here, under the floorboards, where his efforts couldn't be seen.

Of course, just as she was touched by Karel's invisible kindness, a tear on her cheek, Anna noticed that he was sitting on the steps watching her.

"What are you doing?" He jumped down the wobbly steps and thumped to the dirt floor. "I didn't think you came down here."

"It was you, wasn't it? That cleaned up. And hung my wires to save them."

Anna moved next to Karel to touch his shoulder. His shirt was damp and his skin red. She could almost hear his heart pumping. "Is it hot out?" she asked. "You're soaked."

"I had to run home."

"Oh." She stepped away and poked around some, told him that she loved it down in the cellar and she saw why he did too. She was babbling, but she didn't care. She could babble if she wanted. It wasn't the sole right of Herr and Maria to babble on about nothing whenever they felt like it. She told Karel this. He looked at her like she was strange. "Oh, you know what I mean. Just to have an hour alone without someone picking on you. That's all. But I'm glad to see you, Karel. I wasn't talking about you."

She noticed how he was holding something behind his leg. The dagger. He went to put it away, picked up the case the violin was in. Anna had no interest in the dagger—it wasn't the least bit odd that Karel would borrow a knife, the kind of boy he was—but the old violin caught her eye.

"What's that?" she asked.

"Nothing."

"No, it's a violin. Let me see it."

"You'll break it," Karel said. "Don't touch. It's fragile."

139

"I won't. I know how."

"Don't come down here and ruin things." Karel latched the case before Anna could touch the violin, before she could even really see it. He was angry for some reason.

"I wasn't going to ruin it."

"You don't know anything."

He lifted the crate that held the violin case and set it high on a stack where Anna couldn't reach. She'd be too weak to get it.

Anna couldn't believe him. How he turned and smirked at her and waited to see what she'd say about that. She felt like she was sinking into the floor, her legs failing under the light of her brother's cruelty.

"I'm sorry. I wanted to see. That's all," she said. Him staring at her. "You did good here. Cleaning. Putting the cellar in order."

"Yeah. That's what you said." He was put off even more after she apologized. "None of this belongs to us. It's Maria's things."

"I know that," Anna said. "What isn't mine belongs to Maria."

"Why should I care what happens to this junk?"

"You do. That's all. Don't yell at me about it. Answer your own question."

"I don't know what's wrong with you," Karel said. "You're always sulking. You're mad, that's all. Jealous."

"Jealous? Of what?"

"Of me, that's what. Because of how things worked out here."

"In Omaha?"

"In America."

"Oh. I don't think so. That's wrong."

"Listen," Karel said. "I know how it is. Let me fix things for you. I've been thinking it over. You need to come to school with me. That's what it's going to take."

"What are you talking about?"

"For you to feel better!"

Karel had it all worked out. She had until next autumn to build her strength, to find one of Maria's potions that worked. If Anna was just a little better they'd let her come to school in the fall. She'd have something to look forward to then. Something worthwhile to work at instead of wasting time like she had been.

"We'd be in class together. We'd see each other all day. Isn't that what you want?"

"But I'm older than you. I'd be a grade above."

"No, you wouldn't. With what schooling you missed already, they'd let us be together. Maria could work it out with the principal. I'd be there to help. Introduce you to kids."

Anna wasn't so sure. She unhooked a wire work, the pony, and took it to the steps to sit down. She'd consider what Karel suggested, she committed herself that much. Sat there and bent the components of the pony, made its tail wend upward and wild like in the wind.

"What do you do all day anyway?" Karel asked. "Why wouldn't you come to school?"

"You know I do lessons. Every morning. In the books Herr bought."

"Sure. The primers. But they're old. None of the kids heard of them."

"Is that true?"

"That's beside the point. You don't go to school for books. You're missing out on being a friend. That's what I mean. You'll turn out weird like *Herr Mühlstein* is." Karel slapped up at a floorboard as he said this, gestured to the attic. "It will be better," he insisted. "School isn't so bad. The kids aren't dirty. You'd feel better if you weren't hid away so much."

"You know that's not true."

"It's only Herr who thinks you got to be locked up—and even he's not sure why. Maybe if Mom was still around she'd tell him how it needs to be."

"You don't know what you're talking about."

"Sure I do."

Anna swept her skirts flat and laid back on the steps. She rested her head on the worn riser a moment, before she stood and put the wire pony back where she found it. She was tired of all this. She said to Karel, "Am I the one who has to tell you? You should listen to Herr. He's a good man. He adores each of us."

"What do you mean?" Karel rubbed his arms. He looked cold, a film of dried sweat covering him. He rubbed where there were goose bumps. "I don't understand," he said after a moment. "Are you mad?"

"You think you're all grown up, yeah. You should find yourself lucky if you end up like Father. If you weren't pigheaded, you'd know this."

She'd never talked to him this way, her voice sharp with contempt. She was making him angry, reminding him that he was still only a boy. She decided to tell him about their mother—all the things their older sisters had told her in confidence and made her swear to secrecy. Anna made herself sound bored to tell it; she sighed and shook her head at him, like Karel was stupid for not knowing that their mother hadn't been killed in the war, not really.

"She was older than Father," Anna explained. She should have stopped talking. She felt this, her stomach turning over, her guts contracting. "About fifty when you were born. She was an actress a long time before she married, that's why."

Anna told how it had happened. Once Karel was old enough to be left on his own part of the day, their mother changed. They were still in Austria, where they were from, but she wanted to move to Galizien, where a theater needed taking over. In Salzburg directors wouldn't cast her. She was commanding and loud, which was necessary when performing, but not otherwise. No longer was she a summery thing, not libidinous and lithe like when she'd earned her stage name: the Sparrow's Nest, later shortened to just Sparrow, some kind of joke a Viennese producer saddled her with when she was young and desperate. The producer was a lout, but he put a star on her door, and that was all she needed. That was what she needed again when she moved her family to Galizien, far away from Salzburg, where an old colleague, a Bohemian, a washed-up actor himself, had sought her out.

Once they were up there with the Hungarians and Poles, Herr Miihlstein was never happy. He hated Galizien. When war broke out with Russia, he was eager to leave.

"It's because Father's a Jew," Anna explained.

"Aren't we Jews?"

"In a way."

"That's why she died? She wouldn't go? And Cossacks got her because they hate Jews?"

"No," Anna said, rising from the steps to clasp Karel's shoulder. "Silke made that up because you wouldn't understand the truth. Mother was murdered. But not by Cossacks. The man killed her before the Cossacks even attacked."

"What man?"

"The one who led us there. The actor. Some Bohemian man. She was seeing him. They had a romance. Everyone knew that. When war started and Father wanted to leave, the actor went into a rage. It was he who did it. Not the Russians. The actor stabbed her one night and ran off."

Karel looked sick to his stomach, like he couldn't fully believe what Anna said. "You're lying," he said, but she didn't respond to the accusation. All she needed to do was set her lips in a line and wait for him to come back around. It was obvious he believed her.

"Did we bury her before we left?" Karel asked.

"Yes. She's buried in a church courtyard there. Don't you remember? The three handfuls of dirt on the coffin?"

"No."

"You were there, Karel."

"No, I wasn't. I don't remember."

"Such a little boy. So pathetic. We wanted to bawl like you, but it was difficult for us. We knew what had gone on. You understood nothing. That's why we let you go on like a baby."

Karel left the cellar as soon as she finished the telling. He stomped up the steps and out through the kitchen to the back door and was gone. Anna stayed awhile under the floorboards, moved deeper in the cellar, where it was dark, and sat on a crate. She didn't understand why she said those things. She didn't know any better than Karel about their mother or what happened in Galizien. Those rumors she passed on were just what Theresa said. Anna didn't know them as fact. She sat on a crate and looked at her shoes. They were ugly shoes. She hated them. The straps torn at the stitches. The shine worn off. She saw her legs and hated them too. Her skinny legs, bowed a little. The way her knees knobbed out wider than her shins. That was why she stayed under a quilt so much, even when it was hot, so she didn't have to see her legs.

Anna stayed in the attic even more the next week. She felt bad about what she said. That Karel had bawled. That he was a baby. Silke and Theresa teased Karel too much about that. Anna should have known better. She laid under a quilt on the sofa and felt her legs hurt. That was right, she thought. That was what she deserved.

K arel and his friends were at a lot of SOSA meetings that month, the nights Emil Braun spoke. It never hurt to have the buddings of a crowd stirring when Emil rose to bellow "Oyez! Oyez!" to silence the old-timers. He passed around a tattered copy of *Prison Memoirs of an Anarchist* and claimed he knew its author, Alexander Berkman, personally, grinning across the cigar-smoky room, his back to the pink-armed barkeeps, the balding top of his head in the mirror.

"If we want to see real progress in action, we got to knock Tom Dennison and his stooges out. What we got now's a government that's protector for corporate and monopoly interests only. Along with that comes a toilsome life, poor health, broken families, hunger, disease. Trust me. All government will be shown to be useless in the end, and only we can do the showing."

Karel tried following what Braun said, he did, but watching the amassed coalition of immigrants at a meeting was more interesting to him—being an immigrant himself. The kind of folks Karel met on the boat over and in the Bowery. Undesirables compelled to move on down the line again and again. From Rīga to Warszawa, from Danzig to Leipzig, from Wiesbaden to Le Havre, to the Lower East Side, to Montréal, to Chicago, to smaller cities in the Midwest if they couldn't afford to ride all the way to San Francisco. Foreignness showed in the denim jacket a tenement hopper wore, in the sickly sparse mustache he grew, in the military hat he filched off a dead soldier somewhere along the way in Europe. Most people didn't want these types around. They caused trouble. There was trouble enough already. But Karel paid attention to them. How they sang "The Internationale" and quoted Proudhon and wore red shirts to honor Garibaldi. How they fought sometimes in the alleyway after meetings and spread rumors about who among them was plotting to kill a politician. They sounded insane. That was why Karel liked them. They weren't afraid of doing something drastic.

Meetings were crowded those months. The approaching municipal election had everyone worked up. It wasn't always clear to Karel how a vote in Omaha had anything to do with massacres in Serbia or the liberty of sand-whipped Bedouins in Arabia, but he went along with an idea when he saw Emil Braun do the same. What did it bother Karel to sing an anthem, to raise fists and stamp feet? "Yeah! We'll show them what's what!" What did it bother him to shout, to hooray and hurrah, his mouth full of frankfurters and sauerkraut? Emil showed him hospitality, after all. Emil was the guy who introduced him to baseball players. Karel owed him this much at least.

When he wasn't in school or at a meeting, Karel was down at Rourke Park to help out the Omaha Baseball Club as a shag boy, running down balls in the outfield afternoons before supper. He liked to stretch his legs after sitting in a school desk all day. To get in the sun and feel his hair lighten. Karel felt important, catching fly balls during batting practice. This was different than when he played with boys his own age. The baseball spinning high in the air. A grown man hit that ball and Karel caught it. His ears were trained to diagnose how hard a ball was struck and how far it would fly, so he moved quickly to the spot it would land, knowing instantly if he should rush in or lope back, and whether a fly would hook or slice away, as if the most natural thing in the world, into the cradle of his glove stretched open.

Karel kept the ball Josh Joseph had given him in his back pocket, even during practice with the men's club. Some of the players asked Karel why he carried it, seeing the orb bulge his pocket, but Karel wouldn't tell why the ball was important to him. These men were rivals with the ball club from the Northside. They wouldn't like how Karel carried around a baseball gifted by a Negro hurler, even if Josh Joseph was the greatest Omaha had ever seen and was remembered on both Northside and Southside. Josh was seen either as hero or villain—depending on where the person doing the remembering had grown up. And, of course, anybody in Omaha who cared a whit about baseball knew what happened to Josh Joseph after he shipped off to Cuba during the Spanish-American War. How he lost both legs, how he became a shoeshine boy, scuttling along the walkways outside downtown banks—how all his athletic talent was blown away in a single mortar blast. Josh Joseph was more famous for what he didn't become than for what he did.

Most of the time the ballplayers didn't care what Karel had to say. They weren't there to find out what he knew. He was there to listen to them, how it should be, as they joked and discussed points of anatomy, a woman's or their own. The ballplayers told stories about nasty acts they'd pulled as boys and even nastier ones pulled as men. Bill and Ducky Sutez. Jap Marceau, the third bagger. Ralph Snyder, the pitcher. Jimmie Collins, who managed and played some first base when he felt like it. They were fine men.

Karel earned an invitation to join them at a saloon one evening after practice, a notorious little dive over on the other side of Deer Park, up in Gibson, where stockyard workers drank. A saloon where factions from rival political machines held bare-knuckle boxing matches on Saturday nights, out back, where creosote-soaked ropes were squared into the dust to make a ring. Karel knew he shouldn't go with the ballplayers to the Purple Pig, not after his father had caught him in a saloon once already. Things were fine between him and Herr Miihlstein then, they left each other alone, and Karel wanted to keep it that way. Coming home with beer on his breath might mean he couldn't play ball anymore, and that wouldn't be worth it. Karel had a remarkable talent on his hands. That was why fortune brought him to Omaha. He knew this.

He went along anyway. The ballplayers hooked his arms and pulled him in that direction. They said he had to come. That it wouldn't be the same without him. So he walked with them to the Purple Pig, a few blocks down Thirteenth, along the park. It wasn't all that far, not in a group, leather equipment bags strapped over their backs. Not in how they talked loud and joked and laughed, and how people in Deer Park smiled when they recognized them, the Southsiders, because people in that neighborhood were proud of their team. This showed in how the ballplayers took over the bar. The guys who'd taken up residence on the bar stools didn't mind making way for these guys. Why, they were probably thirsty, working up a lather out in the sun, getting ready to play. The ballplayers were well known all over this neighborhood. A few of them had played in the B leagues before having to quit and find real jobs. Of course, certain benefits came along with playing for the local team. Maybe Ralph didn't have to work so hard at the quarry job team organizers found him, or at the stockyard job where Jap mostly sat in a shaded warehouse all day, resting up for a game, or had a catch with the owner's boy, sure. The ballplayers got to throw a little weight around in neighborhood saloons, at least in season. "Go on," a rummy might say. "Take my seat. I was only keeping it warm." And the men did. They bellied up and ordered draught beer. First round on the house. Karel along with them. Just a boy, thirteen, but Karel wouldn't be a boy much longer. He sat at the bar and took his freebie and drank the top off. He listened to the men boast in this dark low-ceilinged saloon, a little shack in Gibson with congested gaslights that gave off more smoke than light.

"It's good you came," Bill Sutez told him. "We got a present for you."

Karel laughed it off at first. He wasn't really listening. Light-headed from the beer. Blood rushing through his ears because he was in a saloon with the brothers Sutez and Jap Marceau. The best the Southside had to offer in the way of baseball players. And they got Karel a beer because he was one of them. They circled around him, said, "It's the truth, kid! Here!" And handed over a package wrapped in tissue paper. "Go on. Tear it apart. Nothing to be scared of." Ducky put his arm around Karel and shouted in his ear, "It's a present, dummy! Open it!"

Karel put his glass on the bar and tore the tissue in two. Out fell a set of wool clothes, pinstriped and white, with a black-brimmed cap. He recognized it immediately but didn't quite believe. It was the uniform of the Southside.

"That's for all you done to help the team," Jimmie Collins said. He was the manager and was compelled to speech making on occasions like this. "You're a member as far as we're concerned. Now you are."

Sure, Karel thought. He was around all the time. He practiced. He went to the tavern. Karel was one of them.

"Well. What do you think?"

"Yeah. Say something, kid."

Ducky held the jersey to Karel's chest. "It'll fit," he said.

"Goddamn," Karel said. "Let me have that."

He jumped from his stool and right there at the bar ripped his shirt over his head so he could try on and button up his jersey. The men cracking up in laughter, saying, "I guess he likes it." Karel dropped his pants so he could get the rest on then tucked the jersey into the knee-highs. "This is great," Karel said. "I mean it." Fastening the rest of the buttons so it spelled *OMAHA* across his chest. Then "Another round." "A toast." They had Karel climb up to the bar top from a stool and raised their glasses to him. The men were so happy for Karel, to see him in their uniform, the baggy hat on his head, the pinstriped whites all crisp and fit, maybe a little tight, tucked into black socks. Karel looked sharp. He smiled back at his compatriots, his teammates. Bill and Ducky and Jap and Ralph and Claude Nethaway. Their hair combed back in a paste made with sweat and dust from the infield. Muzzles black with stubble and grease.

Karel was in a saloon because he belonged there. He too was swarthy. His hair black, hand-swept off his forehead. His broad shoulders stretching a uniform, his tanned skin and palms swelled thick from the beating they took catching fly balls.

He was late to supper that night. That was unavoidable. Usually he cut it close, with rushing up from the field, but going to the saloon put a kink in things. Supper began without him. Karel heard from behind the kitchen door. Forks and knives working in the dining room. Before they noticed him, he lingered to take in the aromas—broth reducing with a wisp of steam above it, fresh bread cooling, a skillet browned by meat. Maria wasn't in the habit of setting a plate for those who didn't bother showing up on time, but she let Karel eat in the kitchen. There was some gravy left. She spooned it over bread for him, pulled an apple from a box where she kept them. Karel ate with his hands, standing at the counter in his new Southside uniform.

"You stink like beer," Maria said, her eyebrows raised as she dunked a saucepan in soapy water at the sink. "You drink with the ballplayers?" He nodded. "Well. What do I care?" Maria said. "This doesn't surprise me. The age you are. Boys always want to drink beer. Beer doesn't bother me. So you work it out with your father."

"I'm not going to tell him." Karel sopped the last bit of gravy with his bread and stuffed it in his mouth.

"Ah. I see." Maria took his plate and put it in the sink. "And he isn't going to notice? Sure. You bet."

The girls were at the table when Karel went by, leaned back in their chairs to talk and digest. Karel wanted to rush by them to the stairs, but there wasn't much chance of that.

"What in the world?" "Look at him!"

"Where did you get baseball clothes?" Theresa asked. "Let me see you," Silke said. The two older ones cornered him at the stairwell. They took his hat to examine it, felt along the pinstripes of his shirt to see if they were sewed on or were a print. Grabbed the bundle of clothes he'd worn out of the house that morning and tossed them out of the way.

"Look at you," Anna said. "Did you make the team after all?"

Of course they would notice him in that baseball uniform. Of course they would notice there was beer on his breath.

"Little brother," Theresa laughed. "Didn't you learn your lesson the first time?"

"Piss off," he told her, then leapt up the first three steps to get away. The girls chased him, Theresa and Silke on his heels, Anna pulling up the rear. What did Karel think? His sisters would just let him come home in a getup like that and not pester him?

"Where did you get that outfit?" Silke asked. "Did you buy it?"

"They were a gift."

"From who?"

"The team."

"What team?"

"Omaha!" Theresa shouted. "It says right on the front."

"The Southsiders," Karel corrected. "I'm part of the team. A real ballplayer."

"No, you're not," Theresa teased him. "The clothes don't make the man. The boy!"

"There's this." Karel plucked his baseball from the back pocket of his new pants. "I got this from a guy. He gave it to me, from his own hand. Said if I wanted to be a ballplayer I needed to carry a ball with me everywhere. I'm a real ballplayer. It's a hell of a lot better than cleaning streetcars all day."

The girls gasped. "Klutz! Don't be cruel!"

Karel went red as they laughed at him. He couldn't convince them of anything. "Josh gave me this ball. The Southsiders gave me this uniform. They took me out for a beer. How's that for you? Does that sound like a real ballplayer or not?"

That was a dumb thing to say and he knew it. Their father was there in the attic, as he almost always was. Tinkering away while he munched his dinner, his back turned to them. Herr Miihlstein ate sardines most nights, a slice of bread with hard cheese and mustard. Food he could eat with one hand while he worked. "What are you shouting about?" he asked, finally disturbed by the commotion. He talked over his shoulder as he painted a music box. The same music box he painted over and over, one textured by the overlaying designs he made. Miihlstein set the music box on his worktable and screwed shut the lids to his jars of paint.

"What's the hubbub?" he asked, walking to the staircase. He liked when they teased each other, smiled at them with pride, so long as they were laughing. As a matter of fact, on the occasions he happened to look up from his table, Miihlstein seemed to like having kids around.

"Someone tell me what's going on," he said. "I don't want to have to guess."

Anna spit it out first. "Karel drank beer."

Miihlstein glanced over to his son and nodded his head, like he wasn't all that surprised. None of them were. With how much Karel was gone all the time, this was no shock.

"And the costume? Where's it come from?"

"I was telling them," Karel said. He'd backed to the stairs to run off if he needed to. But he didn't need to. He stood his ground and told them, "These were gifts."

"The ball too? Or is it stolen?"

"The ball? Look at it," he barked, the outrage back in him all at once. "There's stains all over it. It's old. Who would I steal something like this from?"

"I don't know." Miihlstein turned half away from his kids. He straightened his tie and snugged it under the brass clip. "Who gave it to you?"

"Josh," Karel answered. "He's a friend of Emil Braun."

Karel couldn't help himself. It was the beer working him over, or maybe that he didn't care what his father thought. He was thirteen, after all, his self-assurance budding, becoming arrogance. Drinking with the ballplayers, wearing the uniform home. Now uttering the name Emil Braun. Karel wasn't helping himself at all. He was about to explain who Josh was, the great Negro hurler, but stopped himself there at least.

"Well," Miihlstein deliberated. He picked his shoes off the floor, walked over to the sofa. "Given the origin of these items. Emil Braun, you say. I want them returned. They'll bring trouble. You'll see. Whether they're stolen or not."

"No," Karel said. "I want to keep them."

Miihlstein grabbed his suit jacket from the railing. "Let's go, Karel. Take me to this man Josh. We'll see what he has to say about it."

"You don't understand. Josh doesn't live around here. We can't just barge in on him."

"You will explain on the journey. I'm quite convinced we're leaving."

They took the streetcar north. Caught the Lake Street line near the post office. Karel told his father where Josh lived once they were out on Clandish, but the reveal didn't faze Miihlstein. "That's no trouble" was all he said. "I know how to get there."

Karel was surprised how calm Miihlstein was. Way up there past Cuming Street, what the boys called No Man's Land. Karel didn't think his father had ever been to this part of the city, but maybe Miihlstein had a surprise or two up his sleeve as well. And why wouldn't he? Not only black people lived on the Near Northside—as Karel thought—but it had long been dominated by Eastern Europeans and Jews. For years the most common tongue spoken here was Yiddish. "Many clients live here," Miihlstein told him as the streetcar rumbled north. Miihlstein reached up to raise a window sash and let a breeze in. "I know my way around."

Once off the streetcar Miihlstein went to a little grocery shop in a corner brick building with green awnings. The shopkeeper knew him. Greeted him. "Shalom," they said. Miihlstein asked what the shopkeeper knew about a Josh Joseph who lived around there. *"Der schvartze?"* "Yeah. The baseball player." "No. He shines shoes." "That's him," Karel said. They went on, Herr Miihlstein with his boy straggling behind, embarrassed, sluggish, to a shack set back in the weeds, one with a broken latch, so the door hung ajar.

Karel didn't know what to think, headed here with his father. He shouldn't have worn his new uniform up here, the jersey of the Southside team. He might get trouble for wearing the wrong color letters that spelled out *Omaha*, the white cloth and pinstripes, instead of the solid gray of the Northside. But this didn't really matter. Nobody said a thing to Karel about it, even if he did get some second looks from doorways. It was no surprise, the jersey he wore. Was he—a Southsider—supposed to wear the jersey of the black Northside team? That made no sense. What did anybody expect from him? What was Karel to think? Going past these little shacks with Herr Miihlstein, his boxy hat, his straight-laced shoes and skinny black necktie. Kids on the corner watched with equal parts anger and amusement. Miihlstein didn't seem to notice.

"Is the man of the house at home?" he asked when the woman answered.

This was the same woman as before, Karel was sure, though she didn't wear the red kerchief over her mouth. She dressed nice this time, in a skirt-suit with brass buttons, her hair done up neat. "You mean Josh?" she asked, and waved them inside. "He's here where he always is." She led them in and pointed to Josh in the room, said to him, "I don't know how they find you."

Karel watched the woman. The kitchen was quiet this time. A carton of fruit on the table. The woman grabbed her bag and went in to say good-bye to Josh. Kneeled to where he sat on the floor, whispered something to him, then kissed the top of his head. "I got to get." She smiled to Karel a moment, like she recognized him, or boys like him. "Nice shirt," she said.

"We've never met," Miihlstein said once the woman left.

"They call me Josh."

"Do you know my boy?"

Josh looked Karel over but only shrugged.

Miihlstein wasn't fazed at all being here or seeing a man like Josh, the two stumps where his legs had been, his long, bone-skinny arms. It was so muggy in the room that Josh went without a shirt, so they saw his ribs, a long pink mark across his stomach where he was scarred. Miihlstein kept his upright way even here. He sweat, anybody would have, it was wet in there, but he hardly acknowledged his perspiration, just pulled a handkerchief from his pocket and wiped away and that was that.

He elbowed Karel in the shoulder. "Give me the ball."

Once Karel handed it over, Miihlstein gave the ball to Josh and asked if it was his. "I'm suspicious this ball was stolen."

Josh smiled at the suggestion, like how did this man expect him to recognize one baseball from another after he'd held thousands of them in his lifetime? But Josh took the ball with his colossal left hand and looked it over anyway, perched by the seams on his fingertips like on a pedestal. Black Shinola was smudged on this ball, which gave away who its former owner had been.

"I gave the boy this ball. I remember. He came to see me one time."

"Emil brought me," Karel said. He turned so Josh could see the uniform he wore.

"Yes. That's right. One of Emil's kids. From the boat to a ballfield. I see you."

Josh tossed the ball back to Karel then turned to what he was looking at, the latest weekly digest unfolded out over the floor. The *Monitor*, which was for black folks. His finger traced over the lines on the page, how the NAACP was having a campaign drive to enlist new members and how colored troops were going to be included in a military parade in Baltimore at President Wilson's request. Josh's brown-and-orange eyes going back and forth.

"Who is this Emil Braun?" Miihlstein wanted to know. "He introduced my Karel here to you, but I don't know him. What's Braun up to?"

"What do you mean? I played ball against Emil. That's it. He helps me sometimes."

"The man who brought my son here. I'm asking you about him. My son tells me nothing. So I'm asking you."

Josh folded the newspaper and set it aside, his face twisting at the question. He leaned forward to sweep his body along the floor a few feet closer to look at Miihlstein. "No," he said. "You're not this boy's father. Emil takes care of this one. This is one of Emil's boys, I know."

They stared at each other, both set back by what the other had said. What could Miihlstein think about all this? Karel was knocked out for an instant, that was what it felt like, seeing the look on his father's face, a little glance between Karel and Josh, then like the wind was thumped out of him. Miihlstein's mouth giving in to a little droop, his mustache, his eyes beady, sad, behind the bent frames of his glasses. It was just an instant, Karel slipping out of himself. How Miihlstein must have glimpsed that he was losing Karel, there in a dark shack with some legless *Schwarzer* ballplayer, a hero to the boy, who couldn't recognize the boy's father.

"It's okay," Karel said. It was up to him to set things straight. He grabbed the baseball back, took Miihlstein by the arm, and pulled to the door. "He doesn't know what he's talking about, yeah. He's just a guy. He gave me a baseball. It's no big deal."

"Whatever you say, Karel. But we're here. You brought me here."

"He's a guy, a ballplayer. That's all."

"That's all," Josh echoed. "Just some *schvartze*, some darky. Whatever you folks say. Go on. Act like I'm the one who doesn't know what he's talking about. Coming in here wearing that! That set of rags! You're wearing the wrong colors, boy, for this neighborhood."

Karel peeled out of his knickers and the Southside jersey and his high-ankle shoes once they returned to the attic of the Eigler house. In just shorts and undershirt he collapsed to the bed and rolled the quilt over himself, hoping his father would leave him alone now.

"I'm glad you're home," Miihlstein said. He sat at the edge of the bed and put his hand on Karel's leg. "We miss you around here. Anna thought it might have been something she said that makes you stay away. Is that it? Is that why you're a bad boy all the time? You're insulted?"

Karel said it wasn't that. It was nothing. It was the spring weather. He didn't look up but stared at the pattern of the green and gold quilt, a puzzle he couldn't master. Maybe there wasn't a pattern. It didn't matter. His father kept moving across the room, little by little, stopping to look around until he rested his hands on the bed frame.

"I did wonder if little Anna could sour you so. I'm lucky to have such children. Silke and Theresa, Anna and you. Two complete pairs in your manners. What luck, yeah?"

Karel wouldn't say anything. He should have run away from Miihlstein before they came up here, but he didn't think his father would trap him again. The whole streetcar ride back from the Northside they didn't say a word to each other. They were silent under the rattling of the window sashes, the tinging of the bell. Miihlstein maybe learned better than to ask these kinds of questions, Karel thought, on the streetcar, after the strangeness with Josh. But he was wrong.

"Anna, you know, is not getting better these days," Miihlstein said, starting at it again. "The winter here was much worse than I thought it would be. It's my fault, I suppose. More should have been done to learn what we were in store for coming here, don't you think? Yet. The house suits us. You have friends. You've taken to a sporting life, which is just as well."

Miihlstein stopped talking and looked to the stairs, one set of fingers in his mustache. The girls were coming to see what was wrong, but he waved them away.

"I'll explain someday. What happened with your mother. Why we were in Galizien in the first place, why we had to leave the way we did. It ruined us, Karel. It nearly did."

"I don't want to know."

"Anna told me she blurted out. She botched all she told. The Swallow, you know, that's what the theater called your mother. It wasn't the Sparrow, like Anna told you." Miihlstein laughed to himself. "Surely there's more she botched. Mädel Anna. She's an artist's temperament. Feebleminded when it comes to most plain details."

"Shut up," Karel said, quiet as he wound tighter in the quilt.

Miihlstein surely heard, but he said nothing in response. "There was something special about your mother" was what he said.

THE UNINITIATED
Spring 1918

E veryone knew Jake was with Evie. Even if they didn't go out on the town together, folks saw him on the street and figured he was headed her way. They knew he wasn't spending his nights at the Eigler house, that he only stopped in to shave and change clothes, though he did bring Evie there to visit once. He hired a car to drive Evie over to Clandish on Saturday evening. A bunch of boys were on the sidewalk staring as he helped her out. She dressed formal, something conservative by her standards, laced to the top of her neck, with skirts that brushed over the grimy bricks of the walkway, a dress made from purple crepe with a velvet sash tied across her middle.

"Jeez, Jake." "She looks nice. Doesn't she?" the boys remarked. "What's the occasion? Your birthday or something?"

"That's right," Jake laughed. "Who told?"

Jake introduced Evie to the Miihlstein girls. A mere "How do you do?" before Silke and Theresa fingered the lace and crepe of Evie's dress and asked how she got her hair to curl like that. "She's beautiful, Jake," Theresa said. "Where have you been keeping her?" After dinner they played a game that was typical here. A newspaper and map spread out on the rug to see where the war was, a silly thing to keep up with most days, as the trenches didn't actually move. But the girls remembered enough of Europe to despair over what had been destroyed. Silly little Anna rested against the wall and sniffled, her legs straight so she could rub where her knees bumped out. "It's sad, isn't it?" she said. Everyone agreed it was sad. Except she didn't need to cry. Crying was theatrical. That was little Anna for you. Nobody knew what to do with her.

The girls doted on Evie that night. "Evie Chambers. What a lovely name." "Where do you come from, Evie? Where's your family from?" "Oh. Kansas. That's where. Just Kansas." The Miihlstein girls, Maria Eigler, even Herr Miihlstein when he came downstairs—embarrassed because he forgot there was company and had been applying lacquer and now couldn't shake her hand because his were sticky—they all loved Evie. They said so. Only Karel was gone, and nobody knew where he'd gotten off to. But the rest of them were charmed. The girls walked Jake and Evie to the street when the evening was over and lingered there on the walkway as the two young lovers strolled away.

That week people on Clandish talked about Evie and Jake a lot. Why didn't they just get it over with? Why didn't he ask her to marry him and put her up in a house of their own? Jake flaunted the fact that he had money. It wasn't his money, of course. Pretty much everything he had belonged to Tom Dennison, but that didn't seem to matter. He was in love. Life was good. He should marry his girl.

Of course, things would get worse for Jake.

Tom Dennison looked like an old priest when he confronted Jake about the money. The way his lips twisted his words, how he cracked his knuckles, ready to berate a sinner. "Fess up, son. Don't embarrass yourself by saying you didn't do nothing. We both know that's a lie."

Jake was confused. He thought everything was going swell. So he played dumb and asked what Tom was talking about.

"You're sneaking money to your girl. Billy told me about it. He had a line on you. This is what came up." Jake's face went blank then. He couldn't pretend. "That's stealing. If it's for your girl, that's stealing. Don't ask me what you did. If you want to throw away your own money, that's your business. But don't waste what's mine."

Tom stared at Jake a long time to see what he'd do. Jake didn't say a word. He couldn't even look at Tom, sitting there, as he tried to imagine what would happen next.

"You got to drop that girl," Tom said. "I saw her. She's not so pretty. Find a new girl. Promise me that and we'll be square."

Tom explained things to Jake. How he wanted to believe in him. He wanted to believe Jake was smarter than the other guys, more grateful. This wasn't the first time Tom had been betrayed by a young man whose star seemed to shine brighter than it really did. There were others who thought they could pull one over on the Old Man. These things were solvable. If it only cost money to get through this trouble, Tom didn't care. Money wasn't so hard to get. Jake was a disappointment. But when you counted who had the most to gain and who lost what, there was no way of figuring that Tom Dennison was the loser of this gamble. It was Jake who'd miscalculated. It was Jake who'd lose if he didn't drop that girl and put himself back in Tom Dennison's good graces. That's how simple it was. Even Jake should have been able to see that.

But Jake didn't know what to do. Tom had it out for him. He'd been caught stealing—a cardinal offense, though everything they did was stealing in one way or another, wasn't it?—and he wouldn't even try to make things right. Tom wanted to let him off the hook. All Jake had to do was end it with Evie. But he wouldn't.

A few weeks prior, Dennison had sent a new summer-gray suit to the Eigler house with a thousand-dollar bill tucked in the breast pocket. On the charge slip it read *Happy birthday, sorry it's late. —T.* Maria found the money. Jake didn't believe it when she handed him the thousand. How was so much money held in a single scrap of paper? He'd received gifts from Tom before—liquor, theater passes, front-row seats at fights and ballgames—but nothing like this. If Tom was so concerned about Jake taking money, why give him a thousand-dollar bill? It didn't make sense. Jake thought of giving the cash to Evie—to pay her rent out over a year—but then Tom would have his ass for sure. He was trapped. The way he figured, there was nothing to do but hold on to the thousand and remember who gave it to him.

He was a mess those days before the vote. Unable to keep his thinking straight. Sensitive. He worked nearly twenty hours a day. Trudging through tenements. Up all night in social clubs, imagining lying on Evie's sofa and listening to records. He imagined making love to her. He tried to convince himself that he should break it off with her until things cooled down with Dennison—the reasonable thing to do. But then he'd recall the way her body fit into his, her shoulder under his shoulder, the flat front of her hips on his legs, the way she walked barefoot on the crooked knuckles of his back, how she soaked his feet in alchemic water when they ached, how she'd cared for him when he was knocked down with the flu. He'd miss her scent in the morning, before she perfumed, a reconfiguration of burgundy wine and sweet rolls.

Screw it. He couldn't stand this anymore. What did anyone expect of him?

He went and bought a ring before he lost her. The jeweler said it was a nice one. The ring had a silver band, which cost less than some of the gold ones, but there was a diamond chip, and that was a special thing, uncommon for an engagement those days. He blew just about every cent he had on the ring. She'd have to be his. Once he had the ring, Jake went home to get the thousand from under his mattress. They'd run off. He and Evie would take a car to Lincoln then catch a train to a city where the Omaha machine had no influence. He'd get out with Evie. They'd leave town. They'd make love in a sleeper car.

There was a meeting at the Santa Philomena that night. Jake was required to be there, but then he'd sneak off. Tom, Billy, all those machine men who could hurt him, they'd be too busy with the vote to notice. This was his chance.

Evie acted strange those days. Once Jake got better from the flu, Evie saw herself do plenty of odd things. She was used to lovers who thought they were performers, particularly young men like Jake. While a middle-aged man with middling ambition might be comfortable with what he could and couldn't do in the sack, a young man never was. Jake aimed for grander feats. Unfavorable body positions. Methods a guy had described to him in a barroom. He never understood that those men were tricking him. Or maybe they were as cruel in the ways they screwed as they were in all other ways. The manner of pinching and poking and tweaking and slapping Jake brought to her rooms. What on earth could he be thinking? And then there was his competitive streak. He wouldn't let her take control, like she ought to have. She knew how to do things he couldn't have even dreamt of, if he'd let her. Instead he made sport. He wanted to be on top. He wanted to win. He even said these things to her sometimes in the heat of the moment. "I'm deepest! I'm filling you up!" Evie could deal with his being weird—after all, the sex could be pretty good if he forgot himself long enough to let it happen natural—but she acted peculiar too, she had to admit, and that was the stranger thing. She battled back. She wrestled him under her. Tried to deny him her greater depths. Would come loud and often (sometimes fraudulently) then insist she hadn't just to tease him. "Eh. I've had better." They were often uncomfortable when finished, somehow not quite spent. They were holding back. Why deny that?

They argued about whether they should go elsewhere or stay in Omaha. And where the money would come from if they left. This was never a problem for Evie before. If the man had no money, no rent, no food for her, then it was clear she should move on. It couldn't go on like that forever. Evie was bound to change during some year of her life. Fall in love. She was bound to become strange eventually.

She fantasized that Jake wanted to run away with her and, before long, found herself pestering him about it. They could start over in San Francisco. He resisted whenever she brought that up, not understanding why she wanted to leave. "I have a job here. I just started. Why would I want to leave?"

"You'd do interesting things if we left," Evie insisted. "Pick oranges. Lay on a beach."

"It'd be awful. The money not so good."

"Is that so?" she said, a sure sign of trouble. "Then maybe it's time for me to find work. Get a share of the *good money*. I know you don't make enough to pay for my rooms, not on an election worker's salary."

She was right, but Jake didn't care. He chuckled when she brought up money.

"Don't be stupid," she said. "If you're sneaking from Tom and Billy, that's a bad idea. You'll get hurt."

She leaned over to take his hands and put them to her face and kissed the cracks of his knuckles. Jake looked young when she glanced to him. His face soft, his eyes dreamy in the light of a kerosene lamp. He was only twenty-one. She was twenty-seven and had lived a lot more in that time than he had. Evie didn't know what she could say to convince Jake to leave. The whole original purpose of their relationship was to make him comfortable in her rooms; now she was trying to convince him of the opposite.

"I'm asking for help," she said. "That's all. They want references when you answer an ad. I don't have any. But you could vouch for me. If we can make our own way without having to go to those gamblers for help, we won't have to keep things from each other."

"There's no secrets," Jake claimed. "We just met. What could we be hiding?"

She smiled, resigned, maudlin. They kissed. Neither wanted to own up to anything that could bring down the party.

So she put it to him. "You'll figure out how to make this work. If you won't leave Omaha. If you won't help me find a job. Then it's up to you. How are we going to keep going?"

Most of the time Jake didn't see the point of working for Dennison either. He complained about situations he was forced into. It became tiresome. The jawing with reformers. Nobody would ever change their mind about things they believed in.

Evie was miserable hearing Jake go on about what the gamblers were teaching him to do, how they were initiating him to the underworld. She wanted him to talk about himself—about who his father was, his brother, why it was he ran away from home. But Jake refused. "That's my secret," he said. "Maybe you don't have any secrets. That's up to you."

She wanted to tell everything, but this was impossible when he said idiotic things like that.

The day before the vote Jake came to her rooms in the afternoon. He wore his best suit but was otherwise a mess. He hadn't shaved all week. His shirt was wrinkled and stained with mustard.

"What's wrong?" she asked.

"There's a problem," he confessed. "The money dried up."

He crawled to her on his knees and begged forgiveness. "But I know what to do," he promised. "Don't you love me?"

He produced a ring. "See what this is? We'll get married, yeah. That's what we'll do."

The ring scared Evie. Something awful had happened, she knew it.

"Take this," he said, pushing the ring on her finger. "We'll leave tonight. We'll get hitched. I'll take care of everything. We'll get out."

They'd go to California, like she wanted. But first they'd have to lay low in Texas a few weeks, down by the border. His rambling made no sense. Jake said he had a thousand dollars but wouldn't say how he got it.

Evie knew anyway. There was only one place a guy like him could get that much cash.

"Okay," she said.

"You'll come with me?" He lifted her from the chair and carried her around the room. "I knew you would. What else can we do? This is our only chance."

Evie wasn't sure she'd go with him. She'd think it over. She had six hours. Jake was going to the meeting at the Santa Philomena and then would come for her. She could always change her mind before Jake returned. There was a chance, a fair probability, she knew, that he wouldn't make it back at all.

Josh Joseph died that week. Seeing as the boys had met him, Emil Braun insisted they attend the funeral. Josh was the best ballplayer the city had ever seen, for his race. If Karel was any kind of ballplayer, he owed it to the game to pay respects to such a hurler when he had the chance.

Services were at Zion Baptist, up Twenty-Fourth Street all the way. Past the shacks of No Man's Land, a nice block here or there broken up by weeds, neighborhood folks in their yards watching the four of them, some kids playing ball in an empty lot where the weeds were knocked down by their daily game, an endless match for the kids of this block that was measured over whole summers rather than single innings. "That's right. A fit thing to see along the way," Braun said, and the boys agreed. Those black kids kept up the chatter as they waited for the ball. A staccato chorus crying out in tribute.

Braun ranted to the boys as they went. How Josh had died. He'd been shining shoes downtown when he was knocked off the curb in front of a streetcar. Nobody risked their own neck to save him, a man without legs, though if any of those bystanders had acted fast rather than gawking, they could have saved him. If they'd waved their arms and put themselves in danger, the streetcar would have stopped. But the driver couldn't see Josh arm-limp over the rails. He only stopped when he heard the screams. No way to die for anyone. Particularly not the best ballplayer to ever put on the Negro uniform in the Fourth of July game. "Shame on them. For nobody to help. After he gave his legs to San Juan Hill. Then they watched him killed."

Braun spoke with a sharper tooth that day and the days after.

In the packed church he told the boys to stick to the back, to leave pews open for those who must sit. Maybe there weren't many folks who knew what became of Josh in Cuba, or when he returned from the hospital in Washington, DC, but most everyone of a certain generation remembered Josh Joseph from his prime. How he kicked his front leg shoulder height when he wound up to throw off the mound; how determined he was; how a grin broke across his lips when he busted a hard one in on a batter's thumbs; that he was such an athlete, the fastest runner, the hardest puncher, the best dancer too, and he could have done anything, played any sport professionally (if that had been possible) and he would have been a star from coast to coast. Even if they didn't grow up here, as most black people in Omaha didn't, they knew somehow. They grieved. If not for Josh Joseph, then for someone like him. The prodigy back south they'd never see or hear of again. Karel watched amazed at all the mourners in their suits and dresses and hats—the way the choir swaggered up behind the coffin to sing—and wished he'd dressed better, instead of his high pants, dirty socks, a wrinkled shirt on its second week, one he'd played half-a-dozen school yard games in without washing. He had clean clothes folded in a stack at home but didn't think to put them on. He'd never really been to a funeral before.

His mother's was the only other, but he'd been too young to remember much. All he could picture about that day was unhewn dark, damp black, his sisters standing in their raincoats silent, embarrassed by it all, by his bawling. That was what Anna had told him. There were no red roses, no curtain call. Karel couldn't picture what she'd looked like in the coffin. There was a photograph of his parents they had. Frau reared erect behind an easy chair where Herr sat, sunk into himself. One of Frau's hands was clenched in a fist on the back of the chair.

That funeral would have been different than this one. No shouting and laughing, not in a sunken churchyard in Galizien. Nothing like Josh Joseph's. Women wailing rounds. What Jimmy said were slave songs. Ballplayers from the Northside team made their way around to joke with people. One of them, a second baseman Karel thought was white at first, but was *pale black*, if that was a thing, asked what positions the boys played, then laughed when they told him. "If you boys ever come running at me," he said, "you keep your spikes down."

The line wrapped around the church, made of black and a few white men, Braun among them, waiting their turn to step up to the bier and pay some due. Many of them squeezed baseballs. A few had mitts they flipped around to stare at the stitching gone stiff, to give over to Josh. *Here, my man. My ratty ole mitt. I want you to have it.* But so many of them had mementos, the funeral director wouldn't allow it. What was he going to do with all those relics? Put together a team? Give them away to the kids playing stickball down the street? "Of course! That's exactly what you should do." "What do I look like?" "Wouldn't take much to do it." "I say. What do I look like?"

Josh clutched a ball already, his hand did, inside the coffin. They'd put him in a uniform, a new set of solid grays donated from the Negro team. Karel felt better about what he was wearing when he saw Josh in uniform. There was no shame in having dirt in your clothes so long as that dirt came from a diamond.

Karel became dark watching: maybe the next funeral would be for Anna. How could he think these things? Did he want to make himself miserable? Did he want to put a bad omen on his sister? Dear Anna. How many people would even come pay respects? Maria, Jake. Only five Miihlsteins lived in Omaha—it would be four without her. Would there be music? Herr Miihlstein's Parisians, his hurdy-gurdy friends. A client of his father's might steer by out of duty. It would be nothing like this here at Zion. There wouldn't be a service at a church but a wake in the parlor at home. Then a procession from the Eigler house, the family in the back of a rented truck with the coffin. Would traffic stop as her body passed?

Sadness closed in on Karel. The color drained from his face. "Karel? What is it?" Alfred asked. "You okay?" They thought he was broken up about the ballplayer and didn't understand how that was, since he'd only met Josh once, as far as they knew. "Jesus," Jimmy said. "Who knew you were so sensitive?"

"Listen," he told Anna that night. "I want to give you something special."

"What is it?" she asked, sitting up on the sofa where she slept. Her skin had gone dark around her eyes and mouth, her eyes grayish.

"I don't know. A Kewpie doll. Or a pet to keep you company. A duck."

"What?"

"I'm teasing. I don't know. A new coat. Would you like that? A new purple overcoat?"

"Sure," Anna said. She looked down, under the quilts, surprised that she was wearing her old lavender coat. The elegance had gone out of it. Holes had worn through the crease in the collar. "Can you get one?"

Karel and his friends hung around the Santa Philomena all day a few weeks later. Braun arranged for them to help with a political rally. Josie Washburn was going to speak. If the boys came early to put out benches and folding chairs in the hall, he'd get them half a dollar each for their trouble, and half more if they cleaned up after. Braun assumed they'd want to see the speaker while they were there. He rambled incessantly, broken up about Josh Joseph, and swore upheaval was coming. Karel didn't know what to think, but there were omens Braun spoke of. Word reached Omaha that week how Manfred von Richthofen—*the Red Baron!*—had been shot down and killed by a single bullet near the Somme. The death of Germany's national hero, the ace of its Flying Circus, was a portent of the war's end and revolution across Germanic domains. The Kaiser's army was scuffling. A desperate spring offensive had moved their forces within seventy-five miles of Paris, until supply lines dwindled and they were pushed back, and were still being pushed. German cities ran out of bread in the meantime. There had been no meat for over a year. Things were even worse in Austria-Hungary. Rumors spread that the war might end. There would be disorder, disruption, mayhem. After what went down with the Bolsheviks in Russia—the Red Army, the imprisonment of Romanovs, a photo of bejeweled and fleeing tsaritsas in the papers every week—who knew what else would happen? Global revolution? Was it possible?

Here in the States the situation was difficult. The Espionage Act made it easy to convict an agitator of treason. Braun went on about this in the cellar where SOSA met. President Wilson was threatening to have the labor activist Gene Debs locked up for speaking against the war as the Sedition Act rode a rail through Congress, and Emma Goldman was already serving a two-year sentence in a Jefferson City penitentiary for urging young men to shirk the draft. So it was up to Emil to keep going, with Red Emma out of circulation. The threat was the same for all agitators, for Alexander Berkman, for Kate Richards O'Hare. "Most real leftists are locked up already," Braun said. "Deported. Silenced." This was why a local street screamer and reformist like Josie Washburn attracted attention. She would still speak out, something rare that spring, and the activists of SOSA weren't going to miss hearing her.

By evening a carnival had erupted at the Santa Philomena. There was no wind or rain to move people inside, so families staked out patches of grass to eat off a blanket. Italian clans who lived nearby clustered the walkways and lawns. One stood outside with a whetstone to offer his services. Street vendors sifted through to improvise a buck—tobacco and wine kids transplanted from the flats, trays strapped over their shoulders; register girls from bakeries and delis with crates on their hips, selling half loaves of bread and sliced meat, almond cookies and empanadas. A boy from their school came into a watermelon and sold chunks of its sticky guts for two cents each, his shirt doused pink as he carried what remained on his shoulder. Closer to the hall were men of a different cast. Mill workers in greasy black overalls; slackers in felt caps sat along a brick wall with legs stretched out to reveal their shoe bottoms. A delegation of black stockyard workers, dung caked and bloodstained, trying to find something to eat. Whispers trailed them.

Some Russian warehouse workers leaned against the hall. They wore denim jackets and bit at sandwiches wrapped in newspaper, cheese and onion pressed between slices of cottage white. Smears rubbed into the bread. Between their thighs sat tin cups that brimmed over with sudsy heads of beer. Some boy flitted along with a clay jug hugged to his belly. The boy made wisecracks to the Russians. They replied in kind. To Karel, every word from a Russian sounded like an insult. These thick-chest serfs whose mouths closed in satisfaction over their vittles, whose lips curled venomously under bloodshot eyes. They were sizing Karel up, like they knew where he came from, that he was Austrian, Jewish. Even though he was just a boy, they must have pictured what it would be like to punch him in the face, and how little it would take to beat Karel and his friends. Karel hated Russians. When one whispered to another, when they leered at him and laughed in their native cackle, he too dreamed how it would go down in a brawl. He'd be beaten badly, sure—three boys couldn't rout a dozen cruel Russians—but Karel thought it might be worth the pain to find out for certain. In reality there was nothing he could do except flip up his collar and hope the Russians ignored him.

The boys returned to the Santa Philomena and waited for the door to open so they could find a good spot. The hall couldn't hold the hundreds wanting to get in, so they had to hurry.

It wasn't long, waiting, before Karel saw Jake Strauss push his way to the front and order the doors open. The machine men swaggered like they had big guns tucked in their belts. Karel rushed to the front with his friends, but Jake stuck to the side of the hall, looking nervous, like he and his men had something planned. Election men were scattered all over. Karel knew some of them: Joe Meinhof, Ingo, Paul, Heinz.

"Do you see?" Braun asked, sneaking next to the boys. "Tom Dennison's men all over. I told you this would be worth watching."

A Sicilian gentleman popped up to the small stage to make an announcement. Karel hardly understood a word the man said. *Nicosia* and *America*, and, at slant, the name of the speaker they waited for. The emcee had an inch-thick walrus mustache that weighed down his face, the kind only a cad from some far-flung principality would wear—like the officials Karel's father talked about sometimes, the exiled-from-Wien bureaucrats they'd been afflicted with while getting out of Galizien, officials who stole nearly all their money, Miihlstein claimed. The man onstage wore a village getup of inexplicable distinction. A yellow jacket and ruffled shirt. He raised a peculiar coat of arms—headless fish, crossed sabers, a mule. "What the hell is that?" Jimmy asked. Nobody knew.

The crowd quieted when Josie Washburn emerged at the podium, wide-eyed as the emcee helped her up from a back passage she'd been smuggled through. She was announced. *Here. Signora Wauzboon.* Her hair was dark, a pyramid of curls atop her squarish head. She wore a purple skirt with gold brocade, a metal amulet on a chain. Her complexion was soft, her skin a shade whiter than her blouse, her hazel eyes live and darting. There was a Danish stoutness in her shoulders and jaw, in her heavy clothes and hips. She parted her lips several times as she looked the crowd over but said nothing. She tried to wet her lips with her tongue then flushed so fierce her face turned the same purple of her skirt. Some folks in the crowd became restless in her silence. "What's this? Why doesn't she say something?" There was a rumble all over the hall. Dozens questioned her because she left a gap for them to. "Come on," Joe Meinhof shouted. "We're here! Let us have it!"

Josie Washburn cleared her throat and released the podium.

"You know my name, but you don't know who I am," she shouted. Karel felt a vacuum behind him, the crowd shutting up, sitting down. "I stumbled into Omaha in August 1871. I was seventeen and found myself in the establishment of Anna Wilson on lower Douglas Street. I must be brief, but I will say that I helped her accumulate some of the half-million dollars she left to the charitable organizations of Omaha when she died. I'm not ashamed to admit this. I've changed my ways from that time—but not in the name of reform. No. Reform is a word for ministers and politicians. I am neither. I know little about the so-called *reform* slate and their current campaign. But I do have special knowledge of the underworld these reformers nominally oppose, so this is what I will talk about."

Her penetrating stare peered out from the podium, that look of intention progressives practiced in those days swept east wall to west, front bench to back. Each time her gaze crossed Karel, he wanted to pull his cap over his eyes, to dip his head and stare at his feet.

"As in all cities, there are factions in politics which take turns governing and which are always at war with each other. Each faction charges the other with misdemeanors and crimes of some sort. The charges are usually sustained by the facts, but campaigns for change never succeed. They are never meant to succeed, because the underworld means large profits and quick returns. Meanwhile, you're all as poor as Job's turkey!"

Karel was preoccupied, thinking about his mother, as he watched Washburn. Was this what his mother had been like? What would she have done in Omaha, he wondered, if she'd somehow ended up here? If Anna had been lying about the thing with the actor, the knife in her back a myth, would his mother shout in halls like this? Would she profess and proclaim an honorable cause?

". . . and as if to prove my point, the King Gambler has set up shop on this very ward for twenty years. Little progress has been made to loosen his grip. Do I dare mention his name? No. I'm not so stupid as that. But you know who I mean. The tenement builder, the patron saint of saloon owners. Why else would a pint of beer cost five cents and a liter of milk twenty? The King Gambler is why. Violence is used against the working poor, the disabled, the immigrant, the Negro, our women. The King Gambler and his men protect a system designed to make innocents a commodity. His is an industry of bondage and human chattel. What else should we expect from a man who lives on the backs of fallen women?"

The crowd was quiet until Washburn mentioned the King Gambler. It was Joe Meinhof who started the dissonance, shouting, "Shame! Shame! You're not poor!" Then other of Jake's friends broke in with catcalls. "How'd you get your money, Josie?" "You're no saint!"

Emil Braun shouted back at the election men, "Shut up!" *Bastards*, he called them, spitting slurs. *Prussians.*

". . . yet worst off is the poor marked girl enlisted in an assignation home or brothel. If you have seen such women, as everyone has, then you know it's true." Washburn persevered, surer in the face of resistance. Karel turned to see what Jake shouted, but Jake was enrapt. He strained to hear what Washburn said. ". . . when you contemplate the sorrow and degradation it brings to these girls who are kept in dark rooms, it should be no surprise that our suicides are many."

Meinhof and Ingo on their toes to bark through cupped hands. "Then leave! Get out if you don't like it!" Braun had enough of it. "Come on," he told the boys. "We won't put up with this."

Braun pushed through the crowd, knocking benches with his knees, holding Alfred by the arm. Jimmy Mac and Karel followed, backs to the stage, headed straight for Jake and his friends. Karel felt sweat run down his sides. Jake standing there listening.

"Look," Jimmy said. "There's cops!" Half a dozen policemen were in the doorway. Karel recognized one of them, Harry, who picked Jake up from the Eigler house sometimes in Tom Dennison's car. Why weren't the cops doing anything?

". . . let the error creep out of your mind that a woman seeks the life because she has degraded tendencies, or that she is of low origin. But rather try to comprehend that she has not shared the same advantages and protection by which you have surrounded your own home. If the ministers had devoted as much energy to prevent boys from growing wild oats and teaching men to protect women, as he has in assisting the politician, thousands of souls would have been saved from the yawning abyss of the underworld."

Election workers hunkered down, muscles flexed, eyes wide and dilated, lips drawn taut. Jake lifted a mitt, motioning for his men to wait. He stared at Karel, confused, his hand up. *What are you doing here?* he seemed to say, his mouth moving, washed out.

Meinhof and Ingo grabbed opposite ends of a bench to dump its occupants. Election men yelled, "Josie! How many virgins did you sacrifice for that dress?" Nearly everyone in the crowd turned from the stage to see what the commotion was, again rushing up Karel's heels. It wasn't just machine men shouting. Others joined the tide. "Shame! Shame!"

Braun still pulled the boys along. Karel shouted, "Stop it," to freeze the swerve, to catch his breath, but it was no use. He felt sick as Braun rushed at Jake.

"I know you, Jake Strauss," Braun shouted, jabbing a knuckle under Jake's chin. Jake didn't see it coming. "You whup folks that don't agree with you. Is that it?"

The cobwebs of Braun's hair strew over his head. "Some country ignint, you are. Trying to corrupt a good boy like Karel Miihlstein. You should hate yourself."

"Get lost!" Jake slapped the hand away.

Braun's knuckles were back in Jake's face. He was slick, like he could dislocate his arm from the shoulder. "I'm Emil Braun," he said. "I'm an organizer. This is not how it's done—breaking up a meeting. This isn't civility."

Jake twisted away, but Braun was fixed to his chest. Everywhere Jake turned it was a fog of greasy hair, knuckles jabbed under his chin.

Something came loose in Jake. He grabbed Braun by the front of his shirt. "Piss off!" His men surged, their muscled arms at his back, knocking Jimmy and Karel away, pushing Alfred to the floor.

"My name is Emil Braun! I'm the deacon of a tenement on Pierce Street!"

Jake's friends tore at Braun's clothes. "That doesn't matter," they shouted. "No one will miss you!"

"It's your fault," Braun declared. He circled, trying to face them all, his shirt stretched around his face. "It's Prussians like you what give good Germans a bad name!"

The belligerents closed in. They wanted blood. They wanted Jake to come loose. It was too easy. There was nothing to stop him.

Jake swung at Braun. His face red as the blood pumped in. His eyes bugged. He swung again and knocked Braun to the floor.

Alfred tried to stop his father from going back for more. It was no use. Braun regained his feet and charged at Jake to be walloped again. Feet slick under him, Braun collapsed into a clump of Reds this time, taking one of them down to the floor with him.

The police at the door didn't move. "Please, stop them." Jimmy pled with his fellow Irish to do something, but they wouldn't. They laughed as the Reds encircled Braun. Braun tried to explain how he was a friend of Josh Joseph. "That means something!"

"You can't run into a man's back," one of the Reds explained. "Not at a meeting. We're the South Omaha Bolsheviki! We deserve more respect than that!"

Karel felt it, the rising chaos. The Sicilian gentleman tugged Josie Washburn to the exit, but she wouldn't budge. She watched like others watched. Karel did too. He wished his father was there to pull him away.

Jake looked at Karel again. His face fell in embarrassment. There was nothing Jake would do to stop this. He turned out from the circle to the door.

"Wait!" Karel grabbed his arm. Jake was red and sweaty. He tried to say something, but Karel couldn't hear what. "Make the cops stop them," Karel begged. "Do something."

"I can't," Jake said.

"You're lying."

"I got to go. I'm sorry for your friend, but there's nothing I can do."

Jake pulled away and left. Where was he going? Why did he get involved with all this just to leave once it got hot?

Emil Braun was going to get it. Ingo and Rudi shoved him into the ring. Meinhof jabbed him with a cane he picked off the floor. They shouted, "Did you hear? He cursed America! I heard!" This was a lie—or maybe it wasn't, who knew with Braun?—but the chorus was ready to agree. "Get him! Teach him a lesson!" All it took was a second. A stockyard worker pulled off his shirt. The crowd, hungry for a rout, pushed Braun in. They had him corralled. They smacked him when the rhythm compelled. Members of all groups closed in. It didn't matter who they were, if they'd heard Emil Braun give a talk in the cellar of a saloon, if they'd sung "The Internationale" to the tune he set. They wanted blood—that was what mattered.

He was quiet, they all were. A terrible quiet. Braun was silent, except for his wet breathing, his soaked shirt unsticking from his skin as his diaphragm expanded.

The boys had helped carry Braun up the tenement stairs. There weren't enough volunteers to convey a mobbed and beaten man. For what if the mob came back, then what would happen? "What about the hospital?" Jimmy asked. But there was no money. Braun gave everything the family had for Josh's funeral, the coffin, the choir. There was nothing left. There was sad little to begin with. If they did more harm than good bumping his broken body up the stairs, the boys were sorry. There was no other way. In the room was a table where they could lay him at least. An old woman could be called. Maybe not a doctor, but a wise old woman. Maybe not wise, but at least old.

The old woman and Braun's wife toweled off blood. Where something was broken they tied tight with a dressing ripped from his clothes.

All the election men gathered in a switchyard southwest of the German tenements, near Twenty-Fourth and Hickory. They leaned on the fenders of cars that straddled the tracks until the wall of their bodies fractured so Dennison's Olds 45 could pass through to their middle. Jake watched from inside the car. He was afraid of what was going to happen.

It was up near Capitol Avenue where Tom found him. He had a suitcase and was going to Evie. They would buy train tickets. He had the thousand-dollar bill. They'd get away. He believed this. His heart still raced in his ears, his hands alive where he'd struck Braun. It was Maria's suitcase, an old leather one he'd stuffed some clothes in. She'd wrapped a sandwich in wax paper and sent him on his way once he told her what he was planning.

The sky was overcast as he rushed north. Searchlights danced on the screen of low, churning clouds from the army's balloon training field north of the city. It was in the dailies how there would be elevations and maneuvers throughout the night to practice for surprise blimp attacks on the Western Front. The searchlights made Jake skittish. Clandish Street itself resembled a military zone after the fight at the Santa Philomena. Cops pacing walkways. Paddy wagons stationed at intersections. The streets nearly deserted save for nervous police.

Jake was going to Evie. He'd always been trouble. Falling for her was different. He'd marry her, and that would be the first useful thing he'd do.

But up on Capitol Avenue he heard the growling motor, the squirming rubber against the curb. He looked to the sky, saw the clouds, hoary and gray, and searchlight circles dancing. He heard the door unlatch. Jake slipped inside the Olds next to Tom, next to Tom's machine gun.

They didn't say a word in the car. Not even Harry. The car drove south out of downtown and in the silence Jake was left to guess what was going to happen. On the night Tom's men finished off the Cypriot, Jake had heard, they'd taken the body down this way.

It was Joe Meinhof who opened the door when the Olds stopped at the switchyard. The way Meinhof smiled, his spiteful eyes, Jake thought he was finished. They'd caught him going to Evie. If they searched his pockets, they'd find the thousand-dollar bill.

Jake rushed into the men once he was free from the car. He ducked around, trying to hide. Dozens of men in the crisscross beams of headlights. They cleared away where he walked. No one let him get close. Jake needed to stand next to someone, but the men kept moving away. Dennison was following Jake—that was why he couldn't hide. The men made way for Tom.

Tom went right up to Jake. He said, "Don't forget your luggage," and held out the suitcase. "You wouldn't want to be without extra shorts on the trip tonight. Might need those." The others laughed at Jake. Tom staring him down. Jake couldn't look into those steel and flint eyes, so he looked at the scar on the Old Man's face instead. Fighting back tears, he was so scared.

"I was worried you couldn't hack it with the dirty work." Tom spoke in his big voice so everyone heard. "But they tell me you broke up the reception tonight, Jake. Almost started a riot single-handed." The men laughed like Jake was one of them, he realized. "Some union stooge tried to give you grief and you brought the hammer down. I couldn't have done better myself."

Tom put his hand on Jake's shoulder and spoke softer. "You're in the truck to Red Oak. Then I want you at Mecklenburg's tomorrow. I haven't forgotten you."

Jake caught his breath and grinned back. It was the night before the election. Tom wouldn't be worried about him and Evie now. They were safe for the moment.

Tom moved to the center of the cars, where Billy Nesselhous waited. The priority of the moment was to cross into Iowa to retrieve the hired votes. Every rental car in the city had been reserved for this purpose, with only men on the payroll having access. Jake and Evie couldn't have gotten a car anyway, even if Jake had tried renting one for their escape. So Jake learned. Every man in the machine had a job to do. Jake was to ride in a flatbed truck with Joe Meinhof.

Meinhof hummed under the noise of the highway as he drove, hand limp over the stick shift ball as it jolted from side to side. Jake held to the bottom of his seat as they bounced along because the latch of his door was loose. If the truck turned too sharply, like when they pulled into Red Oak, his door flew open and he had to reach out into the rushing wind to slam it.

The truck, borrowed from a service station, smelled like grease and chewing tobacco. Potato chips crumbled on the rubber mat under their feet. The wood planks that made up the bed rattled behind the cab, the chains too that wrapped around the tops of posts, where the men they'd picked up at a Red Oak saloon held on. Others sat out of the wind, on the boards, but had nothing to hold. Everything shifted and lurched, going fast down the middle of a rutted gravel highway. The headlight beams were the only light in front of them, as far as the wends let them see. Behind them and to the sides there was nothing, an echo of light in the dust clouds they left behind. Jake wanted to sleep, to talk, to do something other than wait and see if a deer, a person crossing, would pop into their light in the road.

"Do you think it's worth it, Joe? Driving all night, for what? A dozen votes?"

"Why wouldn't it be?"

"I don't know." Jake saw pairs of headlights up ahead, the bigger highway that led along the river to Omaha. "It's a lot of work."

"You're young. You don't know any better than to feel that way."

"I was thinking of quitting. Did you know that, Joe?"

"Sure I know. You got that girl. We all know. You spent money that wasn't yours to keep her happy. Evie got you all worked up, and you did something you shouldn't of. That's all."

"I guess that's right."

"What were you thinking when Tom took you down to the tracks in his car? Did you think he was going to do bad things to you?"

"Was I shaking?"

"Yeah, you were."

"That's why I got to go. I don't like that. I got better things I could be doing."

"No, you don't." Meinhof sped up to blast through a crossing. "You don't have to quit. Just square things. Make it up to the Old Man. Talk to Billy. He'd have some idea of what you got to do to make it right."

"If you say so."

Jake was talking too much. He knew this. But Joe Meinhof was his friend. And what did it matter anyway? They'd all seen him with the suitcase.

"You can be such a kid about things, Jake. Honest. I don't know what Tom sees in you. Sometimes I really don't. There's more to what we do than you think there is."

"Sure. I know that."

"You bullshitter. Those reformers want to tear apart our home. They'll take everything we love away from us. Clandish. The saloons. Our jobs. What will we do if they win? You ever think of that?"

"You want my spot. That's all. I know what you're about."

"You don't know. How long have I been telling you these things? And you never cared enough to listen. Why am I surprised you fucked up?"

A man from the flatbed watched them argue through the back window. His face pressed the glass, lit up white. The man stared at Jake. He was shivering.

It was quiet on the River Ward that morning. Any player who seriously disagreed with machine politics was arrested in the days prior on suspicion of vagrancy or some other trumped-up nonsense that took forty-eight hours to clear no matter how evident his innocence should be. The melee at the Santa Philomena was the perfect excuse to root out men Tom Dennison wanted in jail on the seventh of May. All stops were pulled on the Ward. Voters on the payroll of the Pendergast machine in Kansas City would arrive throughout the morning to cast their ballots, along with others recruited from towns in Iowa. Red Oak, Glenwood, Griswold, Walnut. Every barroom on the Ward was rented and stocked with liquor. Bootleggers who owed their survival to Tom Dennison saw to these parties. And it wasn't just bootleggers and machine men. Every favor granted over the past three years was cashed in during polling hours. If a family received coal over the winter, if a grocery bill or bar tab was covered, if someone was granted leniency from a judge, then a car would appear outside their home on Election Day to shuttle them to a poll.

When Jake returned from Iowa, Mecklenburg's was already half-full. The barroom would be packed by 6 a.m. Trucks lined the curb, with dozens of voters crammed on hay-strewn flatbeds. Streetcars from the train stations were full of Pendergast's men. Joe Meinhof and Ingo Kleinhardt lined them up inside and meted out booze. Suitcase still in hand, Jake stayed in the back until it was time to instruct the voters, when Ingo escorted them to two basement rooms separated by a narrow doorway. The basement had been an afterthought, dug roughly and bricked in. As a former tunneler himself, Jake recognized the work. A light hung from a rafter. Its wire snaked in from a hole drilled in the floor above.

"Listen up!" Meinhof slammed the door. Each election man held the standard issue: a baseball bat with the handle cut short, the barrel splintered and dented rusty from past elections.

"The polls open soon and you got to know what to do. You're going to vote today. Here's who for." Ingo passed out cards that had the names of the Square Seven printed on them, and—as these were voters from Kansas City—he gave each a paper slip that had a name and address, so they would know on whose behalf to vote. "We can't help once you're in there. That's against the rules. You got to sign the registry—"

"We know what to do," one of the voters cut in, a squatty Swede with a flat scar scored into his chin. "Cut the shit. We've done this before."

"Shut it!" Meinhof poked his bat under the Swede's chin. "Do as you're told or the big Hun will take you outside." He pointed to Jake. "You understand, yeah? He was a storm trooper before we got him. Don't think he'd hesitate to stick you if you don't do like we say."

Only a few of them had the guts to look Jake in the eyes, if they wanted to see what a real murderer looked like. Jake's blond hair trimmed up the side of his skull, his eyes grayish, bloodshot, scanning the room for threats. Jake's mastiff hands in fists at his side, this son of the Prussian flag. In their sheepishness, the way one of them shook—a young one, a teenager—Jake could see these men believed what Meinhof said. He didn't challenge the conceit. He too was struck dumb, standing back, mysteriously holding a suitcase in one of his giant fists.

Meinhof smiled his nervous smile, his grimace-grin. The bat was raised to see if any voter had the backbone to say more.

"It's close enough to time. Start the roll."

The polling room was an airless ten-by-twelve-foot cell on the other side of the door. This was a gambling room any other day of the year. There was a phone on the wall, used to call in bids on a policy game. Behind the table, where the roll was taken, two slot machines sat dormant under green blankets. Jake stowed his suitcase under the blankets too. He felt eyes on his back as he did this, as if the men dreamed what ingenious new weapon he carried.

Voters crowded to sign the roll book. They were given a ballot and shuffled to a corner to fill in the blanks. An election official was there, some junior clerk from the county courthouse, to make sure each voter knew the address that corresponded with the name he was claiming (that he read it off a slip didn't matter) and that the voter filled in the ballot on his own. These were the only rules that needed to be enforced. As far as the official was concerned, there was no other room at Mecklenburg's than the one he sat in. He was deaf to the instructions Meinhof shouted, deaf to the barroom hopping above. After a voter finished marking the slate, the ballot was exchanged for a slip that certified he'd voted. This wasn't anything official. It entitled him to whiskey and sausage at the bar upstairs.

It was like this all day. Jake and Meinhof moved them from room to room. Bouncers pushed the rowdy ones to the curb, to streetcars running express back to Union and Burlington Stations. These voters would be out of state before anyone else knew they were here.

The sun shined through the front windows in the afternoon. This surprised Jake when he came up to the barroom. He'd been underground since 5 a.m. Before that he'd been riding in the dark most of the night. He soaked in the sunshine that washed through the big front glass. More than a few election workers sat on car fenders in the street. They drank Irish coffee and pawed at plates of sausage and cheddar cheese. Most of these had never owned a vehicle, so the pride of driving a new car—Model Ts and Packard Twins—showed on their ruddy faces. Even if they were exhausted from working thirty hours straight, the exhilaration of Election Day kept them going. This was something they'd talk about the rest of their lives. The time they drove a Studebaker around the Ward on behalf of Tom Dennison and their beloved, infamous mayor, Cowboy Jim Dahlman. The lieutenants traded stories. It was boyish fun. To see them joking, staying up night and day to help a politician. One could almost forget what happened at the Santa Philomena. There was no stain of violence in a man's smile as he chatted up a potential vote. No melee on Clandish, no sabotage, no Cypriot dying. (Not unless you had the eyes to see them.)

Jake sat at the bar until the votes needed to be counted. He picked at some fried potatoes and ham, a beer in front of him he didn't drink. It was late afternoon. Many election workers made their way to Mecklenburg's, having finished for the day. Jake saw them in the mirror behind the bar. Some were his friends, Ingo and Rudi, men he'd hired. They didn't invite him to join them. They were busy boasting of capers they pulled. A smutty poem about a priest and nun they'd printed—with a forged endorsement from the opposition on the back—and distributed in Catholic neighborhoods. A circular they mailed last week in hostile districts, falsely notifying voters that the election had been moved to Wednesday, and that a man could vote by phone if he wished. All of them buzzed at how they busted up Josie Washburn's speech the night before. They marveled at how they'd pitted rivals against each other, at how quickly fighting was stoked and debate stifled. They tipped beers in celebration. Unbuttoned their shirts halfway. Let cigarette smoke drift out their nostrils.

Ingo saw Jake watching. He smiled and lifted his drink. Ingo was amused at what he saw, Jake realized. He understood this amusement once he saw himself in the mirror. He looked like shit. He was tired, decrepit in a way. He hadn't shaved in a week. Jake had been on a mad dash two days and accomplished nothing. He hadn't even managed to run away. The suitcase was in the basement waiting while he sat on a bar stool eavesdropping. The truth of the matter was that Jake was at war in Omaha. He owed money. He'd crossed people who shouldn't be crossed—and they knew about his escape plan. No amount of imagination could change this.

Once the polls closed, the election official went upstairs at Ingo's request and drank on the house while Jake and Meinhof counted votes in the basement. The ballots were kept in a steel lockbox, but Meinhof had a key. He dumped ballots on the table when they were alone. "Let's get to it," he said.

The first time through they separated the ballots into two piles— those supporting Tom Dennison's Square Seven and those supporting the reform slate. The counting was easier like this. Few ballots split either ticket. The first count showed a victory for Dahlman and the Square Seven, but before they restored the ballots to the box, and the box to the clerk, Meinhof called Dennison's office with the numbers. From the way Meinhof's face dropped, it was clear there was a problem. The numbers weren't coming in right. Districts outside the River Ward were going to their opponents in staggering numbers. Normally the machine relied on something close to a split in the outlying districts— with the Ward tipping the results in their favor. That wasn't the case this time. The reform politicians, the churches—they'd gotten their people out. It put pressure on the Ward to produce.

"We've got to do it again," Meinhof said, the telephone on its hook.

"Again?"

"Yeah! That's what I said. Go through the box. Find more that aren't right and toss them out. Make them wrong yourself if you have to. That's what Billy said."

Meinhof called again after they recounted. Jake knew the gain wouldn't be enough. He'd heard Tom talk about what might happen on Election Day, and he knew, as Meinhof slammed down the receiver, that the worst-case scenario was coming true. The deficit was insurmountable. No matter what margin the River Ward delivered, it wouldn't carry the day.

"Screw it," Meinhof said. He stomped around and swore. His face twisted as he rushed to the table and swept a mound of voting slips to the floor, ones marked for the reform ticket. "We'll make the numbers," he said. There was nothing wrong with these ballots, they hadn't been altered. Meinhof tore them in half and kicked them in among the carpet of stomped cigar stubs, then stopped, hands gripped under the beveled edge of the table, the flop of his hair undone. Meinhof smiled, maybe aware of the furniture turned over, the dust prints from his boots on opposition ballots. He dropped the table on its feet and looked like he might laugh.

"What are you doing?" Jake asked. "If you were going to fix the numbers, why—?"

"Get out," Meinhof said. "I'll finish without you."

Jake squeezed the suitcase handle. He tried to relax but couldn't. His anger embarrassed him. So he turned and climbed the stairs without looking back. Let Meinhof fix the numbers. It wouldn't make a difference, not even if the machine claimed the Ward was unanimous in its support of Dahlman. The switch was in. It was over.

E vie didn't know what she'd say if he came for her. She didn't really want to go away and would have to explain her change of heart. How she'd needed a job—that was the way it started. How the math had been simple in those days, but then things changed. It wasn't right to take money from Billy Nesselhous after Jake was sick. After she fell in love. So she told the gamblers to shove it, she wouldn't take their money anymore. She thought Jake had something to get by on. He was stealing from the gamblers, she knew that, but she'd hoped he could keep his strings running, because if he couldn't, she didn't know what they'd do to survive. Maybe Jake didn't understand how things worked, he was young, but Evie should have known better. Life intervened in all plans. Her life intervened and changed the rules. That was what the gamblers counted on, in their way of thinking, that a guy would let something slip he wouldn't otherwise to a girl he fell for. Only natural. The gamblers played the odds that way, bringing in a chaos girl as a hedge. They ran interference on their own schemes, on their own men, as a way of finding out who was strong and who would fail. Evie found out too, by and by, because she was in the middle.

Evie should have known better than to let things go as far as they did with Jake. She knew there was a limit to love, but she ignored what she knew and then went and did something stupid like tell off the gamblers. What would she do now? Her own money was running out.

She had to go away, didn't she? Even though it was a harebrained plan. That was what she thought on election night—she was going to run with Jake—at least early in the night. She was. She'd talked herself into it. But then he didn't show up, and that gave her time to think. Where was he? Was he dead? Did the gamblers get him? Would he still come for her? Did she want him to? Did she wish he'd never come back?

She was in bed when Jake found her, spread out on her stomach. Her pink kimono rode up her body to expose an arc of hips, the sloping meadow lines of ass and thighs. An old habit, posing like that. She heard him come in but didn't move. She tried to not even breathe. A paper lamp made the room glow orange, particularly her. Her bare legs and feet. Jake held a hand to her mouth to feel if she still breathed. She wanted to laugh but she wouldn't move. He pinched a bead of sweat from her top lip and rubbed it into his fingertips.

Evie held her breath but smiled in spite of herself. She'd tricked him, hadn't she?

Jake shifted his weight off the bed to remove his jacket. She took a heavy breath, silk sliding over her legs as she rolled to watch him. He parted the lace curtains and glanced down at the street below but didn't bother to raise the window. She didn't like to have the breeze come in at sundown. It gave her a chill.

"Is this for me?"

He'd left a wax paper package on the bed. She was eating when he turned around, Muenster and mustard on white rye. It was good, warm and formed, the cheese soft. She tore a sliver of cheese from between the bread and smiled as she tasted it. She plucked a rye grain off the blanket and crushed it between her front teeth. Her hair clumped lopsided.

"You like it?" Jake sat next to her on the bed and took her hands between his. He was much calmer than before. All the urgency was gone out of him. "If you want more," he said, "you can send out. Get whatever you want."

"I'm half-starved. A whole apple orchard sounds nice."

"Sure," he said. He bent and kissed the top of her head. "Make it two."

She went to the other room and stepped behind the divider to change clothes. She felt safe behind the divider. Its etched parchment made the light white, it removed the incandescent glare. She felt safe, hidden, but not comfortable. Jake asked why she hadn't packed.

Her rooms were as always, she realized. The high-backed chair and low-slung sofa. The kitchen, her bedroom with the brass bed and leg-less vanity and mirror. All more or less the same. A lamp in front of the divider. In a corner was the cutting table, the woman-shaped wire cage. Around the doorway were several bolts of bright fabric. She was so handy with a needle and those giant shears. It would take some plan-ning to package the tools and bring them along somewhere else. The heavy oak table would have to be left behind if she moved.

She slipped around the screen in the same stained robe she wore before and nudged the suitcase with the side of her foot.

"Where'd you pick this up from?"

She smiled in a far-off way.

"It's late. I'm sorry." He pulled a single bill from his pocket. "Don't you believe what I said before? I have this. It will take us a long way from here."

She took the note and examined it in the orange light. "Is this play money?"

She handed it back. Who'd heard of such a thing as a thousand-dollar bill? Jake tried to make her hold the money, but she wouldn't. The thousand dropped in among her blankets.

He sat sideways on the bed, leaning crooked over his hip. "I told you. We can go off someplace we've never been. We've got that thou-sand. It's cash. We could get some land somewhere and farm. It's enough to get started on anything we—"

Evie waved him off. She went to the kitchen, where the ring was, and handed it back to him. "I don't want this," she said. She left him standing there. His face lengthening. He was terrified, she saw this. Evie didn't know what she was doing. She hadn't convinced herself to break things off—giving back the ring just happened. She didn't know why Jake was late in coming for her. He could have done so many things against the gamblers, stupid things. He could have sealed his fate for all Evie knew, and hers too. He could be in real trouble, and the smart thing would be to distance herself. She saw this. Jake couldn't protect her.

She ran water for the tub. Under the sink basin was a green bottle. She tipped it to her mouth until she reached the dregs then let it clunk against the tile floor as she eased into the water. Hot water filled over her, splashing off her feet as it dumped from the spout.

Jake followed. He sat on the toilet cover, the room filling with steam. The toilet chain hung down from a sweaty upper tank.

"What am I going to do with you?" she asked.

"We agreed already. We'll leave. Then we won't have to worry."

"There's two alternatives, you should know." Evie spun to wet her front, then over again. "Either I jump in the river or find some way to pay the rent. That's how it is. Frankly, I don't care much for the drowning option."

She took on a mocking accent, like she'd grown up on Broadway instead of in Kansas. "This isn't the farm you came from," she said. "We do things different down here in America."

Jake rubbed the shape out of his hair, head in his hands. He was shaking. He was falling apart.

"You got a lot to learn about keeping a woman. I'll tell you that much."

"Why do I deserve you talking to me like this?"

"What makes you think it's about deserving? You think anyone deserves what they get? You think I deserve this?"

Evie knew there was nothing Jake could say that would make things better, but she wasn't going to let him off the hook. Her anger was coming out, and she couldn't stop. This was his fault. She felt a tear pool on her cheekbone, then drip off. She'd begged him to find her a job.

Jake straightened to look Evie in the eyes. She sucked her tears back and reached under the water to feel her legs.

"You deserve too, Jake. Did you forget about Ugo? Is that why you ask about injustice? Because you got no memory? Did you ever think what it was like for him? Running for his life. All those strangers trying to kill him because of a rumor. Only a rumor. And they'd cut his throat in case there was a reward."

They didn't really know each other, did they? She'd been with other men longer, probably knew more about them. Why did Evie presume she loved this one?

He'd never asked about Ugo, and she never volunteered information. Jake didn't know how they met. Whether Ugo picked her off the streets or out of the dance hall where she worked, or whether their meeting was smartly arranged by the gamblers to feel like serendipity, as was the case. Jake never asked where Evie lived before she came here. He didn't want to know how she'd come to be the Cypriot's kept woman, did he? But she was unavoidable in the tub. Alive and present. A complication to his scheme.

"How did you meet Ugo?" he asked. "What did you do for money then?"

Evie let her face drop. He was such a disappointment.

"Were you still a dime-a-dance girl? Or am I missing something?"

She drank from the bottle. She saw a tear on Jake's cheek, which was the last straw, him thinking he deserved to cry.

"I worked for them too. For Billy Nesselhous," she said. "It's the truth. Billy hired me out of a dance hall. Paid me to seduce Ugo and keep tabs on him. Not only Ugo. There were more before him."

"How many?"

Evie laughed. "A few. The first one lasted two years almost. It was easy. Make a man fall in love with you. Let him buy you fancy things. Billy pays for the rooms, so there's plenty of dough for other things too. Things I wanted."

"You were a snitch?"

"I guess so, sure. Ugo never said much. He wasn't up to anything. Don't you know that? Ugo knew people called him the Cypriot. He liked having a reputation, but he was no instigator. I don't know why they had to kill him."

"I don't know either."

Evie crossed her arms over her chest and gave Jake hell with her eyes.

"You got a lot to learn. There has to be money to live on. There has to be some way to make dough. That's just business. Don't be simple about it. A guy pays your way, you owe him what he paid for."

Evie turned her head. Her mouth dropped open. She had to suck her lips. "I want you to go. It isn't right, you being here."

"Is it the thing about the job? Our fight? Is that it?"

She was quiet a long time, him asking questions but not waiting for her to answer. He didn't understand. He didn't see her rooms, her wire dummy, the cutting table. He didn't even really see her, not how she saw herself.

Evie wanted Jake to say the right things, to understand her and what she wanted her life to be like, to convince her that they should stay together and that life would be good if they stayed together. Her shoulders collapsed, compliant to this yen, her eyes went wet. But she repeated "You have to go" until he lifted the suitcase and left.

Anna had her own trouble that spring. Somehow her file flittered up to the top of a stack of suspicious cases at the local education office. She caught the notice of a state inspector.

He came unannounced in May. There was a knock at the door, and when Anna went to answer, a fat man in a brown suit was standing there. He was bald, she saw, when he removed his hat. He asked if Mr. Miihlstein was at home.

She nodded yes. "But he's busy." This was true. Herr usually was busy in the attic and hated to be disturbed.

"Go get him anyway," the man said.

"What do I tell him this is about?"

Anna jumbled her English when she had to speak to a stranger like this, one who had the unmistakable look of a government man. A man who could make trouble. She'd been reading in the parlor, which was a mistake. She couldn't hide when she was in the parlor—he'd seen her though the window and she had to answer.

"Are you Anna Miihlstein?" he asked, bungling his words too, the pronunciation of her last name. Mill-stine. Anna acknowledged that this was her. "I'm here about you," he said. "You don't attend school and I have to find out why that is. Education is mandatory for the children of this state. Nobody told you this, I'm sure, but that's no excuse."

"The school?"

The man nodded. He peered down at Anna to look her over. Anna knew she was in trouble. She wanted to call for Maria, but Maria was out. Only Herr was home.

"Go on. Get your father. I need to speak with him."

Anna had to turn and walk. When she did, she knew the inspector would see everything about her. Her illness. How she had to gird herself to start moving then hurry her legs along to keep up with her torso. How she pulled herself up the stairs by the railing. The man from the state would see that she wasn't at all well, and then he'd repeat himself, that this was no excuse, she was sure. Her illness would make her absenteeism worse. She'd seen this when they lived in the Bowery. The state took sick kids away. Sick kids didn't come back.

Anna sat on the staircase landing when Herr went to speak with the inspector. The front door hung wide open, the inspector waiting on the porch.

"Come in! Come in!" Herr urged him inside. "What are you waiting for?"

The inspector sat hesitantly on the parlor sofa next to Herr. "I'd offer you tea," Herr said, "but I'm afraid it's been doctored."

"What do you mean?"

Herr laughed to himself and, searching the man's face, became silent. This was a dumb thing to say, of course. There was the prohibition.

"I'm not unsympathetic to your plight," the man said. "You surely have your reasons. But the girl must be educated. The law is quite clear on this."

"She is being educated," Herr insisted.

"Two years she's lived in this state, and not one day has she been in attendance at a school, public or private. There are records on file that speak to this fact."

"Herr Inspektor. There's a explanation for this." Herr leaned back on the sofa and folded his hands in his lap. He was a reasonable man.

He would explain. "You have seen my dear Anna. She has trouble. She's sick. So because of her illness I've been teaching her myself."

"Is that a fact? What's the curriculum you follow?"

"Poetry, music, art. This is how she spends her time. I assure you it's being addressed."

The inspector's weary face lit up at this suggestion, like it was becoming clear to him that he was being hoodwinked by immigrants after all.

He explained that the program Herr had devised was hardly up to the standard of what the state prescribed.

Even as Herr invited the inspector upstairs to examine the attic, Anna having to scuttle up the stairs with her eavesdropping found out, the inspector was not impressed. Anna's uncanny crafts, the entire days listening to music, the recitations of German poetry. No. This didn't fit any course of study except in the imagination of Herr Miihlstein.

Anna tried to perk up before all was lost. She snuck away to the bathroom and splashed water on her face, tied a ribbon in her hair, to look better than she was, to fool the inspector. He was stout and spoke with a griping tenor. Anna tried to calm him to the ways of her education by speaking to him directly, instead of letting Herr misguide the conversation. Twice already Herr had misspoke that Anna heard, bringing up liquor and that she'd been trying to speak Hebrew. Her English wasn't so great. She lagged far behind Karel since she was never out in public.

Anna suggested they move back to the parlor, where it would be more comfortable. There she'd show the inspector that she was being educated. That there was no problem.

She set her posture erect on the edge of the parlor sofa seat and played the violin. The inspector sat back and listened. Maria home then, with a plate of ginger snaps and a lemonade. There was no mention of doctored tea, just Anna playing her scales flawlessly, then a simplified étude of Schubert's "Ave Maria." And yes, another ginger snap for the inspector.

The inspector took notes in a book the whole time Anna played. What could he be writing about, all the notes he was taking? He'd ambushed them, showing up like this to observe and record. They were unprepared. It wasn't fair.

"I had no idea this was such a special case," he said once Anna was finished with the violin. "You're going to cause me a lot of trouble. I can tell."

"I assure you we won't," Herr said. "We're not that kind of people."

"Is the boy around?" the inspector asked.

"Karel? He goes to school. Not now. It's summer."

"Yes, I know. But there's some notes about him here, from his teachers." The inspector reached down and patted his briefcase. "Karel is a troublemaker, it says. A bad egg."

"I don't believe that. Karel's a good kid. It's his friends. They're the bad egg."

"He's the ringleader. That's what it says. It has no bearing on Anna's situation, only gives a clearer picture of what's going on."

The strain of pretending for the inspector took a toll on Anna. She was exhausted. The bags under her eyes dropped low, were bluer, her hair hung in strings over her forehead. And now the inspector saying these things about Karel! Anna felt like she was going to collapse by the time the inspector said he had to leave.

"I'll be back," the inspector promised, packing up his briefcase. "You can expect me."

"This did not go well," Maria said. "God in heaven. What will we do?"

Anna hid in the cellar when she was home during the day. This hiding wasn't too much different from her typical day. Working down in the cellar. Twisting around her metal works, until sometimes she overworked a piece and the wire snapped from being bent this way then that too many times. It was summer, though, and cool down below the floorboards. Nobody would see her, like they might if she was reading on the parlor sofa.

The state inspector stopped by on occasion, every few days. "We haven't forgotten about Anna," he'd say to Maria, who was the only one allowed to answer the door thereafter. "Is Anna at home?"

"No," Maria would lie. "Anna isn't expected back until dinner. She's gone playing with her friends."

"We're processing her. Do you understand what that means?"

"Show me her file. Don't come here and say things like that with no proof."

The inspector wouldn't show Maria anything, because he didn't have to. Maria wasn't a blood relative to the girl.

"Listen," she said. "Don't make me beg you. Something can be worked out to keep Anna at home. I'm no fool. I've seen how things work."

"I don't like that implication."

"There's no implication. The girl has friends." Maria leaned her face out the doorway, lowered her voice. "A young man who lives here is a close associate of Tom Dennison. Does that mean anything to you?"

The inspector put his hat on and stepped back on the porch. "Ma'am. That name means plenty. None of it good, I'm afraid."

And yes, the inspector promised, that too would go in the file.

If Anna wasn't in the cellar, she was in the attic, staring out the window. Anna never quite knew what she was looking for. Just watching the street. How bustling things got at lunchtime. Cars bounding past and leaving behind clouds of black smoke. How most every kid in the neighborhood made his way home for lunch. Straggling boys most of the time, given a little hustle at that hour by the hunger pains in their guts. There were a few she knew. Michael Hykell and Nathan Shapiro and Louis Weaver. Boys who wore the same set of wool trousers year round. Cowlicked boys, dusky boys, boys who came skidding around the corner on the heels of their shoes like they were up to something. Until they came to the Eigler house and stopped to peek up at the attic window. And there Anna Miihlstein was. She saw the recognition in a boy's eyes, how he loitered on the walkway to get a better look.

Anna wondered what it would be like to know these boys, to know all the kids on Clandish as Karel must know them. If she did go to school, she might not be so nervous around real kids. This was the way she thought of them, the *real kids*. Not dolls, like she was only a doll. It was quite possible that Karel was right about this—that the reason Anna stagnated physically was because she was trapped in the attic. She'd grow too if she went to school. She'd learn to take care of herself. To not have such thin skin. She'd run. She'd play in a juniper hollow. What else had Karel promised? A pet duck? A new lavender overcoat? A new hat?

Karel wasn't likely to follow through on a promise. And he was likely wrong that the neighborhood school would cure Anna's deficiencies. At any rate, the state inspector would leave them alone if Anna were to enroll, if it wasn't too late for that.

Anna was sure the state inspector was scaring Karel away. He hadn't come home in weeks. Nobody in the house knew where he was. There'd been little word about him at all. Snippets from neighbors about how they'd seen Karel on such-and-such street the day before, or cruising around with the Braun boy in Jobbers Canyon. Of course, Karel was playing baseball. It was summer. Five afternoons a week he had a game at Rourke Park with a junior team sponsored by the Omaha Printing Company. Besides that there was practice with the Southside team. Karel Miihlstein wasn't all that hard to find those days, if they'd dared to go down to the field and grab him. The rougher business would have been pulling him off a ballfield without raising Cain.

None of that mattered much to Anna. She wasn't going to take a streetcar to Rourke Park. From what she'd heard (and what she saw her one trip there) South Omaha wasn't all that pleasant. Anna didn't care to subject herself to the mean spirits of its environs. No. Karel was afraid of coming home because he thought the state inspector could be a welfare cop there to send incorrigible boys to reformatory school. It could have been true anyway. Anna worried about that. The inspector hadn't mentioned Karel after that first time, but maybe it was a cover. Maybe Karel had done something bad and the authorities were going to send him away. Anna considered this a distinct possibility, even though she hadn't heard that Karel was mixed up in any trouble besides drinking alcohol (which there was plenty of going on in the house already, between Herr, Maria, and Jake). Other than that the only concern was what Karel did with those ballplayers. Which was play baseball, by all appearances. He got a blackened thumbnail from an inside pitch that hit his hand where he gripped the bat. Grass stains on his pants. Nothing the inspector could charge Karel with. The realization set in after a while. The inspector truly was there for Anna.

She held her hands in the light from the window, up in the attic, to look at her fingers stretching. She felt bad about how she'd told Karel those things about their mother, the actor their mother had a thing for, how she'd been stabbed and bled to death, and Karel's bawling. She was sorry for the way she told him. She'd felt sad about it every day since. And Karel wasn't there for her to apologize.

It wouldn't be all that awful if she wasn't around. If she wasn't buried up to her neck in all that junk in the cellar. Maybe it wouldn't be so bad if the state inspector took her away.

✳

Whenever Maria left the house, from then on, she took Anna along. The inspector might snatch Anna from the house when Maria was out. She wasn't going to let that happen. Anna followed her around the house in the morning after breakfast, as Maria washed dishes and then shrunk into a wooden chair out front to roll a cigarette and catch her breath before heading to the market. The Eigler house sidled up to the big buildings of downtown—Anna could see them from the porch—so it wasn't far to the market. They walked slow down the steep hill of Clandish, the brick walkway full of chucks and gaps. If they hurried, one of them was liable to trip. Maria was in no hurry anyway. She gabbered to Anna. Told who lived in the houses down the block. Stefan the furrier. A merchant named Rudolph who lived at home and cared for his parents. The McPhees, who were Irish. Maria talked about families who used to live in the houses they passed. Krugs and Fischers and Kountzes. She told about a garden party on Constitution Day in 1892. Anna gibbered back with questions. What clothes were in fashion then? Was it only adults at the party, or kids too? How late were kids allowed to stay up that night? Cars rumbled by on Clandish as they talked. Every once in a while Anna peeked around a house and saw a woman hang laundry.

In the market Anna trailed behind as Maria browsed the stalls. A cabbage plucked out from a stand of them, some fruit. She felt a little better going out on errands with Maria. It had been over a year since she'd done this regularly. Those days, new to Omaha, Anna, Frau, and Karel stepping out for fruit and veggies, whatever else was needed and could be gotten in season. Anna had forgotten how nice it was to get out. Exhilarating as well as aggravating. Her muscles sore. Once she was out in the market stalls, the shouts of callers, the purchasers, a buzzing feeling overcame her objections. She had to stand tall and straighten her back or else she'd be trampled. She liked being out in the sun, in the market, where women complimented her on how smart a white straw hat looked on her, and how cute she was. Some neighborhood boys saw her and could hardly believe their eyes. *Yes, it's Anna,* she wanted to say to them. *Out for a walk. With necessities to buy at market.* So she went to fruit stalls and Hiller's Grocery. The proprietor behind the counter, silent, near a glass case filled with tobacco, pens, and other sundries. His four daughters in a back office with a phonograph and a record that told fairy tales. Anna sneaked over to hear what came from the horn. Baba Yaga and her house on chicken legs.

She carried packages for Maria. Fruit, strawberries, veal cutlets folded in a newspaper. She waited as Maria chatted up merchants, as Maria chatted up women her age, friends, or anyone. Maria liked to talk, so long as she looked busy in the process, a cloth bag snagged on her elbow, her pocketbook unclasped but clutched to her breast, how she made the person behind her in line wait as she fished for coins and counted pennies. Somehow surprised to find she had enough money to pay after all. But always chatting. Asking for news, sharing news. *That's too bad. But she's okay? You never know. A woman like her. Too proud to ask for help.* Maria would help anyone so long as they asked and the solution wasn't money. There were pies that could be made, fresh bread, time-tested remedies. She could sit in a room with someone who was ailing.

One day out on the street, in fact, a man grabbed Maria by the elbow and requested help. A sick woman was dying—an elderly woman with no family, the man said. A woman in the tenement building where he lived. Could Maria go sit with the woman? Until the pastor arrived? The woman was seventy-something years old with pneumonia. There was nothing else to do.

A crowd was at the top of the stairs, men familiar with each other, in the way they whispered, hands gently on each other's shoulders. They cleared the narrow doorway to let Maria and Anna through. None of them wanted in, not really.

The husband sat on a cot next to his wife. A dry little man, he stared at the cap in his hands and muttered something in a Slavic tongue, giving over the only chair in the room to Maria. She set her bags down and took the seat. It was a minuscule place, even for a tenement. Neither of the old couple was large, however. The cot cradled them both, they were so slight.

The men in the doorway said the couple had only lived here a month. He was a Serb, she a German from Alsace-Lorraine. Somehow they ended up here. The husband, the men told, was confused at the mention of Omaha or Nebraska, as if these were faraway places he'd never been. Maybe they'd been looking for Milwaukee or St. Louis but boarded the wrong train at Grand Central in Chicago. If they arrived here lost and broke, in some unknowable wend of the map, there was little that could be done to right their course. Anyway, the wife was dying.

Maria tried speaking German to the husband. He nodded, closed his eyes, then muttered to himself. Maria shrugged and looked to the others. "He doesn't understand. She's gone. She's dead."

Anna didn't know what they'd do. She'd backed under the eaves, where the ceiling sloped lower and lower to refract the angle of the roof. Wool blankets sagged from the rafters where someone tacked them there for insulation, stinking wool that smelled like coal oil and fish, mildew. Anna crouched over herself so the wool didn't rub her hair. She watched as the old husband muttered his prayer. The wife lying there, her face uncovered. Her eyes closed. Her lips sunken and toothless. Under the blanket was her body, a black silk dress exposed, a crucifix on her flattened breasts. Maria leaned near the husband. She whispered something short, a Psalm in Plattdeutsch, then pulled the blanket over the woman to make clear she was gone.

The old man wrung his cap harder. He said something no one understood then felt along a ridge in the blanket where his wife's chin and nose marked a difference in the fabric. He repeated the something no one understood.

The men in the doorway entered. They were a group of singers, one of them explained, a touring Liederkranz from Bremen that was stranded here because of travel restrictions. They rehearsed across the hall twice weekly to stay in practice for the day they could tour again. Each doffed his cap and offered condolences to the husband. They were his friends as much as anyone and now lined up to lay hands on his shoulder. The leader nodded and they began singing, the baritone first, then the rest of them. It was "An der Weser." Anna recognized the song. It came out of nowhere. Anna, Maria, the old husband, they turned to the singing men, their somber faces, and then to the floor because the rendition was sad and spare, sullen and beautiful too. The melodies intuitive and precise. Anna put a hand to the eaves, to the old wool, to keep from falling, her body forgetting itself. Everyone who heard must have stopped in their tracks. Each of them glassy-eyed, faces drooping, longing for homes unreachable, for friends long gone. The singers rolled it out magnificently. Anna let herself get carried away. She let a remembrance of Europe slip into her mind, the burial of her mother. The song was miserable and satisfying. She wished it could last forever.

When they returned home, there was a black Ford waiting at the curbstone. The front door of the Eigler house was cracked open. Herr sat inside with the inspector and a woman in a stiff blue skirt and jacket. The way Herr sat humped into himself, his eyes rimmed red, there was no mistaking what was going to happen.

"I tried to make them tea," Herr said. "I don't know where you keep the kettle down here, Frau Maria. Isn't that embarrassing?"

"There's no need for that," the woman said. She was annoyed, like she'd had to repeat this to Herr already.

"That's right," the inspector agreed. "Will you go upstairs now, Anna? And make up a suitcase to bring? We've told your father here and now it's time."

"Your papers have been processed," the woman said. "Now you're to come with us."

From upstairs Anna could hear them arguing in the parlor. Maria wasn't going to put up with this. This was America, wasn't it? They couldn't just come and take a girl away.

Anna packed her suitcase like the inspector told her to. This was something she'd thought about before so she'd be prepared when the time came and would know what to bring. She only had the one suitcase and it wouldn't even hold all her clothes. So she packed pajamas, two sets, and a few books, and a nicer pair of shoes in addition to the ones on her feet. Still the adults argued in the parlor, Maria louder and louder because the two from the state wouldn't listen to her. The woman made the mistake of telling Maria that she had no say in the matter. Then Anna packed a couple dresses and a week's worth of undergarments. The suitcase was nearly full. Her straw hat wouldn't fit. Anna worried the inspector would take the hat if she tried wearing it out, so she took it off her head and hung it on the baluster for safekeeping. She'd come back for the hat. If she wasn't gone for long. If the state didn't keep her forever.

They were still at it when Anna came downstairs.

"It's my recommendation," the inspector insisted, "that Anna be moved to a state home. The situation is clear. You know very little about the actual condition of Anna's health. That's the deciding factor."

The woman walked across the room and kneeled to Anna. "Has anyone told you that you have rickets?" Nobody had. Anna didn't know what that was. They'd explain it to her in the car. A bone disorder. Calcium deficiency. An absence of vitamin absorption. Knock-kneed, bow-legged. "Now give me your suitcase. Nobody will steal that. Hand it over."

The woman walked Anna across the room.

"But what's the place for?" Herr wanted to know. "Is it for the terminally ill? For the mentally strange?"

"None of those," the inspector said. "Mr. Miihlstein, I'm beginning to think it's you who is deficient. Anna will be taken care of. She is sick in her bones and only the doctor will know what to do."

Anna told herself she'd be all right, she'd be okay. She hugged her father good-bye, let Maria lift her and kiss her on the cheek, then heaved herself into the backseat of the government Ford. There was no time to wait for Silke and Theresa to come home. Anna had a train to catch, the woman explained. "It's better this way. No bawling over each other. You'll see your sisters soon. Believe me." The woman rambling now that she was alone in the backseat with Anna, this sick girl who'd been removed from home.

"It's for your own good. Save them from bawling good-bye and let them get on with their day. Let them forget sooner."

A letter was left at the house that told where Anna's family could visit her. She shouldn't worry.

RED SUMMER
Autumn 1919

J ake had cause to leave Omaha. They left him no choice.

Working for the machine lost all propriety without the veneer of the election. They'd lost the vote and reality came crashing back. Reformers cleaned out the police department and held judges to task. There were crackdowns in ethnic zones, from Clandish to the neighborhoods surrounding the stockyards. With Ed Smith as the new mayor and Dean Ringer calling the shots for the police, the city focused on cleaning out the River Ward. Ringer established something called the Morals Squad, a coalition of his own cronies who were tasked with throwing out Dennison's cronies. There were outrages in the dailies with all relevant clergy and politicians consulted—the same confederacy that won the vote—and something had to be done. Paddy wagons were filled with bartenders to be booked on charges of public depravity. Kegs of beer were chopped in the gutter for newspaper photographers. There would be no drinking for a night, but by morning a machine captain would make bail for the bartenders and pay their fines. New kegs could be procured. Business would be back to normal by shift change at the mills. It was all theater.

Sometimes Jake was the guy who made bail. That July, 1918, a kid came to get him early one morning. It wasn't even five yet. Jake could tell from the way the kid rambled that he'd been up all night, sick on chewing tobacco and snuff. The kid said there'd been trouble with the cops.

The courthouse was elegant early in the morning, when it was quiet. Jake waited inside the bronze doors to see the vaulted dome. Its panes glowed like emeralds in the first light. He paced the rotunda and stared up at the murals, waiting for a judge, and lit a cigarette to see its tails of smoke twist in still air, one of the few times he liked to smoke, alone like that, the building alive with morning sun. He felt that the space belonged to him. In a way it did. If the clerks weren't there, or the nuts debating their fines, or all the real estate people and lawyers, the cops and government men, the street girls being held up to fork over a percentage of what they'd made. Jake stared at the murals—mosaic plowmen, broad-shouldered balers of hay, a Sioux chief in headdress defending a teepee camp—but a judge never came. A police captain did. The police captain said to follow him to a fourth-floor room. Inside was a body on a table bound in a wool blanket.

Jake walked to the end of the room and stared out the window, not even slowing when he passed the body. His fingertips were on the glass before the captain had the door closed. He faced south and could see a long way. There was the library across the street, the Flatiron and its tan bricks, a red boardinghouse that looked like a barn, Clandish Street and the tenements south of there, then freight lines and long, winding boulevards that led to Deer Park and South Omaha.

The police captain thought Jake was stupid. "You still sleeping?" Jake grinned like a clodhopper, in no rush to reveal how he was feeling, to let his face twist up or cry or shout and take a swing at the police captain in revenge. He just wanted to run out the door, to not have to face that body in the blanket. His chest was tight; he could hardly breathe, holding all that in, making himself grin.

The captain explained how there was a fight. Men from Jake's crew were caught with alcohol outside a club downtown. When confronted by police, they refused to surrender the liquor. One of them took a swing at a cop. That's what cops always said, and it was probably true. Most machine workers weren't afraid of reform cops. But the skirmish went too far this time. Shots were fired.

Jake asked who it was. "See for yourself," the captain said. He was there to transfer custody of the body. Jake was to take the body away and arrange for burial. "We won't make a big deal out of this," the captain said, "if you and your boss don't either."

Jake lifted the blanket. It was Ingo Kleinhardt. Ingo was a man Jake hired. The cops shot Ingo through the mouth. His teeth were shattered.

Jake lost his stomach for the work after they buried Ingo. He went up to the office above the tobacco shop and told Tom Dennison he wanted to quit. Jake expected Tom to try and talk him out of leaving, but Tom did nothing like that. Tom was as bitter about how things had turned out as Jake was.

"Those men are your responsibility," Tom said. "Whether you're running the crew anymore or not, you hired him. You brought him in."

"You got to leave," Billy Nesselhous said. "Either do something to get back at Ed Smith or get the hell out of town. We don't need useless men."

"What should I do?" Jake looked at Tom like they were the only two in the room. Other men lined the walls, the toughs. Their heads dipped as they glared at Jake.

"Do your job," Tom said. "This wouldn't of happened if you were on top of it."

"Make up your mind and get in the game," Billy goaded him, "or we have no use for you anymore."

"I can quit? I can leave?"

Jake leaned forward in the chair opposite Tom's desk, hands in his lap.

"It's not that easy," Billy said. "There's the money you owe."

"The thousand," Tom said. "What about that? You think you should get to keep it?"

Jake couldn't have paid back a tenth of what he'd siphoned off, and he'd left the thousand at Evie's the last time he'd seen her. She'd probably spent it. Jake knew it wasn't right to take that money. Nobody had to tell him that. But so much of what they did was questionable. It was all illicit money they trafficked in. All under-the-table, all off the books. There were worse things he could have done.

He kept his mouth shut about Evie. What Jake said was that he'd give back everything he had left. He emptied his pockets onto Tom's desk. "There's thirty here, some change."

"What about that ring?" Billy picked out what was once supposed to be Evie's ring. The silver band with a diamond chip. "This too."

"It isn't worth much," Jake said.

"It's something."

Jake didn't mean to dump the ring, but it was too late to take it back. "Fine. There's all this. Another fifty in my room. You can sell the clothes."

"There were others like you." Tom swept the money back across the desk to Jake. Billy kept the ring. "There were others with promise. You ended like they all did. A disappointment."

Jake couldn't believe it. Were they really going to let him walk?

"Am I done?" he asked. "Can I leave?"

"If you can live with it, keep what you owe." Tom motioned to a trio of thugs along the wall. "Get him out of here," he said.

"To the train station," Billy added. "That's fair. If you had what you owe us, we'd be square. Since you don't, you got to leave town. That squares us."

They put him on the evening train to Lincoln. After that Jake could go as far as the thirty he had left would take him.

There wasn't time to say good-bye to Maria or the Miihlsteins before his train embarked. He didn't have a chance to tell Evie he was leaving. They put him on the train and he was gone.

Returning to his father and the farm in Jackson County crossed his mind. If the war had ended that moment in July—if it ended a few months earlier than it did—Jake might have gone home. But things didn't happen that way. Jake was run out of Omaha. Lincoln was where they sent him. For the second time in his life, he arrived in a new city with only a little money and the clothes on his back. He'd be smarter this time.

And life would be easier here, in a way. Lincoln was safe and bland, its people mostly prohibitionist dry staters, self-flagellating Protestants, Anglicans, Methodists, government workers, students and instructors, young academics, pioneer lawyers, ministers. Its streets emptied at night. And the war was almost over. The German army was on the retreat. There were riots in their cities, famine, discontent. Civil war gripped Berlin. Once it was clear Germany couldn't win the war, the tenor was different in America.

As it happened, Jake met Frau Voight, an old German who ran a lunchroom at the depot in Lincoln. She was plump and little. Frizzy hair fell in her eyes. She wore one of those drab dresses from the Old World, even in July, even in the kitchen, despite its layers and petticoats and white apron starched stiff. She ran around crazed, a pack of boys in her place for supper. A chicken had just finished roasting. She served it with sweet potatoes and yeast rolls and gravy. Frau Voigt watched her patrons eat, laughing and talking to herself. Young men were in her lunchroom, ranch hands headed west, college boys with nobody to cook for them, and Jake. She was happy to have them. "Ders plenty good gravy on dem sweet pertaters, yeah? I was waitink for yah boys to sit der." She didn't try to hide her accent; maybe she played it up. This wasn't such a strange thing to Jake after living on Clandish, but her voice rang different in Lincoln. Frau Voigt had a lilt that made every phrase sound like it was plucked from a popular song. She called the boys *meine Jungens* and slipped them cookies from her apron after they soaked up the last drop of gravy with their last bit of bread. Jake laughed when the college boys teased about her accent, because she laughed too.

Classes were out for the summer, so most houses around the university lacked roomers. Jake took the front room of a white bungalow on Vine Street. It was shaped like an oval, with the front porch wrapped around. There was a big window on the street side. A family of five, the Jeffries, lived in the main house.

That first evening Mr. Jeffries offered Jake work. He was a bricklayer and repaired walkways and streets that had sunk in the dirt. Most of the time he worked alone, he said, but he liked having a helper. His three boys were too young. Jake said he'd do it.

Jeffries had a truck they used to pick up bricks from a furnace near the train station. Jake liked to ride in it. Folks gawked good-naturedly as the truck went by, its engine belching, its springs springing. He waved hello if they smiled at him. The rest of the day he'd dig up old pavers and pack dirt. They worked outside in clean air.

He'd never really seen a place so flat. Lincoln was nothing like home—which was sandy and hilly, with streams and creeks hidden all over—or Omaha, with its bluffs and swampy backwaters. There was grass everywhere here. Jake saw why they grew so much wheat.

In Lincoln, Jake worked. He lived in that room. He went to a football game on Thanksgiving Day when the Cornhuskers played Notre Dame. The game ended in a 0–0 tie, and Jake couldn't figure what good the struggle did either squad. For hours they pushed and shoved and threw bombs downfield as hard as their might allowed. They punched and scratched and shouted and swore. Traded territory.

Were injured. And for nothing. Not even one lousy point. But Jake got to shake hands with Knute Rockne afterwards, so that was fine. In winter he walked to the university library to read in its heated crannies. When the weather was nice, he went for long runs along the Missouri Pacific railroad tracks between Vine and Holdrege in the evenings. The air cleaned his lungs of black phlegm. Those who lived near the tracks must have thought Jake was some mad consumption patient trying to cough up diseased sputum, the way he hacked up the gunk he'd breathed in Omaha. He grew a beard after seeing the Swedes there with beards. His came in tinged red. He trimmed it every Sunday with grooming scissors. He improved his body. He couldn't sleep otherwise. His brain wouldn't shut off. He had to keep busy. Maria sent him letters from the Miihlsteins, from herself, and that helped him get along. Jake answered with a polite, stiff tone. He'd rip up half of what he wrote and cut it down so he wouldn't embarrass himself by saying too much or writing too gaily. He didn't understand why it was so hard to write the way one spoke. His writing always got in the way of what he was trying to say.

Jake fantasized about Evie coming to find him. The thought crept up on him as he kneeled to work after lunch sometimes. Her waiting on the Jeffries' stoop that night or following him on the street. He hung around the station on weekends when trains came in. They could meet up and it would turn out all right. She'd have him back.

Evie never came to Lincoln. Nobody came to visit Jake, and that galled him. He knew then what a heel he'd been.

He was reading in his room when the Armistice was signed on November 11, 1918. The siren from the power plant blared the moment news was wired from France, at 2:20 a.m. General Foch met a delegation of German officers and politicians in a private railcar in the Forest of Compiègne to sign at the eleventh hour of the eleventh day of the eleventh month. The generalissimos maintained their flair through it all. Four years of industrialized warring, genocide, and slaughter, sixteen million deaths worldwide. Jake later read of great bonfires in Omaha that were lit to celebrate the Armistice that night. An effigy of Kaiser Wilhelm burned in Farnam Street outside the courthouse. The dummy was carried in a coffin through the streets, then laid out to be plugged through with rifle shots by the Omaha Gun Club before being set ablaze. The big whistles of the Union Pacific repair shops blew the moment it was known that Germany had come to terms with surrender. The celebration in Lincoln was more subdued. With Spanish flu at its devastating height, most people stayed home rather than risk infection dancing arm in arm with a yawping celebrant. It was much the same through the holidays. There were no Christmas pageants. Stores were mostly empty. Mail was still delivered, streetcars still ran, although all postmen and trolley drivers wore surgical masks while they worked. Some nights Jake had the run of the city.

He didn't do much. He saved money and planned what would come next. He thought of carrying through on his plans to run, sans Evie. To California or Texas, wherever he wanted. In pamphlets and travel books he learned about the interesting life one could have in places other than Nebraska. It was all just dreaming. Jake didn't have the money to leave. He'd been sending half of what he saved each month to Dennison's office in Omaha. Not to make it up to Tom, nothing like that. Jake just felt it was right to send the money. He felt bad having stolen. A guy like Billy Nesselhous might think something like this was pathetic, but doing the right thing was important to Jake. Eventually, at least.

Jake thought about how things had been in Omaha.

Sometimes Evie had betrayed herself by saying she knew Jake would hurt her someday. She was afraid he'd leave, and she'd be stuck alone. "That's the way it is," she said, "for a girl kept in her rooms."

Most nights he tried to be happy his plans didn't work out. So many things could have gone wrong if they'd eloped to San Francisco. What did he know about marriage? This was a rational tack, one he rarely convinced himself of. When he was lonely, on the other hand, when he woke in the middle of the night, Jake felt different about him and Evie going separate ways.

Nights in Lincoln left ample space for regrets. Jake saw how much of his life had been blind luck. All he'd done was make an awful mess of what he'd been given.

Anna quit asking about Karel after her first year at the state sanitarium. The grounds were a few hours northwest of Omaha, but a train came through the town, Heller, to drop off passengers midmorning and returned in the evening with the reverse heading. Herr visited often, as did Maria. When they came to catch her up on news from the neighborhood, Anna stopped them if they talked about Karel, rare as news about him was anyway. "I don't care," she'd say. She'd carry on without him. Women from a local Presbyterian church brought string and canvas to work with. There were lunches and teas and other sick girls. Anna had all she needed to keep herself going.

The state sanitarium wasn't so bad. She had friends. She had teachers. She had treatment. What the doctor prescribed at the home wasn't all that different from what Maria tried already. A steady diet of cod liver oil, fresh dairy milk, mushrooms of three seasons. Anna pursued this diet in earnest at the country home, a prickly nurse pacing over the girls' shoulders during the four daily meals to ensure they cleaned their plates and downed three pints of whole milk. No girl was allowed to leave dinner if even a single morsel was uneaten. The most notable change was an order to take three hours of sunlight in daily absorption sessions. That was what made the difference for Anna. The air on Clandish was too clogged up with industry and had only been worse in the Bowery. Anna's illness first appeared when the Miihlsteins arrived from overseas, although insufficient nutrition on the ship over was partly to blame, Dr. Emmett surmised. Secreting Anna away in the attic had only made her symptoms worse. "Proper nourishment. Fresh air and sunlight," Dr. Emmett told her. "That's the only cure." And it worked, over time. Her case of rickets wasn't such a bad one. Under the care of a capable physician who had a sound, rational mind and was aware of modern science, rickets was usually overwhelmed.

Dr. Emmett kept up a competent, starched front. In his black suit and prim Windsor knots. His bushy white mustache waxed so it extended outside his cheekbones, with matching white hair combed to the right. He kept a big office at the southeast corner of the building, what they called the lodge, furnished with varnished birchwood pieces, where he signed papers most of the day. His Model A was kept in front until he drove home in the afternoon, the residents wishing him off from their lounging chairs as they sunbathed on the lawn. Dr. Emmett sometimes gave girls rides around the grounds after lunch, particularly on icy winter days when he could make the Ford fishtail, four girls clinging to each other in the back and screaming for joy. Emmett bouncing along in his own seat up front, laughing just as loud, just as joyously, throughout what he called his *automotive treatment*. He claimed to have patented the technique.

A day went by fast at the home. There was so much for Anna to do. Wall-to-wall activities, the grounds to explore, a red oak forest, a stream. The absorption sessions on the lawn. The treatments and meals and chewing mint leaves if she felt nauseous and lining up to sip cod liver oil off the tablespoon a nurse held and the long soaks in zinc bathtubs. All required by Dr. Emmett. Add on what the sanitarium teacher demanded. Lessons assigned for the girls' benefit (and mandated by the state) in the chalk-dusty classroom on the third floor of the lodge, across from where the girls slept. Elocution. English, French, and Latin vocabulary. General Math. American History. Typing. Biology and Social Problems. The girls loved speaking French after a mademoiselle from the town came to school them. Mademoiselle, not much older than the girls, married a doughboy and came over with him. After she came to teach, for the next week at least, the girls practiced their nasals nonstop, proud of the way they sounded, and tried to sway their hips like the mademoiselle did when she sauntered the halls of the girls' sanitarium.

There was the gymnasium, built in an annex to the back of the building, where girls learned to heave a basketball toward its hoop. There were social clubs led by girls, in cliques of different ethnic groups, where cooking, sewing, and domestic science were emphasized. There was the art club, whose leaders swore in Anna as a member during her first meeting with them. In the art club's charter was a line about "imitating and emulating great European masters," added at Dr. Emmett's behest, but this dictum wasn't strictly adhered to. They gathered around tables in the cafeteria three afternoons a week and broke open crates where the supplies were stored. Oil pastels and India ink and aluminum cans of shellac and a glass jar of acetone begged off the groundskeeper and blocks of clay and wire gouges to slice the clay. Balls of yarn and twine and oddly angled patches of fabric that were donated by the Lutheran women.

Not that it was easy to make friends. It had been a long time since Anna spoke to a child she wasn't related to. There were awkward moments. Who to sit by at meals. Sleeping in the vaulted dorming hall, where iron bed frames lined the walls and only eight inches separated her mattress from those on either side. Worst of all was Anna's first experience in the bathing room.

Three nights a week, on a rotating schedule, the girls soaked in one of the large zinc tubs that were packed into the room. The experience was pretty much like it sounded, Anna supposed. Warm mineral water, a bathtub. Like any bath. Except for the three other girls who shared the room with her and the nurse who made sure each girl submerged completely and spent the requisite forty-five minutes soaking in the mineral solution.

Nurse Methfessel half pulled off Anna's dress her first evening assigned to the baths, undid the buttons, and slipped off the shoulders before Anna objected and covered herself. "Don't be ridiculous," the nurse snapped. Anna held desperately to the bust of her state-issued dress. She wouldn't budge, no matter how Methfessel hectored her.

The other girls chased out the nurse. "We'll take care of her," they promised.

Anna was fifteen, although she hardly looked ten, the hollow look around her eyes, her chest sunken between the arrested buds of her breasts. The thought of exposing her deficiencies was stultifying. Anna was aware of her absurdity. But the other girls didn't make demands like the nurse had. They let her alone in the corner while they disrobed and got in the water. Anna watched the three girls tiptoe over dewy tile and climb in without peeking. Anna had yet to discover that she could trust these girls. "Go on," one of them said. Her name was Mina. "We won't watch." The three turned their heads, their bodies, so Anna could uncover in peace.

It had been a long time since she'd been naked in front of anyone. And now it was required in front of these girls. Mina with her hair tied with ribbon so her ears stuck out. Her large eyes made her look nervous. She was the tallest, the most developed, and you couldn't tell anything was wrong except for her hips, her giant rump, and the flab around her knees. None of them were perfect. Kate's left elbow jutted severely, and her long body could twist nearly all the way around like a contortionist. Sylvie was stuck crooked in the shoulders and hips, like she was posing on a pageant stage, and all that hair under her arms and on her privates. These girls had been residents longer than Anna. There was meat on their bones. They lay submerged up to their chins and stared blankly at the ceiling.

Anna peeled her undergarments over her flange of hipbone, her knobby knees, and crawled over the high side of her zinc tub to sink into the mineral water then float back to the surface. The water was amniotic and warm.

"There you go," Mina said. "We told you. Listen to us. We'll take care of you."

Visits to the bathing room soon became the best part of living at the lodge. Four girls floating with water over their ears, long hair adrift around their heads. It was sort of quiet. Anna heard pipes clank inside the walls. How there was someone clacking down the hallway outside, back and forth, Nurse Methfessel with the towels. These noises louder to Anna with her ears under the water. Subterranean and baritone noises. She imagined being someplace else, her ears under the water, in that enveloping white noise of the state sanitarium for girls.

They lined up on the cedar bench after, the bathing room opaque with steam, crisp towels wrapped around their frail, tanned bodies. It took a while to come back from wherever they'd gone under the water. Until one of them said something, "It's hot in here," and broke the spell.

The treatments worked. Anna was getting better. Her family saw this each time they visited—how she stood straighter, how she moved more natural, her steps more fluid and assured. If not strong and lively, she was stronger, livelier. Even Karel saw how she improved. He came in September 1918, the only occasion he visited.

They rented bicycles at the train station and arrived around lunchtime. Herr, Karel, Theresa, and Silke. Anna met them on the veranda and led a tour. First around the lodge, the lobby with its green upholstered sofas and shelves of paperback books, a pitcher of lemonade asweat with condensation. Then to the dining room, a cook setting out places for lunch. Up to the classroom and the hall where the girls slept. Back to the lawn until lunch was served. Anna didn't know what else to say. All but Karel had visited before, several times. Her sisters didn't need the tour and were bored walking the halls, mocking admiration at the woodwork, how clean everything was. Karel didn't care either. He straggled behind, waited in doorways, chewed a hangnail in his thumb the whole time. He was too busy looking at the other girls. Girls who whispered to each other and giggled when Karel stopped to see them. It wasn't very often a real live boy was up in the hallways of the lodge. One who was tall and swept wild hair off his forehead with his hand.

At least on the veranda they could sit in rocking chairs and stare out into the woods. There were katydids to listen to. Anna didn't need to speak. They breathed deep because the air was fresh way out here. The aroma of walnut trees was strong this time of year, and it was cool on the veranda, where ceiling fans spun above them, the blade mechanisms connected to a single motor by a long rubber belt. They could smell trees. They could investigate how a ceiling fan worked. They didn't have to talk.

Karel was much bigger. Broader in the shoulders, his voice deeper. He didn't hardly look like Karel, except he did, of course. He was dark, hollows under his eyes, like always. His hair long, down past his ears, and undercut on the sides. He was just older. He'd grown.

After a while Herr and Silke and Theresa went inside to see what was holding up dinner. They hadn't brought anything to eat on the train and then that bike ride. Now lunch was late. What had they been thinking? It was a Sunday, and lunch was often late on Sundays. There were no treatments either. Most of the staff was at home or at a church picnic, besides a cook and Nurse Methfessel. What was the rush? The girls who lived here looked forward to a lazy day.

The two of them alone, Karel asked Anna how she liked it at the sanitarium.

"It's fine," she told him, so quiet she wasn't sure if she'd actually spoken or just moved breath over her lips and thought the words. "I feel better up here. It's the truth."

"Yeah? That's good."

Karel was quiet too. He looked exhausted, the way he slumped in his rocking chair, one close to the railing, where the sun angled in to wash over him. His words sounded forced out, his voice straining to civility. Anna supposed he was trying to be nice to her.

"I didn't get to say good-bye," he said. "I was a little sore about that for a while."

"You were mad at me?"

"Yeah. But don't worry. I forgave you for it. Herr told me it wasn't your fault."

"Of course it wasn't my fault. They took me. How on earth could you be mad at me?"

"Don't get angry. We didn't say good-bye. That's all."

He bit at his hangnail and stared into the trees.

"Yeah," she said. "That's factual."

"Well. I'm happy to see you. I missed you."

"That's nice of you to say."

"And I felt bad. I promised to buy you an overcoat. Purple. Just like the other one. I'll still get one. I'll get you one for winter."

"Don't," Anna said. "They tossed out that ratty thing when I got here. Some ladies from the town make sure all the girls have coats. It's nice of you. But don't bother."

Anna let herself get worked up for a moment. She breathed deep the attar of walnut bouquet and made herself sound bored talking to her brother. She didn't know how she was supposed to respond to what Karel told her, his impossible promises. His trying to get her excited for what would turn out to be nothing. She didn't know at all what to say to him. That he looked like a hoodlum? That hair. That she was embarrassed? That she didn't approve of his habits? What she'd heard about him anyway.

She'd already accepted that he wasn't going to visit. He shouldn't have come.

✳

And then Theresa put it to Anna at lunch. "What'd you say to him? I've never seen him so upset." "There's no reason to be rude," Silke said. "He takes how you treat him so hard."

But Karel didn't look upset to Anna. He looked fine. Some girls wanted to sit by Karel. They grabbed his arm and bade him to their table. He shook them off and sat next to Anna instead. Anna didn't think he was upset. He didn't care about her. She knew this. How could he be mad? Anna didn't need to counteract all that, not like Theresa said. She wasn't being harsh to Karel, she didn't think. They didn't say much while eating, but it wasn't being rude. They had nothing to say. Anna was polite. She passed the salt when asked. Buttered a slice of bread for Karel. If she was short with him she didn't mean to be.

There was more sitting on the porch in silence after lunch. There was Dr. Emmett pulling his Ford behind the school, a new girl with him, the nurses rushing through the halls to find out what had brought him in on his day off. Emmett busy with the new girl all evening in the infirmary, which wasn't all that uncommon, Anna explained. There were more snide comments from Silke and Theresa, until they were too bored sitting on the porch to even complain. There were more girls who came to talk to Karel, asking if he'd been for a stroll in the woods yet, twisting blond curls around their fingers, and would he like to stroll with them. Girls who tossed their heads and whinnied when they laughed. Silke and Theresa were tickled about the way those girls acted around Karel. Their train didn't leave until dusk.

Maybe she shouldn't have given Karel the cold shoulder. Anna considered that as she tried to fall asleep. All those iron beds in a row. The girls tossing because it was hot up there, even with the windows at each end propped open to catch a breeze, when there was a breeze. This attic was not much different from the attic at the Eigler house in that respect. A group of them lined up to sleep. She couldn't help but listen to the others. Their sighing, the way some of them got upset at how they were still awake, like they could conquer wakefulness with more intense exertion. Karel was frustrated so easily as a little boy, and always preoccupied. He wasn't much different now, Anna thought.

She didn't need anything from him. They'd been trained to grow apart. Anna was preserved for posterity in a series of attics; Karel was set free in the city, a boy with wild oats to sow. Isn't that how it goes? Things had changed so much from how they used to be, when Karel was still a precious little boy, when they were precious together. He used to climb into bed next to Anna and put his ear to her back to hear her breath, because their breathing in chorus allowed him to sleep. When he was four years old, five or six. Not when he was thirteen. More than halfway to being a man. They were born to grow apart, as all siblings were.

Anna chided herself to not worry about it. She'd made so much progress. Had become her own person. In two years she'd leave the state sanitarium, with a diploma to boot. She'd be healthy, Dr. Emmett promised her this, if she kept on with the treatments, if she ate enough and absorbed ample vitamin D and kept her spirits up. A sunken heart could ruin someone's health as fast as any physical ailment. Anna didn't need Dr. Emmett to tell her that.

It was then, after her family left, trying to sleep on a humid mid-September night, that Anna noticed the girl in the bunk across the aisle. The new girl, uneasy in her sleep.

She turned with a sigh, the girl, lifted her knees to lie prone. Her blankets fell. That was when Anna noticed the panties she wore, white cotton and lace, no cheap things, and certainly not wool ones like the home issued. This girl was different. She didn't look sickly like the others. Neither skinny nor fat. But ruddy. A rumor had spread in the bathing room that this girl had been made pregnant by her cousin and that was why she was here. In protective custody.

Anna knew she should roll away and grant the new girl some privacy. The rumors should have been violation enough. But Anna inched her vision from the girl's knee to a bulb of thigh. And then the white. She stared dead center at the white, at what was there, like she could tell if the girl really was pregnant.

The girl was young, maybe twelve. Anna bet she was pretty. Too bad she ended up here.

She moaned and rolled so one leg fell and the other rose. Anna should have told Methfessel about the new girl moaning, just to shut her up, if nothing else. And there might be something wrong. Anna should say something, but she'd wait to see what was wrong first. A spot appeared on the white. Anna saw. The spot grew a little and showed red. It was blood.

A nurse there suddenly. "Anna!" Methfessel hissed. "Shame."

Anna turned away and pulled the blanket over herself and curled to the wall. Glanced back to see Nurse Methfessel change the girl's bandage. How she pulled off the old ones, that cotton gauze with a tract of blood cannoning down the center.

Anna was ashamed. For the both of them, because of what she'd seen. What a strange thing to feel.

It wasn't so hard for Karel to forget the anarchists after Emil Braun was beaten at the Santa Philomena and confined to his bed. Karel had the ballplayers.

Ballplayers who lined the dugout steps to slander jokes out the sides of their mouths during games. Who talked quiet and laughed loud, shared from the hip bottle one of them doubtlessly had. Who couldn't wait to hear the mean stories that sprouted anytime they were together. What things the shortstop's sister, the one from St. Joe, would do with a guy if she got one alone a few minutes. How Claude Nethaway couldn't play Saturdays because of religious observance. Who it was that shit in that men's room sink in Hannibal when the roadside cafe ran out of beer, and what maneuvers were required for a guy to perch up there in the first place. And most prominently in July of 1919—this the ballplayers' most side-splitting chatter—how the bride Dwyer came to find out she'd accidentally married a Negro.

It was in all the papers. The girl sued for an annulment once her scandal was discovered. This man Dwyer, it turned out, was of African lineage. He'd fooled everyone for years before his bride revealed his secret. What a joke it became. Not even the fact that the judge threw out her suit for lack of evidence could slow the players' mocking. According to judicial decree, she'd have to stay married to him after all, this Negro Dwyer, which is how they all saw him.

That this was the month of the Interrace Game at Rourke Park played no small role in their orneriness. There was always plenty of talk between the lines during this bout of Northside Negroes v. Southside Bohunks. Now the white team wouldn't let up about bride Dwyer. What a shock it must have been to find out she hadn't married a *man* like she thought she had. The ballplayers had laughed about it for a month already and roared louder at the start of the Interrace Game. They'd planned out their barbs weeks in advance and daydreamed how humiliated their black opponents would be.

To their surprise, the Northsiders found the whole thing just as funny as anyone. "Sure enough she took a shock at what she found," they laughed, slapping their gloves. "That girl lucky she lived to tell the tale. Believe that." "Why you suppose it took so long to figure it out? Why didn't she have a clue until her honeymoon night?" The Northsiders howled about how her jaw must have dropped once Dwyer revealed his Negro self. Only on a ballfield would they dare say such things in mixed company. The blacks in their solid grays, the Southsiders in their pinstripes. Both teams with *OMAHA* across their chests in felt patches of either red or black.

Jap Marceau, the Southside third baseman, didn't like how the Northsiders teased back, but it didn't matter. The game went on. The Southsiders shut up about bride Dwyer then and forever. And the less they talked, the louder the black ballplayers from the other dugout became. The game itself was as close as it could get, 2–2 after three frames, but it ate up the hotheads on the Southside how grievously they'd misplayed the shit talking.

Karel and his friends leaned into the rail at the end of the dugout during the game. Rourke Park held seven thousand people when packed. If it wasn't for Karel's status with the team they'd have been stuck out in the grass beyond the outfield fences, straining to see each pitch. In the dugout they could see everything. Karel rose to the rail to note the weather, to tilt his cap and check out the clouds, the flags, to decode which way the wind blew, if it swirled, if there was a glare that could conspire against an outfielder. Karel in his pinstriped whites and black-brimmed cap. He went through his routine just for fun, since he was a spectator, the same as the masses beyond the fence and in the grandstands. The Interrace Game always attracted attention, and even more so this year, after the riots in Chicago and Washington, DC, after so many doughboys came back to find their slaughterhouse jobs had been filled by blacks. And nothing had been done about that. Karel checked the grandstands, all white. In the bowl beyond the outfield fence it was a different story, where a section for black spectators took hold from left field alley to right. Beyond that, streetcar lines ran double time to bring in more and more who couldn't even get into the park, folks who followed the game by trying to decode uprisings in the crowd, from the section the cheering or groaning was coming from. Karel fix-ated on the crowd. He faced the wrong way when a foul ball lined over his head, spun just in time to see a blur sail by and peg a man in the shoulder. Karel knew better than to not pay attention, but this was his first Interrace Game, his first Fourth of July really, out free in the city.

The rest of his family had gone to the country. His father and sisters, even Maria, to visit Anna. Anna had been gone a long time by then, over a year. Karel had visited only once. The grounds were kept nice enough up there, he remembered, and had been told. Shady and cool. Croquet was played evenings. There was a lobby with fine furniture and books. A sweeping veranda with ceiling fans churning. Five-course meals were served to visiting families on Thanksgiving, Christmas, and Easter. Even that night there would be a fireworks display, which was why the rest of Karel's family was there. No matter how pleasant the grounds were, Karel acted sour. His sister ignored him the one time he visited her, wouldn't hardly say a word to him, only the required cour-tesies, which was worse than saying nothing. He refused to go again because of the way Anna treated him.

Karel spent all his time on the ballpark, or tagging along with ball-players after a game. Since Herr Miihlstein and Frau Eigler visited Anna in the countryside most weekends, Karel was left to spend his time in Southside saloons. He became one of the ballplayers that summer, truly. He was fourteen and had grown into a tall, loping creature. If he wasn't running, he tripped over his feet, so he tried to be running all the time. The ballplayers commended his hustle. He liked that. Even his friends belonged by then. This was the summer Jimmy Mac spent mornings at a boxing gymnasium to learn what it meant to be River Ward Irish. His hands grew thick from swelling, his shoulders and neck and forearms too. He talked all the time about how Jack Dempsey was going to be the new champ once he got his shot. This was the summer Alfred squared off. His shoulders grew. His hips, mercifully, slimmed. Even though his father couldn't come to see him—Emil Braun was laid up at home from the beating he took at the Santa Philomena, and might be forever—it gave Alfred more than a bit of pride to man second base for the junior squad, and to do it well. He could move his feet now. He could dance the bag to bring the ball around the horn. All three boys fit at the end of the Southside dugout. They belonged.

As the game moved into the late innings, both teams struggled to take advantage of good fortune. The Southsiders failed to score in the fifth even after the black hurler walked the leadoff man. The Northsiders rapped into a double play with the bases loaded to end the top of the sixth.

The game itself was tight, but that wasn't the worst of it. The blacks carried on about bride Dwyer. "Didn't she know her man's secret before she felt what he was packing?" "Judge shoulda took mercy on the poor woman." "She'll never be the same." Their second baseman worked his mouth relentless. It changed how Karel saw an infielder in the ready position, how the man let his arm dangle crudely between his thighs. Down the Southside dugout, faces lengthened as the ballplayers watched and heard what the Northsiders jibed them with. "No joke she sued. Sore as she'd be, who'd blame her?" That second baseman jawing. Fowler was his name, a small light-skinned man. Karel wished the man would stop talking. Jimmie Collins, a skinny man with jug ears who managed the Southside team, rose to the lip of the dugout and shouted, "Shut up now about that. We've heard plenty." It only made things worse. "What's that, Jim?" Fowler asked. "Now, she wasn't *your* daughter, was she? That'd be an awful shame."

The Southsiders would have to win the game. That was the only way about it.

They went up swinging for homers. They crashed into second base as hard as they could. They blistered the knuckles of the blacks with inside fastballs. But the blacks could play this game too and give as good as they got. They could blister a white's knuckles if they wanted, out there afield in Rourke Park, this game their yearly chance to bean a white in the back, or come in sliding with spikes high and get away with the aggression. When Jap went hard into second on a steal attempt and nearly spiked Fowler, Fowler tried to land a punch on Jap, but the ump wouldn't have it. "That's the end of it," the ump warned, a finger up in Fowler's face. "I'll call the game off if the rough stuff don't stop."

Jap was nearly forty. He'd played a dozen seasons in the minors and was dropping back now, after he'd been cut from a B league team that summer. He was small and had dark, bushy eyebrows, a swollen pug nose that made him look like a fighter. He wouldn't ease up. The Northsiders wouldn't either. That's why everyone prized this tradition the whole year over. It was their one chance. It was sanctioned. Whatever violence came.

It wasn't until the eighth that the whites broke through. Bill Sutez was on third after a double and an error when Ducky brought him home with a sacrifice fly to left. The score was 3–2 in favor of the Southside going into the final frame. "We're almost there," Karel said. They didn't dare relax as the Southside took the field. They would shut up those boys from the Northside. They'd earned this.

Still, as the first batter struck out on four pitches and the second batter popped to third, you couldn't blame any of those Southsiders if they eased up in the field. Only that Northside second baseman stood in their way.

Fowler worked his jaw as he stepped in the box left-handed. He was short and scrawny, not much bigger than Alfred, so the Southside outfielders snuck closer to urge on their pitcher, Ralph Snyder. Ralph looked like he should have been working a broom in a sawmill instead of trying to get the last out in a game like this. Unremarkable in his uniform, thin and grubby, his soiled jersey flagged out over his belt in back. Tobacco juice dripped off his chin as he leaned in for the sign Ducky Sutez put down. But Ralph had value—a side-arm lefty who threw junk and wasn't afraid of anyone. He went right after the Northsider, throwing a fastball for strike one, then a curve for strike two. Even as Fowler took the first two offerings, he still ran his mouth. The next pitch from Ralph was hard, up and in, to knock Fowler off the plate and change his eyes, and was followed by a breaking ball down and away in the dirt. Fowler didn't flinch. "Don't waste nothing on me. Bring it here," he said, pointing to the middle of the plate with his bat. With the count even, Ralph would come back over the plate. Everyone knew this. Fowler didn't have much power, but he was fast. Walking him was out of the question.

Ralph didn't exactly look fresh out there on the mound, but he had enough left to pound three more fastballs on the outside half that Fowler could only spoil. All Fowler could do was hold the count even. Out in the bowl beyond the outfield fence, all the black folks cheered him on. He was their only hope, that Fowler. He had to keep the game going. It didn't look like he had much chance, but he spit into his hands and stepped back in anyway. He choked up on the bat and jumped on the next pitch, a fastball that straightened out on Ralph and stayed up. Fowler got into it. This the only time he stopped talking, stumbling out of the box, head down, just running, not even seeing as the ball rocketed over Bill Sutez into the right field corner. They'd played him to hit the other way, not believing he could pull a fastball, but that was exactly what he did. He cranked it into the corner. He was off to the races.

. Karel jumped to the top step of the dugout—they all did—to see the ball skip to the fence and carom into foul ground. Fowler was already around first, chugging to second, running hard, headed for third the whole way. He should stop at third. But the way this guy swaggered, the way he talked, Karel knew the play wouldn't end until Fowler scored or was put out. And the ball was stuck in the corner. Bill Sutez was botching the play. By the time Bill found the ball he'd overrun it, and then fumbled it, and then launched wildly to the infield. It was all Jap Marceau could do to knock the ball down as Fowler turned third. The ball squiggled from Jap, spinning in the dirt not far away, but far enough. Fowler would tie the game.

Everyone saw what happened next. How Ducky, catcher's mask at his side, prowled up the line from home plate. There was no throw coming, but Ducky blocked the plate anyway. As Fowler started to strut, knowing he'd score, Ducky put a shoulder into him. Fowler didn't see it coming. Ducky dropped him to the chalk. The guy's legs still kicking as he hit the ground. By then Jap had the ball raised to his ear and let fly. Ducky took the honors himself and tagged Fowler, the black, as he still lay there in the dirt.

"Ducky did that on purpose, didn't he?" Jimmy said. "Jeez. I'd say he did."

They all looked to the ump for a ruling, the air gone from the field. He took his time giving one, thinking things through as Fowler turned in the dust to see. The umpire squeezed a fist near his chest. Fowler was out. It was over.

It was the wrong call, wasn't it, but who was to say? The ump, surely, and he said out. Now the ump was running off the field. It was over. The Northside manager chased after to beg a fair ruling, but it was no use. Once the ump crossed outside the foul line, the manager couldn't grab his arm to slow him down. Once the ump made it to the grandstand, with the other stunned thousands, the manager couldn't even quarrel, for then the ump was a white man.

The ballplayers remained on the field, all out of the dugouts, palms up in question, unsure what to do. It wasn't fair. Nobody was sure if the game was really over.

"Three outs," Jap screamed, throwing his glove into the air. "That's all you get!"

The Northsiders weren't convinced. "You can't do that. You can't knock a guy out like that."

"Sure can. He did it, didn't he?" "Would of been an inside-the-parker otherwise. Not our fault your guy don't look where he's going."

Both teams pressed together, one half against the other on the spot where Fowler had been flattened. The ballplayers were all over each other, trying to break up the fight or instigate, Karel couldn't tell, the crowd on their feet shouting, no longer stunned, louder than they'd been during the game now that there was brawling. Alfred and Jimmy Mac screamed from the dugout too, flinging anything at hand out to the field. Paper cups, gloves, bats, the pine tar rag.

Fowler limped in the direction of his side's bench, shaking out his legs as he went. There was something strange in how Fowler walked. He was in no hurry. He wasn't agitated as he went down the steps to grab his mitt from under the bench then spun to the field. He pulled something from his mitt—a razor—and headed back to get Ducky.

"Shit," the blacks shouted, backing out of the scrum as they saw. "You getting it now."

Most Southsiders ran back to the dugout or scrambled to the outfield grass to watch. Fowler said he'd kill the guy who took a cheap shot. He held up the razor so sunlight caught the blade. He said he'd be happy to skin that thieving catcher if the thieving catcher wasn't too chicken. "That's fine," Ducky shouted. "I'd like to see you try."

Only a few players remained on the spot—Fowler and his shortstop, Ducky and his brother. Fowler and the Sutez brothers jawed, but nobody moved. The realization of what they were headed for dropped its weight over them. There was a sort of emptiness. Fowler looked like he wanted to put the razor back but couldn't. He had to hold out the blade and explain his anger with more anger. He had to hold a razor to a white man's throat, because that's what had started.

Karel was out on the grass. He didn't know why. Just found himself closer and closer to what would happen. He'd gone headlong and there was no reason, standing right next to the Sutez brothers. He peeked around and saw the blade. Fowler noticed him, the boy. Fowler stopped arguing to stare at Karel, to look him straight in the eye. Karel in his Southside uniform. Did they know each other? Was Fowler one of them he'd met at Josh Joseph's funeral? Josh in his grays inside the coffin. Was Fowler the ballplayer who joked around with the boys?

How should Karel know? Fowler was nobody, out there holding a razor up to a man.

"Are you crazy? Put that thing down!" The Northside manager ran up to Fowler. He snatched the razor away and pushed Fowler and the others to their bench. "Going to get yourself killed! Your teammates too!"

They all came out of it then. The game was over.

Joe Meinhof spotted the boys after. "What were you doing on the field, Karel? Did you get a piece of the action? Is that what you were after?"

The boys laughed. "He'd of liked to," Jimmy said. "They had it coming."

"Pulling a razor? What in the world."

Along with thousands of others they waited outside the park for a streetcar. They'd be stuck awhile in traffic. A barricade had been erected to ease the passage of black spectators and their team back to the Northside, with a police escort the whole way—so why not feel good for a while if you had to wait? Why not shout? Why not taunt those on the other side of the barricade?

Joe Meinhof chatted about the game and other things. He was a captain with the machine now. The delight of his position showed in his posture and how he combed his hair back over his head with a bump of pompadour. He wore an expensive suit, with a green silk tie and handkerchief, with shined dress shoes. A small man, short in height and slight in build, he wasn't much larger than the boys. "I been trying to spot you guys," he said. "No use pretending. I got something to tell you." Karel didn't pay attention. Meinhof was weird and uneasy. Karel didn't like him, even if there was something about the man now. Some gravity.

Karel was lonely in that crowd squirming with glee. The scrum didn't bring him the happiness it should have—not since he'd walked out on the field. People recognized him. Some of them slapped his back and congratulated him for being so brave, facing down that Fowler with his razor. Others despised Karel for being stupid, thinking they knew what was going on, that he'd moved only dumbfounded, following his eyes. But how could anyone know what went on inside Karel? He didn't know himself. It was embarrassing to have strangers wonder if he was stupid, brave, whatever. Nobody should think about him at all. How the game ended was unfair anyway. Ducky had cheated. Fowler should have been awarded the run and the game resumed. Karel knew that. Nobody except black people seemed to care that the result was fraudulent. This bothered Karel too. He thought about Josh Joseph and the ball Josh gave him and insisted he keep, which was in his back pocket right then. The baseball with shoe polish rubbed in its hide.

"Listen," Meinhof said. "No trolley is coming, not in this mess. Let's walk. My place isn't far. I got something to eat."

Sure, the boys agreed. They went along. Karel didn't have anywhere else to go, nothing better to do. He went along.

✳

241

The walls of Joe Meinhof's room were plastered with posters he filched from around the Ward. Advertisements for wrestling matches from years ago, menus from places he ate at, ads for women's athletic clothing, for Norma Talmadge movies, for comic operettas. There were doodles Joe penciled in lunchrooms and Happy Hooligan cartoon strips he tore from the *World-Herald*. The papers were yellow and curled at the edges, this fossil record of things that caught his eye. Joe layered posters and clippings over each other, three or four deep.

He sat on his cot to appraise the collage, the boys there with him. Karel watched without interrupting, as if Joe was a great artist at work. He spun paste in a cracked ceramic bowl, dropped ashes into the mixture from his cigarette, to affix a poster from the Interrace Game.

"There's beer," he said, remembering the boys. They were thirsty. Joe rattled in his cabinets and came back with some crackers and sardines. He put more beers on ice then started talking. It was a hot day. The boys wouldn't mind listening, would they, not with cold beer and a breeze lifting the drapes? Joe told how he and his half-brother Charlie had to run from their town. They grew up in a religious collective in the central part of the state before Joe got them kicked off the farm. He'd looked at the neighbor's wife taking a swim in a pond. He snuck up a mulberry tree and watched as her dress dropped. She pinned her hair, waded in, then floated on the surface. There was no mystery why Joe did what he did. "I was nineteen years old. I reached in my trousers. So what? What I didn't notice was that the neighbor was there too. He saw what I was doing and heaved this stone into the pond to stop me. Splash! I nearly fell out of the tree." Over the next week the man told half the county about Joe touching himself. It wasn't the first time Joe got in trouble for something like this. He and Charlie often snuck into town to see girls dance when tent shows came through, on nights they were supposed to stay out with the cattle. The herd could fend for itself as far as they were concerned. When Joe's mother heard, she packed bags for both Joe and Charlie and locked them out of the house.

Kings of Broken Things

"It isn't so bad here like it was out there, is it, boys?" Joe asked. "If you know the right folks here, you got a chance at least."

It was pleasant enough in Joe's room. Outside, people shopped from a merchant who'd set up there. Joe leaned out the window to see. "But I got to say, things are getting worse off than they were before. There's all sorts of rumors now about what's going on. As a man who'd know, boys, I'll tell you it's true."

"Sure," Jimmy agreed. "A guy hardly goes out anymore unless he's looking for trouble."

"You can't trust nobody," Alfred said. "I hear gunshots all the time. Warning shots."

"The city commissioners are coming after us, that's why," Joe said. He went to the kitchen and took a drink of cloudy liquor from a bottle. "The Morals Squad? Ha! All they do is make people suffer. You boys know. You get around more than most, I bet. Fighting all over at night. In tenements. In Jobbers Canyon. Clandish is a ghost town. You don't hardly risk going outside. That's just what those reformers want."

The boys became drunk.

"Those new cops ain't got a clue."

"We had it good before, didn't we? And didn't even know it."

"Sure we did."

"Something bad's going to happen," Karel said.

The others stared at him. He hadn't said anything since they'd come to Joe's room. He'd sat quiet in a corner; now that he spoke up it sounded like shouting.

"You're right," Joe said. He passed the bottle to Karel. "Something bad's happening now. There's the rapes. A few a day, yeah. It's in the dailies. It's the *Schwarzers* that do it. They filled the packing plants during the war and now we can't get rid of them. I don't know what the owners wanted blackies for in the first place. Nobody wants scabs around."

"We know that," Karel said. He took a drink.

243

"Some of the time they aren't even blacks that do this, yeah, but some white guy with cork soot rubbed into his skin." Joe laughed. "I heard about a few guys who did it. If you boys are interested. Rub on a black face and you can put it to a girl. You can really abuse her and get away with it because it's a blackie they'll be looking for."

"That's a joke, yeah?"

"A guy doesn't even think twice anymore, boys, not about that kind of stuff."

"Maybe all those blackies would think twice if the cops did the job like they used to."

"They're just strange about it," Joe lamented. He held the neck of the bottle with both his knobby hands. "If you cower in a room like we are, like cockroaches, the cops might leave you alone with a beer. But they shut down all the *Vereine* and beer gardens. Even Krug Park is different. There's nowhere to dance. Nowhere to hear singing while you drink. Nowhere for a whole family to eat on the Ward where they know they'll be safe. Clandish is a worse place to live, yeah. Maybe that's their aim. We can't live like we did. That's what they wanted."

They drank into the night before Karel left. It was easy to drink with Joe. He had good stories and didn't ask for anything in return, like some men did, like a boy always had to fear when a hard-drinking man asked for company in his room. Joe wasn't like that. He knew jokes boys liked; he talked to them about what plagued their city, like they were men; he didn't act like he was better than them, or make fun; he didn't make them drink too fast, like the ballplayers did when Karel went to a speakeasy with the team, and then laugh when he was sick in the alleyway. Joe made sure the boys ate as they drank and sat up straight to let out their belches when the pressure built. Joe even apologized for what happened to Emil Braun at the Santa Philomena, and Alfred appreciated that, said it wasn't Joe's fault, so forget it, Alfred heard from everybody how his father had it coming. It would have been easy to drink all night, but Joe didn't allow that either. He sent them home when it was time to stop.

"Look here," he said. "Don't go straight home, okay? Walk around a little. Let the stink blow off you a bit. Trust me."

Karel wasn't going home anyway. He didn't stay at the Eigler house more than a few nights a week. There was a boys' dormitory he found west of Thirteenth Street, not in the tenements but close to there. The building looked like a barn, maybe it was once, with broad boards painted red and an open loft upstairs. Two rows of beds lined the walls. Union Pacific had built the home for its workers, but the machine, it was said, owned the building now and kept it for street kids. Any boy could find a bed here, and breakfast. There was often work to be had too. Machine lieutenants stopped in around suppertime. Karel recognized some of them, those who'd been buddies with Jake Strauss when Jake was still around. (Sometimes Joe Meinhof was there poking around, although Karel hid under his blanket if he saw Joe. Karel didn't want to be seen by Joe in the dorming house.) "Want some fun? There's money in it too," the lieutenants said. "Sure you do. It's easy. Do what comes natural to a boy." They flipped coins to the boys to show they were legit. Karel didn't know what the work was.

Before the dorming house opened it wasn't so easy for a kid out on his own. In summertime there were doorways a boy could lean in, or managers of lunch counters who didn't mind if a kid laid his head on a tabletop so long as he cleared out for the rush. Winter was more complicated. A boy could rent a man's bed during the day if that man worked a day shift, but that cost money. A boy might even stay home a few days if he forgot why this was his worst option.

Karel stuck to the quiet end of the loft. At the other end boys played cards or threw dice or learned to curse in a dozen languages. All of them smoked corncob pipes, another amenity the house provided. Those boys stayed up all night talking from nicotine. The misfit boys of Clandish. But Karel came here to sleep. At home in the Eigler attic he couldn't find peace. After Anna was taken away, Miihlstein rehung many of the wire monstrosities she'd made. In the dark Karel could see their silhouettes hang, the jagged legs of a wire elephant, the gaping hole among the cords of a raven's middle. He couldn't stand to be haunted.

Karel wished the feeling he had on the ballfield could somehow follow him home, but it couldn't. There was too much weight in familiar places. The stuff about his mom he didn't want to believe. What happened with Braun and, not long after, Jake being run out of town in disgrace, a thug, a thief, good riddance. And Anna.

Karel switched on a lamp to take off his shoes and tuck them under the mattress. The light might annoy those around him. They could roll over and grumble for all he cared. They could say, "Oh, you again." He'd tell them to fuck off.

Karel sat in the lamplight. That was all. The room looked strange to him, the way shadows took hold in corners, under beds, in the airy loft above him where the rafters crossed. The room reminded Karel of when he'd visited Anna at the state home. She too slept in a hall like this one. The two rows of beds. All strangers to one another, which made them compatriots in a way. It was always lonely to fall asleep in a row of beds, particularly if you were bracketed by silent neighbors. If he couldn't hear his breathing, Karel feared that the boy next to him had died in the night, what he'd feared years before when he shared a bed with Anna, when he fell asleep to her delicate snore but awoke to silence, her snoring stopped. The terror of that.

Karel would stay up late and stare into the rafters. He'd listen to the cardplayers. This night he'd leave the light on.

S omething wicked must have come over Tom Dennison after they lost the vote. He always hated losing—he'd gone red-faced and toppled faro tables in Denver as a young man when he lost at cards— and was even worse as he aged. Losing left him speechless. He had no idea what to tell Frank and the others about Jim Dahlman and the whole coalition falling. That this was expected? That there was nothing he could have done to change things? Why people voted like they did wasn't always something Tom could explain. Maybe it rained too much that spring, or too little. Maybe it was too cold for their liking, or too hot. Maybe they lost a job or found out their wife was cheating or their in-laws wanted to move into the spare room or their boss was a prick. Men had this effective weapon—the vote—but rarely understood how to use it. Tom took advantage of this when he could, but that didn't mean he could say why people voted one way or another. The only hard fact of the matter was that they did. This was shown in numbers. The reform slate carried six of seven spots on the board. Tom's Square Seven took only one.

Things would change in Omaha. There would be upheaval in city hall, in the police department, on the bench. Almost every seat of control they had was in disarray.

Frank didn't say much when Tom saw him on election night. Frank fingered the foil tops of unopened champagne bottles and flipped his class ring from one finger to another. He barely even nodded when Tom said hello, and Tom knew enough not to push against the mood of his benefactor. Frank could look pure evil when mad, in his finely tailored suits, his unamused, aristocratic glower. Tom had clashed with Jay Gould before and could attest that Gould had nothing on Frank.

Of course, it was Billy who broke the silence—"We lost. What's to say about it?" Frank shrugged. "Isn't that what we pay you for, Billy? To talk?"

Tom admitted that he couldn't make heads or tails of losing. "Give me a week," he said. "I'll decide what to do."

He paced the brick drive outside his house that week, thinking. Bullet straight and tree lined, the drive gave the impression of something extraordinary as his house slipped into view. The house was wood framed with finishes of granite at certain edges, the cellar and foundation limestone, highlights of plaster festoons above the front door. Off the second-floor bedrooms were balconies as wide as the patios below, where tiered gardens overlooked the industrial valley. There were pergolas holding grapevines, arbors abloom with creeping red ivy. Everything here was made for looking at, for admiring, like it was unreachable, a mirage. Years before, an enemy left a bomb on Tom's doorstep. An ingenious design, the bomb, a simple wooden crate with six sticks of dynamite and a pistol inside. A string was tacked to the porch and connected to the trigger of the pistol. If someone had lifted the box—Tom's wife or daughter—the whole house would have been blasted clean off the earth, his wife and daughter too. Frances found the crate. A smart girl, she didn't touch anything. Tom noticed the trip wire when she brought him to see. He had police dismantle the device. After that Tom closed the grounds. Bodyguards were kept outside around the clock. You had to be a close friend, a known friend, if there was such a thing, or else you couldn't get close. The bomb changed things. That was when Tom put a machine gun across his lap in the car. That was when everything here, all this bounty he'd won, started being lonely.

He wouldn't give up what he'd earned. No matter if it was lonely. He wouldn't go out on a loss. The mere idea drove him nuts. He could only think of one thing: how to get back what was taken from him.

Tom knew it was big trouble when the people elected men like Ed Smith, a self-righteous prick who messed up deals. Ed Smith wanted to clean out the police department and city hall, and that meant firing people. It meant taking benefits away from folks who were used to having them. Jobs, pensions, kickbacks. Arrangements everyone was used to. As far as Tom was concerned, Ed Smith and his cronies were the greedy ones. Greedy for laws. They wanted to take over the River Ward because they didn't like what happened here—but already there were so many laws that a man was either a lawbreaker or a hypocrite. Tom hated the reformers. Any guy might do bad things, just as all males of the species did, but a real man owned up to his sin. That was the difference.

Almost overnight Mayor Smith had cops enforcing every little law to the extreme. Arresting the jobless for vagrancy, putting people in jail for traffic violations. His idea was to show how much control the police had over all crime in the city, but it didn't work that way. Folks didn't trust the police now. Nobody ever trusted them, but this was different. At least with a cop who worked for Tom, a guy knew where he stood. With one of Smith's cops you had no clue what to expect. And still there was crime. There weren't enough police west of the Mississippi to close all the speakeasies on the River Ward, because there was demand for them. If one closed, nine more opened before the kegs from the first were axed in the gutter. And there was still rape. Still murder. The stuff that really made folks worry. A cop might clip you for jaywalking and toss you behind bars. It was a little much for jaywalking, but you got caught. Fine. Then you read in the paper how four girls were attacked by blackies the week before and the police had no leads, no arrests had been made. That made folks think. What if the police didn't worry so much about jaywalkers? What if they didn't have fifteen men watching traffic and another forty shutting down neighborhood bartenders? Maybe then the cops could catch a rapist.

Tom had to save the city from its reformers. He'd ruin things for Ed Smith. For any and all of those damn reformers. Those damn hypocrites.

Joe Meinhof set it up with some boys who could cause trouble. Tom was going to turn them loose.

"I wouldn't want to be Ed Smith, I'll tell you that much," Meinhof said. "There's soldiers coming home from France, and already they're not happy. Lots of folks ain't happy. Their jobs been filled by blacks. We're doing something about it. Ed Smith and his cronies won't do shit."

"I think you're right," Tom muttered. "Let the bastards have it their way for a while. Then they'll be glad to see us back."

Tom didn't know if boys needed encouragement to do bad things in the first place. This might be their natural state. To go out and destroy property. To fight a cop. To paint their faces and stick it to a girl. The whole country was different after the war. They were all changed. In particular those boys who grew up knowing nothing but war, mustard gas, tanks, biplanes with machine guns strapped to the wings; boys who couldn't remember anything else but bad feelings let loose and fighting like fighting was the only thing, and how blackies were around to mess things up for the people who were supposed to have the good life.

Maybe it was wrong to take advantage of the circumstances. Who's to say?

Tom saw how it was different for these kids. Billy told him what was going on. What a success the dorming house was, how the boys Joe Meinhof kept there were abler than most lieutenants. Tom didn't believe it at first but it was true. Those kids did what you told them. It was glorious and simple. A thing of beauty.

E vie had plenty of friends who did themselves in. Girls from the neighborhood who did what they felt they must once the party ended. Dried up. Lonely. States of affairs to be avoided at all costs. But a girl grew older. All folks did, the world over, forever, of course. There was a difference, though. If a girl had strange predilections, her habits led to darkness. If she was used to druggings, to self-abuse, to absorbing men's cruelty in good humor. All this led to one thing.

Evie always swore she wouldn't end up like that. She never worked a big palace, for instance, and had never seen the inside of an opium den. At her lowest she made herself attest to having self-respect, even if she didn't believe she did, another of her habits. She'd never give any love away—she promised this too. She'd keep all the love she had for herself. She wouldn't think like those girls who did away with themselves. Evie had other, greater talents besides the things her body could do. And Jake had left her a thousand-dollar bill whether he'd meant to or not.

She started in on business the summer of 1918, a series of small jobs for girls who owed her a favor, just enough to get by until she could figure out what to do with the thousand. It wasn't that she didn't want the money. Who wouldn't? That much cash could take her anywhere, in theory. But, in reality, the thousand was invalid. Tom Dennison was watching. Jake was still in Omaha then, but they weren't talking and it wouldn't have been worth it to bring this up. Dennison was the only one who could change money like that, so Evie brought the thousand back to him.

He ordered her to sit once she was up in his office. "This won't take a minute," she said, refusing the chair. She plucked the thousand from her handbag and slapped it to the desk. Dennison stared back at her. "What do I want with this?"

"It's yours," she said. "Take it."

"Who gave this to you? Did you steal it?"

"Say I found it. It's yours, so what's the difference? You got it back."

"Don't try to be smart. I know where you got it. Do you think you'll get Jake out of trouble, bringing this to me?" Dennison turned to Billy Nesselhous. "I'm not sure who's buying off who anymore."

Evie looked down at the chair where he'd wanted her to sit. Tiny, low to the floor, a chair for a child. These men played such games, always picking at and belittling each other. No wonder they trusted no one. Thugs lined the walls. They made a point to stand behind her, to make her want to sit. Evie felt their eyes where her dress clung to her hips.

"What does Jake want you to do?" Dennison asked. "Are you going to marry him?"

"Not a chance. We're through."

Dennison and Billy looked to each other again. Billy shook his head, like he thought she was lying. "Say you don't get married. Then what will you do?"

Evie said she sewed for the girls on her block, which was true. There wasn't much business, but she made do.

"Hmph," he said. That was the end. A man hmphing himself was all. She didn't need to be there for that. Evie turned to walk away, but Dennison stopped her.

"You get ten percent," he said. "A finder's fee."

On the table was a hundred dollars in small bills. "I'll set you up with a woman. She makes dresses and she's got a lot of business. More than she can handle. If you're being straight with me, you'll get the excess."

Evie couldn't figure why he was helping her. "Is it Jake?" she asked. "Is that why?"

"Don't go around thinking I owe you anything, or you me. That's all. Don't talk to him again and we'll be square. You understand?"

Evie didn't care. "Why would I want to see that rube again?"

She regretted putting it like that, like she really had been conning Jake, like she'd tricked him into thinking the love she offered was anything but real. She wasn't bothered for long, though. She counted the hundred and made the deal. She'd be set up fat.

She didn't even wait a day before meeting the dressmaker, a lady entrepreneur who could teach Evie how to deal with merchants, how to keep accounts, how to make deadbeats pay. Evie had dozens of things to ask, and there were a thousand more she'd learn along the way. It was one thing to sew for yourself, to create your own fashions, and quite another to impose an intelligent design on an unsuspecting client. The dressmaker wore a demure black suit that fit over her smoothly. She was happy to tell what she knew about the trade and the craft. Evie was surprised by this kindness. In every trade she'd trafficked before, a girl tried her hardest to keep a fresher face out of the game, to reduce competition. There were mean tricks all girls were trained in from birth. It wasn't so hard to make a girl feel bad about herself if that was what you were after. But the dressmaker wasn't like this. She advised Evie to never let a man hold her money if she could avoid it, especially not a bank, where the regulations were designed to rid a businesswoman of what was deemed her excess capital. The dressmaker sounded persecuted and crass at times, but Evie saw how this was necessary. This woman was a success; she'd become one by keeping the fact of her success a secret. Nobody could take from her what they didn't know she had. From the outside it looked like she kept a shabby shop, with gaps in the window glazing, a small showroom where a client undressed in the open. To an outsider her company was nothing to be jealous of. It brought in cash all the same. A small but dedicated clientele was convinced of the dressmaker's vitality. Quality was high. This was enough.

"Maybe you're not such a nice woman at heart," the lady told Evie. "But you'll be all right. It was smart going to Tom Dennison. You did well."

Evie was busy with her own shop before long, making dresses, slips, camisoles, and scarves for working girls. So maybe it didn't matter when she heard that Jake skipped town. She accepted his leaving. Keeping her end of the deal with Dennison would be easier if Jake was gone. As Evie saw it, she and Jake were the separate legs of an X. As one's fortune rose, the other's fell. While rumors spread about Jake and the scandal he'd brought on himself, Evie set up shop out of her rooms on Capitol Avenue and was making a killing.

Her main room was cleared of the lounging furniture. The dimensions redesigned with new purpose, the room made longer. Evie had a box couch and small table constructed at the window, one with only room enough for her. Curtains lined the couch so she could block out the workroom—something she almost never did—to sit quietly alone at the open window, to look down at the street. If she was home, she might as well be working. Evie ate breakfast at the nook table, but that was all. Otherwise, she indulged her vocation. The old worktable was preserved, of course, and the wire dummy acquired fresh cousins to accommodate the several garments Evie worked on at a time. She bought a new treadle sewing machine now that she had room for one, and kept it at the center of her rooms, its oiled wood and iron pedal. Her mother had owned something similar, so Evie knew how to make it work. Around her bed in the other room, she stored bolts of fabric and bins filled with sequins and beads.

To look at her rooms one might have believed it was a lonesome life Evie lived. (Why, she wondered, didn't anyone have such thoughts about her loneliness when she was a kept woman?) But her rooms were always busy those days. With madams coming in to place orders for their girls, and the girls trying on dresses or stopping in to see how the work came along, to escape their own petty cell in a palace. To enter a workshop was no idle thing for these girls. Here they were allowed to linger and observe craft coming together, instead of being spritzed endlessly with perfume, or popping champagne corks, or the nonstop washing and checking of their bodies by the state examiner. To sit and gossip was a fine thing. To be treated like a lady.

The girls teased Evie about the money she must be bringing in. They knew what expenses the madam passed on to them for garments, which was never the same as Evie charged, but she still made plenty. "With what kale you got, why don't you go see some far-off corner of the globe?" "Paris." "An island someplace." "Shit. Even a day in Kansas City got to be better than sitting around here."

"Why not get with a family?" one girl always asked. A new girl, or an old one, ones on adjacent points of a cycle. "Have some babies. Let me live with you! Ha! I'd be your kid."

"That isn't for me," Evie replied. "I like it like this."

"What about your mother then? Send for her."

Evie told how her mother had taught her all about needlework and the making of clothes. The girls thought it would be a great thing to send for her if she was poor. To enjoy the profits and help with the work. It wasn't like that, Evie explained. "My mother couldn't get along here. There's one spot in Topeka she's been allowed to live her whole life, and that's where she'd want to stay." Evie didn't know if what she said about her mother's wishes was entirely true. She didn't want to find out what her mother would think of all this, the way Evie lived. That was all.

The girls asked about Jake.

In a way those girls admired Evie for what happened. It was said that Jake had been bamboozled by her, that he was done in because of the things his girl demanded. That poor, bewitched boy—a wicked, conniving woman was behind it all. If this was true, the girls said, good for her. "If a man can't give what's needed then he gets what he gets."

Evie didn't feel that way. It wasn't that Jake didn't give what she demanded; he couldn't accept what she could provide. Not such a small distinction, after all.

He returned to her in late September 1919, on a Wednesday. She'd received a letter from him a few weeks before in which he asked permission to stop by and say hello. He was going to take the Miihlsteins to a carnival on the Ak-Sar-Ben midway, he said, and wouldn't be in Omaha long. By contract, Evie shouldn't have allowed a visit. But she replied without thinking. In a note she dashed off immediately, she told him he could say hello if he was going to be around.

When the day came, Jake arrived early because the kids were gone from the Eigler house when he went to surprise them. "Only Herr Miihlstein was there. Anna's still at that home. Miihlstein didn't know where Karel was. He hardly comes around at all."

His voice was shaking. He was outside in the hallway because she didn't ask him to come in. He explained that he didn't work for Tom Dennison anymore and had just come to visit.

Evie knew Jake was living in Lincoln, something that surprised him, since nobody wrote him there, he said. "There was a lot of talk after you left," she said. "Rumors you'd been run off, or killed for being unfaithful to Dennison, that you'd gone back where you came from, that I gave you syphilis and the both of us were committed to a sanitarium to lose our minds. Folks said you killed a man and ran to Kansas City until the heat wore off. But I got to the bottom of it," Evie said. "Maria Eigler told me the truth."

"The truth?"

"Tom ran you out, didn't he? For you not being who he thought you were."

He laughed at that. "I hoped nobody would know. I lost that thousand-dollar bill and it was all over. Nobody is so dumb they'd forgive that, yeah. Tom let me leave. That's something."

Jake doesn't know, Evie realized. Nobody ever told him that she'd given the thousand back to Dennison, even as they ran him off, and that was what saved his hide.

"Tom's a forgiving man, isn't he?" Evie said.

"A thousand dollars. More than that." Jake's eyes wet thinking of all that money. "Did I ever have so much as all that? Seems impossible now."

At her suggestion they went for a walk. Neither knew how long they'd go or where. He led down to the Flatiron. Reinhold had sent him a letter—*There's one letter,* Evie thought—telling how the big project under the city was nearly done. "The tunnels aren't being used yet," Jake said, "but they're close." They walked without looking at each other. Strolling in half strides, staring at the pavement. He detailed things she didn't really care to know about the tunnels. How permanent lighting was wired in and gravel spread over the bottom of the corridors. A spiral staircase replaced a dumbwaiter from the hotel kitchen. "It's all just piddling now. They don't even dig. Not since last week."

Jake stopped to have a look around. He paced the pavement, led Evie across the street to stare down at the bricks in one spot, then back across to another. Somewhere around here, he explained, was where he struck down Ugo with the backside of a spade.

"Is this the spot?" Evie asked. "Below us? Where we're standing now?"

Jake said he'd know if he were under the surface. He'd remember the bend, the dip in the tunnel floor. But he hadn't been down there since, and it was impossible to tell otherwise.

"Then why say anything? Is this why you came back? To dig up the business with Ugo?"

She saw that Jake was shaking again. "There's no reason," he said. "I wanted to see you. You understand that."

"Come on," Evie said, leading back into downtown. "Where else does the tunnel go?"

They followed along the surface. Around city blocks and buildings, as diagonal as he could navigate the squared city grid, north on Eighteenth Street to Douglas, near bustling Hotel Fontenelle, then down Dodge to Eleventh. They were moving liquor in the tunnels, into hotel kitchens, all the way to the terminus north of Capitol Avenue, where a new red light called the arcade was open for business. The arcade was in an alleyway between two brick buildings where Tom Dennison's infamous Sporting District used to be, years ago, before that was shut down by a previous generation of reformers. Iron gates were posted at each end now, painted red and decorated with lights. There were dozens of cribs, small chambers that held women. Each crib had two areas, an entryway, a cot beyond the divider. A door and window formed the projecting front, the whole thing about six feet high, shorter than Jake. Girls waited in windows to have their shapes appraised by whoever moved along the line. Businessmen over lunch hour, high schoolers skipping class. This was what passed for discreet, even in this reform era, at least in the context of what had gone on so publicly for years down on the river flats.

There was nothing on the river where the flats used to be. Evie knew this. Mud and garbage. All the tents gone. There were the pig iron mills, the river and its spit foam, its blackened tree trunks floating along, gray mud slick across its banks. The tents with girls inside had been replaced by this glittering fantasy. The girls in the arcade had on silk robes and their hair was pinned up. They joked loud like they'd spent the morning drinking. One of them looked familiar to Jake and he said so to Evie. He thought the girl was named Doreen. "The girl in the red dress."

He pointed her out. "Raped in Riverview Park two years ago. Had her fiancé run out on her. I know her."

This girl wore what was supposed to look like a cocktail dress but was really a slip that enabled her to fuck quick. Evie had made it for the girl and knew she wasn't Doreen. This girl, tall and slender, Mary, walked right by the both of them. She had a rigid jaw, a small mouth, narrow eyes. Jake followed her to the gates. "I'm sure it's her," he said.

"It isn't Doreen," Evie said. "It can't be. Doreen killed herself."

A chippie taking her life wasn't news, but Evie remembered how it ended for Doreen. She'd wandered the streets until someone grabbed her and said they'd take care of her. They fed her, bought her some clothes, some liquor, led her down the basement stairs of an opium den. Doreen lasted a year on the flats. That was long enough. She grabbed the exposed circuit wire that ran through her tent and took it in her mouth. A john had just walked in. Lights flickered all along the river before going out, the length of the flats and on Capitol Avenue. Doreen bit into the wire and broke the circuit. She had to be cut loose because her teeth fused to the metal.

"You knew her?" Jake asked.

"We weren't friends. I just heard, that's all. The lights went out one night. If you lived on this block, you heard how that girl was the reason why. Doreen Jungjohann. How's a girl walk around carrying a name like that anyhow?"

Evie asked if Jake had a place to stay. He could head to the Eigler house for the night, he said. Maria would take him. But he didn't angle that way. Evie and him walked the gloaming instead, to the edge of the tenements, to the top of a Little Sicily bluff to see the river at sunset. They circled back north of Dodge, north of Capitol, to the brownstone where Evie lived, close enough to the arcade to hear an electric piano pound out ragtime, keys falling one on top of another in whimsical rhythm. She'd left the lights on in her rooms. The curtains were closed and glowed yellow from the bulbs. Her ears throbbed trying to hear something from the other rooms, some grunt or sigh, if the girls were busy with clients. What she heard was traffic. Pops of motorcars, rhythmic mill pounding, a train whistle in the distance. The building was quiet.

She remembered the last time Jake was up in her rooms, fourteen months before, and how she'd told him off. *You don't understand,* she'd said. *I worked for them too.* It was embarrassing how stupid the two of them were those days.

Evie went up to the bathroom and locked the door. She was crying and didn't want Jake to see. She didn't know what he was here for or what she could give him to make him go away. Through her tears she looked down and saw her hands and really cried. Gouges where she'd slipped with a needle. Her nails unpainted. Calluses spread over her fingers like glaciers. She'd moved on, hadn't she? She was freer to live how she wanted to without worrying what trouble Jake might drag her into. She was doing well. She was making it. Except that she was locked in the bathroom again, and Jake was there outside the door.

He asked her to let him in after a while but she wouldn't.

"Did you miss me?" she asked through the door. "Is that why you came back?" Her voice was soft and halting, her syllables muted because it felt like she was choking.

"Let me in," Jake begged. He slipped his fingers under the door. "What did you do with the money? You could of bailed me out. They would of let me stay. I could of kept my job." He was such a fool. "What did you do with the thousand-dollar bill?"

He didn't leave, but he didn't say more about the money, and that was wise. He was better when he kept his mouth shut.

She'd quit crying a long time before. She calmed down, all that shameful grief out of the way, and she began to think—if he wasn't leaving—what it was she wanted from Jake, if anything.

"Didn't you wonder about that girl Doreen before? How long did you say? Two years since you saw her last. What did you think happened to a girl without a way to take care of herself?"

Jake said he wanted Evie to open the door. He wanted to see her face. To end the waiting.

"Anything you could say would be useless now," she said. "Don't you know I take care of myself? I have my business." Jake said he had no idea. "I make garments for the girls around here. Quite a lot of them too. The girls don't have to go down to the muck anymore and can have nice things to wear. Didn't you wonder how I'd manage to keep up the rent? Didn't you worry if I'd be long gone when you came to knock? Or if some new dick would answer? Or if I'd be out on the street?"

"That's great" was all he could muster. "What you're doing."

Evie didn't need him. She'd figured it out on her own and didn't need some poor yokel to take care of her.

She opened the door and was in the kitchen by the time he realized she'd gone by. She checked the icebox, pulled out some milk and poured a glass for Jake. She poured another for herself and took a bite from a plum.

"Look," she said. "You can't stay here. You're imposing. I don't like it."

He drank the milk in three gulps and set his glass next to the bottle. "I'm not asking to stay."

"I'm not offering either. Yet you're still here."

Evie shouldn't have answered his letter. She shouldn't have let him in, but it was too late to go back on that. He washed the glass in her sink and dried it with a towel. "Look at all this stuff you did around here," he said. "Must have kept a carpenter busy most of a month. New tables. Doors!" He looked so much older now. With a beard, the way his hair was cut short up the sides. How his shoulders were bent and his arms hung lower. He was tan too, his skin dark and cracked where it bowed around his eyes. His nose sunburned.

"I'll be around a few days," he said. "I want to go to the carnival. On Sunday there's supper at Maria's."

"I'm not going to Sunday supper," Evie said.

He pulled out a near-empty billfold to count his money. He couldn't stay long.

The Ak-Sar-Ben carnival was in full swing, its midway congested and loud. Traffic was slowed by meandering farmers on vacation, kids in truck beds, hair full of nits and dust. They wanted to see clowns and have their stomachs drop on a whirl-a-whirl ride, to catch a vaudeville routine and eat caramel apples and laugh at tiki men in grass skirts. They wanted merry-go-rounds, dancing bears, a Ferris wheel. There would be a big parade, theater shows put on nonstop, a coronation ball to crown the new King Ak and his queen. It was a great honor among the hoity-toity to be crowned or have a teenage daughter subjected to the king during the festivities.

Evie took Jake that Wednesday afternoon. She wouldn't hear of a bricklayer spending his few dollars on her, so she bought rock candy and apple cider for the both of them as they cruised the midway. In all the time she'd lived on the River Ward, this was the first time she'd been to the carnival. Both sides of King Ak's Highway were lined with billboards and booths and theaters. A massive dancing pavilion was put up to accommodate those who wanted to try the Skip Fantastic, the latest dance craze, to shimmy and jazz in an unashamed way. Performers worked the crowd for tips. The Byak Headhunter growled at people—a black man with his scalp dyed in blood and a three-inch tuft of hair that stuck up in the middle of his bald head, he pounded the butt of a strange-looking spear to the pavement and took money for the thrill this provided. There were actors dressed up like jesters and clowns, like maidens. Buxom women strolled in bathing suits to promote the show they worked in. There was a man dressed like Bacchus, his cheeks and nose rosy, in leather sandals and what probably doubled as Tarzan's loincloth another year; a man in a red cape and bull's horns who answered to Beelzebub; an old woman dressed as a Southern belle; girls in peasant dirndls and flowery aprons; a man made up like a hobo, trousers torn, a hat with the top punched out, rags wrapped around his feet, who might have been a real hobo, Evie thought later; a man in blackface with ballooned drawers, a minstrel player with a tenor sax. Evie and Jake argued about which show looked most interesting. At first Evie wanted to see Mack Sennett's collection of Bathing Beauties, sportive girls in tank suits and rubber caps, but then she saw a flyer for something called Yankee Doodle Bertha that looked good. They saw neither. Jake argued it was better to stroll the midway and watch oddballs perform for free. There would be more money for food that way. She had enough cash for whatever they wanted to do, but he didn't like the sound of that. "You're cheap," she said. He agreed with a dopey smile, walking with his shoulders back. "Call me old-fashioned. I don't mind."

With two military installations nearby—Forts Crook and Omaha—there were a bunch of soldiers in the crowd. Evie saw them around the year after the Armistice. Doughboys come home. Some loitered along the midway. Husky kids in uniform, long green socks and puffy breeches, like football players lost afield. Some twitched with war neurosis and struggled to keep their eyes open, or shuffled along in painful, halting gaits, like they were slipping on ice. Evie didn't want to think about what doughboys had seen or had done to them over there to make them this way. Bombardments, nerve gas, horses disemboweled on barbed wire, the still-twitching charred grist of a man caught by a flamethrower. There were doughboys who'd been buried alive when the man next to them stepped on a landmine, trapped when four tons of earth thrown up by the explosion landed. Girls heard these things and more from doughboys who came back looking for comfort in a woman—and Evie heard when the girls needed a turn of their own to unburden. A flyboy, crazy-eyed, sun dazed, whose timorous hands curled and shook, forever gripped on the controls of his biplane's yoke and machine-gun trigger. One who skimmed his hands over his face like a preening cat. It was too sad to see them. Most boys cultivated a wish to die in glory rather than become stock clerks or broom boys, and after that, hideous adulthood. Evie had talked to hundreds of them in the dime-a-dance hall she started at and knew how they thought. Boys gave themselves expiration dates too. How many of these suffering doughboys would have gone over if they knew what waited for them was not death in the heat of battle but lost limbs, hand tremors, waking nightmares, begging for buffalo nickels outside a shop where they otherwise might have worked? Those shops where merchants lived mundane lives and were cursed by the young. These same shops that were the envy of old men who knew better.

A doughboy without legs lay on the pavement, struggling to stay upright as he sold souvenirs from the war. Pith helmets were common now that the fighting was over. Doughboys called them Kaiser hats, black Prussian helmets with the spike on top. They brought back thousands of them to keep and to sell. Jake bought one. It wasn't much, only two dollars. He bought it just to destroy it. "With a sledgehammer," he figured. "That would be worth it."

That evening she worked at her table as he made spaghetti for dinner. He had no idea what he was doing and cussed from the kitchen in German, something Evie couldn't help but laugh at, it was so quaint. His German made her think of how he'd asked her to call him old-fashioned at the carnival. It was a strange thing, and amusing, what different people they were now. How it was Jake who suggested they head to Little Sicily, and he who further suggested they stop in at a bakery for pasta and cannoli, and that he cook. "My brother did most of the cooking on the farm," he said. "But what's to it?" The noodles were broken and mushy, and there was too much butter (it sopped into Jake's red beard as he slurped) and too few capers, so he tried to add more, too late. But it was food, and they ate it. There were the cannoli, which couldn't be ruined so long as he didn't drop the package. Besides, Jake redeemed the whole thing as they finished dessert. He uncorked a new bottle. He pointed out that they'd never been on an outing before. The carnival was their first.

"We could have more," he said. "We don't have to. But we could."

He sipped his wine and waited for her to answer. She just hmm'd to him.

I t was in the dailies the next day—the thing that happened to a girl
named Agnes Loebeck in the weeds near Riverview Park. The *Bee*
ran her account of it. A black man stuck a revolver in her sweetheart's
ribs. A black man in a white felt hat robbed the sweetheart, Milton, of
his watch and the sixteen dollars he carried, and the rings Agnes wore.
They didn't have time to fight back. He ordered Milton to go ahead fifty
feet and sit down. Milton did that. Milton sat on a curb to watch what
would happen. The black man dragged Agnes Loebeck into the weeds
by her hair. He had his way. She was nineteen years old.

There was a minor sensation about what happened. That same week
President Wilson had collapsed from exhaustion in Colorado and was
being rushed back to Washington to recuperate. There was speculation
in the papers that the president might die. The Ak-Sar-Ben carnival was
nearing its apex, which was big news in Omaha, with all the visitors in
town and the high-society ball only days away. But there was this other
item in the papers—a blip about what happened to Agnes Loebeck and
her friend Milton as they walked home on Scenic Avenue. Her picture
was in the *Bee*. Short black curls barely covered her ears. Square jaw,
full cheeks when she smiled, dark eyebrows. She wore lipstick. She was
Milton Hoffman's girl. Milton worked in a Nesselhous crew of runners;
most of the boys on Clandish knew him. The article said Milton was a

cripple. This was partly true. He fell out a tree when he was a boy, and the broken bone in his leg never healed right. He walked with a cane.

Milton said the black man stuck a revolver in his ribs and went through his pockets to rob him. Agnes screamed. The black man slapped her with the meat of his hand, knocked her to the ground, covered her mouth. He kept the gun on Milton when he dragged Agnes into a gully. The whole time he kept telling her to shut up. Milton couldn't wholly see what he did to her. The grass was tall. The weeds were thick and yellow. Stalks bent in the breeze, in Riverview Park, up on the bluffs. The black man stopped and looked at Milton before running off. The black man made no effort to hide his face. Agnes confirmed what happened in the weeds was real bad.

Some Union Pacific men came up from the roundhouse they worked in down at a sprawling yard by the river, not far from Riverview Park. It wasn't hard to raise a search party. Not even a week earlier a UP conductor had been murdered out in North Platte in a robbery gone wrong. He was shot dead with a .32 automatic. This was big news in Omaha. The Union Pacific employed over two thousand men here, settled and itinerant, and a similar number across the state. These men took an interest in the murderer being found. It was Leon Darling who murdered the conductor. Darling was a tramp. A black man. His roommates turned him in for the reward. The gun was in his trunk when the railroad detectives found him, a .32 with the same number of bullets missing that had been fired into the conductor. Railroad detectives got a confession out of him. He'd only meant to rob the conductor but lost his nerve in the heat of the moment and fired. The trigger stuck. Three shots fired instead of one. The detectives had Darling up in a jailhouse in Grand Island. A lynching had been planned, if the yard men there could bust in, but it didn't go off.

You can bet those railroad men in Omaha thought of this when they looked for whoever robbed and abused Agnes Loebeck. Practically all the shop workers rushed the bluffs when they heard what happened. They carried crowbars and iron pipes and pieces of lumber. Railroad men rushed the Missouri bluffs from their turntable, work abandoned to find the man who'd held a revolver at a cripple and abused a girl. They ran high-kneed through stands of weeds and fell face-first when the yellow loess dirt gave way. They evaded trees and rattled windows they passed. Once word spread of what happened to Agnes Loebeck, the whole Gibson neighborhood was swarmed by railroad men. They knocked down fences and tore up gardens looking for the one who did it. The girl said she could identify her attacker if they got hold of him. *He isn't a large man, he's short. I think he's a hunchback.* All night they knocked on doors and questioned whoever was inside. Railroad men who kept awls and block tobacco in the sagging bibs of their overalls, who flexed watermelon-sized biceps to carry wrenches, thirty-pound, three-foot wrenches that were their jobs. Some teenage boys from the Southside joined in. The dorming house emptied in a rush, Karel up in front. Once they got over the shock of what the manager was waking them up for, the boys thundered down the stairs and into the streets to Gibson. Once they heard that the baddest men of a Union Pacific rail yard had formed a party, all teenage boys who wanted to be bad were keen to join the search. Boys, fourteen, fifteen, sixteen, who'd been too young to fight in the Great War. Some stopped at home to grab Pop's shotgun.

Lots of these kids knew Agnes Loebeck and her sister. The family was liked in Gibson. That meant a lot to people there. To the boys. To the men of the Union Pacific.

The party wandered and shouted and kept Gibson awake. They sloshed liquor. They dipped cloth in coal oil and lit torches. But they didn't find any black man that night.

The party reconvened at the Bancroft school late the next morning. Nearly three hundred searchers. It was Friday morning, a workday, a school day, but that didn't matter. Surely no manager would hold it against one of his men. A bunch from the slaughterhouses showed up, jobbers from the River Ward, concerned parties from all over the county, to find the one who did it—a short black man who looked like a hunchback and wore a white cap. Lots of folks had seen a man sneaking around Gibson who looked like that. One guy said he'd been robbed by a black hunchback two weeks before. They got weapons to shoot the black hunchback if he came around again. They waited on the trampled diamond where baseball was played after school, or ducked under crab apple trees to escape the sun, or below the hanging beans of catalpas. Karel was in the outfield near the Bancroft school. He smoked cigarettes with men, shared their flasks, and shook his head in disgust as they traded stories of how these new police couldn't do the job. They fluffed their shirts away from their backs because it was hot. They told Uncle Remus jokes. Some kicked up dirt practicing their footwork and punching.

A kid rushed into the crowd in the evening. He shouted the news.

"The cops got him! He's up at the Loebeck house now! They got him!"

Somebody told the police she knew the one who grabbed that girl Agnes on Scenic Avenue. A neighbor. She pointed out the shack where he lived, at Fifth and Cedar, with another black man in a white woman's house. She called it "the trouble house on our block." Two black men, one white woman. If something bad happened, this neighbor figured it must have been done by one of those men.

It was late in the evening. Cicadas were cranking loud. The other two abandoned him once they saw police detectives on their street. They caught sight of the cops and took off. The one the police were looking for was under the bed—that was where they found him. He said he didn't own a revolver, but they found one in the room. A long-barreled kind, like they were looking for. They grabbed his arms and told him to confess.

"Don't you know that girl Agnes?"

"I didn't do nothing."

"We'll see." "What if she recognizes you, boy? Then what?" "Something tells me she's going to remember."

"I didn't do it."

"You think she'll know you? You think she'll remember your face?"

He was guilty enough then for most people. But the cops took him over to the Loebeck house, not far from Gibson Road, up on Second Street, to ask Agnes if this was the one who did those things to her. She screamed when she saw him in her mother's lamplit parlor, the one she said raped her, twisting his cloth cap in his hands. She collapsed to the sofa when she saw him. "Yes! That's the man," she shouted. Her sister repeated it. "He's the one! That's him!"

Milton Hoffman was there and he confirmed this was the man without a doubt.

One of the neighbors sent his boy over to Bancroft to tell the party the cops got the one who did it. They were told what Agnes said. She knew from his hat and clothes and shoes and from his face and his size. He said, "It wasn't me that did it," and she recognized his voice instantly. She remembered that voice telling her to shut up as he pulled her into the weeds. Agnes Loebeck rubbed her face as she said these things, her head aching, bound in a scarf. The little sister stayed close to keep a shawl over her shoulders.

They weren't inside twenty minutes. The house was surrounded by the time they went to leave—10 p.m. on Friday night.

The mob party ran the eight blocks from Bancroft to Second Street and waited for the cops to bring out the one who did it. Karel was with them, one of the three hundred whose throats burned from running. They packed like grain around the house. They climbed trees and to roofs. That was when they saw him for the first time. They had a face, a name. Will Brown.

The mob, that first one, tried to lynch Will Brown right then, once the cops led him into the open. Some boys in the mob party snatched the keys from the police Model T and wouldn't give them back. The phone lines were cut. There was a standoff on the porch. Three police and Will Brown; the three hundred of the party. The party wanted the one who did it. They shouted, "Lynch him!" Karel saw the police and Will Brown on the Loebeck porch. He got as close as he could to see Will Brown. The one black man in a field of white. His dark, spongy hair, his shirt torn from folks pulling. Warning shots were fired from both sides. Stones thrown. Nooses tossed over tree limbs. The party jabbed at Will Brown with long clubs. "Let us have him! A judge won't punish him! We will!" Almost three hundred people were in that mob and they wanted Will Brown. Somebody tossed a lariat around his neck, a lucky shot, and started to tug away, nearly yanked Will Brown off the porch by his throat before a cop was able to slip the loop off. It went on like that for an hour before more police showed up, every reserve in the city. They got Will Brown out of there. They fought through the party and got him in the back of a commandeered truck and sped recklessly away to the county courthouse downtown. The mob party chased after the car and threw more stones, but the police got Will Brown away. Somehow they got him out of South Omaha and into a jail downtown.

Some in the mob party tore off after the police, but most of them stayed to tell tales about what just happened and what would. The little Loebeck sister peeked her face out the door and asked everyone to leave. Most didn't. A mob party like this went on for a while. Most of them were blotto or near it. There were oaths to swear, promises to make about what they'd do later.

Karel found a spot in a tree and listened to what went on. A few ballplayers were loud about what had happened at the Interrace Game some months before and how things only got worse after that. "We should have made an example of that cheating Fowler when we had the chance." A scuffle broke out between some ballplayers, ones who weren't even on the field when Fowler pulled the razor. Karel had been on the field. These guys argued over how they should have got that Will Brown but they'd botched it. The attacks on the front porch weren't organized, no wonder they didn't work. But what to do about it? There was only one thing. The courthouse. They had to get him. They talked and scuffled. They cracked new bottles and drank more, so after a while they wanted to drink more than anything. Near the front porch, maybe down the block, men unzipping to piss on the ground.

Karel went back to the dorming house. He'd stopped drinking.

It was much the same in the streets along the way. The mob party out on a drunk, the speakeasies overflowing. Saloons weren't too secret during the Ak-Sar-Ben anyway. Some who'd chased after the police filtered back to where they lived on the Southside. They'd been too slow to catch up before the one who did it was locked safe in a jail cell. That Will Brown had slipped away. But they'd get him.

Some word was going around how Milt Hoffman set it up to have a friend of his darken his skin with soot then rush them in the park and do those things to Agnes Loebeck—but why would that happen? Was Milt mad at his girl? Why would Milt do that?—and now the underlying interests were just playing this Will Brown for a patsy. Karel had heard enough about those men Jake had worked for that he knew Dennison wouldn't be at all opposed to what was going on, since it made the new mayor look bad. Tom Dennison, Billy Nesselhous, they wouldn't care if a lynch mob roamed. Even if a riot broke out it would suit them.

Not everyone agreed that Milt set it up to have his girl raped. Some thought Agnes was in on the sham too, that she'd been paid off to finger a black, or that she was a prostitute, and maybe she'd wanted those things to happen to her.

Karel heard these rumors. People debated in the street.

And Will Brown could have done it. There was always that possibility. Will Brown could have raped Agnes just like she said, just like Milt said. It was easiest to believe this. Who wanted to accuse a girl of lying about a thing like that? And who was saying those things about Milt anyway? Who'd believe a guy set it up to have his girl raped?

Will Brown did it. That's what most believed, what Karel thought he believed. That's what made sense.

At the dorming house there were organizers from the machine talking to boys. Just inside the door, by the manager's office. Joe Meinhof was with them. Lining up the boys, handing out some coin. Half now, half later. Karel slipped upstairs before Joe saw him. He wasn't looking for a job. Months and months had passed since Karel cared a bit about making money, not since Anna went away. What Karel cared about now was sleep. He'd been running around day and night and figured he'd do the same tomorrow. The mob party wasn't going to give up that easily. They all said so. They'd do anything to get that Will Brown.

E veryone had a theory about who he was. No one knew for sure. He's someone the boys wondered about a lot in the years after 1919, after what they did that September. Will Brown. What was he thinking when the cops handed him over? Could he hear what that mob promised to do to him?

Consider that Will Brown lived in Gibson. It wasn't easy for a black man there. Not far from Rourke Park and right next to Riverview Park. He was forty years old. Pockmarked with a small mustache. He came from Cairo, Illinois. Some said Will Brown got a girl pregnant and a judge in Cairo was going to order them married. That was how he ended up in Omaha, running out on that girl. Men like him moved around so much it was hard to say what made them go from one place to the next. Most of them in Omaha worked in stockyards, a lot of them scabs who took the jobs of doughboys.

A black man was guaranteed nearly two dollars a day in the yards. With some money to spend, a place to live, life would have been good enough for Will Brown. But he was getting old that summer. He felt bad in his back, his legs and arms. His neck would have always been twisted. Some days it wasn't all that bad if he didn't get work, if he could rest on a park bench and look at a newspaper. Otherwise it meant staying home.

He and another black man lived under the same roof with a white woman that year. Their place on Cedar Street wouldn't have been much, in some backwater ward bisected by freight lines, a shack so close to the Missouri that Will Brown could sit on a tar paper roof with a bottle and watch the river swell in the late hours if he wanted to. He could have seen riverboats float downstream at night, electric lights shimmering on the water, heard cornet calls echoing off the cottonwoods on the Iowa side. There wasn't much legitimate fun a black man could have down in South Omaha besides going to a lunchroom for beans and coffee. Sitting on a roof and listening to a jazz band play a riverboat was a jubilation most nights. If he felt sick and sore, it would be. People on those boats wore white suits and dresses and bathed in electric light. They drank illegal booze and danced to hot music. Everybody else had to sit down in the muck to listen. If they lived down in the muck they'd hear by and by, like Will Brown would have.

He was in his cell on the fifth floor all night Friday. He was there all day Saturday. Never once did he confess. Never once did he say anything but that he was innocent of raping that girl. He had to know it was over. He'd already had a noose around his neck. If you'd been accused of rape and had to rely on the police to protect you, then you'd know it was over. They had him rushing away in the back of a truck, people trying to get him, bottles breaking, the uproar at the courthouse. God in heaven. They claimed he didn't say but six words the whole time all this happened. *It wasn't me that did it.* They put him in front of that girl Agnes and that's all he could say. He nearly got carried off by a lynch mob, had to be saved by the police. Will Brown would have known what kind of trouble he was in. He'd have known there wasn't much he could do about it. Men in a fix like that almost never said something to defend themselves. They knew what was coming.

A few blocks away the Ak-Sar-Ben carnival carried on. The prisoners could hear a calliope from the midway, the dying murmurs of faraway laughter, from an open window at the end of their row. There were traveling shows in theaters, musical revues, strong men, and novelty acts. Folks ate candied apples and hot dogs. The parade and coronation ball were still to come. Not a single room was vacant downtown; there was record attendance all week. The arcade was bustling busy all night Friday and all night Saturday, tens of thousands of visitors downtown to see what kind of action they could find in the city.

Will Brown was in his cell Sunday morning. It was quiet. The carnival wouldn't open until noon. City and county offices were closed. The only commotion inside the courthouse came when breakfast was carted around and the drunks from the night before were let out of the tanks.

No more than fifty people in the whole city would have known him the day before he was arrested. The day after, up in a county jail cell, Will Brown's name was on the lips of everybody in Omaha after what that girl said he did to her.

A guard showed Will Brown first thing that morning, the three Saturday editions draped over an arm like shaving towels as he rapped the bars with his cudgel. "You read?" the guard asked. "I guess you recognize your own name at least."

It would have been different for Will Brown to see his picture in a paper. He was known. What did he think about that? Maybe he convinced himself that someone good could save him. He knew whether he did what that girl said he did or not—him being one of the holy few who would ever know the truth—but he'd hoped to be saved even if he was guilty, even if he did do things to the girl. Seeing his name in the dailies, maybe he believed it for a while, that something could save him.

J ake and Evie stayed in Saturday. They didn't know what to do. They read the papers. Jake wished he knew what Tom Dennison had going. Things had moved on without him while he lived in Lincoln those fourteen months. They would move on now despite his being back.

He went to the Eigler house on Sunday. There was lunch at noon. Hamburger steaks and beet salad. They sat on the front porch after and listened to the noise coming from the mills, the clanging bells of streetcars, the shearing of a hot wind kicking up dust. Maria and Jake and Theresa and Silke and Mühlstein—Karel hadn't been seen for weeks. It was a thing they'd done a thousand times before, watching the day wind down, watching the families across the way on their porches watch back, seeing groups of friends walk Clandish in twos or threes, debating some point of gossip or philosophy that was important to them and perhaps no one else in the world. Jake never quite knew what folks said as they walked by, murmuring from crooked mouths, shoulders touching as they swayed. *They're going to get that boy.*

It was hot and humid for the time of year. It would probably rain, the air was so thick, maybe overnight. The clouds were low and hazy. They blended together and formed continent-like masses, gray, amorphous, never-ending. Jake hoped it would rain. Just sitting on the porch made him sweat. He felt drops roll down his back and tried not to move at all. Silke and Theresa sat sunning on the porch steps. "I like your beard," Theresa said. One of them had to say something. When he arrived, they'd all stared at Jake and his wiry red beard.

"Yeah?" He played along. "I like it too. It gives me an excuse to scratch."

The girls beamed as he dug into his jaw with his fingernails, their faces pink and glazed in the sun, in their heavy dresses, the only kind they had. Sleeves rolled, skirts to the knee. The girls were content like this, as if on a beach in Atlantic City, modeling bathing suits in a Harold Lloyd picture. Theresa swept hair off her forehead and tilted her chin skyward. Silke leaned back on her hands to stick her chest out. Jake couldn't help laughing, looking at them.

He asked Silke how many boys were chasing her. She shook her head and blushed, then cleaned the thick lenses of her glasses with the fabric of her dress to avoid looking at Jake. He blushed too, seeing how uncomfortable he made her.

"There's boys who talk to her plenty." Theresa ratted her out. "The boys who live down where they keep the streetcars at night. Italians, around there. Poppa wouldn't like them. They're sweaty and grow stupid mustaches."

"They're gross," Silke claimed.

"Who's gross? Those grimy boys who work in machine shops?" Jake had spent enough time in Little Sicily to know what Theresa meant. "They unbutton their shirts when they see you two coming, yeah?"

He saw it clearly. Both girls would have babies of their own before they knew what. It pleased him to think of something so usual.

Maria asked if Jake had been to see Evie yet. Evie had come to visit the Eigler house a few times since he left. Requested his forwarding address. Maria asked if Evie ever wrote. "No," he said. "I never heard from her."

Maria shrugged.

Jake didn't say more about Evie. It was Sunday and she hadn't asked him to stay. He'd only wanted to see her again—that was why he wrote that letter asking if she'd let him come by—and he saw her. Four days he stuck close by her side. They walked and ate. There was the carnival. Evie made him sleep on the couch at night—she'd reattached a door with a lock to the hinges of her bedroom—but that was fine. This was more than he hoped for. To be near her. To hear her voice. Of course he wanted to stay. Of course he wanted to share her bed, to have her in the bathtub at least one more time. But that didn't matter. He'd return to Lincoln that afternoon. He could go even further, all the way to California, if he wanted. These old things he told himself. Promises still valid in their ephemeral way.

It was then he saw the boys march across Clandish. He noticed the mass of them first. Teenage boys in lines a dozen wide going up the street, across lawns and abandoned, rubble-strewn lots. They blocked a streetcar. A few police kept up at the flanks, lecturing the boys, it looked like, trying to get them to turn back. Milton Hoffman manned the point. Jake recognized Milt. The boys' mob was only half a block down Clandish, Milt shuffling along with his bad leg as he shouted some slogan.

Jake crouched in the lawn to watch. The Miihlstein girls scrambled to the porch. They understood what was happening. They didn't have to stumble to the walkway and squint down the avenue. The girls had experience. Jake remembered when he saw their cowering. They'd come from the Eastern Front during the war. Their glassy eyes and pinched lips were what caused him to react. He told them to get inside.

"Make them stop." Silke was on the top step, pleading with Jake. "Don't you know those boys? Weren't you the boss of them? Tell them to go away. We don't want them here. We want them to leave us alone."

"Don't worry," Jake said. "They're not after you."

"It's Karel," she sobbed. "Karel's out there!"

He put them inside and had Maria clasp the locks. He heard them on the other side of the door before he followed the noise. "Is Jake going to find Karel? Is he going to make them stop?"

It was 2 p.m. when the boys got to the courthouse. They marched from Bancroft, fifty or sixty of them in the beginning, boys one and all. None were older than sixteen, except for Milt Hoffman. Some were as young as ten. They added more before they got downtown. Hundreds of boys. All feeling strong. Worthwhile and mean. Shouting school slogans and war songs they knew by heart. Karel sang along from the middle. It was boys who first battered the courthouse doors—on the north side—and demanded Will Brown be handed over.

"Give him to us!" they shouted. Some of the voices high-pitched, some cracking. "We'll take care of him!"

The guards locked the doors. It was Sunday, the building was closed. "There's a way these things are done," a police detective told them. "You got to let the courts do their work." He ordered the mob to disband. Boys laughed in his face.

A towhead named William Francis was one of the leaders. He wore the military uniform of his high school cadet squadron and riding breeches. William Francis was from Gibson—he stopped around the boys' dormitory sometimes but never stayed—and was a good friend of Agnes, everyone knew. That gave him some authority in the matter. He was tall and slim. His hair was shaved up into a mess atop his head.

They were all friends of that brown-eyed girl, Agnes. If not before, surely now. She was pretty and modest. She worked in a steam laundry with her mother. She was a hard worker. She attended mass at St. Patrick's, the nine o'clock service. Everybody knew these things.

Boys promised to take matters into their own hands, since the grown-ups had bungled things. It was up to the boys there. Alfred Braun and Jimmy Mac. Gangs of street kids in matching baggy suits and bowler hats, in felt caps and dark shirts dusted white with billiards chalk. High school kids from the Southside. Wide-shouldered Bohunks in denim pants. Football players in letter sweaters. Boys from slaughterhouses with hands bleached white and shriveled from pickling tanks. Leather-skinned boys who prodded sheep and cattle all summer in dung-layered stockyards. Boys of all stripe and affiliation. They chatted across the street from roadsters, traded cheap cigarettes. All sorts of boys Karel knew from baseball games. Roy Teeter, who would fight anyone and had the scars on his face and hands to prove it; Michael Hykell, who was a talker; Ernie Morris, a small fry who usually took the first punch in a fight; Nathan Shapiro, whose Jewish mother locked him out of the house for the night if she heard him swear; and Louis Weaver, whose older brother died of the flu on a transport to France. All boys like Karel, who wanted to prove they too were salty.

None of the authorities paid much mind to the boys. Mayor Smith observed from the courthouse with the city commissioners, the chief of police, the sheriff. They expected a lynch mob to come for Will Brown—an extra fifty policemen were on guard that Sunday to keep him safe until the arraignment on Monday—but when the mob arrived and it was only boys, the authorities couldn't bring themselves to disperse the crowd. The courthouse was built with lynch mobs in mind, billed as riot proof only seven years before, with heavy stone blocks, bronze doors, and unscalable walls. Will Brown was at the top of their battlement, in the fifth-floor holding cells. They believed he'd be safe until the trial.

※

Jake didn't follow the boys. He ran to Tom Dennison's office.

His mind was a frenzy. He doubted there was anything he could do, as Silke implored him to. He needed to see Tom's face. Only Tom could take control. Jake needed to look in the Old Man's eyes; then he'd know what was going to happen.

The office was empty when he got there. The safe was gone, the card cabinets, the signed photographs of movie stars and pugilists. The walls bare except for nail heads sticking out. The desks and chairs gone, marks worn in the floor where they'd scraped. The place was abandoned. No bodyguards outside. No men taking hedge bets over telegraph wires. No Madge Holloran at the pinewood desk near the door. Jake was alone. The office was cleaned out, every presence deleted.

The tobacco shop still operated below. A man behind the counter waited as Jake stumbled back down the stairs.

"Where'd they go?" Jake shouted. The man knew him. Jake had passed through this shop hundreds of times before.

"What do you want me to say? There's nothing here but my shop. You see that."

The mob grew throughout the afternoon. It wasn't something Mayor Smith counted on, that the rough men of the River Ward and Southside would follow the lead of the fifty boys who first struck out to make demands. But by 5 p.m. thousands more joined in. Once the railroad men and jobbers had salved their hangovers, they heard what had started at the courthouse and wouldn't be left out.

For a while they weren't sure what should be done. The counterargument that all this had been set up by Milt Hoffman made its rounds again. There was some dispute whether Will Brown had really done it to Agnes Loebeck. Will Brown was a hunchback. It said this in the papers. He could barely close his hands into a fist, could hardly walk, much less spring from the bushes on a hilltop above the river. How could he rape a girl like that? It was a mystery. Folks wondered why Milt hadn't stopped a cripple from doing things to Agnes. Milt worked for the Dennison machine. Even though he walked with a cane, Milt was a thug. He'd been known to beat a guy with that cane if his temper got the better of him.

A chorus of panic echoed over the River Ward once it started. Paddy wagons screamed by with a cop on the runner to churn the siren. Jake followed in their wake. The closer he got to the courthouse, the more fighting he saw. It was like the melee on Clandish in 1917—kids fighting police, police trying to push bystanders off the block—except the kids enjoyed fighting more than they did before. The cops were desperate. Groups of raiders formed in the mob party. Ten, twenty boys, a man to lead. They charged the courthouse doors and had to be beaten back. One group fell and another stood. There were thousands in the mob party and only a few dozen police outside. Some doughboys moved to the front to give advice. Then the mob party threw bricks at the police who guarded the courthouse doors, a bombardment, before the raiders charged. A few cops were hurt. Nobody made it inside.

Injured raiders sat along the curb when Jake reached the courthouse block on the Farnam side. These were high school kids. They sat on the pavement with hands in their hair to keep the blood in, joking about where they'd gone wrong and which one of the cops it was who got them. They talked like this was a football game with a rival team. These weren't street kids. They wore letter sweaters and had good teeth. "Do you think it will scar?" one asked. He removed a handkerchief to show the swollen blemish over his eye where he'd been walloped by a cop. "I hope it scars."

Bill and Ducky Sutez raised a new party, and Karel grabbed Alfred and Jimmy to follow along, the band the ballplayers made, thirty or so of them, to rush the vestibule. They surged the doors to see what they could do. Soldiers, ballplayers, boys from tenements, from the dorming house, from Jobbers Canyon, some Karel didn't know. A German artillery cannon captured from the Argonne Forest was on display outside the courthouse—a gift from the War Department to commend the city's enthusiasm for selling bonds. It had an eight-foot gun. The raiders lifted the hitch and wheeled the carriage as fast as they could to batter down the doors, and it worked. They rushed in and demanded Will Brown be handed over.

Karel could see only a few feet in front of himself as their bodies pushed forward. There was constantly someone stepping on his foot or pulling his shirt until it stretched off a shoulder. Police fired warning shots down the elevator shafts, and that drove the raiders crazy. Bill Sutez screamed into the atrium sky and pulled a revolver. Karel pushed anyone who came near him, whether cop or raider, because he couldn't find his friends. A cop caught a bullet in his shoulder and screamed until another was there to hold him. Did Bill Sutez fire the shot? Karel didn't know. A few more cops were beaten unconscious and carried out. Onlookers rushed out too, unsure why they'd gone inside in the first place. Everybody wanted outside. Formaldehyde and ammonia bombs had been thrown down the stairs. At the first scent of them, Karel ran, which was fine. It was easy. Fire hoses punched at his back, washed him and the others out the vestibule, over each other where the German artillery cannon was stuck halfway in the door. Raiders stumbled, ammonia blind, over their legs, ones at the front who'd been hit with fumes, some with dangling broken arms, until someone led off to the hospital. Cops poked hoses out the door and blasted anyone who was close.

Mist from the spray freckled Karel's face where he stood near the curb. There were thousands on the north side of the courthouse. With hardly any space to stand, men and boys passed bootleg whiskey and swigged from tilted bottles because there wasn't room to raise their arms. They stashed flasks in hip pockets. Hundreds of bottles out of thin air. Crates of booze had materialized at a corner newsstand.

There was shattering glass, shotgun fire, windows breaking. All of it punctuated by a woman's carnal cheer. That was what Karel heard, the noises he had to brace himself against. The screaming and laughing of those hurt and those in the mob party. He wasn't a kid anymore. Not now for sure. If he could find his friends, he'd tell them how he saw two people fucking in the back of a car, how he too swigged whiskey from a flask. It was all okay, whatever people put themselves to do. He let his mind cloud over with the flash of small arms, the police sirens, their useless, barking orders, the shouts of celebration and calls for revenge. He had the sense (they all must have) that whatever was going to happen would be okay, that it was sanctioned by some wanton authority.

Speeding cars rushed into the crowds with young men on sideboards, to find where the action was. Cars with Sicilians, Lithuanians, Greeks, Serbs, Germans. Once word of the riot spread, anyone who wanted to take a swing at a cop made a beeline to the courthouse. A gang hijacked a streetcar and wore out the bell as they plowed into the mess. Musky husbands rushed from houses with whatever hammer or club or bat they could lay hands on and then hopped a taxi to get there fast. Jalopies swung recklessly around the blocks. They swerved and skidded to miss bystanders and each other. Karel heard motors hammer at full throttle a block away, spreading echoes between the high-rises of downtown, while trucks hopped hot over the pavement to load up with furniture or produce or women's garments, whatever could be looted. Crammed full inside, passengers on the footboards, taxis slumped cockeyed and labored up hills, running for free. "The fare is already paid for. As long as all this goes on, it's paid for!"

People shouted out any news they heard. Smutty details of the rape. Conjecture about Will Brown's body in relation to the girl's. They made him out to be huge, a towering man with mountainous shoulders, arms like a gorilla, legs like a mule. Karel had seen Will Brown when they had him cornered on the Loebeck porch, but he couldn't recall if what people said was true. Karel shook as he remembered Will Brown. A voice came to him through the drunk of the mob. The voice of a stranger god. They talked about Agnes Loebeck as if she were a little girl, pious and pure, like she only ever wore long, white Sunday dresses; like she picked berries in a pristine field; like she'd never even heard of anything resembling a dick before. They made jokes about black sex, about slicing off Will Brown's organ and stuffing it in his mouth. About shooting it off with shotgun spray at close range. About sledgehammering his balls and feeding them to a hog. They talked about that woman Will Brown lived with down in Gibson, Virginia Jones, and what kind of woman she was, shacking up with two black men. What did anyone expect to happen when things like that went on in a city?

Towheaded Will Francis rode a white horse. Its hooves struck streetcar rails, whose glint showed down the block. Somehow he'd acquired a white Arabian, an erect, regal horse, muscled and ghostly beautiful. A rope hung from the pommel of his saddle. "We want the Negro and we're going to get him," Will Francis shouted. He rode back and forth to excite the others. "I got the rope! Get us the Negro, men, and us boys will do the rest!"

The man next to Jake collapsed. He dropped like he was nothing. People fired warning shots—both police and hotheads in the mob. Some fired until they ran out of bullets, then yelled until more were found. A bullet fell from the sky and dug into the top of the man's head. Jake was next to him when he dropped, a body crumpled into his legs. Jake tried to help the man to his feet, but it was no use. His hat fell off, and they saw what happened. A woman poked her finger out the top of the hat to show where the bullet went through.

They circled in to look, the body facedown, a man in a blue suit, neither old nor young. There was hardly any blood. He'd been standing watching and a stray bullet came down on his skull. "He was next to me," the woman holding the hat said. "Then, kaput." This made sense. Nobody questioned it. A truck came along, they laid the body in the back. The truck drove off with the body.

Raiders stormed the courthouse again, and a few made it up the stairs this time. They found Chief Eberstein and made him address the mob from a window. Eberstein urged them to let the law take its course. Nobody listened, nobody could hear.

Jake had been at the back of the crowd, but now he was surrounded, with nowhere to go, just people everywhere, talking and jeering and telling each other what they thought should happen. Jake couldn't find the boy. It was impossible. Who knew where Karel could be in this mess? Karel could be one of the raiders, could be inside the courthouse swinging a brick at a cop. Jake had to push and shove just to hold his ground, just to watch as a ladder was raised up the side of the courthouse. A few of the mob climbed in a second-floor window, none of them Karel. They didn't last long before the police forced them down.

You're not judge and jury, a sergeant rushed out to tell the mob. He was grabbed and punched in the mouth. They took his nightstick and beat him. Sheriff Clark tried to talk some sense into the mob—all those government men and their logic—and he was greeted by a girl who slung a skipping stone upside his head.

Jake saw Karel. The boy had bore out a circle for himself. Nobody wanted near him—hopping on his toes, swinging his arms—but people watched. Jake pushed through to see. Black-haired Karel had muscles in his neck and had grown a voice, and Jake wondered if it was really him. "Karel!" Jake shouted. The boy stopped to look around; it was him, hair stuck to his face, his shirt nearly torn from his body, how he swayed in a drunken swagger. "What are you doing?" Jake shouted. Karel looked at Jake but didn't answer. What on earth could he say?

Not far from them the mob bombarded the courthouse. Jake couldn't hear for all the glass breaking. Police sprayed fire hoses from a third-floor window—that was how it escalated—and the mob threw rocks in return. Nearly every window was gone through with a rock or stone or brick, shards hanging from the casements. Any police who tried to stop the mob were stoned—they couldn't stop six thousand from smashing out windows or rushing the doors, not if the mob party would risk getting hit with rocks too. Rubble rained on every-one near the building, not just the cops. Girls filled tin buckets with stones from a vacant lot and carried them to throwers. Cooks from a hotel kitchen carried dishpans filled with bricks from a demolished building.

There was an explosion on the west side of the courthouse, a fireball and plume of smoke. Karel took off sprinting in that direction. Jake tried to follow but couldn't. He didn't want to be there. Karel did.

When Karel got to the front he saw what caused the fireball: someone got the bright idea to steal gasoline from a filling station in a tin can. He was going to toss it through a window and start the courthouse on fire, but the gas exploded in his hand. Scorches marked the grass where it happened, charred earth, a trail through the mob where the burned man was being led away.

Evie stayed home as long as she could stand it, knowing from the start that Jake would find his way to the courthouse to see what was going on. With her window open Evie heard the masses simmer throughout the day and knew it had something to do with that Will Brown the police had captured, the one who did bad things to a girl. Evie saw folks run down her street to go join the action, saw a madam lock her door up tight, which meant real trouble on a night like this, when there was a lot of money to be made. But if it was too much trouble, if the money wasn't even worth it to a madam, then something bad was going to happen.

Evie locked her windows at the sash, and her doors too, to head out in search of Jake, although she wouldn't have admitted that. She walked a few blocks to see what was going on up near the courthouse. She heard the noise echo between the buildings long before she could see anything. All those people. The puffs of smoke. The sun setting behind the buildings in all its fall glory. These people were gruesome. Evie knew she should hurry back to her rooms—that she should be smarter; she had too much to lose trying to pass through a lynch mob to find Jake. What if someone in the mob picked her out? Jake Strauss would be fine. Evie should get out of there, because she was shaking and should listen to her fear, and it was no secret what kind of blood the mob wanted to spill.

She stayed only a minute. Climbed with wobbly legs to the top of a stoop outside the Omaha Building to look for Jake. She couldn't see him in among the thousands of hats and faces and flops of styled hair in the mob party. This was no surprise. What was Evie going to do if she found him anyway? Drag him out of there? She just wanted to see what he was doing. If he was part of the mob or not. If he incited the crazies on or tried to talk them out of what they were going to do. Like this would show who Jake really was.

Evie had no hope of spotting him. She snuck away as fast as she could. Looking for Jake wasn't worth the risk of being caught up in something bad, she told herself. She had to get out of there.

※

Jake noticed boys going in and out of the Bee Building. All these boys hustled up the front steps and through the door and nobody stopped them. The building was guarded by private security. Nobody in the mob touched it, their attention focused in the opposite direction, on the courthouse. Except for those boys who hurried in and out—boys who weren't rioting. Jake recognized one of them, then another. All these boys were runners for the machine. Billy Nesselhous's boys, in dungarees and short wool jackets, with grime-smudged faces and penny cigars. A boy army that worked for nickel tips. The runners bound in and out of the Bee Building. It was Chip Lee who was at the door to keep out unwanteds, Chip who normally guarded the door to Dennison's office.

It didn't take much to get inside. Chip had always liked Jake and let him pass. He chased the boys up to the top floor. Billy and Meinhof were there, waiting to hear what was going on.

Billy jabbed Meinhof in the shoulder and winked when he saw Jake on the landing.

"I won't make trouble," Jake promised.

"Great," Billy laughed. "He won't bother us, he says. What a relief."

A small group of men were in a sparsely furnished office, backs turned to peer out the windows. Tom Dennison was at their middle. "What do you think?" he asked, grinning. "Would something like this happen if we ran things?"

Jake didn't answer. A space opened at the window and Tom bid Jake to stand next to him. He put an arm over Jake's shoulders as they watched what unfolded. All of them were drunk, even Tom. All of them festive for the occasion. A crate of the same booze from the street was up here, half-empty by then. They pointed out what looked interesting from the window. A fistfight. A woman who bared herself to raiders and made promises. The sunset made spectacular by the smoke. Anything the men said was half covered by the racket. Mostly it was Billy talking to boy runners who rushed up three steps at a time to tell what happened:

How a black was chased down Seventeenth Street and caught outside the Omaha National Bank. A mob tried to lynch him, but police stopped it. Tom shook his head as he heard. How a black was pulled off a streetcar on Farnam, this one with a pistol in his belt. He holed up in the basement of an iron foundry until police removed him to the city jail for his own good.

Around 8 p.m. a runner told how the Townsend Gun Company had been raided, and that street kids had broken the windows of sporting goods stores to scout for baseball bats and weapons. Several doughboys filched guns and ammunition from pawn shops, and soon they began firing on the courthouse.

The women prisoners were released. Over ten thousand citizens were trying to destroy the courthouse and murder a man—whatever these women had done couldn't be worse than that.

A sixteen-year-old leader of a mob party was killed in a gunfire exchange with police, or from friendly fire. An insane man escaped from the prisoners and dashed to the river. Taxis ran hot, packed. Thousands hustled in from neighborhoods nearby before they missed the lynching.

And then word came about what happened to Mayor Ed Smith. The runners were barely coherent they were so excited. Smith was inside the courthouse doors amid the sound of gunfire when he fired at a rogue doughboy in uniform. The doughboy confirmed this, holding up his quivering, bloody hand where the bullet went through. When Smith emerged, he held a small pistol. The mob became unglued at his holding a gun.

Smith was going to talk some sense into the crowd. That was why he came outside in the first place. "Lynch me if you got to lynch someone!" He was hit on the head with a baseball bat before he could say more then struck with the butts of revolvers. They slipped a rope around the mayor's neck and dragged him to the corner and before long had him hanging from a light pole at Sixteenth and Harney, hatless and bloody, his feet clear of the ground, his eyes bugging out of his skull. This was the mayor. Two men tugged the rope to lift him higher.

Three police detectives cut down the mayor and rushed him away. His head was badly beaten. There were rope burns on his neck and he could hardly breathe. He might die at the hospital.

Tom's mouth shrunk as he heard what happened to Ed Smith. His eyes narrowed. He felt the change in his face and couldn't control it like he'd always been able to control his expression. He was dumbfounded, he wanted to be less drunk. He tried to figure out the balance that was being created. A calculation he couldn't figure. Could he repay what he owed? And to whom would he tender compensation? How could he even imagine he could square this chaos?

Tom fell into a state his men had never seen before and needed to compose himself. He was a man who valued control over all else, a gambler aware of the angles. Anarchy wasn't something he stomached easily. "All we did was have Milt march with the boys," he said.

"We sure did," Billy said. "The taxis, some liquor. But goddamn. Look at this! Who would of guessed it?"

Some in the mob complained how they'd let Mayor Smith get away. They were angry with how those detectives slipped in and cut Smith down from the rope and drove off with him. Some yelled about how they should have done more. When they had the mayor in hand, they should have finished him off, because he protected that Will Brown.

They rocked a police car back and forth until it tipped. They put a match to a stream of gasoline so the car exploded. A group of boys fled around the corner, hair singed off.

Karel saw where these boys came from, and that was where he went. All he could do was follow the desire of the moment, the voice of the mob, and he wanted to be where people were set to their sharpest edge. The hanging of Mayor Smith changed them, the ringleaders, the loudmouths. It made them realize their capabilities, that great violent mass of them, explosions in their ears. They were serious about what they wanted. All police were in the courthouse. None were left outside. The sheriff and his deputies, the prisoners, Will Brown too, all trapped on the top floors. There was no escape unless the mob granted escape.

Gasoline cans were brought from a filling station. Some men lifted the cans to a windowsill and splashed gas through. A torch was thrown in after. The mob didn't let firemen get close to the building. Pumper trucks were blocked in the traffic of bodies. Kids cut the fire hoses with knives. Nobody was allowed to leave the courthouse, armed members of the mob stationed at every door. They held looted .22s and more ammunition than could be shot. The rooms filled with smoke.

The prisoners were driven to the roof. Almost the whole inside of the courthouse was wood, its rooms packed with paper, county records, land deeds. It burned quickly. The prisoners lay flat on their bellies because snipers across the way buzzed bullets over their heads. One prisoner who peeked over the edge had his face sprayed with buckshot. Two others were hit by rifle slugs, their bodies jumping even as they lay flat. Half the mob was armed. It didn't matter if a man had a rifle or a pistol, he took a shot.

Prisoners pled with the deputies to hand over Will Brown. They didn't want to die for the sake of Will Brown going to trial. They picked him up and were going to throw him off the edge before Sheriff Clark made them think better of it.

Alfred and Jimmy Mac had been looking for Karel, and they found him on the south side of the courthouse. They stole a ladder from a fire truck and were going to scale the east side of the building. Jimmy Mac asked Karel if he wanted to climb. Of course he did. What else could he do? They'd need help lifting the ladder. Karel could climb to the second story, the others right behind. Spotlights from cars played on the boys as they clambered over ledges to pull themselves up. Fire bit at their heels. The other two formed a human ladder to reach a third-floor window ledge, Karel on their shoulders, hanging sixty feet above the pavement to show his shoe bottoms to the crowd as his legs swung free from Jimmy's shoulders. A cheer erupted when he pulled himself up. Standing in that cheer, that noise of approval from the mob, Karel couldn't stop. He dropped a rope for Jimmy and Alfred. All the windows on the third floor were smashed out. Inside the offices burned, so they started over again to reach the next floor.

Jake couldn't see much of what went on from where he was, the dappled texture of hats and white faces, bodies packed around the block. He heard explosions and shouted demands, smelled gunpowder brimstone and gasoline smoke that poured out windows. He and Tom Dennison sat and watched. Nothing but people for blocks and blocks. They shuffled and pointed. They stood close. This was happening. They were burning down the courthouse, they were destroying the city. All this to get Will Brown.

Policemen trapped on the fourth floor waved a white flag. When Karel pulled himself to that ledge, the cops begged to be rescued. They'd been forced up the stairs by smoke and were being overcome. "Sure," Alfred said, crawling up behind. "There's ladders. But we got them." He gestured down to where the mob now held bigger ladders than what were stolen by Alfred and Jimmy. "We got all the ladders." Alfred smiled. "But we don't rescue a cop for nothing."

Those cops promised anything. There was only one thing the mob wanted.

Jimmy Mac shouted down the news, but it was useless. The cops shouted too, but nobody could hear them from up there. Finally a cop in a blue uniform threw a note to the crowd. There was mass ecstasy when the note was read. *Come to the fourth floor of the building and we will hand the nigger over to you.* Ladders were raised, the police saved. Once the police reached the ground, raiders began to climb. Karel waited from his ledge. He felt at home on the ledge, how it was when he slid to make a catch in centerfield, like he wouldn't leave this place until someone made him, and no one could make him. Young men—those from the boys' mob who could taste their triumph—gripped the rungs as they climbed and showed rope nooses to the crowd. Karel helped raiders through the window before he entered. The raiders searched for Will Brown, but Will Brown wasn't there.

He was on the roof and the roof was going to collapse. There was an iron stairway on the backside of an elevator shaft. Sheriff Clark started his men down this way.

Will Brown was told to stay put, to crouch in a corner where nobody could see him. He'd have no chance in the crowd. The others might make it.

Clark and his deputies went first down the stairs, the prisoners except Will Brown behind them. They were met by raiders on the fourth floor. Ducky Sutez was first among them. "We'll kill every one of you unless we get that Negro," he said. The sheriff was trapped between the mob and the prisoners. Clark refused to hand Will Brown over. There was shoving on these narrow stairs bolted to the backside of an elevator shaft, inside a burning building. Clark didn't move. He wouldn't let the raiders by.

Prisoners at the rear broke away to get Will Brown. They passed him over their heads, from hand to hand, down the iron stairway to where the raiders were. They got Will Brown. The raiders. Karel was there. He reached up at Will Brown but couldn't touch him. Men had taken over again, their arms longer than Karel's, their hips heavier when he tried to move them. Karel stretched but couldn't reach—all at once Will Brown fell, and it was Karel's hands that tried to catch the weight of the man and pass it off. But Karel couldn't hold. The weight crashed through him, crumpled him into a corner. Will Brown on top. Karel saw Will Brown's eyes as the raiders grabbed and lifted him and carried on. Will Brown's white eyes popping out of his skull. Raiders lifted Karel to his feet, but Karel's legs didn't work. His legs and hands were numb where he touched the black. He flattened against the wall to watch raiders tear off down the stairs. He couldn't follow.

They held Will Brown out a window. They ripped his clothes off. They had him.

Thousands rushed to the south side once word spread. Jake watched as Farnam Street emptied outside the Bee Building, on the north side, the masses hurrying, pushing, scuttling over to see Will Brown strung up on a traffic signal at Eighteenth and Harney. He was dragged through the crowd at the end of a rope, bleeding and bruised, to where a boy climbed a pole and tied a noose over the iron beam. The noise was awful. Rifle echoes, pistols. Mothers pushed to the front. They lifted babies to see a body flounder at the end of a rope.

※

A bullet sliced the rope. The body fell from the traffic signal and was tied to the bumper of a police car and dragged down the street. Karel was back on his ledge to watch where the car went. Down Harney to Thirteenth. Thirteenth to Douglas. Douglas to Fifteenth, on and on. Karel heard praise for the parading car. He heard guns, alone with his back against the burning building. The granite scalded him, but he didn't pull away. He leaned into the heat.

He caught a glimpse of the car as it came down Seventeenth Street. He saw the body dragged behind. The driver went slow so others could run along or pose for a photograph.

A boy sold pieces of the noose for ten cents. He sliced off segments with a knife.

Will Brown burned in the middle of Dodge, on Seventeenth. The car stopped and a pyre was built. Pallets were smashed to pieces and thrown in a pile. Brown was put on top. He was doused with coal oil from a street lantern and lit.

They dragged the grist until martial law was declared and troops from Fort Omaha and Fort Crook flooded the city. The boys went home. What remained of the body was found hung in front of the Beaton Drug Company store at Fifteenth and Farnam, just around the corner from where Tom Dennison once kept an office above a tobacco shop.

Jake stayed with Tom Dennison the whole night. They sat next to the window. They watched embers smolder through the smashed-in maws of the courthouse and heard the hammering of pistons from the car with Will Brown's body behind it, the motor echoes between buildings, the victive ovations of teenage hooligans. They smelled wisps of burning flesh in the breeze. They watched as soldiers trucked in, as machine-gun nests were built on street corners.

Jake twisted an early edition of the *Bee* in his hands. In the years after he would deny even being in the city during the riot—claiming he was in Lincoln that night.

There were thousands of questions Jake could have asked once it was over. Why did Milt Hoffman lead the boys' mob? Why did the taxis run for free? Who supplied the liquor? Why didn't the machine do anything to stop this? Why was Tom Dennison in this office to watch, this front-row seat?

Jake didn't ask Tom any of these questions. He asked about the Cypriot.

"What are you talking about?"

"The Cypriot," he said. "Ugo Daniel. Why was there a bounty?"

Tom didn't laugh, as Jake thought he might. He looked Jake in the eyes. He was tired, his flinty eyes ancient. There was a scorched smell even though it rained. Firemen searched the courthouse for cinders that still flickered in dark rooms. A boy sat on a ledge, rocking himself.

"Who was the Cypriot?" Jake repeated. "What did he do?"

"He was nobody."

Tom turned to look out the window. He was quiet a long time, as if remembering that morning two years ago when he arrived at his office to the news that the Cypriot had got the works. He walked in to see Jake Strauss waiting, the kid who'd taken care of it.

"I don't know who he was. That's the truth of it. Some fast talker. Nobody important. He didn't work for us, or for Pendergast, or anyone. Who'd even heard of him until the rumors spread? My guess is he was some loser. Some confidence man. Billy had a girl working to find out who he was, but she didn't learn squat. Nothing important. He never stole from us, I can tell you that. He had his own money. He never did anything but draw attention to himself."

"Why did you give the bounty then? What was the point?"

"I didn't care who he was. The rumors were doing harm. The man was nothing. Everyone said he was getting the best of us. The longer he lived, the weaker we looked. That was all."

Jake looked Tom in the eyes. There was gravity to his features, more than usual, this man who trafficked in human lives. He was fighting himself, clinging to something he felt was law.

"What did it hurt to give him the works? Did you think of it that way? It did us no harm to get rid of him, I'm certain. Tell me if I'm wrong. How did it hurt us?"

He came down from the ledge once the firemen spotted him, a few hours before sunrise. They lifted a ladder and he toed each rung until he was on the ground. They thought he was stuck. Karel didn't think of it that way, even if he wasn't certain how he'd get down. He was just sitting there, the baseball out of his pocket so he could roll it in his hands and feel the laces, the scuff marks that still held polish from Josh's fingers. He didn't need help. Sure, the building was burning. There was martial law. Karel saw from the ledge. How a man was burned and dragged behind a car. How the mob party went on for a while, and then it was ended by their army. Machine guns set up on corners. Lorries rumbled by with a company of soldiers who put a stop to the party. Then the fires were put out. Karel knew the courthouse wouldn't crumble.

He was unsteady on solid ground, at the bottom of the ladder. Karel couldn't make sense when he spoke. The firemen asked if he needed a doctor and let him go when he shook his head to say he didn't. They must have known he was involved. Surely they could smell the smoke on him, the whiskey on his breath. And why else would a boy be four stories high—where the raiders went in—if he wasn't deep in the bad shit? But they didn't question him. They didn't turn him over to the authorities, which would have meant handing over an Austrian boy to soldiers of the American army. Maybe that's why Karel could hardly stand on his own two feet. Surely these firemen had it in for him. They should have torn him apart for looking like one of the boys who'd cut their hoses. But it wasn't like that. Karel was alone on that ledge, fourteen years old. He'd flipped his baseball in his lap when they held the spotlight on him. He was afraid, he was crying. They freed Karel. A white boy. They told him to go home.

Karel couldn't go to the Eigler house. Not with his hands shaking. Hands that remembered when the weight of a man balled into him and they'd collapsed to the floor, up there on the secret staircase.

The first place he tried was the boys' dorming house, but the front door was boarded over, the windows shuttered. All signs that the building had been occupied were removed. The rules posted outside. The manager, who liked to sit on the steps and smoke what smelled like chocolate cigars. All those machine recruiters were long gone. The only sign of activity was the trampled grass. Each of them rushing around like crazy until now. A curfew was in place, part of the military's demand as they secured the city. Soldiers zipped around on motorbikes and ordered everyone home. Where were the boys who stayed in the dorming house supposed to go?

Alfred's tenement room was close, so Karel tried there. He didn't like the idea of imposing on the Brauns. But what else could he do?

The door inched open as Frau Braun poked her nose out and asked who it was. The bed had been moved to block the opening, this the heaviest furniture they owned, particularly with Emil lying on it. Emil Braun hadn't recovered from what happened at the Santa Philomena. His back was broken. This was what he said. His heart too.

Emil cursed from the space in the door, edging his wife away. "It's me," Karel insisted. "Stop saying those things, Herr Braun. It's Karel."

"I know who it is. Do you think I can't smell a rat?"

Braun said he knew what they'd been up to, the three he used to call his boys.

"Why couldn't you stick with me?" He smacked the door frame. "This wouldn't of happened. Boys out rioting, destroying government, but for nothing. Less than nothing. To ruin another man. To ruin a working man."

Karel didn't argue. He only asked that they open the door a foot more so he could squeeze in out of the hallway before a real rat got him. Braun said, sadly, that letting him in would be impossible.

"This is your friend's fault, isn't it? That Jakob Strauss who took aim on Emil Braun." Braun pressed his face to the opening. "Was it a lynching, Karel? Did you lynch a man?"

"Jake left a long time ago," Karel explained.

"Oh, don't believe it for a second. That Prussian. He's got something to do with it. He's at the heart of this evil. I promise you."

Karel remembered then. He'd seen Jake outside the courthouse.

"Leave us alone, son. Leave us in peace. I'm sorry. There's nothing we can do for you. I tried. You know I tried. But now it's too late. There's no room here for your struggle."

There was nowhere else to go. If he wouldn't go to the Eigler house, if he wouldn't turn himself in to the police, then nowhere. Karel hopped the fence at Rourke Park and laid flat in the outfield grass. Rain fell in his eyes, which was just as well. The turf had wilted in the heat and needed rain. Down there on the Southside, not far from where the boys' mob started to march. Doughboys made patrols. They shined truck lights into yards and parks looking for hooligans. The curfew must be enforced. The lights played over Karel. If he moved, they'd see him.

He didn't care. They could take him away. They could send him back to Europe if that's what they'd do. It felt better to give himself up, even just dreaming, because he was young and alone and didn't understand why he did the things he did, why he'd been a part of what happened, and if maybe he'd be better off locked up somewhere. Karel didn't want to think about having to run from the police or hiding from soldiers. The whiskey he drank hours before had worn off and he felt sick to his stomach. Karel wondered if they'd hold him responsible for what happened. A man was killed. He didn't know if there would be trouble for that, if any one person out of all of them would be accountable. Why shouldn't it be him? he wondered.

He felt the weight of Will Brown's body on his hands. Will Brown had still been alive then, for another minute. Karel had never felt the weight of a man. He'd believed he could put his hands up and pass off the black like it was nothing. But the man was heavy, more than Karel could hold. The others took over to do what they all said they were going to do. Karel ran the other way. He didn't scream, he didn't cry right away either. *Oh,* he said to himself. That was all. The animal fury drained from him all at once, like his heart lost its rhythm, having the man, that Will Brown, crash into him. He crawled out to the ledge and waited for others to join him. Nobody did. They all went down the back stairs, and by the time Karel regained his senses enough to look in, the way was blocked, the offices in flames.

Karel stood to heave his baseball as hard as he could into the dark. He didn't deserve to keep a baseball once owned by Josh Joseph. He threw and stumbled forward from the effort. No sound returned for a long time, then *tunk* as the ball hit the wood of the backstop on the fly. The report echoed off the houses around there. Standing, Karel waited for a searchlight to find him, a headlight, even a porch light from one of the houses to turn on. No eyes peeked out window shades, though. The noise was gone.

He laid down, the grass wet underneath him. He dreamed about the first time he hit a home run. How his bat crushed into the ball and sent it sailing. What he remembered, the feeling, was how his hands echoed back after he made contact. When he watched a teammate hit, the swing looked like a smooth motion, an uninterrupted arc. But it wasn't really. There was a moment when the hitter's clout was questioned, the bat knocked faintly off path by the ball. This isn't something that can be seen. You can only feel the vibration when it's you up there hitting. The slight knocking back. Like the skip of a heartbeat.

Once the ball was off in the air, his heart came back to its rhythm. He had to run, didn't he? That was how the game was played.

Herr Miihlstein found Karel at the field. Karel never would have guessed it would be his father who snuck over the fence into the grandstand then crawled down to a dugout. Whispering around, tripping over himself in unfamiliar terrain. "Karel," he called. "Where are you?" Karel could stay in the outfield on his belly and his father wouldn't find him. He could observe the man bumble and claim no relation, not even proximity. Herr Miihlstein was about to give up, to search elsewhere or be arrested, perhaps, an obvious foreigner flouting the curfew. But then he bent to the ground near the pitching mound. Miihlstein picked up something and held it into the bleeding light of a streetlamp across the block. The ball Karel had thrown. His father found it.

Once Karel's shoes hit the clay and sand of the infield, Miihlstein turned to see what the noise was. When he saw, he rushed to clutch his son by the arms.

It surprised Karel how his father was still larger than he was.

"It's you," Miihlstein said. "I promised your sisters you would be here, my Karel. I'm so happy you are. What a lucky man I am."

"How did you find the field?" Karel asked. His father laughed. Of course he knew how to find Rourke Park.

"Come, come. Let me rest here in this shelter. It's raining, you know."

They went to the dugout.

"I owe you," Miihlstein said, sighing as he sat on the bench. "Was it last year I promised to tell you about her? Or longer than that? Your mother. You were upset about her."

"Don't," Karel said.

"What do you mean?"

"Don't tell me. I don't want to know."

Miihlstein was baffled and came to stand by Karel at the screen. "This is yours," he said. He handed the baseball to Karel.

Karel took the ball—Josh's ball. Scuff marks on it, grass stains. The ball smelled like smoke, like the fire inside the courthouse.

Miihlstein pulled Karel along by his arms toward home. Soldiers stopped them three times along the way to ask where they'd been and where they were going. Each time Miihlstein explained how they were lost and just trying to get back to the house where they lived. Each time the soldier struggled with Miihlstein's accent but finally said, "Fine. You're okay. Go home."

Epilogue

She paged through the dailies while breakfast cooked. She read about the riot, the army coming in, the mayor whisked out of the city, barely alive after being hung from a light pole. There was a photo on the front page of the *World-Herald* of rioters mugging with the charred remains of Will Brown. She bent close to the print and studied the faces to see if anyone she knew was in the lynch mob. Maybe she searched for his face, to see if that was why Jake Strauss was at her door at sunrise, distraught, smoky and exhausted, his face waxen and cinder specked, lately born from the riot. She let him in. Took him by the hand and pulled through the door and held him.

It rained that morning. A quiet but heavy rain, no wind. She waited while Jake slept and thought about what happened. She watched the coffee boil up brown in its pot. The smell didn't wash out of the air for a long time despite the rain. She sat there smelling the smoke from the courthouse turn stale and hoped a cool wind would rush along the river to sweep the damning air away. She looked out the windows. Kids snuck from door to door to sell postcards of the hanging.

She'd led him to the bathtub after he was inside. She sat on the tub edge and plugged the drain. She drew fresh water and stood to let him hug his chest to her thighs, his head to her womb. She undressed him. She tossed his jacket out the doorway and unbuttoned his shirt, pulled off his smoky clothes, held his hand as he stepped into the water. She soaked a cloth to wet his arms and neck. She poured powder in the water and swirled with her hands to make it bubble. A sleeve of her nightgown soaked to the elbow.

It calmed him to lie in the bathtub, in the steam, his body weightless underwater. She lifted his foot and washed the backs of his legs. She savored him. They didn't need to say anything. It was fine if his eyes shuttered and closed, if his breathing slowed.

He pulled her to the water when she washed his chest, like asking, one hand on her wrist, the other on her elbow. She went behind the divider to undress, naked when she returned to slip into the water with him. The wake her body made spilled over the sides to the floor.

He took her face between his hands and kissed her. Her face cradled. His fingers brushing her skin. He caressed the pouch of her chin before they kissed again.

He was falling asleep in the water. His eyes closed, holding to her as he slid on the porcelain. She said they should get out of the bath. They did. She said they should dry off and go to bed, and they did. They moved to the bed and swept off the covers. She laid in the curve of his body, letting him hold her. He buried his nose in her hair and breathed it.

She read about the lynching in the newspaper and knew she had to leave. She couldn't live in this city. She had to get far away from any place where people knew her.

She came to wake him when the food was ready. Watched him in that big bed that nearly took up the whole room. Evie knew he was pretending to sleep. She watched from the doorway until he rolled over and looked back at her.

"Spell it out for me," she said. "Tell me where we'll go. What we'll do once we get there. Is it San Francisco? Is that where we're going?

I'm going to have a shop there. What will you do? Will you lay bricks? Will you dig?"

He tried to keep his mouth shut and be happier for it. The way he pinched his lips tight and rolled away and closed his eyes again, like he could take back being awake. But she was on the bed next to him. There was breakfast. She would listen. She said, "Tell me." There was nothing else he could do.

Within the month Evie and Jake were off on a train headed west. She worked night and day to arrange things. She packed up what she had—the wire dummy, the cutting table, all her tools and the bolts of cloth, the jewels and sequins and feathers, the half-finished garments that would have to find an owner in another city, every penny of money she'd saved—and she figured out what they could do somewhere besides Omaha.

They found a small city out west called Beaufort. There were jobs for Jake. Farmwork around the countryside. They'd meant to go all the way to San Francisco, but on the train he heard about the unions there, the IWW, and that scared him off. He just wanted to farm some. It didn't have to be his own farm, and was probably better if it wasn't. The biggest farms he ever saw were in California. However much help he could provide was good enough for an orange grove owner, or the overseer of a spinach-green valley, they could always use more. Jake a day laborer; Evie with a shop in town at the back of a little house, a two-story with a fence and a matching carriage garage, where the car was parked, once they bought a car. Jake collected garden tools in there. Forks and hoes and hand clippers and a five-tine cultivator and a machete. He kept a garden behind the house. Strung lines for green beans and tomatoes and chili peppers, pimentos, poblanos, and most of what they ate came from that garden. He learned to cook what grew here and was good to eat.

A quiet kind of life. Even though Jake was still young, and would be young for a long time yet, he felt like they'd earned this, Evie and him, after everything they'd gone through to get here.

And even though Evie sometimes could agree with Jake, that maybe they'd earned a quiet life, there always remained what they saw happen in Omaha when they lived there, so Evie knew they deserved nothing. Nobody did. As far as Evie was concerned, it was shameful to live like they did in Beaufort. Happy. Smiling to strangers on the walkway. Making friends. Shameful. To make money. Her own money. To design and sew and have customers with the means to pay cash for the extravagant things they wanted. That kind of quietness of mind, that kind of life, had a way of erasing a black mark from a person. After all those years Evie knew about this. Evie felt bad. She was embarrassed. It changed a person to see how things really were. Made her feel different about herself.

Every once in a while she'd get to talking to a black person—on a side street in Beaufort or at the back door of her nice house, painted lime green, with a second story where the nursery was, her shop in the parlor—and it would come up how Evie was from Omaha. "Oh, missus. I heard about there."

She felt disgraced. That they could just do that to a person, in Omaha, and lots of other places. That some rowdy boys could start trouble outside the courthouse anytime they wanted and nothing could put a stop to it, because a man with no power was the target, a man who couldn't escape how he was marked. His body broken from working stockyards. His skin. It was easy to see why Will Brown had been picked out by the police, by the mob. Knowing all this made Evie sick, even if she never let this show in her face. She was ashamed. Even if she didn't say so, it was a disgrace on them all.

✳

It isn't like Jake forgot all about those things. The riot. The lynching. But he didn't like to talk about his ramshackle days down on the River Ward. He kept a garden and tuned up a Model T in his spare time. He loved his woman, they were married, they had a little bit of money, and then a boy and then a girl, both children with his blond hair and coarse Prussian skin. Jake had his woman. He had his kids. So what else was there to talk about?

Sometimes people, white people, if they found out Jake Strauss was from Omaha, they asked what he thought about the burning of the courthouse, the stringing up of Mayor Smith.

"Oh, sure. Just one of those things."

Sometimes Jake came across somebody from Omaha. "Did you know Tom Dennison?" that person would always ask. "I mean personally. Did you ever meet him?" And Jake would tell the truth, at least partway. "I knew Tom. Worked for him for a little while."

Then it could only follow: "You think Tom Dennison had anything to do with that riot?"

"Well," Jake would say, "the way I see it." He'd hesitate, but would tell them. "Of course he did. There's no other way all that happens without Tom Dennison having a hand in it."

The machine was still strong after the riot and would be for another decade. Those days, Tom Dennison had his hands in everything—everything except the mayor's office during Ed Smith's solitary three-year term. Tom had something to do with the newspaper coverage that year, in 1919, how they played up every detail of those twenty white women that were raped in Omaha and the hundreds more around the county and the lynchings from coast to coast. The Red Summer. Tom always had a hand in the papers. At least half those rapes weren't committed by black men at all. Whether those were Tom's men in blackface or not, who could say? But it wouldn't surprise anybody to find out that they had been. Tom and his men did all they could to discredit the rule of law under the Smith administration. So Tom had something to do with the state of agitation. He had something to do with the riot. How the taxis ran all night, rushing downtown whoever wanted in on the action. The machine controlled the taxi firms. Tom had something to do with all the liquor passed around the crowd. He ran the liquor syndi-cate. And the boys' dorming house. People wondered about that later. How a boy could find work if he stuck around a dorming house long enough, not moving boxes or cleaning out a house after the old lady living there died, but breaking windows. Going to demonstrations to cheer on a man who said bad things about the trouble black workers were causing. There was a different tin to things then. It was a fixed game. Machine lieutenants knew who a misfit was and recruited him. Fed him. Gave him a bed to sleep on. It was Tom Dennison who set this all up. Everybody knew that. Tom's men organized things. Maybe he didn't know how upside down the whole city would get. How could he have? Tom thought he was just like anybody else who was trying to ride out a spell of bad luck. He was desperate. Thinking it would be just one more concession, one more of his own personal rules he'd have to break, then that would set his world right again.

Maybe Tom Dennison didn't lynch that man, Will Brown, not with his own hands. And he didn't. But you couldn't say he wasn't involved. You couldn't say Tom had nothing to do with the riot, nothing to do with the lynching. Who'd believe you? You'd be wrong.

He didn't have to give an order to riot. He didn't have to order the mob to smash out the courthouse windows and dump gasoline inside. He didn't have to tell them to put a noose around the mayor's neck. He didn't have to tell them anything.

The men who ran things may not have caused the riots, but they certainly benefitted. Cowboy Jim Dahlman would win reelection in 1921 and remain in office until he died in 1930. Tom Dennison would enjoy his position of power another ten years before retiring. He would die in a San Diego hospital, in 1934, after driving his car off the road.

The boys on Clandish wondered about these years as they grew older—the war years, the riot year—and how their city wasn't so splendid as they thought it was when they were young.

The boys took jobs when they were old enough to get them. Some in Jobbers Canyon warehouses, some in South Omaha stockyards. A few finished high school; even fewer went to college, became lawyers and insurance executives and city administrators. Some moved far away. Most of the boys on Clandish stayed close. They had kids of their own who went to battle in Europe in what seemed like only a short time later. Sons who died on the beaches of Normandy.

Those boys thought of what happened to Will Brown. Will Brown, who was buried in a potters' field at Forest Lawn Cemetery. They knew so little about him. There wasn't much of an effort to know more. Men like Will Brown just sort of disappeared those days. It was easy. A poor man might carry a state certificate in his billfold to prove he did in fact exist. He might only have one photograph of himself, alone in that billfold because nobody else would want it. A man like Will Brown. Who was he supposed to give a photo to? Even for a man like Will Brown, who was lynched, whose name was in all three local dailies and the *New York Times*, the situation was only marginally different. They had his photo in the newspapers. A reporter must have found it in a drawer in his place after the cops dragged him out. Unless it was his mug shot. Will Brown in his overalls. In a denim shirt and what passed for his good hat, one that had a solid brim at least. A man with no family around. With no friends who could stand up to defend the man as a man. Nobody to eulogize him. No funeral. No words at his burial unless the grave digger said something. Unless the grave digger spat on his grave, which was more likely. Nobody thought speaking on Will Brown's behalf was worthwhile, the boys guessed. They didn't know. Sure, the boys thought a lot about Will Brown, but they didn't know him. To them, he was unknowable.

As the boys moved around once they were older, they'd see other towns that had lynchings. Towns that had a certain prominent tree on the square, a hanging tree. A point of pride in these towns, maybe, a sign that read *33 Men Hanged Here.* A stranger traveling through might think about what it did to a person to walk by that tree every day, to have a tree like that in your hometown. White or black or red or whatever. Just walking by that tree and knowing what was done there and what the purpose of that tree was, at least according to the people who ran that town. A tree that would outlive everybody.

Will Brown came from Cairo, Illinois, an island of a city at the confluence of the Ohio and Mississippi. This was in the papers. How he'd lived there a long while. He'd probably been there when Froggie James was lynched in Cairo a decade earlier. He'd have been there when they chased Froggie to a residential neighborhood and pulled him from the shed he was hiding in and burned him alive in an alley. Maybe Will Brown walked those streets to get to work. Maybe he went by that very alley sometimes. Where there were fire stains on the pavement and the eaves of houses.

Like there were bullet holes that marked the stone facade of the courthouse in Omaha.

The neighborhoods of the River Ward would be demolished piece by piece, Clandish in particular, until there wasn't even a Clandish Street anymore, no tenements, just more rail yard with a bridge overhead to let cars go over without seeing. The maps amended, Clandish deleted from the index. Growing up, the boys thought they really came from somewhere, but it would become clear they came from nowhere. Some of them were around to see the big buildings downtown razed to the ground too. The old Gothic post office, the Bee Building, city hall, the Hotel Fontenelle, Jobbers Canyon itself. These monuments of their youth, that had once been of primal importance, held no importance. Only the courthouse remained. The courthouse, where the riot had been, where a man had been lynched, was the only monument that survived.

Both Jimmy Mac and Alfred hung around Clandish for a while, the same as ever. Sure, a guy like Joe Meinhof or Milt Hoffman could just disappear, and they both did—caught a train the evening of September 28, as a matter of fact, the riot still boiling, and were out of Omaha before any arrests were made, never to be seen or heard from again.

It wasn't so easy for a boy like Jimmy McHenry. Jimmy had his picture in the *World-Herald*, that famous photograph of folks posing with the burned remains of Will Brown. Jimmy right up front, grinning large and proud. His cheeks all red from liquor. Surrounded by folks from all walks of life. Businessmen wearing the gaudy rings of their fraternal order; housewives with felt flowers on their hats and big ebony buttons on their pea coats; jug-eared mill workers; pissed-off men in trench coats; a guy in a tuxedo and bow tie; an Irish kid beside himself with self-importance. Jimmy couldn't walk away from that. A picture of him in the paper, one that was reprinted on thousands of postcards sent all over the country. And what people wrote on the back of these postcards: *See what folks in Omaha had going? A cookout at the courthouse. All OK here now.* Maybe Jimmy didn't know what he was

getting into. How, as a result of that photograph, police were able to
track him down. All the boys (all girls, women, and men, for that matter) who took part in the riot had to worry about being identified. It was
a simple thing when it came to Jimmy Mac. His face in the paper. Still,
even if he was identified as being present at the lynching, it was a more
difficult matter to prove he was a party to the lynching. The county
attorney declined to press charges, because he couldn't prove Jimmy
did anything other than pose for a photo, and plenty of folks did that.
It wasn't illegal to do so. Two weeks later a firefighter came forward and
said he recognized Jimmy as one of the boys who stole a ladder from a
fire engine as the courthouse burned. But the next day an anonymous
donor sent a check to replace all equipment that was damaged in the
riot, and suddenly the fireman wasn't so sure after all that Jimmy was
the boy who took a ladder. Jimmy was off the hook so far as the county
attorney was concerned, but he still had to face his mother. He didn't
foresee his poor mother having to think about her son front and center
at a lynching, and dumb enough to get photographed to boot. And
then Mrs. McHenry being the subject of whispers at mass. The target
of sidelong glances every day for months on the street. All because her
boy had his picture in the papers. What a shame.

For Alfred Braun things were a bit different. He wasn't in the photograph of the lynching, for one thing, so he didn't have that to live
down. Not in such a specific way.

After the riot Alfred reconciled with his father. After months of
living in the dorming house, he apologized for everything. Said he was
sorry for getting mixed up with that bunch of fascists in the Dennison
machine, for what happened at the Santa Philomena, and how the
Interrace Game was besmirched by a rotten play. Alfred was sorry for
the courthouse, for Will Brown. He bawled his eyes out on the hallway
side of the door to the Braun tenement room. Emil wouldn't let him
in, as he hadn't let Karel in either. But Alfred didn't slink off elsewhere,
as Karel had. Alfred collapsed against the door and howled about how

sorry he was until Emil couldn't take it anymore. "Come here, my boy! What am I saying? Get inside! Get inside before the rats get you for good!"

Emil Braun was rejuvenated a degree after that. He stumbled along with a cane but was upright and moving at least. An improvement over being stuck in bed like he'd been the previous sixteen months. Braun needed Alfred's help to get around. So they stood together in the cellars of Southside taverns that hung the black flag of anarchy, so Emil could speechify on the misdeeds of Omaha's King Gambler and reminisce about the greatness of Josh Joseph, Braun's friend, the best there was from a time when even a slaughterhouse floor worker knew how to respect the game.

None of the Brauns starved during the lean years to come, nor during the even leaner ones after that. Alfred was killed in 1927, in Seattle, Washington, when a riot-busting cop's baton cracked his skull. Alfred Braun was decried in the *Post-Intelligencer* as a common thug, which he probably was. Most anyone who'd known him in Omaha agreed that this was right.

The Miihlsteins stayed on Clandish awhile. Silke and Theresa married and had kids, as Jake once predicted, and moved to further-out subdivisions and new kit houses that came mail order from a Sears, Roebuck & Co. catalog and arrived on a railcar to be assembled.

Anna lived in the sanitarium until she was eighteen. Over the course of those three years, her health improved greatly. She grew some but would always be small, always a little knock-kneed and fragile. But at least when she lived at the sanitarium she received some proper schooling, in between meals and absorption sessions out on the lawn in the lounging chairs. The girls there asked Anna about the riot when it happened. "That's where you're from?" "Yeah. Four blocks from my house!" Some of them treated her with respect after, girls Anna tried to keep clear of from the start. But her friends, Mina and Kate, they understood Anna and her temperament more after news of the riot reached them. They felt sorry about what happened, but not just that. They conveyed something more. Understanding, commiseration. "Did you hear from your brother?" Tears in Kate's eyes as she asked, Anna shirking half a turn to sit taller and brush her dark hair back. Of course Anna hadn't heard from Karel. She didn't have to answer that question. "I'm so sorry," Mina said. "You should write him and tell him what you think. Tell him it's an abomination to have that happen."

Mina and Kate were good friends. Anna always believed these girls were the real reason she was cured at the sanitarium.

Anna did so well over those three years at the home that she went off to a Lutheran college in Kansas upon her release and later took a job in Kansas City as an actuary at a life insurance company and made a career out of that. Kind of funny really, to the people on Clandish who heard where Anna wound up and what she did to make a living.

There isn't much more to say about Karel Miihlstein. For how much pride the other boys on Clandish invested in Karel and his talent for baseball, he was a disappointment in the end to many of the boys, those who'd believed one day Karel Miihlstein would be as well known as Ty Cobb or Cy Young or Tris Speaker.

Karel didn't talk much to the other boys after the riot. He was the quietest and strangest person they knew, through the end of their schooling. Karel still played ball those years, even though he severed ties with the South Omaha ball club and played only for a high school squad. Once he was sixteen, he signed a contract with a pro team and moved to Minnesota to play ball all summer and worked a job in a timber mill the rest of the time. Eight years later the boys on Clandish heard about him. His name showed up in a box score in the newspaper. *KMhstn rf.* That had to be him. He played four innings for the Detroit Tigers at the end of a season, in Yankee Stadium, had one turn at bat, in which he made an out.

His father had gone back to Vienna by then. Nobody could guess if Herr Miihlstein would have cared or not that his boy made it, at least briefly, to the big leagues.

A week after the riot, Karel had moved back in with his family. Silke, Theresa, Maria Eigler, and Herr Miihlstein. They picked up the damage. Almost every day they removed rubble from Clandish, like pretty much everyone did. Like this was the new life here.

The US Army sent in trucks once martial law was lifted. (Tom Dennison sent trucks too. Whatever that's worth.) Soldiers and members of the state militia were there to help, but for the most part it was people who lived on the River Ward who were left to put things back together. People like Maria Eigler, like Ignatz and Ingo Kleinhardt's widow and the Miihlsteins.

Maria kept Karel hidden in the attic for three days after the riot so he wasn't grabbed by the authorities. If Karel had been taken in for questioning, if there was some witness or informant who could finger him, like had happened with Jimmy Mac, it was possible that Karel would be deported without even being convicted of a crime. Something a native-born boy didn't have to worry about. With Karel's involvement in the South Omaha Social Anarchists, people knew about that, his actions on the night of the riot were clear violations of the Sedition Act. Boy or not, he could have been stockaded inside an outbound steamer by the end of the week. So Maria didn't ask if Karel was involved, or what he was doing during the riot, or why he'd been hiding on the dark ballfield when Miihlstein found him. That was his privilege. If he was able to keep his mouth shut he could shed the indecency of what he'd done. Anyway, he had to squeeze his shaking hands together to keep them still when Miihlstein brought him home, and that told all. Nobody had to guess if he'd been up to bad things. And if it was worse than throwing a brick through a window, folks didn't want to know about it.

The police never bothered Karel. He was never brought in front of a grand jury like some boys were—like happened with William Francis, who rode a white Arabian horse and raised a noose to urge on the mob party—so Karel helped out. He pushed a wheelbarrow. He scooped up debris with a broad-mouthed shovel. He was even at the courthouse when militiamen hooked chains to a flipped-over, burned-out police Model A and hoisted the vehicle to a flatbed truck. Maria was mad about that—Karel close to soldiers, at the scene of a notorious crime. She wanted him to stay home. But Karel didn't worry. If they hadn't grabbed him yet, he figured they never would.

The four remaining Miihlsteins swept up glass. Washed at gasoline stains on the walkways with buckets of soapy water. Which was futile. They rested on the Eigler porch like they'd done so many times before. Watching their neighbors. Little boys stomping around with nobody minding them so long as they stayed out of the way. Folks were pretty tired of boys causing trouble just then, but these boys—five, six, seven years old—they couldn't help themselves. They paraded around in damaged hats they found laying around, a homburg made soggy and caved in from the rain. They wrestled and took bricks from the rubble piles, lifted the bricks over their heads to show how strong they were. These imps. These kings of broken things.

After a few days of clearing debris, Maria saw an opportunity to have the junk in her cellar trucked off for free. She wasn't the only one with the idea. Broken chairs with the upholstery torn found their way into government trucks as property damaged in the riot. Sacks of clothes that had been moldering in some damp cellar corner. Bent bicycle wheels, automobile tires with rubber that wouldn't take another patch. The streets were clear enough, the people of Clandish must have figured, so they turned to their junk rooms.

Maria sent Karel and Herr Miihlstein down to pluck out the worst of her collection and carry it to the end of the block. An empty keg of beer and crates of dry bottles—evidence of how she'd flouted the state prohibition—dried flower stems, watercolor paintings left by Anna. A pony Anna bent out of scrap wire, a wood elephant, a June bug of orange yarn, stacks of journals with poetry written in girly script. There were August Eigler's army uniforms from the Civil War. Root vegetables that were too dry to be eaten. "Get rid of it all," Maria shouted down the steps. "What do I care? Most of that I forgot about a long time ago."

Karel found the instrument case where the dagger was. He'd put it right back where he first found it, August Eigler's dagger, that Karel had held up impotently to Ignatz two years before. He opened the case. For some reason he thought the dagger would be gone, that Anna would have snagged it for herself when nobody was looking, but the dagger was right where he left it. Black gum on its blade, the handle holding together, tucked next to the violin. Karel reached into the case, but this time cradled the violin in his hands. A violin without strings, the fingerboard loose with the blond of its wood showing where the stain had faded. He'd never asked Maria about the violin, because he didn't really care who it belonged to. If it was August Eigler's, or Maria's, or hidden in the cellar by the deceased luthier who lived here before the Miihlsteins. Karel was sure the violin would crumble in his hands if he picked it up. He grabbed the violin and it didn't crumble. He held it up to the light from a window and saw an inscription on its back, one so faint it hardly showed, the sprucewood was beaten so badly. It read *Treue der Union* and *Theodor Bruggemann* and *1st Nebraska Volunteer*

Infantry. This violin hadn't belonged to August Eigler. Karel had no idea who this other man could be. A deeper mystery.

Karel waited for Herr Miihlstein to come down then showed him the violin.

"What's this?" Miihlstein asked. "This can't be one of mine, is it?"

"No. I found it here." Karel pointed to the case, empty except for the dagger and bow.

"Well," Miihlstein said. His eyes lit up behind the lenses of his glasses. He lifted the violin, as Karel had done, lowered himself by bending at the knees so he could hold it above his head. "Can we save this one? Shall we take it to my table?"

Karel shrugged. He didn't know the first thing about that.

"It isn't so nice. The vintage is poor. Maybe I could make it sing again. Maybe not." Miihlstein put the instrument to his side, held it only by the neck, and it didn't fall apart. "Bring it up," he said. "I'll ask Maria if she knows anything. If the violin has some importance, I'll fix it."

Karel took the violin with both hands, shuffled it across the cellar to where the case was, and laid it to rest in the velvet. Closed the lid and twisted shut the brass clasps.

"What was it about her?" Karel asked.

Herr Miihlstein breathed in when Karel said this. "What is what?"

"My mother. You were going to tell me."

"Yes. I was, I was. I was going to tell you, but you made me stop. And now you want to start again." Miihlstein laughed in his flat way. He went to the steps to sit and wiped his hands on his trousers, then brushed at the filth that had rubbed off on the fabric. "I don't like being down here," he said.

"You like the attic."

"It's nice up there, yeah. You know that."

"What were you going to tell me?"

"Oh," Miihlstein sighed. "I've been wanting to tell you a long time. Your mother. They called her the Swallow. A vile thing to call a woman.

She hated they called her that. Sometimes she didn't mind, if it was a joke. She played along. I did too. Like I didn't care."

"What do you mean?"

"Nothing. I shouldn't say that. I'm going to tell you what a wonderful woman she was. Because you heard some bad things. That's why. Sometimes your sisters get excited about these things, the stories about your mother. They were old enough to hear what people said. Bad stories for them to know. I want to tell you her best qualities. What she smelled like when she cared what she smelled like. Lilacs. That's what she smelled like."

Miihlstein told what her voice was like first thing in the morning over breakfast. Nearly a whisper, as light as smoke. These her best qualities. How she stayed out late when possible. How she wore her hair up when younger, down as she aged. That she once played Cleopatra and kept the brass armband she wore for the role. She wore the armband until she was too fat. It was like their wedding band. Miihlstein had made the armband for the production, one of his first jobs, and stole it from wardrobe to give her once the show closed, because he knew she loved the prop. Like Cleopatra would have loved it.

"We ran off to Venice after we married—didn't you know that? Of course not—before we had you kids. To make connections and find work. But I became deathly ill. The porter had to carry me out of the hotel because the manager thought I was contagious. I was going to die. But your mother took care of me until I was well again."

"Herr," Karel interrupted. "Do you miss her?"

Miihlstein looked confused, like he could cry.

"I don't understand these words. Of course I do. She was my love. My only love."

"She left us."

"Yeah. That's precisely right. There was only one of her and now she's gone."

AUTHOR'S NOTE

This book is a work of imagination. While many passages are based on historical personalities and events, the scenes depicted are a fictional approximation of what life was like in Omaha during the last years of World War I and how the Omaha Race Riot of 1919 was experienced. In order to serve the story, I altered reality, placed real people in imagined spaces, invented dialogue, and dramatized events. That being said, I tried to stay true to the historical record when possible, particularly as this pertains to the character of real people. Mostly I used primary sources in these cases. Many hours were spent in the microfilm rooms of the Omaha Public Library and Creighton University's Reinert Library parsing *World-Herald*, *Bee*, *Daily News*, and *Monitor* archives to ensure that these pages best represent the spirit of the River Ward in all its complexity.

Several books were invaluable while conducting the research that fed the novel. *The Underworld Sewer: A Prostitute Reflects on Life in the Trade, 1871–1909*, by Josie Washburn, and *River City Empire: Tom Dennison's Omaha*, by Orville D. Menard, both from University of Nebraska Press, are vital resources about many of the shadowy figures who lived in Omaha during those years. *The German-American Experience*, by Don Heinrich Tolzmann, *The Gate City: A History of Omaha*, by Lawrence H. Larsen and Barbara J. Cottrell, and the WPA-produced *Omaha: A Guide to the City and Environs* are also great resources. Likewise, this book couldn't have been possible without the work of local historians, archivists, and preservationists, particularly those at the Durham Museum, Douglas County Historical Society, and Nebraska State Historical Society.

To this day there is controversy and conspiracy about what caused the Omaha Race Riot of 1919 and lynching of Will Brown, and whether these tragic events reveal something significant about the humanity of this city, or if troubled times should be forgotten. This book is an act of remembering.

ACKNOWLEDGMENTS

Thanks are due to everyone who helped make this book possible, whether through collaboration, support, or other means. Foremost to Cleo Croson (my maternal grandmother) and Billy Wheeler (my paternal grandfather) for stoking my love of storytelling and history by sharing so honestly the stories of their lives. They were born decades after the events depicted here, in towns far away from Omaha, yet their stories keep me thinking about who I am, how families end up where they do, and those who were left behind along the way.

As always, thanks to Nicole, Madeleine, and Clara for bringing light and adventure to my life. To my family, Marta and Dennis, Karen and Bill, Matt, Shannon, and everyone, for their support, love, and humor. To Stephanie Delman for her unfaltering enthusiasm and tenacity in finding the best publisher for this book, and Vivian Lee for her insights and fearlessness as an editor.

To my closest friends and conspirators, Bill Sedlak, Amber Mulholland, Drew Justice, Ryan Borchers, for their patience in developing the early and late drafts of this story into something far more significant than I first imagined it could be. Along these lines, many thanks to Dave Green, Jenn Ladino, Devin Murphy, Doug Rice, Sam Slaughter, Kwakiutl Dreher, Susan Aizenberg, Ngwarsungu Chiwengo, Miles Frieden, Arlo Haskell, Gregory Henry, Julie Iromuanya, Jean-Baptiste Joly, Lee Martin, Mary Morris, Dave Mullins, Timothy Schaffert, Lucas

Schwaller, Brent Spencer, Mary Helen Stefaniak, Robert Stone, Travis Thiezsen, and Shannon Youngman.

To the journals and presses who published excerpts from the novel in progress: Edition Solitude (*On the River, Down Where They Found Willy Brown*), *Boulevard* ("River Ward, 1917"), *Artful Dodge* ("The Hyphenates of Jackson County"), and *Four Quarters* ("In Her Place on Capitol Ave, 1917").

This book wouldn't exist without the generous support of amazing arts organizations and the people who run them, like Akademie Schloss Solitude, which for three months put me up on the grounds of a German castle to ponder beingness and the place my art can occupy in the world; Key West Literary Seminar, which thrice brought me to paradise in the dead of winter and challenged me to think big; Kimmel Harding Nelson Center for the Arts, which gave me space to write during the early days of drafting; and the creative writing program at Creighton University, which was a second home—one I could return to.

ABOUT THE AUTHOR

Photo © Travis Thiezsen

Theodore Wheeler is a reporter who covers civil law and politics in Omaha, where he lives with his wife and their two daughters. His fiction has been featured in *Best New American Voices*, *New Stories from the Midwest*, the *Southern Review*, the *Kenyon Review*, and *Boulevard* and received special mention in a Pushcart Prize anthology. A graduate of the MFA program at Creighton University, Wheeler was a fellow at Akademie Schloss Solitude in Stuttgart, Germany; a resident of the Kimmel Harding Nelson Center for the Arts in Nebraska City; and a winner of the Marianne Russo Award from the Key West Literary Seminar. He is the author of *Bad Faith*, a collection of short fiction. *Kings of Broken Things* is his first novel.